Adam Blake is a pseudonym for an acclaimed, internationally bestselling novelist based in the UK.

THE
DEAD SEA
DECEPTION

ADAM BLAKE

sphere

SPHERE

First published in Great Britain as a paperback original
in 2011 by Sphere
Reprinted 2011 (twice)

A CIP catalogue record for this book
is available from the British Library.

ISBN B 978-0-7515-4573-9
ISBN CF 978-1-84744-465-3

Typeset in Sabon by M Rules
Printed and bound in Great Britain by
Clays Ltd, St Ives plc

Papers used by Sphere are from well-managed forests
and other responsible sources.

 MIX
Paper from
responsible sources
FSC
www.fsc.org   FSC® C104740

Sphere
An imprint of
Little, Brown Book Group
100 Victoria Embankment
London EC4Y 0DY

An Hachette UK Company
www.hachette.co.uk

www.littlebrown.co.uk

To Chris, my father
And Chris, my brother
And Chris, my soul-brother
And Sandra, my sister – but maybe we
should call her Chris to avoid any ambiguity

Prologue

When despatch called to tell Sheriff Webster Gayle about the plane crash, he was at the bowling alley, just about to sink a spoon into an enormous bowl of ice cream. One of the thoughts that went through his mind as he listened, along with the first gripes of pity for the dead and bereaved, and dismay at the shit-storm this would bring him, was that this seven-dollar sundae was now surely going to waste.

'Emergency landing?' he asked, making sure he understood. He cupped his hand around the phone to shut out the rever-berating sounds of pins falling and being reset in the adjacent lane.

'Nope.' Connie was definitive. 'No kind of landing at all. That bird just fell out of the sky, hit the ground and blew the hell up. Don't know how big it was or where it was coming from. I've put calls out to ATC at Phoenix and Los Angeles. I'll let you know when they get back to me.'

'And it's definitely inside the county limits?' Gayle asked, clutching at a feeble straw. 'I thought the flight path was more to the west, out by Arcona.'

'It came down right by the highway, Web. Honest to God, I can see the smoke right out the window here. It's not just in the limits, it's so close you could walk to it from the Gateway mall.

1

I already passed the word along to Doc Beattie. Anything else you want me to do?'

Gayle considered. 'Yeah,' he said after a moment. 'Tell Anstruther to get up there and rope it off, a good ways out. Far enough so we don't get anyone stopping by to rubberneck or take pictures.'

'What about Moggs?' Meaning Eileen Moggs, who comprised the entirety of the full-time staff on the *Peason Chronicler*. Moggs was a journalist of the old school, in that she drove around and talked to people before she filed copy, and even took her own photos with an over-sized digital SLR that made Gayle think of a strap-on dildo he'd seen once in a sex toys catalogue and then tried to forget.

'Moggs can go through,' Gayle said. 'I owe her a favour.'

'Oh yeah?' Connie queried, just blandly enough that Gayle couldn't be sure there was any innuendo there. He shoved the bowl of ice cream away from him, disconsolate. It was one of those fancy flavours with a long name and an even longer list of ingredients, leaning heavily on chocolate, marshmallow and caramel in various combinations. Gayle was an addict, but had made peace with his weakness a long time ago. It beat booze, by a long way. Probably beat heroin and crack cocaine, too, although he'd never tried either.

'I'm on my way over,' he said. 'Tell Anstruther a good quarter of a mile.'

'A good quarter of a mile what, chief?'

He waved to the waitress to bring him the check. 'The incident line, Connie. I want it to be at least five minutes' walk from the wreck. There'll be people coming in from all over when they get a sniff of this, and the less they see, the sooner they'll turn around and go home again.'

'Okay. Five minutes' walk.' Gayle could hear Connie scribbling

2

it down. She hated numbers, claimed to be blind to them in the way some people are blind to colours. 'Is that it?'

'That's it for now. Try the airports again. I'll give you a call when I get out there.'

Gayle took his hat from the empty seat beside him and put it on. The waitress, an attractive dark-featured woman whose name tag said MADHUKSARA, brought him the cheque for the ice cream and for a hot dog and fries he'd had earlier. She affected to be scandalised at the fact that he hadn't touched his dessert. 'Well, I'd welcome a doggy bag if it was a practical proposition,' he said, making the best of it. She got the joke, laughed louder and longer than it deserved. He creaked a little as he stood. Getting old, and getting rheumatic, even in this climate. 'Ma'am.' He touched the brim of his hat to her and headed out.

Gayle's thoughts were on idle as he crossed the baking back-lot towards his battered blue Chevrolet Biscayne. He was entitled to a new car on the police budget whenever he wanted one, but the Biscayne was a local landmark. Wherever he parked it, it was like a sign saying, THE DOCTOR IS IN.

How was *Madhuksara* pronounced? Where did she come from, and what had brought her to live in Peason, Arizona? This was Gayle's town, and he was attached to it by strong, sub-terranean bonds, but he couldn't imagine anyone coming from a great distance to be here. What would be the draw? The mall? The three-screen movie theatre? The desert?

Of course, he reminded himself, this was the twenty-first century. Madhuksara didn't have to be an immigrant at all. She could have been born and raised right here in the south-western corner of the US of A. She certainly hadn't had any trace of a foreign accent. On the other hand, he hadn't ever seen her around town before. Gayle wasn't a racist, which at some points in his career as a policeman had given him a certain novelty value. He liked variety, in humankind as much as in ice cream. But his instincts were a cop's instincts and he tended to file new faces of any colour in a mental pending tray, on the grounds that unknown quantities could always turn out to be trouble.

Highway 68 was clear all the way to the interstate, but long before he got to the crossroads he could see the coal-black column stretching up into the sky. *A pillar of smoke by day, a pillar of fire by night*, Gayle thought irrelevantly. His mother had belonged to a Baptist church and quoted scripture the way some people talk about the weather. Gayle himself hadn't opened a bible in thirty years, but some of that stuff had stuck with him.

He turned off on to the single-file blacktop that bordered Bassett's Farm and came up through the fields on a nameless dirt track where once, a great many years before, he'd had his first kiss that hadn't come from an elderly female relative.

He was surprised and pleased to find the road roped off with an emphatic strip of black-and-yellow incident tape, a hundred yards or so before he was close enough to see the sprawl of twisted metal from which the smoke was rising. The tape had been stretched between two pine fence posts, and Spence, one of his most taciturn and unexcitable deputies, was standing right there to see that drivers didn't just bypass the roadblock by taking a short detour into the cornfield.

As Spence untied the tape to let him pass, Gayle wound his window down.

'Where's Anstruther?' he asked.

Spence pointed with a sideways nod. 'Up there.'

'Who else?'

'Lewscynski. Scuff. And Mizz Moggs.'

Gayle nodded and drove on.

Like heroin and cocaine, a major airplane crash was something outside Gayle's experience. In his imagination, the plane had come down like an arrow and embedded itself in the soil, tail up. The reality was not so neat. He saw a broad ridge of gouged earth about two hundred yards long, maybe five or six feet high at its outer edge. The plane had broken up as it dug that furrow, shedding great curved pieces of its fuselage like giant eggshells along the whole, tortured stretch of ground. What was left of the fuselage was burning up at the far end and – now that Gayle's window was down, he became aware – filling the air with a terrible stench of combustion. Whether it was flesh or plastic that smelled like that as it burned he could not be sure. He was in no hurry to find out.

He parked the Biscayne next to Anstruther's black-and-white and got out. The wreck was a hundred yards away, but the heat from the fire laid itself across Gayle's body like a bar across a door as he walked over to where a small group of people was standing, on top of the newly ploughed ridge. Anstruther, his senior deputy, was shielding his eyes as he looked out over the remade country. Joel Scuff, a no-account trooper who at age twenty-seven was already more of a disgrace to the force than men twice his age had managed, stood beside him, staring in the same direction. Both looked sombre and nonplussed, like people at a funeral for someone they didn't know that well, fearful that they might be called on for small talk.

Sitting at their feet, on the rucked-up earth, was Eileen Moggs. Her phallic camera sat impotently in her lap and her head was bowed. It was hard to be sure from this angle, but her face had the crumpled look of someone who had recently been crying.

Gayle was about to say something to her, but at that point, as he trudged up the rising gradient of the earthworks, his head crested the ridge and he saw what they were seeing. He stopped dead, involuntarily, his brain too overloaded with that horrible image to maintain any commerce with his legs.

Bassett's North 40 was sown with corpses: men and women and children, all strewn across the chewed-up earth, while the clothes disgorged from their burst suitcases arced and twisted above them in the searing thermals, as though their ghosts were dancing in fancy dress to celebrate their new-found freedom.

Gayle tried to swear, but his mouth was too dry, suddenly, for the sound to make it out. In the terrible heat, his tears evaporated right off his cheeks before anyone could see them.

PART ONE

ROTGUT

1

The photo showed a dead man sprawled at the foot of a staircase. It was perfectly framed and pin-sharp, and nobody seemed to have noticed the most interesting thing about it, but it still didn't fill Heather Kennedy with anything that resembled enthusiasm.

She closed the manila folder again and pushed it back across the desk. There wasn't much else in there to look at anyway. 'I don't want this,' she said.

Facing her across the desk, DCI Summerhill shrugged: a shrug that said *into each life a little rain must fall*. 'I don't have anyone else to give it to, Heather,' he told her, in the tone of a reasonable man doing what needed to be done. 'Slates are full across the department. You're the one with the most slack.' He didn't add, but could have done, *you know why the short straw is your straw, and you know what has to happen before that stops*.

'All right,' Kennedy said. 'I'm slack. So put me on runaround for Ratner or Denning. Don't give me a dead-ball misallocation that's going to sit open on my docket until five miles south of judgement day.'

Summerhill didn't even make the effort of looking sympathetic. 'If it's not murder,' he said, 'close it. Sign off on it. I'll back your call, so long as you can make it stick.'

'How am I meant do that when the evidence is three weeks

old?' Kennedy shot back, acidly. She was going to lose this. Summerhill had already made up his mind. But she wasn't going to make it easy for the old bastard. 'Nobody worked the crime scene. Nobody did anything with the body in situ. All I've got to go on are a few photos taken by a bluebell from the local cop-shop.'

'Well, that and the autopsy report,' Summerhill said. 'The north London lab came back with enough open questions to bring the case back to life – and possibly to give you a few starting points.' He pushed the file firmly and irrevocably back to her.

'Why was there an autopsy if nobody thought the death was suspicious?' Kennedy asked, genuinely puzzled. *How did this even get to be our problem?*

Summerhill closed his eyes, massaged them with finger and thumb. He grimaced wearily. Clearly he just wanted her to take the file and get the hell out of his morning. 'The dead man had a sister, and the sister pushed. Now she's got what she wanted – an open verdict, implying a world of exciting possibilities. To be blunt, we don't really have any alternative right now. We look bad because we signed off on accidental death so quickly and we look bad because we stonewalled on the autopsy on the first request. So we've got to reopen the case and we've got to go through the motions until one of two things happens: we find an actual explanation for this guy's death or else we hit a wall and we can reasonably say we tried.'

'Which could take for ever,' Kennedy pointed out. It was a classic black hole. A case that had had no real spadework done at the front end meant you had to run yourself ragged for everything thereafter, from forensics to witness statements.

'Yes. Easily. But look on the bright side, Heather. You'll also be breaking in a new partner, a willing young DC who's only just joined the division and doesn't know a thing about you.

Chris Harper. Straight transfer from St John's Wood via the academy. Treat him gently, won't you. They're used to more civilised ways over at Newcourt Street.'

Kennedy opened her mouth to speak, closed it again. There was no point. In fact, on one level you had to admire the neatness and economy of the stitch-up. Someone had screwed up heroically – signed off way too fast and then got bitten on the arse by the evidence – so now the whole mess was being handed off to the most expendable detective in the division and a poor piece of cannon fodder drafted in for the occasion from one of the boroughs. No harm, no foul. Or if it turned out there was, nobody who mattered was going to be booked for it.

With a muttered oath, she headed for the door. Leaning back in his chair, hands clasped behind his head, Summerhill stared at her retreating back. 'Bring them back alive, Heather,' he exhorted her, languidly.

When she got back to her desk, Kennedy found the latest gift from the get-her-out-by-Friday brigade. It was a dead rat in a stainless steel break-back trap, lying across the papers on her desk. Seven or eight detectives were in the bear pit, sitting around in elaborately casual groupings, and they were all watching her covertly, eager to see how she'd react. There might even be money riding on the outcome, judging from the mood of suppressed excitement in the room.

Kennedy had been putting up quietly with lesser provocations, but as she stared down at the limp little corpse, a ruff of blood crusted at its throat where it had fallen on the trap's baited spike, she acknowledged instantly what she ninety-per-cent already knew – that she wasn't going to make this stop by uncomplainingly carrying her own cross.

So what were the options? She ran through a few until she

found one that at least had the advantage of being immediate. She picked the trap up and pulled it open, with some difficulty because the spring was stiff. The rat fell on to her desk with an audible thud. Then she tossed the trap aside, hearing it clatter behind her, and picked up the body, not gingerly by the tail but firmly in her fist. It was cold: a lot colder than ambient. Someone had been keeping it in his fridge, looking forward to this moment. Kennedy glanced around the room.

Josh Combes. It wasn't that he was the ringleader – the campaign wasn't as consciously orchestrated as that. But among the officers who felt a need to make Kennedy's life uncomfortable, Combes had the loudest mouth and was senior in terms of years served. So Combes would do as well as anyone, and better than most. Kennedy crossed to his desk and threw the dead rat into his crotch. Combes started violently, making his chair roll back on its castors. The rat fell to the floor.

'Jesus!' he bellowed.

'You know,' Kennedy said, into the mildly scandalised silence, 'big boys don't ask their mummies to do this stuff for them, Josh. You should have stayed in uniform until your cods dropped. Harper, you're with me.'

She wasn't even sure he was there: she had no idea what he looked like. But as she walked away, she saw out of the corner of her eye one of the seated men stand and detach himself from the group.

'Bitch,' Combes snarled at her back.

Her blood was boiling, but she chuckled, let them all hear it.

2

Harper drove, through light summer rain that had come from nowhere. Kennedy reviewed the file. That took most of the first minute.

'Did you get a chance to look at this?' she asked him, as they turned into Victoria Street and hit the traffic.

The detective constable did a little rapid blinking, but said nothing for a moment or two. Chris Harper, twenty-eight, of Camden Ops, St John's Wood and the SCD's much-touted Crime Academy: Kennedy had taken a few moments in-between Summerhill's office and the bear pit to look him up on the divisional database. There was nothing to see, apart from a citation for bravery (in relation to a warehouse fire) and a red docket, redacted, for an altercation with a senior officer over a personal matter that wasn't specified. Whatever it was, it seemed to have been settled without any grievance procedure being invoked.

Harper was fair-haired and as lean as a wire, with a slight asymmetry in his face that made him look like he was either flinching or favouring you with an insinuating wink. Kennedy thought she might have run across him once in passing somewhere, a long way back, but if so, it had been a very fleeting contact, and it hadn't left behind any strong impression for good or bad.

'Haven't read it all,' Harper admitted at last. 'I only found out I was assigned to this case about an hour ago. I was going over the file, but then ... well, you turned up and did the dead rat cabaret, and then we hit the road.' Kennedy shot him a narrow look, which he affected not to notice. 'I read the summary sheet,' he said. 'Flicked through the initial incident report. That was all.'

'All you missed was the autopsy stuff, then,' Kennedy told him. 'There was sod all actual policing done at the scene. Anything stay with you?'

Harper shook his head. 'Not a lot,' he admitted. He slowed the car. They'd run into the back end of a queue that seemed to fill the top half of Parliament Street: roadworks, closing the street down to one lane. No point using the siren, because there was nowhere people could move out of their way. They rolled along, stop-start, slower than walking pace.

'Dead man was a teacher,' Kennedy said. 'A university professor, actually, at Prince Regent's College. Stuart Barlow. Age fifty-seven. Place of work, the college's history annexe on Fitzroy Street, which is where he died. By falling down a flight of stairs and breaking his neck.'

'Right.' Harper nodded as though it was all coming back to him.

'Except the autopsy now says he didn't,' Kennedy went on. 'He was lying at the bottom of the staircase, so it seemed like the logical explanation. It looked like he'd tripped and fallen badly: neck broken, skull impacted by a solid whack to the left-hand side. He had a briefcase with him. It was lying right next to him, spilled open, so there again, there was a default assumption. He packed his stuff, headed home for the night, got to the top of the stairs and then tripped. The body was found just after 9 p.m., maybe an hour after Barlow usually clocked off for the night.'

'Seems to add up,' Harper allowed. He was silent for a few moments as the car trickled forward a score or so of yards and then stopped again. 'But what? The broken neck wasn't the cause of death?'

'No, it was,' Kennedy said. 'The problem is, it wasn't broken in the right way. Damage to the throat muscles was consistent with torsional stress, not planar.'

'Torsional. Like it had been twisted?'

'Exactly. Like it had been twisted. And that takes a little focused effort. It doesn't tend to happen when you fall downstairs. Okay, a sharp knock coming at an angle might turn the neck suddenly, but you'd still expect most of the soft tissue trauma to be linear, the damaged muscle and the external injury lining up to give you the angle of impact.'

She flicked through the sparse, unsatisfying pages until she came to the one that – after the autopsy – was the most troubling.

'Plus there's the stalker,' Harper said, as if reading her thoughts. 'I saw there was another incident report in there. Dead man was being followed.'

Kennedy nodded. 'Very good, Detective Constable. Stalker is maybe overstating the case a little, but you're right. Barlow had reported someone trailing him. First of all at an academic conference, then later outside his house. Whoever signed off on this the first time around either didn't know that or didn't think it mattered. The two incident sheets hadn't been cross-referenced, so I'd go for the former. But in light of the autopsy results, it makes us look all kinds of stupid.'

'Which God forbid,' Harper murmured, blandly.

'Amen,' Kennedy intoned.

Silence fell, as it often does after prayers.

Harper broke it. 'So that stuff with the rat. Is that part of your daily routine?'

'These days, yeah. It pretty much is. Why? Do you have an allergy?'

Harper thought about that. 'Not yet,' he said at last.

Despite its name, the history annexe of Prince Regent's College was aggressively modern in design: an austere concrete and glass bunker, tucked into a side street a quarter of a mile from the college's main site on Gower Street. It was also deserted, since term had finished a week before. One wall of the foyer was a floor-to-ceiling notice board, advertising gigs by bands Kennedy didn't know, with dates that had already passed.

The harassed bursar, Ellis, came out to meet them. His face was shiny with sweat, as though he'd come straight from the bureaucratic equivalent of an aerobic workout, and he seemed to see the visit as a personal attack on the good name of the institution. 'We were told the investigation was closed,' he said.

'I doubt you were ever told that by anyone with the authority to say it, Mr Ellis,' Harper said, deadpan. The official line at this point was that the case had never been closed: that had only ever been a misunderstanding.

Kennedy hated to hide behind weasel words, and at this point felt like she owed little loyalty to the department. 'The autopsy came back with some unusual findings,' she added, without looking at Harper. 'And that's changed the way we're looking at the case. It's probably best to say nothing about this to anyone else on the faculty, but we'll need to make some further investigations.'

'Can I at least assume that all this will be over before the start of our summer school programme?' the bursar asked, his tone stuck halfway between belligerence and quavering dread.

Kennedy wished it with all her heart, but she believed that giving people good news that hadn't been adequately crash-tested was setting them up for more misery later. 'No,' she said, bluntly. 'Please don't assume that.'

Ellis's face fell.

'But . . . the students,' he said, despite the self-evident lack of any. 'Things like this do no good at all for recruitment or for our academic profile.' It was such a strikingly fatuous thing to say that Kennedy wasn't sure how to respond. She decided on silence, unfortunately leaving a void that the bursar seemed to feel obligated to fill. 'There's a sort of contamination by association,' he said. 'I'm sure you know what I mean. It happened at Alabama after the shootings in the biology department. That was a disgruntled teaching assistant, I understand – a freak occurrence, a chance in a million, and no students were involved at all. But the faculty still reported a drop in applications the next year. It's as though people think murder is something you can catch.'

Okay, that was less fatuous, Kennedy thought, but a lot more obnoxious. This man had lost a colleague, in circumstances that were turning out to be suspicious, and his first thought was how it might affect the college's bottom line. Ellis was clearly a self-serving toerag, so he got civility package one: just the basics.

'We need to see the place where the body was found,' she told him. 'Now, please.'

He led them along empty, echoing corridors. The smell in the place reminded Kennedy of old newsprint. As a child she had built a playhouse in her parents' garden shed from boxes of newspapers. Her father had collected them for arcane reasons (maybe, even that far back, his mind was beginning to go). It was that smell, exactly: sad old paper, dead-ended, defeated in its effort to inform.

They turned a corner and Ellis stopped suddenly. For a moment Kennedy thought he meant to remonstrate with her, but he half-raised his hands in an oddly constrained gesture to indicate their immediate surroundings.

'This is where it happened,' he said, with an emphasis on the 'it' that was half-gingerly, half-prurient. Kennedy looked around, recognising the short, narrow hallway and the steep stairs from the photographs.

'Thank you, Mr Ellis,' she said. 'We'll handle this part on our own. But we'll need you again in a little while, to let us into Mr Barlow's study.'

'I'll be at reception,' Ellis said, and trudged away, the cartoon raincloud over his head all but visible.

Kennedy turned to Harper. 'Okay,' she said, 'let's walk this through.' She handed him the file, open and with the photos on top. Harper nodded, a little warily. He staggered the photos like a poker hand, glancing from them to the stairs and then back again. Kennedy didn't push him: he needed to get his eye in and it would take as long as it took. Whether he knew it or not, she was doing him a favour, letting him put it together in his own mind rather than hitting him with her thoughts right out of the gate. He was fresh out of the box after all: in theory, she was meant to be training him up, not using him as a foot-rest.

'He was lying here,' Harper said at last, sketching the scene with his free hand. 'His head ... there, around about the fourth stair.'

'Head on the runner of the fourth stair,' Kennedy cut in. She wasn't disagreeing, just wrapping it in her own words. She wanted to see it, to transfer the image in her head to the space in front of her, and she knew from experience that saying it would help. 'Where's the briefcase? By the base of the wall, right? Here?'

'Here,' Harper said, indicating a point maybe two yards out

from the foot of the stairs. 'It's open and on its side. There are a whole lot of papers, too, just strewn around here. Quite a wide spill, all the way to the far wall. They could have slipped out of the briefcase or out of Barlow's hands as he fell.'

'What else? Anything?'

'His coat.' Harper pointed again.

Kennedy was momentarily thrown. 'Not in the photos.'

'No,' Harper agreed. 'But it's here in the evidence list. They moved it because it was partially occluding the body and they needed a clear line of sight for the trauma photos. Barlow probably had it over his arm or something. Warm evening. Or maybe he was putting it on when he tripped. Or, you know, when he was attacked.'

Kennedy thought about this. 'Does the coat match the rest of his outfit?' she demanded.

'What?' Harper almost laughed, but he saw that Kennedy was serious.

'Is it the same colour as Barlow's jacket and trousers?'

Harper flicked through the file for a long time, not finding anything that described or showed the coat. Finally he realised that it was in one of the photos after all – one that had been taken right at the start of the examination but had somehow been shuffled to the bottom of the deck. 'It's a black raincoat,' he said. 'No wonder he wasn't wearing it. He was probably sweating just in the jacket.'

Kennedy climbed part of the way up the stairs, scanning them closely. 'There was blood,' she called over her shoulder to Harper. 'Where was the blood, Detective Constable?'

'Counting from the bottom, ninth and thirteenth stairs up.'

'Right, right. Stain's still visible on the wood here, look.' She circled her hand above one spot, then the other, triangulated to the bottom of the stairs. 'He hits, bang, bounces . . .' She turned to face Harper again. 'Not robbery,' she said, to herself more than to him.

He referred to the file again – the verbal summary this time, not the photos. 'No indication that anything had been taken,' he agreed. 'Wallet and phone still in his pocket.'

'He's worked here for eleven years,' Kennedy mused. 'Why would he fall?'

Harper flipped a few pages, was silent for a while. When he looked up, he pointed past Kennedy to the head of the stairs. 'Barlow's office is at the other end of that first-floor corridor,' he said. 'This was pretty much the only way he could take when he left the building, unless he was going all the way back to reception to drop off some outgoing mail or something. And it says here the bulb had gone, so the stairwell must have been dark.'

'Gone? As in removed?'

'No, gone as in burned out. Bulb had blown.'

Kennedy ascended the rest of the stairs. At the top was a very narrow landing. A single door, set centrally, led to another corridor – from what Harper had said, the corridor that led to Barlow's office. To either side of the door were two windows of frosted glass that looked through on to the corridor, extending from the ceiling down to about waist height. The remaining three feet or so from the windows to the ground were white wooden panels.

'So he comes to the top of the stairs in the dark,' she said. 'Stops to turn on the light, but it doesn't go on.' It was to the left of the door, a single switch. 'And someone who's waiting here, on the right-hand side, moves in on him while his back is turned.'

'Makes sense,' Harper said.

'No,' Kennedy said. 'It doesn't. That's not where you set an ambush, is it? Anyone standing around out here is visible both

20

from the bottom of the stairs and from the upper corridor, through these windows. It's stippled glass, but you'd still see if someone was standing there.'

'With the light out?'

'The light might be out on the landing, but we've got to assume that it's on in the upstairs corridor. You wouldn't miss someone standing right there in front of you, on the other side of the glass.'

'Okay,' said Harper. He paused, thinking. 'But this is a college. You wouldn't necessarily assume it was sinister for someone to be waiting here at the top of the stairs.'

Kennedy raised her eyebrows, let them fall again. 'The murderer would *know* it was sinister,' she said. 'So it would be an odd place to choose. And Barlow had reported being followed, so he might be more alert than usual. But there's a better answer for all this anyway. Go on.'

'A better answer?'

'I'll show you in a minute. Go on.'

'Okay,' Harper said. 'So whoever it was hangs around on the landing here for however long it takes, lets Barlow walk past, then grabs him from behind. Twists his head until his neck snaps, and pitches him down the stairs.'

Even as he was saying this, Harper was smiling. He snorted derision at his own summary. Kennedy looked a question at him, and he pointed to the top of the stairs, then to the bottom. 'You're right,' he said. 'It doesn't make any sense at all. I mean, talk about overkill. The guy was fifty-seven years old, for Christ's sake. The fall would probably have killed him in any case. Why not just give him a push?'

'Interesting point,' Kennedy said. 'Maybe Mister Somebody doesn't want to take the chance. Also, let's not forget that Mister Somebody knows how to break someone's neck with a single twist. Maybe he doesn't get to show his skills off too often and this was his night to strut.'

Harper joined in the game. 'Or they could have struggled, and the twist was a headlock that went wrong. Both that and the fall could have been accidents, more or less. Even if we find the guy, we might not be able to prove intent.'

Kennedy had descended again as he was talking. She passed him, went all the way back to the foot of the stairs. The banister rail ended there, curving down into a thicker wooden upright. She was looking for a specific feature, which she knew had to be there. It was about two feet off the ground, on the outside of the upright – the side that faced the lower corridor, rather than the stairs themselves.

'Okay,' she said to Harper, pointing. 'Now look at this.'

He came down and squatted beside her, saw what she was seeing. 'A nick in the wood,' he said. 'You think it was done on the night Barlow died?'

'No,' said Kennedy. 'Before. Probably a long time before. But it was definitely there on the night. It shows up in some of the forensics photos. Look.'

She took the prints back from him and flicked through them, came up with the image she'd first seen earlier that day, sitting across from Summerhill as he gave her the poisoned chalice. She passed it to Harper, who looked at it with cursory interest at first, then carried on looking.

'Bloody hell,' he said at last.

'Yeah. Bloody hell indeed.'

What the photo showed was a small shred of light-brown cloth caught on the jagged lip of that tiny imperfection in the wood. The forensic photographer had been careful to get it in very clear focus, presumably assuming at that point that he was participating in what could be the start of a murder inquiry.

22

The ragged tuft of cloth had been logged as evidence, too, and was therefore still sitting in a labelled bag in a labelled box on a shelf back in the division's forensic support wing. But nobody seemed to have given any real thought to it since. After all, you usually didn't have to work too hard to establish the presence of the victim at the scene of the crime.

Also in the photo, in the background but still more or less in focus, was Stuart Barlow himself, in a tan jacket with leather pads sewn in at the elbows – the stereotypical bachelor academic, except with his neck bent at an impossible angle and his staring face livid in death.

'I looked through the pack, but I didn't really register this,' Harper admitted. 'I was mostly just looking at the body.'

'So was the investigating officer. You see what it means, though, right?'

Harper nodded, but his face showed that he was still working through the implications. 'It's from Barlow's jacket,' he said. 'Or maybe his trousers. But . . . it's in the wrong place.'

'Jacket or trousers, Barlow shouldn't be anywhere near here,' Kennedy agreed, tapping the spot itself with her finger. 'It's a good seven or eight feet, laterally, from where he ended up, and it's on the wrong side of the stair rail – the outside. The jag in the wood is angled downwards, too. You'd more or less have to be moving upwards into the sharp edge to tear your clothes on it, and that's assuming you're standing where we are. I don't see any way this could happen as the body fell from above.'

'Maybe Barlow flails around after he hits bottom,' Harper speculated. 'Not quite dead. Trying to get up and get help or—' He stopped abruptly, shook his head. 'No, that's ridiculous. The poor bastard has a broken neck.'

'Right. If the loose thread had been from the street coat, then I'd maybe buy that. You can't figure the angles on something that's flapping around loose in someone's hand. But the street coat is black. This came from the clothes the victim was wearing, which wouldn't move upwards when his body was moving down, or do elaborate pirouettes around solid objects. No, I'm thinking Barlow met his attacker right here, at the bottom of the stairs. The guy waited out of sight here, probably in this alcove under the stairs, then when he heard the footsteps coming down he got into position, stepped out as Barlow walked by and grabbed him from behind.'

'And then arranged the body to look as though he fell,' Harper finished the thought. 'That would explain him hauling Barlow upright and catching his clothes on that jag.'

Kennedy shook her head. 'Remember the blood on the upper stairs, Harper. The body did fall. I just think it fell later. The attacker kills Barlow down here, because down here is safer. No windows, less chance that Barlow will see him coming – or recognise him, maybe, if they've met before. But he's thorough and he wants to make sure all the physical evidence is right. So once Barlow is dead, he drags the body up the stairs so he can throw it down again and add that extra touch of authenticity. In that process, as he's manhandling the body, the jacket catches on this jagged edge and a little shred of it gets caught.'

'That's way too complicated,' Harper protested. 'You just have to hit the guy with a pipe wrench, right? Everyone will assume it was a mugging that went wrong. You could walk right out of here with the murder weapon under your coat and nobody would ever know. Dragging the body up the stairs, even late in the evening when there's no one around, is a stupid risk to take.'

'It could be he preferred that risk to the risk of an investigation,' Kennedy said. 'There's the bulb, too.'

'The bulb?'

'On the upper landing. If I'm right, Barlow wasn't killed or even attacked up there. But the light is blown, to make it look that bit more likely that he fell. Could just be a weird coincidence, but I don't think so. I think our killer takes care of that little detail too. Unscrews the bulb, shakes it until the filament snaps, puts it back.'

'Afterwards.'

'Yes. Afterwards. I know, it sounds insane. But if that *is* what happened, then maybe ...'

She started up the stairs again, on hands and knees this time, head bent low to examine the edges of the stair runners. But it was Harper who found it, seven steps up, after she'd already gone past it.

'Here,' he called to her, pointing.

Kennedy turned and leaned in close to peer. Caught on the head of a nail that had been hammered in at a slight angle and remained proud of the wood, there was another wisp of light-brown cloth. It had survived because it was right in close to the wall, where people using the stairs were least likely to tread. Kennedy nodded, satisfied. 'Bingo,' she said. Corroborating evidence. Barlow's body had been dragged up the stairs, prior to falling down them but presumably after death.

'So,' Harper summarised, 'we've got a killer who strikes from the shadows, breaks a guy's neck with a single twist, then lugs him all the way up a flight of stairs that's in public use, and hangs around long enough to do a bit of stage dressing, all so he can fake an accident and duck a murder investigation. That takes an insane amount of balls.'

'Late in the evening,' Kennedy reminded him, but she didn't disagree. It suggested a cold-blooded and self-possessed performance, not a crime of passion or a fight that just got out of hand.

She straightened up. 'Let's take a look at Barlow's study,' she suggested.

3

In Leo Tillman's dreams, his wife and kids were both alive and dead at the same time. Consequently, the dreams could pivot on almost nothing – some tiny detail that sparked the wrong association in his defenceless subconscious – and career off into nightmare. There were very few nights where he made it through all the way to morning. Very few dawns that didn't find him already awake, sitting on the edge of his bed to disassemble and clean his Unica, or reading through online databases in the hope of a sighting.

This morning, though, it wasn't his bed. He was sitting on the seat of a complicated exercise machine in a stranger's bedroom, watching the sun come up over Magas. And it wasn't a gun in his hand, it was a printed A4 sheet with a couple of hundred words of slightly blurry copy. The Unica was tucked into his belt, with the safety on.

A colossal picture window in front of him framed the presidential palace at the other end of a narrow avenue lined with wrought-iron fencing. It looked exactly how the White House would look if you dropped a mosque right in the middle of it and then walked away. Beyond that, Main Street, and beyond that – opening directly off the main drag – the Caucasus Highway. It was a joke to call Magas a town, in Tillman's opinion, in the same way that it was a joke to call Ingushetia a country. No army. No infrastructure. Not even any people. The latest census gave the whole republic a smaller population than, say, Birmingham.

People mattered to Tillman. He could hide in a crowd, and so could the man he was looking for. That made Magas both attractive and dangerous. If his quarry was here, which admittedly was a longshot, there weren't very many places for him to go to ground. But the same thing would be true for Leo if things went bad.

There was movement from the bed behind him: the faint, purposeless stirrings that come with waking up.

Almost time to get to work.

But he watched the sunrise for a few moments longer, caught – despite himself – in a waking dream. Rebecca was standing in the sun, like the angel from the Book of Revelation, and with her, cradled in her arms, Jud, Seth and Grace. All of them as they were on the last day he saw them: not aged, not touched by time. They were so real that they made Magas look like a cardboard cut-out of a town, a bad movie set.

Tillman indulged these moments because they kept him alive, kept him moving. And at the same time he feared them because they softened him, made him weak. Love wasn't part of his present, but it was real and vivid in his past, and the memories were like a sort of voodoo. They made dead ground inside him yawn and gape open, made parts of his own nature that were almost dead rise up. Most of the time, Tillman was as simple as a nail. Remembering made him complex, and contradictory.

He heard a sigh and a fuzzy mumble from the bed. Then a more concerted movement. Reluctantly, Tillman closed his eyes. When he opened them again a few seconds later the sun was just the sun, not really capable any more of warming his world: just a spotlight, shining from a guard post in the sky.

He got up and crossed to the bed. Kartoyev was fully awake now and was coming to terms with his situation. He strained against the ropes, but only once with each one, testing the tension. He wasn't going to waste any energy in pointless struggle. He stared up at Tillman, his teeth bared as the muscles in his arms flexed.

'*Kto tyi, govn'uk?*' he demanded. His voice had a gravelly burr to it.

'English,' Tillman told him, tersely. 'And lie still. That's a friendly warning.'

There was a moment's silence. Kartoyev glanced off towards the door, listening and calculating. No sound of approaching footsteps. No sound at all from the rest of the house. So had this intruder killed his bodyguards or just sidestepped them? It made a difference. Either way, his best option would be to play for time – but the amount of time would be different in each case.

'*Ya ne govoryu pa-Angliski, ti druchitel,*' he muttered. '*Izvini.*'

'Well, that's clearly not the case,' Tillman said, mildly. 'I heard you last night, talking to your girlfriend.'

Belatedly, Kartoyev cast a glance to his left. He was alone in the massive bed. There was no sign of the redhead who'd shared it with him the night before.

'She's downstairs,' Tillman said, reading the Russian's expression. 'Along with your muscle. No sense in making her go through all the unpleasantness that you and me are about to experience. No, she didn't betray you. It was the booze that got you, not the girl.' He reached into his pocket and brought out a small bottle, now mostly empty. It would look to the Russian like gloating, but in fact Tillman was just letting him see how deep Shit Creek was running. 'One comma four,' he said. 'Butanediol. When it hits your stomach, it turns into GHB, the date-rape drug – but if you drink it along with alcohol, it takes

28

its own sweet time to kick in. They're both competing for the same digestive enzyme. So that's why you slept so deeply. And why all your people are tied up in the bathroom right now like so many cords of wood.'

'The boy from the bar,' Kartoyev said, grimly, lapsing into English at last. 'Jamaat. He's dead. I know his name, his family, where he lives. He's dead. I promise you.'

Tillman shook his head. He didn't bother to deny the young Chechen's complicity: the booze was the only common factor and Kartoyev was no fool. 'Too late for that,' he told the Russian. 'The kid's long gone. I gave him a couple of million roubles out of your safe. Not a fortune, but enough to give him a start-up in Poland or the Czech Republic. Somewhere out of your reach.'

'There is nowhere out of my reach,' Kartoyev said. 'I know all the flights out of Magas and I've got friends in the interior ministry. I'll trace him and I'll take him apart. I'll take you both apart.'

'Possibly. But maybe you're overestimating your friends. Once the funeral's over, they'll probably be too concerned about carving up your little empire to worry much about who it was that took you out.'

Kartoyev gave Tillman a long, hard stare, appraising him, taking his measure. Clearly he found something there that he took for weakness. 'You're not going to kill me, *zhopa*. You got that big pistol tucked into your belt, there, like a gangster, but you don't have the stones. You look like you're about to start crying like a little girl.'

Tillman didn't bother to argue. Maybe his eyes had watered a little when he stared into the sun, and the Russian was welcome to read into that whatever the hell he liked. 'You're right,' Tillman said. 'As far as the gun's concerned anyway. It stays where it is, for now. Most of what I had in mind to do to you, it's already done. Except I may untie you if you give me what I came here for.'

'What?' Kartoyev sneered. 'You hot for me, American? You want to suck my cock?'

'I'm British, Yanush. And I'll pass, thanks.'

Kartoyev tensed at the use of his given name and strained against the ropes again. 'You are going to bleed, asshole. You better kill me. You better make sure you kill me because if I get my hands around your—'

He broke off abruptly. Even over his rant, the click had been clearly audible. It had come from the bed, from directly underneath him.

'I told you to lie still,' Tillman said. 'What, you didn't feel that bulge under the small of your back? But you feel it now, obviously. And maybe you know what it is, since it's in your catalogue. In the special offer section.'

Kartoyev's eyes widened and he froze into sudden, complete stillness.

'There you go,' Tillman said, encouragingly. 'You got it in one.'

Kartoyev swore long and loud, but he was careful not to move.

Tillman raised the sheet of paper he was holding and read aloud from it. 'The SB-33 minimum metal anti-personnel mine is a sophisticated battlefield munition combining ease of use, flexibility of deployment and resistance to detection and disarming. Emplaced by hand or by the dedicated air-dispersal SY-AT system – page 92 – the mine's irregular outline makes it hard to locate on most terrain, while its MM architecture (only seven grams of ferrous metal in the whole assembly) renders most conventional detection systems useless.'

'*Yob tvoyu mat!*' Kartoyev screamed. 'You're *insane*. You'll die, too. We'll both die!'

Tillman shook his head solemnly. 'You know, Yanush, I really don't think so. It says here the blast is highly directional: straight up, to rip open the balls and maybe the guts of the poor bastard who steps on it. I'm probably okay standing way over here. But you stopped me before I got to the good part. The SB-33 has a double pressure plate. If you lean down on it hard the way you just did, it doesn't detonate, it just locks. That's so you can't make it blow long-distance, with a mine-clearing charge. It's the next move you make that's going to unlock the plate and introduce you to a life lived like a football match – in two halves.'

Kartoyev swore again, as vigorously as before, but the colour had drained out of his face. He knew this item of his inventory very well, and not just by reputation: during his army days, he had probably had plenty of opportunity to see what the SB-33's maiming charge could do to a human body at point blank range. Probably he was weighing up in his mind the many different ways in which that shaped charge could mess him up, short of killing him. With the mine's upper surface pressed right against his lower spine, it was virtually certain that it would kill him. But there were some truly sickening alternative scenarios.

'So,' Tillman continued, 'I was looking for some information on one of your clients. Not a big account, but a regular one. And I know he's been by to see you quite recently. But I don't know which of your many products and services he was interested in. Or how to reach him myself. And I'm very keen to do that.'

Kartoyev's gaze flicked up, down, sidelong, then back to Tillman by the longest possible route. 'What client?' he asked. 'Tell me his name.' The Russian was too smart and too disciplined to let anything show in his face, but Tillman saw it all the same in those restless eyes – the visible sign of a complex calculation. You didn't get to be as successful as this man was in so many different rackets – illegal arms sales, drugs, people trafficking, the buying and selling of political influence – by ratting out your customers. Everything he said would have to sound plausible and everything he said would have to be a lie. Small, inconsequential details would be closest to the truth, while key information about place and time and transactions would be lies on a spectacular and heroic scale. Kartoyev was building an inverted pyramid of falsehood in his mind.

Tillman waved the question away brusquely. 'Name's slipped my mind,' he said. 'Don't even worry about it. I need to get some coffee, and maybe a little breakfast. We'll talk later.'

Kartoyev's eyes widened. 'Wait—' he began, but Tillman was already heading for the door. When he was halfway along the upper hallway, he heard the Russian say 'Wait!' again, in a slightly more urgent tone. He went on down the spiral staircase, treading heavily on the inlaid wooden steps so his footsteps resounded.

He checked on the other captives before doing anything else. Kartoyev's girlfriend and many bodyguards weren't in the bathroom: it would have taken too long to drag them all from the various places in which they'd fallen into the drug sleep. Tillman had just tied and gagged them in situ or lugged them a little way and dumped them behind furniture if there was any chance that they could be glimpsed from the building opposite. Most of them were groggily awake by now, so he went around with syringes of Etomidate, a dope-fiend Santa with gifts for all. He injected the drug into the men's – and the woman's – left or right cubital veins because their tightly bound arms made them stand out like ropes. Soon enough they were all sleeping again, more profoundly than before.

When it came to killing, Tillman was precise and professional, and his choice of drugs reflected this. The difference between an effective dose of Etomidate and a lethal one was about thirty to one for a healthy adult. These people would wake up sicker than parrots and weaker than puppies, but they'd wake up.

With that business concluded, Tillman went and sat by the window for a while, watching the street. The house was set back in its own grounds, the gates high and the walls topped with razor wire. To discourage uninvited guests no doubt. But he didn't want to be surprised by an invited one, or a colleague or acquaintance coming around to find out why Kartoyev hadn't shown up at some appointment or other. Once that happened, the house, the city and the entire Republic of Ingushetia would quickly become an escape-proof trap for Tillman. He had every reason to act fast.

But he had even better reasons to wait, so that was what he did. And because he was too tense to eat or drink, to read or to rest, he waited in stillness, staring out of the window into the bull grass and the monkey puzzle trees.

Tillman had been a mercenary for nine years. He'd never done interrogation work – he had no particular taste for it, and in his experience the men who specialised in it were profoundly damaged – but he'd seen it done and he knew the big secret, which was to make the subject do most of the heavy lifting for you. Kartoyev was a tough bastard, who'd clawed his way to his current position of eminence using the balls and throats of lesser mortals as handholds. But now he was lying on top of a contact mine, and his imagination would be feeding on itself in ferocious, toxic fast-forward. When a strong man is helpless, strength becomes weakness.

Tillman gave it two and a half hours before he went back up

to the bedroom. Kartoyev hadn't moved a muscle, as far as Tillman could see. The man's face had gone white, his eyes were wide, his lips slightly parted so you could see the clenched teeth within. 'What was the name?' he asked, in a low and very distinct tone. 'Who do you want to know about?'

Tillman patted his pockets. 'Sorry,' he said. 'I wrote it down somewhere. Let me go check my jacket.'

As he turned back towards the door, Kartoyev made a horrible, ragged sound – as though he was trying to talk around a caltrop in the middle of his tongue. 'No,' he croaked. 'Tell me!'

Tillman made a big show of thinking it over, coming to a decision. He crossed to the bed and sat down on the edge of it, placing his weight with exaggerated care. 'The first time you lie to me,' he said, 'I'm giving up on you. You understand me? There are other guys on my list, other people this guy uses, so you're completely expendable – to me, as well as to him. You lie to me, or you even hesitate in telling me everything you know, and I'm gone. In which case, it's going to be a very long day for you.'

Kartoyev lowered his chin to his chest, then brought it up again, a slow mo nod of acquiescence.

'Michael Brand,' Tillman said.

'Brand?' Kartoyev's tone was pained, uncomprehending. Clearly he'd been expecting a different name. 'Brand ... isn't anybody.'

'I didn't say he was important. I just said I want to know about him. So what have you got, Yanush? What does he come to you for? Weapons? Drugs? Women?'

The Russian drew a ragged breath. 'Women, no. Never. Weapons, yes. Drugs ... yes. Or at least, things that can be used to make drugs.'

'What sort of volume are we talking about?' Tillman was

careful to keep his voice level, not to let the urgency show, because the strength had to be all on his side. Any chink in his armour might make the Russian baulk.

'For the weapons,' Kartoyev muttered. 'Not so very many. Not enough for an army, but enough – if you were a terrorist – to finance a medium-sized jihad. Guns: hundreds, rather than thousands. Ammunition. Grenades, one or two. But not explosives. He doesn't seem to care much for bombs.'

'And the drugs?'

'Pure ephedrine. Anhydrous ammonia. Lithium.'

Tillman frowned. 'So he's brewing meth?'

'I sell meth.' Kartoyev sounded indignant. 'I said to him once, if that's what you want, Mr Brand, why take away these bulky and inconvenient raw materials? For a small surcharge, I'll give you crystal or powder in any amount you like.'

'And he said?'

'He told me to fill his order. He said he had no need of anything else I could offer him.'

'But the amounts?' Tillman pursued. 'Enough to sell, commercially?'

Kartoyev began to shake his head, winced. He'd been holding to a position of paralysed rigidity for several hours, and his muscles were agonisingly locked. 'Not really,' he grunted. 'Recently, though – this last batch – much, much more than usual. A thousand times more.'

'And it's always Brand who collects and pays?'

Again, the look. *Why is he asking this?* 'Yes. Always ... the man uses that name. Brand.'

'Who does he represent?'

'I have no idea. I saw no reason to ask.'

Tillman scowled. He stood up suddenly, rocking the bed a little and making Kartoyev cry out – a choked, premonitory wail of anguish. But there was no explosion. 'Bullshit,' Tillman said, leaning over his captive. 'A man like you doesn't fly blind. Not even on small transactions. You'd find out everything you could about Brand. I already warned you about lying, you brain-dead scumbag. I think you just used up the last of my goodwill.'

'No!' Kartoyev was desperately earnest. 'Of course, I tried. But I found nothing. There was no trail that led to him, or from him.'

Tillman considered, keeping his face impassive. As far as it went, that matched his own experience. 'So how do you contact him?'

'I don't. Brand tells me what he needs, then he appears. Payment is in cash. He arranges his own transport. Cars, usually. Once, a truck. Always these are hired, under assumed names. When they're returned, they've been scrubbed clean.'

'How does Brand contact you?'

'By telephone. Cellphones, always. Disposables, always. He identifies himself by a word.'

Tillman caught on this detail. It seemed unlikely: amateurish and unnecessary. 'He doesn't trust you to recognise his voice?'

'For whatever reason. He identifies himself by a word. *Diatheke*.'

'What does that mean?'

Kartoyev shook his head slowly, with great care, once only. 'I don't know what it means to him. To me it means Brand. That's all.'

Tillman looked at his watch. He felt almost certain that the Russian had nothing more to tell, but time was against him. It was probably time to start packing up. But Kartoyev was the best lead he'd had in three years and it was hard to walk away without squeezing the last drop out of him.

'I still don't believe you'd let it go that easily,' Tillman said, staring down at the rigid, sweating man. 'That you'd do business with him, year in and year out, without trying to figure out what he's about.'

Kartoyev sighed. 'I told you. I tried. Brand comes in on different routes, from different airports, and leaves, likewise, in different directions: sometimes by air, sometimes driving. He pays in a number of currencies – dollars, euros, sometimes even roubles. His needs are ... eclectic. Not just the things you mentioned, but also, sometimes, legal technology illegally acquired. Generators. Medical equipment. Once, a surveillance truck, new, designed for the SVR – for Russian intelligence. Brand is a middle man, obviously. He fronts for many different interests. He acquires what is needed, for whoever is prepared to pay.'

A tremor went through Tillman, which he couldn't suppress or keep from the Russian. 'Yes,' he agreed. 'That's what he does. But you say you've never sold him people.'

'No.' Kartoyev's voice was tight. He could read the emotion in Tillman's face and he was obviously concerned about what that loss of control might mean. 'Not people. Not for work or for sex. Perhaps he sources those things elsewhere.'

'Those *things*?'

'Those commodities.'

Tillman shook his head. He was wearing a hangman's deadpan now. 'Not much better.'

'I'm a businessman,' Kartoyev muttered, tightly, sardonic even in extremity. 'You'll have to forgive me.'

'No,' Tillman said. 'There's nothing that says I have to do that.'

He leaned down and reached underneath Kartoyev's body. The Russian yelled again, in despair and rage, stiffening in a whole-body rictus as he braced for the blast.

Tillman pulled the squat, plastic box out from under him, letting the Russian see the blank, inert digital display and the words – ALARM, TIME, SET, ON-OFF – printed in white on the black fascia. A foot of electric cable and a Continental-style plug dangled from the device, on which the maker's name, Philip's, was also prominently emblazoned. The alarm clock was of eighties vintage. Tillman had bought it under Zyazikov Bridge, from a Turk who had his meagre wares spread out on the plinth of the President's statue.

Kartoyev's incredulous laugh sounded like a sob. 'Son of a whore!' he grunted.

'Where did Brand go this time?' Tillman asked, slipping the question in fast and brisk. 'When he left you?'

'England,' Kartoyev said. 'He went to London.'

Tillman took the Unica from his belt, thumbed the safety in the same movement and shot Kartoyev in the left temple, angling the shot to the right. The mattress caught the bullet, and some of the sound, but Tillman wasn't worried about the sound: the windows of the house had been triple-glazed and the walls were solid.

He packed his things quickly and methodically – the clock, the gun, the xeroxed sheet and the rest of the money from the safe. He'd already wiped the room for prints, but he did so again. Then he gave the dead man on the bed a valedictory nod, went downstairs and let himself out.

London. He thought about that dead ground in his mind, in his soul. He'd been away for a long time, and that hadn't been an accident. But maybe there was a God after all, and his providence had a symmetrical shape.

The shape of a circle.

4

Stuart Barlow's study had already been examined by the first case officer, but there were no evidence notes in the file and nothing had been taken. Searching it was going to be a daunting proposition: every surface was stacked with books and papers. The strata of folders and print-outs on the desk had spread out to colonise large areas of the floor on both sides, which at least had the effect of hiding some of the goose-turd-green carpet tiles. Prints of Hellenic statues and Egyptian karyatids, rippled inside their glass frames by seasons of damp English weather and bad central heating, stared down at the shambles with stern, unforgiving faces.

The small, cluttered space was claustrophobic, and indefinably sad. Kennedy wondered whether Barlow would have been ashamed to have his private chaos exposed to public scrutiny in this way, or if the heaped ramparts of notebooks and print-outs were a professional badge of pride.

'Mr Barlow was in the history faculty,' she remarked, turning to the bursar. Ellis had returned as promised to let them in, and now stood by with the key still in his hand, as if he expected the detectives to admit defeat when they saw the intractable mess of the dead man's effects. 'What did that entail? Did he have a full teaching schedule?'

'Point eight,' Ellis said, without a moment's hesitation. 'Five hours remission for administrative duties.'

'Which were?'

'He was second in department. And he ran Further Input – our gifted and talented programme.'

'Was he good at his job?' Kennedy demanded, bluntly.

Ellis blinked. 'Very good. All our staff are good, but ... well. Yes. Stuart was passionate about his subject. It was his hobby as well as his profession. He'd appeared on TV three or four times, on history and archaeology programmes. And his revision website was very popular with the students.' A pause. 'We'll all miss him very much.' Kennedy mentally translated that as: he put arses on seats.

Harper had picked up a book, *Russia Against Napoleon*, by Dominic Lieven. 'Was this his specialism?' he asked.

'No.' Again, Ellis was categorical. 'His specialism was palaeography – the earliest written texts. It didn't come into his teaching very much, because it's a tiny part of our undergraduate syllabus, but he wrote a lot on the subject.'

'Books?' Kennedy asked.

'Articles. Mostly focused on close textual analysis of the Dead Sea and Rylands finds. But he was working on a book – about the Gnostic sects, I think.'

Kennedy had no idea what the Gnostic sects were, but she let it pass. She wasn't seriously considering the possibility that Professor Barlow had been murdered by an academic rival.

'Do you know anything about his private life?' she asked instead. 'We know he wasn't married, but was he involved with anyone?'

The bursar seemed surprised by the question, as though celibacy was a necessary side effect of the scholarly life. 'I don't think so,' he said. 'It's possible, obviously, but he didn't mention anybody. And when he came to departmental functions, he never had anybody with him.'

That seemed to let out wronged husbands or jealous ex-lovers. The odds on finding a suspect were getting longer. But Kennedy had never had high hopes. In her experience, most of the work that solved a case was done in the first couple of hours. You didn't return to a case that was three weeks cold and expect to jump the gap in one amazing bound.

All this time, Harper had been skirmishing around in the books and papers – a token effort, but maybe he felt that having missed the mark with Napoleon, he had nothing to lose by bobbing for insights a second time. This time he held up what looked like a picture, but turned out to be a news clipping, pasted neatly on to card and then framed. It had been leaning against one of the legs of the desk. The headline read, 'Nag Hammadi Fraud: Two Arrested'. The man in the accompanying photo was recognisable as a much younger Stuart Barlow. His face wore an awkward, frosty smile.

'Your man had a criminal record?' Harper demanded.

Ellis actually laughed. 'Oh no,' he said, 'not at all. That was his triumph – about fifteen years ago, now, perhaps longer. Stuart was called in as an expert witness in that case because his knowledge of the Nag Hammadi library was so extensive.'

'What was the case?' Kennedy asked. 'And while we're on the subject, what's Nag Hammadi?'

'Nag Hammadi was the most important palaeographical find of the twentieth century, inspector,' Ellis told her. She didn't bother to correct him on her rank, though out of the corner of her eye she saw Harper roll his eyes expressively. 'In Upper Egypt, just after the end of the Second World War, near the town of Nag Hammadi, two brothers went digging in a limestone cave. They were only interested in finding guano – bat excrement – to use as fertiliser for their fields. What they found, though, was a sealed jar containing a dozen bound codices.'

'Bound what?' Harper asked.

'Codices. A codex is a number of pages sewn or fastened together. The first books, essentially. They began to be used in the early Christian era, where up to that time, the norm would have been to write on scrolls or single sheets of parchment. The codices in the Nag Hammadi find turned out to be texts from around the first and second century AD: gospels, letters, that sort of thing. Even a heavily rewritten translation of Plato's *Republic*. An incredible treasure trove from a period just after Christ's death, when the Christian church was still struggling to define its identity.'

'How did that become a court case?' Harper asked, cutting off the lecture just as the bursar took a deep breath for what looked like another, bigger info drop. Deflected, he looked both indignant and slightly at a loss.

'The court case came much later. It concerned forged copies of Nag Hammadi documents, which were being sold online to dealers in antiquities. Stuart appeared as a witness for the prosecution. I think he was there mainly to give an opinion on the physical differences between the original documents and the forgeries. He knew every crease and ink stain on those pages.'

Harper put the article down and rummaged some more. Ellis's face took on a pained expression. 'Detective, if you're planning to conduct an extensive search, can I please get on with my duties and come back later?'

Harper looked a question at Kennedy, who was still thinking about the court case. 'What was the verdict?' she asked the bursar.

'Equivocal,' Ellis said, a little sullenly. 'The dealers – a husband and wife, I think – were found guilty of handling the fraudulent items, and of some technical infringements relating to proper documentation, but innocent on the forgery charge, which was the main one. They had to pay a fine and some of the court's costs.'

'As a result of Professor Barlow's testimony?'

Ellis made an 'oh!' face, finally seeing where she was going. 'Stuart wasn't that big a part of the case,' he said, doubtfully. 'To be honest, everybody thought it was funny that he set so much store by it. I think most of the relevant evidence came from the people who'd bought the forged documents. And as I said, it only resulted in a fine. I don't really think ...'

Kennedy didn't either, but she filed the point away for later. It would be worth following up if they drew a blank on everything else. Not that everything else amounted to very much, so far. 'Why hasn't Professor Barlow's sister collected all this?' she asked. 'She's the only surviving relative, isn't she?'

'Rosalind. Rosalind Barlow. She's in our files as next of kin,' Ellis agreed. 'And we've corresponded with her. She said she wasn't interested in any of Stuart's things. Her exact words: "Take what you want for the college library and give the rest to charity." That's probably what we'll do, eventually, but it will take some time to sort through it all.'

'A lot of time,' Harper agreed, adding after a beat, 'All good here, Inspector?'

She shot him a warning look, but his expression was as bland as runny custard. 'All good,' she said, 'Detective Constable. Let's go.'

She was heading for the door as she spoke, but she hesitated. Something had registered on her inner eye, without her realising it, and was now clamouring to be admitted to her conscious attention. Kennedy knew better than to ignore that fish-hook tug. She slowed to a halt and looked around once more.

She almost had it, when Ellis jangled his keys and broke the slender thread by which she was pulling the thought up into the daylight. She shot him a glare, which made him falter slightly.

'There are other things I need to do,' he said, with no conviction at all.

Kennedy breathed out deeply. 'Thank you for your help, Mr Ellis,' she said. 'We may have to ask you some further questions later, but we won't need to take up any more of your time today.'

They headed back to the car, Kennedy turning over in her mind the little they knew about this already badly mangled case. She needed to talk to the dead man's sister. That was priority number one. Maybe Barlow really did have a nemesis in the palaeographical arena; or a student he'd gotten pregnant, or a younger brother he'd stiffed in some way that might have left a festering grudge. You were about ten times more likely to catch a killer by having his name given to you directly than you ever were by climbing a ladder of clues. And they didn't have a ladder as yet. They didn't even have a rung.

Yes, they did. The stalker, the guy who Barlow had said was following him. That was the other way into this. Harper was going to hate her, because she was determined to talk to the sister herself, so most of the grunt work in all of this would fall on him.

In the car, she laid it on the line for him, forwards and backwards.

'When Barlow said he was being followed,' she said, reading from the file notes, 'he was at some kind of an academic conference.'

'The London Historical Forum,' Harper said. He had been flicking through the file at odd moments in the course of their visit, evidently to some effect. 'Yeah. He said the guy was hanging around in the lobby and then he saw him again in the car park.'

'I'm wondering if anyone else saw him. Barlow didn't give us much of a description, but maybe we could fill in the gaps. Maybe someone even knew the guy. There would have been dozens of people there after all. Maybe hundreds. The organisers would have a contact list. Phone numbers. Email addresses.'

Harper gave her a wary look.

'We share the cold-calling, right?'

'Of course we do. But I'm going to see Barlow's sister first. You'll have to chase it by yourself until I get back.'

Harper didn't look happy, but he nodded. 'Okay,' he said. 'What else?'

Kennedy was mildly impressed. He'd read her expression accurately, knew there was more to come. 'You're going to take a lot of shit for working with me,' she said. 'That's just the way it is right now.'

'So?'

'So you can get out of it really easily. Go to Summerhill and say we've got personal differences.'

There was a pause.

'Do we?' Harper asked.

'I don't even know you, Harper. I'm just doing you a favour. Maybe doing myself one, too, because if you're in with those monkeys, I'd rather have you outside the tent than inside – and you'd rather be there, because I'll sure as hell pass the pain along when it comes.'

Harper tapped the steering wheel idly with a thumbnail, blowing out first one cheek and then the other. 'This is my first case as a detective,' he said.

'So?'

'Two hours in and you're already trying to kick me off it.'

'I'm giving you the option.'

Harper turned the key and the engine of the antiquated Astra roared gamely – an old house cat pretending to be a tiger.

'I'll keep it open,' he said.

5

As he'd planned to do, Tillman drove the rental car to the outskirts of Erzurum, where he left it way off the road hidden under a few tree branches and armloads of scrub. He'd hired it using a false name, which was different from the false name on the passport he'd shown at the Georgian and Turkish borders.

From a bar on Sultan Mehmet Boulevard, he placed a call – untraceable as far as local law enforcement was concerned – to the police in Magas, making sure they knew about the body. They'd find the bound and gagged guards, if someone else hadn't already, and nobody would die except Kartoyev. Not mercy, obviously: just a habit of mind that Tillman put down to neatness or professional pride.

He wasn't planning to stick around long, but he wanted to make a couple more calls before he went off the radar again. The first was to Benard Vermeulens – a cop, but a cop who, like Tillman, had done both regular military and mercenary service before coming back into civilian life. Now he worked for the UN mission in Sudan, and he had access to all kinds of unlikely but topical information, which he was sometimes prepared to share.

'*Hoe gaat het met jou,* Benny?' Leo asked, the one Flemish phrase that Vermeulens had ever succeeded in teaching him.

'Mother of god. Twister!' Vermeulens' hoarse, burring voice made the phone vibrate in Tillman's hand. '*Met mij is alles goed!* What about yourself, Leo? What can I do for you? And don't bother saying nothing.'

'It's not nothing,' Tillman admitted. 'It's the usual thing.'

'Michael Brand.'

'I heard he was in London. Could still be there. Can you turn over the usual stones? I want to know if his name turns up on anything official. Or anything at all, for that matter.'

'*Joak*. I'll do that, Leo.'

'And the other usual thing?'

'Now there, I have bad news.'

'Somebody's looking for me?'

'Somebody is looking for you very hard. For two weeks now. Lots of searches, lots of questions. Mostly three or four elbows in the chain, each time, so I can't get a glimpse of who's asking. But they're asking like they mean it.'

'Okay. Thanks, man. I owe you.'

'This is for friendship. If you owe me, we're not friends.'

'Then I owe you nothing.'

'That's better.'

Leo hung up and dialled Insurance. But Insurance just laughed when she heard his voice. 'Leo, you're not a risk that anyone's willing to take any more,' she told him, with what sounded like genuine fondness in her voice.

'No? Why is that, Suzie?' he asked. It did no harm to remind her that he was one of the three or four people still around who'd known her when she had a real name.

'If you kill someone on a side street in Nowhere-on-Sea, honey, that's one thing. But killing someone at a major inter-section in the big city where we all live ... well, that's different.'

Tillman said nothing, but he covered the mouthpiece with his hand for a moment anyway, afraid that he might swear or just suck in his breath. Hours. Just a few hours. How could the news have run ahead of him? How could anyone have tied his name to a death that had only just been discovered?

'I thought the world was a village,' was all he said.

'You wish. In a village, it would just be MacTeale's big brother you had to worry about. As it is, it's everyone on his Rolodex.'

'MacTeale?' For a second Tillman had trouble even placing the name. Then he remembered the big, angry Scot who'd headed up his squad for the last year of his stint at Xe. 'Somebody killed MacTeale?'

'You did, apparently. At least, that's the word that's going around.'

'The word's wrong, Suzie.'

'So you say.'

'I didn't kill MacTeale. I killed some no-account Russian middle-man who thought he had friends in high places, but I reckon they were the kind of friendships you rent on a short lease. Listen, all I want is another passport, in case this one got a stain on it. I can pay up front, if that will make things easier.'

'You can make things as easy as you like, Leo. Nobody is going to sell to you, employ you or share intel with you. The community has closed its doors.'

'And that includes you?'

'Leo, of course that includes me. If I start offending the sensibilities of my clients, I'll have a lonely, impoverished old age. Which will still put me ahead of you, sweetheart, because from what I hear, you're on borrowed time now. No hard feelings.'

'Maybe a few,' Tillman said.

'Good luck.' Insurance sounded as though she meant it, but she hung up without waiting for him to answer.

Tillman snapped the phone shut and put it away. He nodded to the barman, who came and brought him another Scotch and water. Someone had gone to a lot of trouble to shut him down, and whoever it was, they'd achieved miracles in a very short time. He tipped back the whisky in a silent toast to his unseen adversary. Your first mistake, Mr Brand, he thought, was letting me find out your name. Now here we are, just thirteen years later, and you slipped up again.

You let me know I'm on the right track.

Tillman was nobody. He'd be the first to admit that: more so as he'd gotten older, as he'd moved further and further away from the one time in his life when everything had come into clear focus and – briefly – made a kind of sense.

It was the mystery on which he was nailed up, these days. The hunt was what gave shape and meaning to his life, and so he was defined by an absence: four absences, in fact. The only things that were real for him were the things that weren't there. Such a long time ago, now. So much blood under the bridge, and more to come, definitely, because the alternative was to stop looking. If he stopped looking, Tillman wouldn't just be nobody, he'd be nothing, and nowhere. Might as well be dead as admit that he'd never see Rebecca again, or the kids. Never come home, was how he put it to himself; admit, finally, that the world was empty.

It had been different when he was a younger man. Being nobody was the easy option back then. Born in Preston, Lancashire, where he lived until he was sixteen, he grew up with a drifter's nature and a drifter's skill set, too lazy to be dangerous or even effective. He wandered into things, wandered out of them again, cared about nothing.

At school, Tillman had been good at most subjects, the academic stuff as well as workshops and sports, but was too uncommitted to any one thing to turn *good* into *great*. Good came without effort, and it was enough. Consequently, he dropped out at sixteen, despite earnest interventions from his teachers, and took a job at a garage that paid sufficiently well to supply a lifestyle of casual vices – drinking, women, occasional gambling – indulged without all that much conviction.

Eventually, though, and maybe inevitably, he'd drifted out of his accustomed orbit. He became part of a generational exodus from the north of England to the south, where there just seemed to be more going on. It wasn't even a decision, really: in the decades after the Second World War, Lancashire's mills and factories had foundered like so many torpedoed trawlers, and the waves thrown up by their collapse had pushed a million people to the opposite end of the country. In London, Tillman had done a lot of things, been ambitious in none of them: a strong man whose strengths were hidden from him. Garage mechanic, plasterer, roofer, security guard, joiner. Jobs that required skills, certainly, and Tillman seemed to acquire those skills very readily. What he didn't do was to stick to any one path for long enough to find out what he was underneath those quotidian disguises.

Perhaps, in retrospect, it ought to have been obvious that a man like that would find his centre of gravity in a woman. When he met Rebecca Kelly, at an after-hours lock-in party given by one of his former bosses in an east London pub, he was twenty-four and she was a year younger. She looked out of place against dark-pink flock wallpaper, but she was so extraordinary that she probably would have looked out of place anywhere.

She wore no make-up, and she didn't need any: her brown eyes contained all colours and her pale skin made her lips look redder than any lipstick could make them. Her hair was like the hair described in the *Song of Solomon*, which Tillman vaguely remembered from a religious studies lesson: clusters of black grapes. Her stillness was like the stillness of a dancer waiting for the overture to start.

Tillman had never encountered beauty so perfect, or passion so intense. He'd never encountered a virgin, either, so their first night of lovemaking was unexpectedly traumatic for both of them. Rebecca had wept, sitting amid the bloodied sheets with her head buried in her folded arms, and Leo had been terrified that he had injured her in some profound and irrevocable way. Then she embraced him, kissed him fiercely, and they tried again and made it work.

They were engaged three weeks later, and married a month after that in a registry office in Enfield. Photos from that time invariably showed Tillman with his arm protectively around his wife's waist, his smile tinged with the solemnity of a man carrying something precious and fragile.

Work had never been entirely real for him. He prospered without effort, meandered without a tether. Clearly, though, love was real: marriage was real. Tillman's life had folded inward on another's life, to make a focus where none had been.

Happiness was something he'd never missed because he believed he already had it. Now he understood the difference, and accepted the stark miracle of Rebecca's love with uneasy wonder. There was nothing you could do to deserve a gift like that, so on some level you always half-expected the boom to drop and the gift to be snatched away.

Instead, the children had come along, and the simple miracle had become a complex one. Jud. Seth. Grace. The names had a biblical ring. Tillman had never read the Bible, but he knew that there was a garden in it, before the Devil showed up and the shit hit the fan. He felt as though he were living there: for six years he felt that.

Part of being happy was that he'd learned to focus his skills and his intellect. He'd set up his own company, selling central heating systems, and he was doing pretty well – well enough to rent a warehouse with a small office attached, and take on a secretary. He worked six days a week, but didn't stay late unless there was an emergency. He always wanted to be there to help Rebecca put the kids to bed, even though she never allowed him to read them bedtime stories. It was the one thing about her that he didn't understand. She had a horror of stories, never read fiction herself, and shut him down within a sentence if he ever ventured on a 'Once upon a time'.

She was a mystery, he had to admit that. He'd explained himself to her in a dozen sentences or so, without the aid of diagrams, but Rebecca was reticent about her past, even more so about her family. She only said that they were very close, and very inward-looking: 'We were everything to each other.' She became quiet when she said these things, and Tillman suspected some tragedy that he was too afraid to probe.

Had he married a picture? A façade? He knew so little. But you could know nothing about gravity and still remain fastened to the earth. He was fastened to her, and to the children, that tightly. Gentle, nervous Jud; boisterous, crude Seth; furious, loving Grace. Rebecca, against whom adjectives leaned askew because there was no way to describe her. If he needed to know anything more, she'd tell him. And whether she told him or not, gravity would still operate.

One evening in September, when the summer had stopped as suddenly as a car crash and the trees were burning bright red and yellow, Tillman came home, not one minute later than usual, to find the house empty. Completely empty. Jud was five, and had just started school, so he thought at first that maybe he'd got the date mixed up and missed a parents' evening. Contrite, he checked the calendar.

Nothing.

Then he checked the bedrooms and his contrition turned to abject terror. Rebecca's side of the wardrobe was empty. In the bathroom, the vanity unit was bare and his toothbrush stood alone in a purple plastic mug that bore the face of Barney the Dinosaur. The children's rooms had been even more thoroughly stripped: clothes and toys, sheets and duvets, posters and friezes and pinned-up kindergarten paintings, everything had gone.

Almost everything. One of Grace's toys – Mr Snow, a unicorn who smelled of vanilla essence – had fallen behind the sofa and been forgotten.

Then he found the note, in Rebecca's handwriting, consisting of four words.

Don't look for us.

She hadn't even signed it.

Tillman was walking wounded, working through the shock of what felt like an amputation. He called the police, who told him he should just wait. You didn't become a missing person by walking out of the house: time has to elapse before you can be awarded that status. Tillman could maybe call around his wife's friends and family, the desk sergeant suggested, and see if she was with anyone she knew. If the kids didn't show up for school the next day, then Tillman should call again. Until then, it was much more likely that the whole family were safe and well somewhere close by than that they'd been abducted en masse. Particularly since there was a note.

Rebecca didn't have any friends, that Tillman knew of, and he had no idea where her family lived, if they were still alive at all. These options were closed to him. All he could do was walk the streets on the very remote off-chance that he might run into her. He walked, even though he already knew it was an empty hope. Rebecca and the children were far away by this time; the purpose of the note was to make sure that he didn't follow or to persuade him – as if that were even possible – that they'd left of their own accord.

They hadn't. That was his starting point. As he stalked the streets of Kilburn like an automaton, he replayed the events of the day again and again: the children kissing him goodbye, with as much spontaneity and love as usual; Rebecca telling him the car might be in the garage for its MOT, so if he needed a lift home she probably wouldn't be able to pick him up (he called the garage and checked: Rebecca had driven the car in at noon, asked them to replace the spare tyre at the same time, and arranged to pick it up the following morning unless it failed its test). Even the contents of the fridge were a speaking testimony: she'd stocked up for the week, presumably in the morning before dropping the car off.

So the note had been written under duress – a prospect that he had to force his mind away from immediately because the dangerous rage it evoked threatened to tear its way out of him in some crazy way.

The police had been no more helpful the next morning. The note, they explained, made it very clear that Mrs Tillman had left him of her own volition and taken the children with her because she no longer trusted him with them.

'Was there some marital dispute the night before?' the desk officer asked him. He could see naked dislike in her eyes: of course there was a dispute, that look said. Women leave their husbands all the time, but they don't up and run with three kids unless there's something seriously wrong.

There was nothing, Tillman said, and kept on saying, but the same question surfaced again and again, accompanied each time by an absolute refusal to list Rebecca as a missing person. The kids, yes: school-age and pre-school-age children can't be allowed to just disappear. Descriptions were taken and photofits put together. The kids would be looked for, Tillman was told. But when found, they would not be taken from their mother, and the police would not necessarily cooperate in putting Tillman and his wife back in contact with each other. That would depend on the story Rebecca told and the wishes she expressed.

At some point in this vicious circle of patronising indifference and bald suspicion, Tillman lost control. He spent a night in the cells, having had to be wrestled away from an impossibly young constable, screaming obscenities, after the little rodent asked him if Rebecca had been having an affair. It was fortunate that he hadn't got his hands around the kid's throat: he'd certainly been about to.

As far as Tillman could tell, there was never any real investigation. He got progress reports, at odd intervals; sightings, which according to the Met were always followed up but always turned out to be false alarms; sporadic news articles, which seemed at one point to be building into some kind of conspiracy theory in which he'd murdered his wife and kids or else murdered his wife and sold his kids to Belgian paedophiles. But that kind of phenomenon has to have something to feed on, and since there was no news after the first day, it petered out without reaching critical mass.

Tillman contemplated the ruin of his life. He might have gone back to work, tried to forget, but he never seriously considered it an option. To forget would be to leave Rebecca, and their children, in the hands of strangers whose agenda he couldn't even begin to guess at. If they hadn't gone willingly, and he knew they hadn't, then they'd been taken, from a populous city without so much as a trace. And they were waiting now to be rescued. They were waiting for him.

The problem with this, as Tillman was intelligent enough to appreciate, was that he wasn't even close to being the man they needed: the man who could find and free his family from the hands of their captors. He didn't even know where to start.

Sitting in the kitchen of their home, a week after the disappearance, he thought it out with ruthless and clear-headed logic. What needed to be done could not be done by him and could not be trusted to anyone else.

He had to change. He had to become the man who could find and fight and liberate and do whatever else was required to restore equilibrium to the world. The resources he had at his disposal were fourteen hundred pounds' worth of savings and a mind that had never yet been tested to its limits.

He took Rebecca's note from his pocket. *Don't look for us.* For the thousandth time he read those words, for surface and then for hidden meanings. Maybe, but only maybe, the space after the first word was wider than the other spaces: Rebecca's yearning for him projected into that minuscule void, begging him to see what her heart was really shrieking as her hand wrote.

Don't
look for us.

I'm coming, he told her in his mind, his hand balling into a fist. It won't be soon, but I'm coming. And the people who took you away from me are going to bleed and burn and die.

The next day he joined the army – the 45th Medium Regiment, Royal Artillery – and began, methodically, to rebuild himself.

6

Back in the bear pit, later, Harper's fellow officers were keen to debrief him on his day out with the ball-breaker. He disappointed them by having nothing of substance to say.

'We were together in the car for like, ten minutes,' he pointed out. 'The rest of the time we were squeezing the scene, two weeks late. We barely even talked. It's not like we were out on a date.'

'If you were,' Combes pointed out, 'she'd just go around afterwards telling everyone you shot off too early.' This got big laughs all round, despite being just another limp variation on the default Kennedy joke that had been running the circuit for the past six months. As jokes went, it earned its keep, turning up in anonymous emails, graffiti in the toilets, bottom-of-the-barrel drunken rambles at the Old Star. *Why did Kennedy leave her boyfriend? What did Kennedy tell the marriage guidance counsellor? Why does Kennedy never reach orgasm?*

They told Harper the story. He knew it already, intimately, as every officer in the Met knew it by this time, but the detectives recounting the legend did it for their own enjoyment more than for his. Kennedy had been an ARU, an armed response unit. She'd gone in as part of a team of three. Guy outside a terraced house in Harlesden at two in the morning, shouting, waving a gun. Neighbours had heard windows smash. One said she'd heard a shot.

Kennedy took point, approaching the guy head-on while Gates and Leakey, her two colleagues, moved in behind parked cars to flank him. The guy in question, one Marcus Dell, aged thirty, was as high as a kite on something or other, and the thing he was waving in his right hand did look like a gun. But his left hand was bleeding like a bastard, and according to Kennedy's statement after the fact, she'd had a suspicion that he'd broken the window by punching it in rather than with a bullet.

So she'd gone in a little closer, talking, talking, talking all the way, till she was ten feet away and she'd seen what Dell was carrying: a broken clamshell phone, its top half sticking out at a suggestive angle.

She called the all-clear and the other two officers came out of covert, full of that mixed adrenalin, relief, anger and slightly surreal buzz that comes with being close to a life-or-death decision and then being told to stand down.

Dell threw the phone at Leakey, hitting him square in the eye. Then both Gates and Leakey cut loose, firing off eleven bullets between them in the space of six crowded seconds. Four of those shots were direct hits: arm, leg, torso, torso.

Amazingly, though, Dell didn't go down. He went for Kennedy instead, and since by this time she was just a few feet from him, he only had to take a step forward to fasten his hands around her neck.

Consequently, it was Kennedy who fired the bullet that put him down: through the left ventricle at a distance succinctly noted on the incident file as 'zero feet'. She'd blown his heart out through his back, more or less, and then stood there robed in his blood while Gates and Leakey confirmed the kill.

This was the story as told by the dead man's wife, the single eyewitness willing to come forward. It turned out Dell had been trying to break into his own house, a result of a marital disagreement that had its roots in the dope he'd ingested and his unwillingness to share. Lorina Dell was very clear about the sequence of events and the respective roles that the three armed officers had played.

Gates and Leakey told the story differently, of course. They claimed they'd fired before Dell threw the phone, and in the still-unaltered belief that it was a handgun.

The story got a little muddy here. Leakey also offered as evidence a handgun, a cheap Russian GSh-18, with a full magazine, which he claimed to have found tucked into the back of Dell's belt. Gates confirmed that this was the gun's provenance, even when it turned out not to have a single fingerprint of Dell's on it.

The testimony that was going to nail them, when this finally came to trial, wasn't that of the dead man's stoner wife. It was Kennedy's. She denied that the GSh-18 had been found at the crime scene (a great many guns had recently arrived in the evidence lockers from a raid on a container ship that had turned out to be smuggling weapons, hashish and – incongruously – cloned viagra pills). She accused both of her fellow officers of having fired on Dell when he manifestly offered no threat.

Kennedy's decision to play the George Washington gambit took everyone by surprise. It meant her own ARU licence got trashed, along with those of Gates and Leakey, and it set her against the department in a fight that ultimately she couldn't win. The guy had died with his hands around an officer's throat: it didn't even have to come to court if they all kept their stories straight.

In successive interviews, Kennedy had been invited to repeat her version of events probably a dozen times, without a single word being written down. Tactful interviewers invited her to consider the order in which key events had superseded each other, and the full extent of the danger posed by Mr Dell's attack on her own person. These review sessions had been used in other controversial cases with positive outcomes for the force and all officers concerned. But you could only do so much for a cop with no sense of self-preservation. Kennedy continued to assert that she, Gates and Leakey had used lethal force against a confused drug addict who could barely stay upright. She invited the crown prosecutor to throw the book at her.

So far, that hadn't happened. The case had now become a three-way running skirmish between the Met, the CPS and the Police Complaints Commission. A full inquiry was underway and would have to report before any charges were preferred. Until then, Gates and Leakey were suspended on full pay, while Kennedy got to stay on in the division, *sans* gun licence, plying her normal trade.

Except that nothing had come back to normal for anyone concerned. Kennedy was in Coventry: a pariah in the bear pit, a walking target for anything the DCIs felt like throwing at her, and maybe, Harper thought, damaged in less tangible ways – holed below the waterline. When she'd warned him off, he'd gotten the sense that it was cold pragmatism rather than quixotic generosity. Something like the way the officers trapped on the *Titanic* had finally told the rescue boats to stand off so they wouldn't get sucked down when the big liner went under.

Harper realised that Combes was still looking at him, waiting for a response to the cautionary tale.

'She doesn't seem like the easiest person in the world to work with,' Harper said, throwing a sop to Cerberus.

'You got that right,' someone – Stanwick? – agreed.

'But I guess she felt pretty strongly about how those other guys messed up the arrest.'

The mood in the room turned a little colder. 'What did the little bastard expect?' Stanwick demanded. 'He assaulted an officer, he went down. Good riddance.'

'Fine,' Harper said. 'And they'll all probably walk on that basis. So Kennedy's not hurting anyone by sticking to her story.'

'Fancy your chances, do you?' Combes enquired, with a definite edge. 'She's a real looker, isn't she?'

Considered objectively, Kennedy had everything you'd need to merit that description: a figure that went in and out in the right places, striking acid-blonde hair that she wore pulled severely back in a way that suggested she could loosen it and shake it out as a prelude to sex, and that this would be something to see, and a face that – although maybe a little too emphatic at nose and chin – still had an intensity of expression you'd have to call attractive.

But she was ten years older than Harper's girlfriend, Tessa, and that relationship was new enough to skew his judgement on all other women. He shrugged non-committally.

'He fancies his chances,' Combes announced to the room. 'Well, you can forget it, son. She's a dyke.'

'Yeah?' Harper was interested now, but only as a detective. 'How'd you know?'

'We did a day-at-the-races thing last March, the whole department,' Stanwick told him, as though he was talking to an idiot, 'and she brought a bird with her.'

'Wouldn't that make half of you dykes as well?' Harper asked, innocently. His tone was light and friendly, but the chill in the room grew: on some level, this was a test, and he wasn't doing well.

'Anyway, you'd better get your jollies while you can, mate,' one of the other DCs summed up. 'She's not going to be around for much longer.'

'No,' Harper agreed. 'Probably not.'

The conversation turned to other things, and flowed around him, leaving him out. He let it. He had a lot of phone calls to make, and he might as well make a start while Kennedy was off interviewing Barlow's sister.

The London Historical Forum was a biannual event hosted by the university. He tracked down the relevant office, which was at Birkbeck, and after doing the phone-tag runaround with a job lot of receptionists and assistants, he was able to requisition a copy of the contact list from the last conference. It came through as an email attachment half an hour later – but instead of a word-processed document, they'd sent jpegs. Each page had been separately mounted on to the copier plate and scanned in, in some cases very sloppily, so that first letters of surnames were clipped off on the left, and the bottom two or three lines of each sheet appeared to have been missed out.

Harper emailed back to ask if there was a Word version of the list somewhere in the system, then printed the scans out. He could work with what he'd been given for now.

As he walked down the corridor to the printer, Harper thought about the conversation he'd just had. Why had he stood up for Kennedy, or at least refused to join in the general condemnation? She was far from likeable and she'd made it abundantly clear that she was happy to work the case solo.

But it was Harper's first case and some atavistic part of him rebelled against backing out of it: the angel who looked down on police work had to take a pretty dim view of officers recusing themselves for fear of rocking the boat. And Kennedy seemed to have good instincts, too: not flashy, but methodical and thorough. Harper had seen flash, preferred the core skill set intelligently applied. However far her mind was off the vertical as a result of the Dell shooting, the pending court case and having to live in exile within the department, she was still trying to do her job.

So he was going to work with Kennedy and give her the benefit of the doubt – for now, at least. If she busted his balls too much, or if she turned out to be more unstable than he'd guessed, he still had the option of shouting up the ladder and pleading PD, as she'd suggested.

In the meantime, being on the other side of an argument from the likes of Combes and Stanwick – who he had already identified as self-serving dicks – was single malt for the soul.

He took the print-out back to his desk and started the arduous and unpleasant task of chasing up some eyewitness testimony that might not even exist.

He was seven names into the list when he found the next dead body.

7

Rosalind Barlow's address was Stuart Barlow's address. The brother and sister lived together – *had* lived together – in a cottage-style bungalow, just outside the M25 ring in the probably-used-to-be-a-village of Merstham. Like William and Caroline Herschel, or the Wordsworths, or Emily, Anne and Charlotte with Bramwell. Kennedy had a brother of her own and therefore had her doubts about these domestic arrangements. Live-in boyfriends were bad enough: having a brother hanging around the place was an even more cast-iron guarantee of arrested development and neurotic co-dependency.

Ten minutes into the visit, she'd shifted that initial estimate a fair distance. Ros Barlow was a tough, confident woman, tall and solidly built, with a head of auburn hair designed to be sculpted into something big and heraldic – the kind of woman who gets called 'handsome' a lot. She was fifteen years younger than her brother, and the house was hers, inherited from their parents. Stuart Barlow had been living in it rent-free for years while Ros held down a job in the securities department of a New York bank. She'd moved back to London only recently, to take up a better position in the City, and so had ended up sharing with her brother for a few months while he sorted something else out. Now, though, she said, she was looking for somewhere else herself.

'I've got a friend I can bunk in with, for a few nights. After that, I'll try to find somewhere a bit closer to the centre. If there's nothing on the market, I'll rent for now. I'm certainly not staying here.'

'Why not?' Kennedy asked, surprised by the woman's vehemence.

'Why not? Because it's Stu's. Every single thing here is his, and it took him years to get it just the way he wanted. I'd rather sell it to someone else who likes this kind of thing than spend the next two years changing it over piecemeal to something that works for me. I'd feel like . . .' she groped for a simile '. . . like he was still trying to hang on to me and I was breaking his fingers one by one. It would be horrible.'

Ros had taken the news that the investigation had reopened very much in her stride. 'Good,' was all she'd said.

They were sitting in the living room of the cottage, which had nineteenth-century Punch cartoons on the walls and a drinks cabinet that someone had retro-fitted from a Victorian roll-top desk. An open staircase in a modern design, with no risers, divided the room in two – not something you expected to see in a bungalow. Presumably Barlow had had some extension work done in the loft space and there was now a room up there.

'You asked for the autopsy,' Kennedy said, putting down the small but extremely potent cup of espresso that Ros had given her when she arrived. 'Was that because you suspected that your brother's death wasn't an accident?'

Ros clicked her teeth impatiently. 'I knew it wasn't,' she said. 'And I told the constable who came out here exactly why. But I could see he wasn't listening, so I had to demand an autopsy, too. I've been around overworked people long enough to know the signs. You have to make a noise – make yourself really bloody loud and obvious – or else they file you under business as usual and sod all gets done.'

Kennedy agreed, as far as that went, but didn't say so. She wasn't here to play 'ain't it awful'. 'That was a local officer, I'm assuming?' she said. 'In uniform?'

'In uniform, yes.' Ros frowned, remembering. 'And I called him a constable, but actually I didn't ask his rank. He had a number – a number and letters – on his shoulder, but no pips or stripes or stars. I've been abroad for a fair few years, but I think that makes him a constable unless they've changed the uniform regs.'

'Yes,' Kennedy said, 'it does.' She liked that Ros could call those details to mind after two weeks. It meant she might remember other things with the same clarity.

'So what did you think had happened to Stuart?' she asked.

Ros's expression hardened. 'He was murdered.'

'All right. Why do you say that?'

'He told me.' Kennedy's surprise must have shown through her professional poker face because Ros went on more emphatically, as though she'd been contradicted. 'He did. He told me three days before it happened.'

'That he was going to be murdered?'

'That someone might attack him. That he felt under threat and didn't know what to do.'

Ros was becoming more strident. In the face of her heightened emotion, Kennedy became deliberately emollient. 'That must have been terrible for both of you,' she said. 'Why didn't you contact the police?'

'Stu had already done that, when he realised he was being followed.'

'At the conference.'

'Yes. Then.'

'But if he was actually threatened ...' Kennedy was tentative. She could see that the other woman disliked being interrogated, was likely to see any question as a challenge unless it was phrased as neutrally as possible. 'Did he explain all this at the time?' she asked. 'I mean, when he called the police and told them that he was being followed?' Or was there something more? Something he kept to himself? I'm asking because I've read the case file now and there was no mention of any actual threats.'

Ros shook her head, frowning. 'I said he felt threatened, not that he'd actually *been* threatened. He told the police everything he could tell them, everything that was verifiable. The rest was ... impressions, I suppose. But I know that he was afraid. Not generally afraid. Afraid of something specific. Sergeant Kennedy, my brother wasn't a level-headed sort of man. When we were kids, he was always the one who'd have the sudden enthusiasms – the collecting crazes, the addictions to comics or cult TV shows, all that sort of thing. And emotionally, too, he was always ... just all over the place. So I had every reason to think he was exaggerating, making something out of nothing. But that's not how it was. This time was different.'

'How was it different?'

'Someone broke in here, late at night, and went through all of Stuart's things. That wasn't imaginary.'

Kennedy's response was automatic. 'Did you report it?' Meaning, is there an evidence trail? Is this documented anywhere?

'Of course we reported it. We couldn't claim on the insurance otherwise.'

'So things were stolen?'

'No. Nothing, as far as we could see. But we needed new locks and the back door had to be repaired. That's how he got in, whoever he was.'

'Was this before or after Professor Barlow noticed he was being followed?'

'After. And that was when I started to take the whole thing seriously. But you evidently didn't.'

Because nobody put the case-work together, Kennedy thought, even after Barlow turned up dead. Barlow's reporting a stalker had only come to light after the autopsy results came in – and any file entries for this breaking and entering were probably still lost in the system. It was farcical. The central criminal register wasn't exactly new, or complicated. It was supposed to operate automatically now, cross-referencing old cases as new ones were entered on the division's database. So long as you filled in your fields correctly in the first place, the old stuff just got flagged up for you without you having to do anything.

But not this time.

'We do seem to have been slow out of the gate,' Kennedy admitted, trying to forestall Ros Barlow's hostility by throwing her a bone of contrition. 'But if you're right, why didn't the assailant attack your brother here, after getting entry to the house? Was he surprised in the act or something? Did you hear him come in?'

Ros shook her head. 'No, we didn't,' she said. 'We only found out someone had broken in when we came down in the morning.'

So assuming there was any through-line at all here, the motive had to go beyond just killing Barlow. He could have been murdered as easily here as at the college; more easily, if he'd been surprised in his sleep.

Kennedy thought again about the spectacular mess in Barlow's office. Maybe that wasn't the normal state of things: someone could have broken in there, too. She looked at the slanted column of sunlight coming in through the parted curtains, the dust motes suspended in the still air. The word *murdered* seemed a bit unreal in this room – and the scenario she'd imagined, of Barlow's corpse being dragged up the stairs at the history annexe to be thrown down again, ridiculous and melodramatic. But unlike Stuart Barlow, she wasn't acting on feelings. She was responding to the evidence, and the evidence was pointing towards something complicated and nasty. A murder preceded by a completely separate break-in meant a plan or a motive that went beyond just wanting someone dead.

'Did you discuss with your brother what this intruder might have been looking for?' she asked. 'If Professor Barlow was afraid, was it because he had something specific in his possession? Something valuable that he thought people might come looking for?'

Ros hesitated this time, but finally shook her head again – an admission of ignorance. 'It's possible, but Stu almost never discussed his work with me because he knew it bored my arse off. He'd been talking to the Ravellers a lot lately. So he was working on something old. But mostly they work from photos or transcriptions, not from originals. There'd be no reason why he'd have valuable artefacts in the house.'

'The Revellers?' Kennedy echoed.

'Not Revellers. Ravellers. It's an internet community, for palaeographers – people who work with old manuscripts and incunabula.'

'Professional academics, then, like your brother?'

'And hobbyists. A lot of them do it for fun.'

'How would I get in touch with them?'

Ros shrugged. 'I'm sorry, I don't know. I only use computers for spreadsheets and email. They're ... a forum? A website? I don't even know. You'd have to ask one of Stu's colleagues. But I think they're definitely where you should start. I can't think of anything else in Stuart's life that could possibly have motivated anyone to follow him, or attack him.'

Kennedy remembered something that Ellis had said. 'He was writing a book. Could there have been anything sensational or controversial in that? A new theory or a refutation of an old one? Something that might have harmed someone else's reputation?'

Ros looked suddenly bleak. She didn't answer for a moment and had a tremor in her voice when she did. 'Stu had been working on that bloody book for the last ten years. He used to say he'd probably be writing the acknowledgements on his deathbed.' She paused and then added, in a colder, flatter tone, 'It didn't help that he couldn't make up his mind what his bloody subject was.

'For a good five years, it was going to be about the Dead Sea Scrolls. Stu was convinced there were still big things to find in there, even though everybody in the field had been all over them for the last sixty-odd years. Do you know how many books there've been on the scrolls already? Hundreds. Literally, hundreds. When I asked Stu why anyone would want to read his, he'd get all mysterious and quote some lines from William Blake.'

'What lines?' Kennedy asked.

'Umm ... something about "we both read the Bible, day and night. But you read black and I read white". Stu thought it was terribly clever, whatever it was. But then he lost interest in the Dead Sea Scrolls altogether. He went into his Gnostic period. All the weird early Christian cults – Arians and Nestorians and the other assorted happy clappers. Then it was about Bishop Irenaeus. And then finally it was about the Rotgut. I think the last time we talked about it, that was where it was at. The Rotgut. It was going to be a complete re-evaluation of the Rotgut.'

Kennedy made a 'go on' gesture, which saved her from having to admit verbally that she had no idea what the other woman was talking about. She assumed it wasn't illicit alcohol.

'The Rotgut Codex,' Ros explained. 'It's a medieval translation of a lost version of John's gospel. About as obscure as you can get, unless you want to research something like punctuation marks. I don't think anyone's reputation was tied up in Stu's book. Not even Stu's. Some universities require you to publish to stay on-staff. Stu had tenure, so he was taking his own sweet time.'

Kennedy asked a few more questions, mostly about Barlow's colleagues at Prince Regent and the friends he'd made online. Ros was vague about both. She clearly hadn't been very much involved either in her brother's public life or in his private enthusiasms.

As she was seeing Kennedy to the door, though, something occurred to her. 'Michael Brand,' she said, as though in answer to a question Kennedy had already asked.

'Who is that?'

'One of the Ravellers. He's the only one Stu ever mentioned to me by name. You might not even have to go too far, if you wanted to talk to him. He's working in London at the moment, or he was up to a few weeks back. Stu met up with him the night before he died.'

'Just socially or . . . ?'

Ros opened her empty hands. 'I have no idea. But he was staying in a hotel somewhere in the West End, close to the college. Close enough for Stu to walk there from work. Maybe they talked about all this. Maybe it's why Brand was here.'

They walked together to the door, Ros visibly still sorting through recent memories. 'Not the Bloomsbury,' she muttered. 'And not the Great Russell. It was around there, though, and it was two words. Two short words.'

She opened the door. Kennedy stepped through, then turned back to face her.

'Pride Court,' Ros said. 'The Pride Court Hotel.'

'You've been a great help, Miss Barlow,' Kennedy said. 'Thank you.'

'Don't mention it,' said Ros, without warmth. 'Just return the favour.'

Kennedy's phone rang as she got back to the car. She recognised the number as being one of the bear-pit phones and was tempted to ignore it, but it might be Summerhill checking in on her. She thumbed it open one-handed as she fumbled for her keys with the other hand.

'Kennedy.'

'Hi. It's Chris Harper.'

'How's it going?'

'It's going great. Seriously, sarge, my productivity rate is going through the roof here.'

The car made a digital clucking sound as Kennedy pressed the key stud, but she made no move to open the door. 'What? What do you mean?'

Harper's laugh carried a tremor of excitement, but he just about managed to get a bored, bravura tone into his voice. 'When I sat down, we just had the one corpse. Now we've got three.'

8

The first zombie stories started to come in two days after the crash, but the real flood didn't hit until day four. These things take time to get up their initial momentum, Sheriff Webster Gayle conjectured, but after they get to a certain point there's no stopping them.

There was only one story on day two – one real sighting, if you wanted to call it that, although in fact that was the one thing it wasn't. Sylvia Gallos, the widow of one of the men who'd died on Coastal Airlines Flight 124, had woken in the night, hearing noises downstairs. Though distraught with grief, she'd still had the presence of mind to rummage in the drawer of her bedside table and find the little .22 calibre mouse gun her husband Jack had bought for her. His business had called him away from home a lot, and he used to worry about her safety.

Gun in hand and hand more or less steady, Mrs Gallos had crept down the stairs to find the house empty and the door still securely locked. But the TV was on, a glass of whisky and water was standing half-drunk on the coffee table, and the air was full of the smell of her late husband's favourite cologne, Bulgari Black.

That was it for day two, but it played well and got a lot of air-time, usually at the end of ten or twelve minutes of more

74

serious and solemn coverage. The authorities were still trying to figure out who to blame the crash on. The black box hadn't been retrieved yet, although a whole lot of people were out looking for it, and opinion was divided as to what exactly had happened up there. Was it a terrorist atrocity? Maybe a long-term after-effect of all the volcanic garbage sitting in the upper atmosphere after that eruption in Iceland a year or so back? Or worst of all, from the industry point of view, a design flaw that meant all planes of that make (it was an Embraer E-195, and only four years old) would have to be grounded for the foreseeable future.

By day three, according to the TV news, they had a part of an answer to that. Still no black box, but the insurance and FAA people had gone over most of the wreckage and it told a consistent if not yet quite complete story. One of the doors had blown open in mid-flight, causing a sudden and massive depressurisation. After that, a whole lot of other dominoes had gone and toppled over: the pressure bulkhead buckled, causing some hydraulic cables to snap, and a few seconds later the vertical stabilisers cut out. The engines stalled, the air flow broke, and the plane – which had an empty weight of thirty-two tons – was from that moment on about as aerodynamic as a great big bag of tyre irons. Gravity did its thing, enfolding Flight 124 into its ruinous embrace.

In Peason, there was still a feeling of shock and grief for the dead strangers who'd come tumbling out of the sky, but for the nation at large there seemed to be a sense that the event was a lot less interesting now it had an explanation. Consequently, on day three the human interest stories took over from the stories about the crash itself. The focus now turned on the woman flying into New York to be reunited with her sister after a twenty-year feud; the guy who was going to pop the question to his childhood sweetheart; the three passengers who, although travelling separately and seemingly unaware of each other, had all been part of the same intake at Northridge Community High School.

And in among all of these sell-by-the-inch soap opera tragedies there were the walking dead. On day four, they came out in force.

A clerk in the New York Department of Public Works, who took Flight 124 to get home from some junket in Mexico City, had swiped in at his office, sent a couple of emails, surfed a little porn and then – without swiping out again or being seen by security or reception staff – disappeared without a trace. He was lying on a morgue slab in Peason at the time, but evidently routine is a powerful thing.

A woman from New Jersey, also a casualty of 124, took her car out of the garage and drove to a local supermarket, where she drew out fifty dollars from her checking account and apparently bought a goldfish-on-a-string pet toy and a tin of anchovies, which were found in the trunk of the car later that day when the store closed and it was still there in the lot. Her boyfriend affirmed that she always bought her Burmese, Felix, treats of this kind when she'd been away.

And maybe the creepiest of all, another passenger, a Mrs Angelica Saville, had called her brother in Schenectady to complain that the plane had been circling for hours in a fog so thick that nothing could be seen outside the windows. The call had come a full sixty-one hours after 124 hit the ground.

'Did you read this stuff?' Webster Gayle asked Eileen Moggs, over their regular midweek lunch at the Kingman Best of the West café, two miles out of town on the 93. He showed her the story about the New Jersey woman and she winced as though it gave her physical pain.

76

'This one gets trotted out every ten years or so,' Moggs said. The look on her face was sour and Gayle was sorry he'd put it there. He found her face – lined, strong-featured, emphatic, topped with a frizz of red hair like low brush fire – an amazing and beautiful thing to look upon. 'They wait just long enough for everyone to have forgotten the last time, and then damn it if they don't go right ahead and do it again. It's a hack tradition. Goes all the way back to the Boston Molasses Flood.'

Gayle thought he'd misheard. 'The what, now?'

'The Boston Molasses Flood of 1919. Stop grinning, Web. It was a real disaster and two dozen people died. A storage tank burst. They drowned in molasses, which must be a pretty horrible way to die.'

Chastened, Gayle nodded, agreeing that it was. Moggs carried right on making her point. 'For weeks afterwards, the papers carried stories about how the dead were still turning up for work. Or their ghosts were. They quoted survivors – colleagues and relatives – as giving all kinds of corroborating details. Yeah, that was John's shirt, Mary always sat in that chair, and so on and so forth. Only they never said those things. Or maybe one or two of them did. After that it was just the hacks making it up and the nut-jobs and hoaxers playing along. That's all it ever is.'

Sheriff Gayle said he took her word for it, as he usually did on most things outside his own very limited experience – which essentially meant outside the Coconino County limits. But it was sort of a lie: on some half-buried level he was drawn to these stories of strange revenants. A whole bunch of people had died all at once, suddenly and traumatically. Was it too much of a reach to imagine that some of them might come back? That maybe their spirits might have passed over so quickly that they didn't even realise they were dead, so they kept right on doing the same-old-same-old until the news caught up with them and they faded away? It was a haunting image. He didn't share it with Moggs, but he kept turning it over and over in his mind.

On the fifth day, the walking dead stories only got a limited airing in the mainstream media, but you could find a zillion of them on the internet. With the help of Connie, who was a lot less sceptical than Moggs, he went looking for them and began to compile a master list. It didn't bother him that they weren't always attributed and that details like names and ages changed from one report to the next. There's no smoke without fire, he reasoned. And since that metaphor raised the hideous, indelible memory of the crash itself, it almost seemed to have something of a timeless truth about it. There were more things, in heaven and in earth. You just never knew, until it happened to you and you suddenly did.

All this time, the County Sheriff's Department was involved in the investigation of the crash, but only in what you'd call a facilitating capacity. They kept the crowd away from the wreckage on the first day and coordinated access for the ambulances and paramedic crews. Journalists by and large were kept well away from the site, except for Moggs who was allowed to wander at will so long as she didn't make a big deal out of it. Nobody begrudged her this privilege: Sheriff Gayle was highly regarded, and most of his deputies and troopers felt kind of a warm glow from the reflection that he was getting some.

Then when the airlines' experts and the FAA's experts and the insurance company experts came in, Gayle and his people took the lead in the search for the black box, which could have been a needle-in-a-haystack deal if it had been left to the out-of-towners. The thing was putting out a signal, and the locators were very fancy majiggers, locked to that one wavelength, so sensitive you could almost feel them pulling on your arm like a pointer dog. You still needed to know the area to get anything out of them, though. If you just kept to the right heading, you'd hit a mesa or a dry creek bed after a couple of miles or so, and have to go around. And then you'd be off of your line and you'd tear away in a different direction, jam your car in a box canyon and so on. So the Sheriff's Department had four people working with those search parties, just helping them to negotiate the terrain, as it were.

They were also officially in charge of what came and what went, laboriously logging the writing-up and removal of physical evidence. It wasn't glamorous policing – very little that fell within Gayle's purview could be called that – but it did keep the crash in the forefront of his mind and brought him into daily contact with the people actually investigating it.

He took the opportunity of raising the walking dead sightings with anyone who'd stand still long enough to listen. Mostly people seemed to find the topic either funny or morbid, and either way they thought it was bullshit. One of the FAA people, though, was more receptive to the idea. She was a tall, nervous woman named Sandra Lestrier, and she was a member of the spiritualist church. That didn't make her credulous, she was at pains to point out: spiritualist wasn't another word for sucker, it meant someone who believed in and was in touch with another dimension of the endless plurality that was life. But she did have a theory about ghosts, and although reluctant at first, she eventually consented to share it. With his impressive height and his rough and ready good looks, Gayle had always had a certain charm with the ladies, which he had never abused: in his fifties now, with his hair turned to silver but still as full as ever, the charm had metamorphosed – to his sorrow – into something avuncular and safe. Women were happy to talk to him. Only Moggs seemed willing to take that further step to pillow talk.

'Ghosts are the wounds of the world,' Sandra Lestrier told Gayle. 'We see the world as a big, physical thing, but that's only a tiny part of what it is. The world is alive – that's how come it can give birth to life. And something that big, if it's alive, you'd expect it to have a big soul, too, right? When the world bleeds, it bleeds spirit. And that's what ghosts are.'

Gayle was rocked. Religion had never been a big thing in his family, but he was aware of it, and he knew that it came in three flavours: regular, which was okay; Jewish, which was sort of okay too, because the Lord appeared to the Jews and gave them what amounted to an all-clear; and Muslim, which was the bad apple. He'd never realised up until then that there could be progress in religion just like in anything else, fashions that came and went.

He asked Ms Lestrier to tell him more about the wounds of the world, but the specifics turned out to be a little confusing and uninteresting. It was something to do with the persistence of life in the valley of death, and several different kinds of human soul that all had their own names and places in a hierarchy. The more technical it got, the more Gayle tuned out. In the end, he was left with the metaphor and very little else. But he did like the metaphor.

Things were getting a little crazy by this time: the black box from Flight 124 still hadn't been found and that was becoming kind of an embarrassment to the federal guys. The signal had started to break up, apparently, and now it was hard for them to get a fix on it, even though they'd brought in a spy satellite of some kind to coordinate the search. The FAA guys on the ground were keen to pass some of the blame along to inadequate support from the Sheriff's Department, and Gayle had harsh words with one of their bigwigs who came into the station to throw his weight around.

It was getting a little ugly and a little political. Gayle hated politics and wanted the box found before anyone from the governor's office got involved. He started running the search recons himself, which had the incidental benefit that he sometimes got to ride shotgun for Ms Lestrier and hear a little more about her newfangled religion.

He was riding solo when he met the pale people, though. He was following the line of a broad arroyo with a whole lot of tributaries – badly broken ground that the feds had already hit and bounced off of. It was late afternoon but still hot, the kind of cloudless day where the shadows are as black as spilled ink and the sun hangs dead centre in the sky like a piece of fruit you could almost reach up and touch. Gayle stayed in the air-conditioned car as much as he could, but had to get out to walk down to the stream whenever the banks were high enough to hide it. Not that there was much of a stream at this time of year: just little puddles here and there on the creek bed, each with a few skinks around it like an honour guard.

There was nobody else in sight. Nobody much would have a reason to come out here in the heat of the day. Gayle had got out of the car a half-dozen times to trek down to the bottom of the arroyo, kick a few rocks around to prove he'd been there, and trek back up again.

Then one time he came scuffling and sliding down the steep bank to find himself abruptly face to face with two complete strangers. They weren't hiding or anything: they didn't jump out on him from cover. It was more like he'd been lost in his own thoughts and the first time he registered their presence they were right there in front of his damn nose, staring him down.

A man and a woman. Both young – maybe in their mid-twenties or so – tall, and lean in a way that suggested a whole lot of effort spent in a gym or on a track. They had incredibly pale skin, almost like albinos, but the man had dark red flashes high up on his cheekbones where he'd obviously caught a little too much sun. They both had jet black hair, the guy's long and loose, the woman's fastened up at the back of her head into a no-nonsense bun the size of a fist. Their eyes showed black, too, although they were probably just dark brown.

But the thing that Gayle noticed first of all, and most of all, was the symmetry: identical sand-coloured shirts, tan slacks, tan shoes, as though they were aiming to blend in with the surrounding desert; identical stares on identical faces, like he was looking at the same person twice, even though they were of different sexes and weren't even physically alike at all. He thought of the Viewfinder toy he'd had as a kid, and how each picture was really two pictures, on opposite sides of the reel. It was like that – and for a second he was almost afraid to speak to them in case they answered in creepy unison.

But they didn't. In answer to his belated 'Howdy', the woman nodded while the young guy gave him back a strangely formal 'Good day to you'. Then they both went back to staring at him: neither of the two had moved an inch so far.

'I'm looking for the black box from the airplane that went down,' Gayle explained, unnecessarily. 'About so big by yay long.' He gestured with his hands, which of course took them away from his belt where his department-issue FN five-seven rested in its worn leather holster. He realised this a moment later, dropped his hands again awkwardly, and still neither of the strangers had moved. Gayle was at a loss to understand why he felt so ill at ease.

'We haven't seen anything like that here,' the man answered. His voice was deep and it had a weird something to it that Gayle couldn't quite get his head around. It wasn't that he sounded foreign, although he did, just a little. It was the tempo, which was sort of sing-song, like someone reading from a book: slightly slower than normal speech, with a weight behind it that a casual remark like that just didn't need. The man also put a slight but noticeable emphasis on the word *here*, which Gayle picked up on and thought was odd.

'Well, I'll take any clue I can get,' he said. 'You see any sign of it some place else?'

The man frowned, seeming momentarily troubled or irritated, then countered with a question. 'Why are you looking for it? Is it important?'

'Might could be, yeah. It's got all the intel on it about how that plane come down. There's a whole lot of people looking all over for this thing.'

The woman nodded. The guy didn't react at all.

'Well, keep your eyes open anyway,' Gayle said, just to make a hole in the silence.

'We'll strive to do so,' the woman promised. Again, as with her partner, there was that measuredness and that weight, like the words had been written down for her to say. And again, the accent was unplaceable but definitely not local. Gayle, for whom *local* was the measure of all things benign, experienced that strangeness as mild discomfort.

The young man reached up a hand to wipe his eye, as though there was a dust speck in it. When he lowered his hand again, there was a smear of red across his face, right under the eye. It gave Gayle a little bit of a shock. Forgetting his manners, he pointed.

'You've got something,' he said, inanely, 'on your cheek there.'

'I weep for witness,' the man said. Or at least that was what it sounded like.

'For what?' Gayle echoed. 'It looks like you ... did you cut yourself or something? It looks like you're bleeding.'

'You could perhaps search over there,' the woman broke in, ignoring Gayle's solicitude. 'Where the scree is. If the box had fallen there, it would have slid down into the weeds at the bottom of the bank. It would be out of sight unless you came very close to it.'

Now the measured pace sounded like a lawyer in court, picking his words to skirmish his way around something he wasn't going to admit to. Gayle wondered whether these two knew something they weren't saying. He didn't have a damn thing to hold them on, though, and something about them was still giving him a crawly feeling at the nape of his neck. He just wanted this encounter to be over, and he was about to give them a nod and a thank you kindly, then move on.

The strangers moved first, both at the same time, and without there seeming to be any signal between them. As slow as they talked, when they moved it was like drops of water running on a greasy griddle. They were past Gayle in a split-second, parting to go around him. Wrong-footed, embarrassingly slow, he turned to watch them go. Saw them walking by his car and on up the road, fast and smooth, falling into step with one another like soldiers.

The nearest building – a gas station – had to be five miles up that road, and it wasn't a walk that anyone would make by choice in the middle of the day. All the same, that seemed to be what the strangers were proposing to do. Was that how they'd gotten here? They just walked from somewhere? How could they do that without having their faces and hands burned all to hell and gone?

Gayle opened his mouth to call after them. A man could die of heatstroke just walking around out here like that, without a hat. But the words sort of died in-between his brain and his mouth. He watched the two figures top a slight rise and walk on out of sight.

With an effort, Gayle pulled his mind back to the task in hand.

This little stretch of the arroyo was empty, too, but he saw plenty of sign that those oddballs had walked around here some: footprints and scuff marks in the sand and the darker dirt of the creek bed, a bit of sage that had been torn up as they walked through it. It looked like they'd done pretty much what he was doing: come down from the road, walked as far as they could along the near bank, then stopped and turned around when they hit a gully they couldn't cross.

Could just be an afternoon stroll. Drug transaction. Pay-off for some political backscratching. Sexual assignation. No, not the last. The two had something about them that made Gayle believe they were related – very closely related – and his imagination rebelled against the vision of stereo onanism that rose in his mind. He tidied it out of sight and tried to forget about the creepy duo. They hadn't done anything out of place; had been extremely polite and helpful, in fact, and didn't have to explain to the law any more than anyone else did what they were doing walking along a dry arroyo on a hot day.

He climbed the bank, abruptly aware that he was sweating like a pig. As he walked back to the car, he could hear Connie's voice chattering on the radio-phone, asking him to pick up if he was there.

He hooked the handset out through the open window and pressed the talk button.

'Checking in, Connie,' he said. 'I'm on Highwash three miles out from 66. Just working my way up the road, here. You need me?'

'Hey, Web,' Connie replied, her voice half broken up with the crackle from the tall rocks up here. 'You can come back in. We're all done on that black box thing.'

Gayle swallowed this information with a certain dour resignation. He'd put a lot of hours into this business. 'Okay,' he said. 'Where'd they find it?'

'They didn't.'

'What?' Gayle stuck his head in through the car window to shut out the sound of the wind, which had sprung up at just the wrong moment. 'What did you say?'

'They didn't find it. It just stopped transmitting, and they gave up on it. But that FAA woman you're always talking to said they got everything they needed out of the wreck. The whole damn circus just up and rolled out. She said to tell you bye. Over and out.'

Gayle shoved the phone back on to its rest, feeling more perplexed than aggrieved – although he had to admit that he was pretty sore, when it came down to it. Just gave up? One second it's crucial, the next it doesn't matter a damn?

Gayle was a stubborn man and that didn't sit right with him.

It wasn't over until he said it was.

9

An incidental benefit of being a cop was that you got to ignore the congestion charge, central London parking restrictions and the speed limit. Kennedy drove back into London along the A23 with the windows open – not quite like a bat out of hell, but fast enough to air-cool her overclocked imagination.

Three dead historians at the same conference. In the words of Oscar Wilde, that seemed to be considerably above the proper average that statistics have laid down for our guidance. It could still be nothing, probably *was* nothing. Even now, an outrageous coincidence seemed more likely than a ruthlessly efficient killer, stalking and striking down people who had strong opinions about the Rotgut Codex and superannuated Christian sects.

But Stuart Barlow's death hadn't been an accident. That was obvious, both from the autopsy and from the physical evidence. Kennedy had mixed opinions about autopsies: sometimes they were more about politics than facts, and politics is the art of the possible. With the physical evidence, she trusted her instincts – and mourned all over again the fact that nobody had bothered to call in a forensics team on the night when Barlow had yo-yoed up and down that stairwell. She could be sitting on DNA, fibres, fingerprints, any amount of serviceable stuff, instead of flailing around in the dark looking for a direction.

Maybe on some level, too, she wished this hadn't come up right now. She'd been living in a kind of suspended animation since the night when Marcus Dell got shot. Or rather, since the night when she'd fired the bullet that put Dell down. It was important to get the grammar right. Heather, active subject, as in *Heather pulled the trigger*. Dell, passive object, as in *the bullet hit Dell in the heart, and tore right on through*.

When you came up for an ARU licence, they tested you for a whole lot of things and mental stability was most of them. They just called it by a lot of different names, like ability to handle stress, emotional intelligence, panic index rating, psychological integration rating and so on. It all came down to the one question: would you lose it if you had to shoot someone or if someone was shooting at you?

And the answer, to put it baldly, was that nobody knew. Kennedy had scored top end on all of those scales. She'd also drawn her weapon on three occasions, and fired it twice, in one case exchanging shots with an armed suspect – a bank robber named Ed Styler who she'd brought down with a bullet in the shoulder. She'd survived all that well enough and never lost a single night's sleep over it.

Dell was different. She knew why, too, but didn't want to go there just yet. It was a can of worms that, once opened, could prove to be impossible to square away again. So she soldiered on without a weapon; relieved, really, to be without it for the time being, until the whole mess got sorted out. The problem, though – the wider problem, which made the pending prosecution shrink into a wrong-end-of-the-telescope perspective – was that she might have lost something else along with the gun and the right to carry it: the iron faith in her own judgement that had made carrying it possible in the first place.

She found Harper in the canteen and hooked him right out of

it into one of the interview rooms. There was no way she was having this conversation with anyone else from the division listening in. She closed the door and leaned against it. Harper sat on the desk, still with half a chicken sandwich in his right hand and a can of Fanta in his left. It was four in the afternoon and he was finally getting round to lunch. From his face, she could tell how happy he was with the way the case was going. The sweat-room smelled of piss and mildew, but Harper didn't seem to mind.

'Take it from the top,' Kennedy said.

Harper, with his jaws working, gave her an ironic *salaam* but said nothing. Kennedy had to wait, with as much patience as she could manage, until he'd swallowed the mouthful and washed it down. 'I got the list and started working through it,' he said, finally. 'Got nowhere on the stalker. Nobody else saw him. Nobody else even remembered Barlow talking about him.'

'Tell me about the deaths,' Kennedy said, bluntly.

'Well, that's where it gets interesting. Catherine Hurt and Samir Devani. They both attended that history conference and they've both died since. Amazing, yeah? And you know what's even better? Hurt pegged it on the same night as Barlow, Devani the day after.'

Kennedy said nothing as she pondered on that timing. It was a very tight spread, by anybody's reckoning. Out of nowhere, she remembered a garbled line or two from Hamlet: someone asking Death what the big occasion was in the underworld that caused him to take so many princes all on the same night.

'How did they die?' she asked.

'Accidents in both cases. Or they were recorded as accidents. But so was Barlow, right?' Harper raised his left hand, knocked down the index finger and then the forefinger as he recited the brief litany. 'Catherine Hurt, hit and run. Devani, electric shock from a badly earthed computer.'

'Did you get the files?'

'There's only a file for Hurt. It's on my desk, but seriously, there's sod all in it. No witnesses, no CCTV footage, no nothing.'

Kennedy took that on the chin. She'd heard on a TV documentary that the UK had twenty per cent of the world's CCTV cameras, but it was a sad fact of twenty-first-century policing that they were never where you needed them to be. 'Is it just those two?' she asked Harper. 'Or are you still working your way through the list?'

'I'm about two-thirds done. Still waiting on a lot of people to get back to me, though – so I've talked to a little under half of them. Before you ask, I've been trying to find a link between the three victims, but I haven't come up with anything so far. Well, apart from the convention itself. They're not even all historians. Devani is the odd one out – he's a modern languages lecturer at a community college in Bradford. Hurt is a teaching assistant at Leicester De Montfort. Their names don't come up together anywhere when you feed them into a search engine.'

Kennedy was surprised at that. In her experience, if you typed any collection of random names into Google, you automatically got a million hits. Maybe the absence of a connection was suspicious and anomalous in itself. 'Are you all right to keep working through the list?' she asked Harper.

His chagrin showed on his face. 'We've got two new victims,' he pointed out. 'Shouldn't we go and do some site work?'

'*Possible* victims. And the sites are as old as Barlow's. Tomorrow we'll go out and do some recce. First, let's make sure we didn't miss anybody else.'

'What are you going to be doing?' Harper demanded, suspicion in his voice.

'I'm going back to Prince Regent's, to have another look at

Barlow's office. His house was burgled a while back. I'm wondering if someone might have gone through his things at the college, too.'

'What would that prove?'

Kennedy was going on instinct – the indefinable sense that she'd missed something the first time she was in that room – but she didn't want to say that: it was too hard to defend. 'For starters,' she said instead, 'it would prove that the stalker existed. And it might give us a line on a possible motive. Old artefacts, manuscripts, something like that. Smuggling them, forging them, stealing them. I don't know. Barlow thought someone was following him and maybe he thought he knew why. I can ask about these other two at the same time – see if anyone at Prince Regent's knows of any connection between them and Barlow.' She paused. 'Do something else for me?'

'Oh, anything. I'll be sitting here with all this time on my hands.'

'Call a hotel – the Pride Court, in West one. Somewhere around Bloomsbury. Ask for contact information for someone who was staying there recently. Michael Brand.'

'Yeah, okay. Who is he?'

'He was in some sort of online club that Barlow belonged to. They call themselves the Ravellers. In fact, it would be great if you could get a membership list from somewhere. If either of these other two DOAs were in the same gang, we might be on to something.'

Harper made her spell the name out before she left. 'When are you going back to Summerhill?' he asked her, as they walked back along the corridor.

'When we know what we've got. Not yet. The DCI threw this to us because he doesn't want to have anything to do with it. When we bring it back to him, the first thing he's going to think is that we're trying to put one over on him. We'll need to make a case.'

'Three dead historians don't make a case?'

'They do if they were murdered. We don't know that yet.'

'Oh, they were murdered all right.' Harper sounded almost cheerful. 'Congratulate me, Kennedy.'

'On what?'

'This is my first case in Division. I hit a serial killer on my first case.'

Kennedy didn't share his enthusiasm. That cluster pattern of supposed accidents was still troubling her a lot. One killer, working his way through a list? Not likely. Not likely at all. You'd need to be really lucky, or else to have done immaculate recon, to get three people in two days and come away clean. Serial killers were often obsessives, and they were very good at finding the victims that matched the needs of their particular psychosis, but they mostly treated each murder as a separate project. And spree killers just exploded, at a time and place of their own choosing. If she and Harper were dealing with a murderer, it was a murderer who didn't seem to fall into either of those categories.

She stopped a couple of turns of corridor short of the bear pit, sparing Harper's reputation, and turned to face him. He was looking at her expectantly. He made a beckoning motion with one outstretched hand, coaxing her.

'Fine. Congratulations, Harper.'

'Like you mean it.'

She punched him on the shoulder.

'Good going, Chris. You rock. First of many, man.'

'Thank you. Makes up for spending the day on the phone.'

'Tomorrow will be different.'

She remembered that promise later and wondered whether he'd believed her.

10

Solomon Kuutma was a mystery, even to himself. A man who revered honesty and transparency, he moved in secret and hid the deepest truths in the deepest wells: seeing all life as sacred, he killed without compunction and ordered others to kill.

If anything about his life troubled him, it was the thought that these contradictions, seen from the outside, could look like mere hypocrisy. Other men might not trouble to think through the paradoxes to the simple truth at their core. They might judge him, and judge him unfairly, and though the judgements of men weighed as much as a feather weighs (those of women, infinitely less), the unfairness – purely hypothetical – was irksome to him.

He had thought, therefore, of writing a memoir, to be given to the world after his death. All names, all circumstantial details, would be removed, but the central fact of a good man bending his conscience to fit through the needle's eye would be clearly explained, and so would be understood by those who read with open eyes and minds and hearts.

Obviously, this was madness. The memoir would never be written, the explanation never offered. Even without names, the truth would be apparent and all his labours of many years would be made meaningless at a stroke. His masters would be horrified to hear that Kuutma had indulged such a wild idea even for a second. They might even call him home – a home-coming without honour, and for that reason unbearable: the greatest joy turned into the most trenchant pain.

All the same, Kuutma composed, within the privacy of his mind, the explanation for his actions. He recited it to himself, not like a prayer, but like a prophylaxis – a ward against evil, because a man doing the things that Kuutma did was at risk of falling into evil without even knowing it. Sitting on the rooftop terrace of a café in Montmartre, with Paris sprawled wanton below him like a submissive lover, he considered the situation that had arisen because of the actions of Leo Tillman, and he explained, to no one but himself and perhaps God, what he intended to do to resolve that situation.

My greatest skill, he thought, *my greatest gift, is love. You can't defeat an enemy without knowing him, and you can't know him without loving him, without letting your mind move into silent sympathy with his. Once that Herculean task is done, you will be ahead of him always and without effort, able to lie in ambush along all the pathways of his life.*

But Kuutma could not love Tillman. And perhaps that was why Tillman was still alive.

Kuutma had been following the ex-mercenary ever since Turkey, trying to decide what approach might be appropriate, given that Tillman had now murdered Kiril Kartoyev and presumably, before murdering him, had spoken with him.

It was a dynamic problem, played out across four dimensions as Tillman moved across the face of the continent. Tillman moved very quickly, but that was not in itself a source of difficulties. Much more troublesome was the fact that he moved in a deliberately scattershot way, complicating pursuit and requiring Kuutma to withdraw and redeploy his teams many times over. Tillman would book a taxi and then walk, buy a train ticket and then steal a car. And as though he knew about the American debacle, which at this stage seemed impossible, he never, ever flew.

Tillman only stayed in Erzurum for a few hours, not long enough for Kuutma to move a team into place around him. Barely long enough, in fact, to change his clothes, to shave and perhaps to check whatever networks he used to see whether there was any fall-out from the raid on Kartoyev's house in Ingushetia that might personally affect him.

Kartoyev's death was inconvenient to Kuutma. The Russian was only a supplier, and a foulness unworthy even to be touched because the things he supplied served the basest impulses of men. Still, he'd been efficient and useful, and had learned long ago to keep to his assigned place in the scheme of things. Kartoyev asked no questions. He sourced difficult items quickly and untraceably. He kept his avarice within acceptable bounds.

Now a new Kartoyev would have to be found, and that was Tillman's fault. Or perhaps the fault lay with Kuutma himself, for not addressing sooner the unique problems that Tillman presented.

I held back from killing you because I wanted to be sure beyond doubt that you needed to be killed: that there was no possibility my judgement was tainted. This was not cowardice but compunction. It does not diminish me.

Still, in Erzurum Kuutma held back a little more. Even if his worst presentiments were realised, there was time; time to move gently towards that synthesis of perspectives that was the heart of his mystery. Time to understand all, and to forgive all, and then to act.

From Erzurum, Tillman went to Bucharest, probably by way of Ankara. Most likely he'd taken the train, or rather a number of trains, doubling back through the mountains north of Bursa on foot. There was a place there where two branch lines passed within seven miles of each other, before veering away sharply to north and west. The traffic on the western line was mostly freight: it would have been relatively easy for Tillman to jump on board on a slow gradient and ride the rods, or force the door of a carriage, and be carried through three hundred bone-shaking miles, across two sloppily guarded borders, to the Romanian capital.

In Bucharest, though, he used his own passport – one of many passports, but one he'd used before and which was trace-able to him – to obtain a room in the Calea Victoriei Hotel. Kuutma weighed his options with a fine discrimination. It was still far from clear what Tillman knew, or what his aims were, and in these rare, ambiguous instances the Messengers' creed was Janus-faced. *Do nothing that is not warranted. Do every-thing that is needful.*

The killing of Kartoyev, Kuutma reasoned, had put Tillman over the invisible, wavering line into the second of those cate-gories. He would need to be removed, and ideally he would need to be interrogated first. Kuutma would take care of the interrogation himself. He contacted local Messengers, and a team of four was despatched to the Calea Victoriei to detain Tillman long enough for Kuutma himself to arrive and take over.

But although Tillman had checked in at the hotel, and had paid for three nights in advance, it seemed to be yet another of the blind alleys he liked to set up wherever he went. When the Messengers moved in, it was to find the bed empty, the room untouched apart from a note that in due course found its way to Kuutma.

The note read, *Cuts both ways.*

Kuutma felt certain the note did not refer directly to him,

even though it seemed to pun on his name. Tillman could not know his name. Only one person Tillman had ever met could possibly have told him, and that one person was secure, beyond reasonable or even unreasonable doubt. No, the note was a taunt – and therefore a juvenile and mistaken gesture on Tillman's part. He meant only to say that Kuutma, and the powers he represented, could not move against him without revealing their hand and making his search easier.

He would learn that it did not cut both ways: it was only in the last and least era of human history, where the extraneous was sanctified, that razors were designed with a double edge.

From Bucharest Tillman went to Munich and from Munich to Paris, by paranoid and complicated means – the stolen car among them. Either he avoided border stations altogether or else he presented a false passport that Kuutma's sources hadn't yet linked to him. There were no official records of his journey, no footprints to follow, any more than there would have been if Kuutma had made the same pilgrimage himself.

In Paris a team had already been deployed, because Kuutma by this time had more than a presentiment of where his quarry was heading. The three Messengers there – chosen and assigned by Kuutma with due consideration for the nature of the task and the target – picked up Tillman's trail on the Boulevard Montparnasse and moved in quickly. They assumed that Tillman was heading for the Metro station and had already decided to kill him there. Instead, Tillman walked into the underground parking garage of the Tour Maine. But when the team closed in to despatch him, he had disappeared. A thorough search of the area revealed no trace of him.

At this point, the team committed an enormous breach of protocol. Under their leader's orders, they dispersed, as was right and proper, returning to their safe house by different routes. But they failed to use the check-reverse-check system instigated by Kuutma to ensure that none was followed.

The next time the Paris safe house was left empty, it was ransacked. Tillman had turned Kuutma's sting back upon himself, with a certain grace. Fortunately, they kept no documents of any kind at the safe house. What documents did Messengers need? Tillman escaped, but he escaped with empty hands.

Kuutma felt he was learning from these failures. Tillman had been a mercenary for nine years and most of his experience had been in urban warfare. He was comfortable in cities, knew how to find invisibility in a crowd, or a doorway where someone else would see a dead end. So clearly, when they next sought to close the net on him, it should be somewhere those skills would be of no use.

Magas. Erzurum. Bucharest. Munich. Paris. The westward trend of Tillman's journey was marked and unmistakable now, and it seemed inevitable that it would end in the one place where it was least convenient to have him go. Kuutma could be paranoid, too. He used all the resources he had ready to hand – not plentiful but certainly adequate – to watch the mainline stations northward from Paris and the ferry ports from Quimper to Hook of Holland.

In the meantime, he reviewed what he knew about the man who had become the most fascinating irritant in his far from serene existence. Most interesting to him, without a doubt, was the period of Tillman's life that began with the day he returned home to find his family vanished and his house cold and empty.

Tillman could easily have gone back to what he was before – a man asleep, made docile first by his own idleness and then by bovine contentment. He could have found another woman, and been equally happy with her, since surely to a serious man all women were alike. But he did not do these things. He went in a different direction entirely and acquired a new set of skills. Seen in context, it formed an extreme but unsurprising response to grief and loss: to become a soldier, a man who kills without human feeling, since nothing in his own life seemed any longer to call for the exercise of such feeling. An extreme response, yes. But now, in retrospect, it was possible to read the same decision in another way.

Twelve years of soldiering, first in the regular army and then as a mercenary. For the first time, Tillman had seemed completely absorbed, completely committed. He had been promoted to corporal, then to sergeant. A commissioned rank had been offered him, but by then he was in a mercenary outfit, and ranks, in such an organisation, were a loose fit at the best of times. Tillman chose to remain a sergeant so he could stay in the field, and his employers were happy to let him stay there because in the field he excelled. The soldiers who served with him gave him their taciturn worship and the name Twister – a tribute to an ability to get out of any situation with his hide and any other hides that he was minding miraculously unscathed.

It seemed like Tillman had found a new focus, a new family. But Kuutma, reviewing the evidence now, suspected that this had always been an illusion. Tillman had no interest in acquiring a new family. He was intent, still, on finding the one he'd lost. Throughout these years, he was equipping himself for a specific task. Building up a skill set that would be supremely and minutely appropriate when he stepped aside from soldiering and launched himself – suddenly and without warning – into his current search.

Kuutma remembered a conversation, with unsettling vividness. The last time … no. Not the last time. There was another time, after that. But close to the terrible end, the indelible moment.

'Will he forget you?'
'Oh God! Why would you care?'
'Will he forget you?'
'Never.'
'Then he's a fool.'
'Yes.'

Tillman's starting point was a name: Michael Brand. Rebecca Tillman had met with a Michael Brand on the day of her disappearance, by prior assignation. Unfortunately, she'd left a note of the name, the time and the place on a pad next to the telephone in her kitchen, where she'd taken the call, and though she'd torn off the sheet and taken it with her, Tillman had been able to make out the impression of the characters on the sheet beneath.

The name led nowhere, of course. The hotel where Rebecca Tillman had arranged to meet Brand was the scene of no carnal or criminal actions, and forensic investigation would unearth nothing there. It was simply the place in which she had been told what she needed to be told, so that the necessary arrangements could be made. It was even late, past the time when she should have been told, and lateness was always to be deplored in such matters. Perhaps if Brand had been more mindful of his duty ... but Brand was by necessity a blunt and uncertain instrument.

Still, it was a blind alley. That should have been the end as well as the beginning of Tillman's quest. He had a name, but nothing to attach to the name. He had the fact of a meeting, but no hypothesis that made sense of the meeting. He should have given up.

Thirteen years later, he had not given up. He had emerged from the red spatter of the world's battlefields, a man given over to violence and death, to resume with unexpected vigour a search that it now appeared he had never really abandoned. He was looking for his wife, who after so long an absence might not even be alive; for his children, who he would not even know if he saw them. He was trying to rebuild by force of will the one moment of real joy his life had ever harboured.

It was of the utmost importance to Kuutma, and to the people who employed and put their trust in him, that Tillman should fail. It was also, in a different sense, important to the fates of twenty million others.

Because if Tillman even got close to the truth, that was the number of people who would die.

11

The bursar wasn't available when Kennedy got to Prince Regent's. In fact, nobody was. The history annexe seemed to be deserted except for a sad-looking man at the front desk, framed against the backdrop of the bulletin board with its endless vista of the gigs of yesteryear: the Dresden Dolls, Tunng, the Earlies. She asked if the receptionist could open the room up for her himself: that was outside his brief. And nobody else was available on-site? Nobody. What about in the main building? The main building was outside his brief.

She flashed her ID. 'Get someone over here now,' she told him, grimly. 'I'm not asking for an extension on my homework, I'm investigating a death.'

The sad man grabbed the phone and spoke into it with a certain urgency. A couple of minutes later, Ellis bustled through the door, annoyed and flustered. 'Inspector Kennedy,' he said. 'I didn't expect to see you again so soon.' His expression said a lot more, none of it complimentary.

'I'd like to take another look at Professor Barlow's office, Mr Ellis. Would that be possible?'

'Now?' The bursar's lack of enthusiasm was palpable.

'Ideally, yes. Now.'

'It's just that there's a degree ceremony tomorrow and a lot to do if we're to be ready. It would be much more convenient if you could wait until next week.'

She didn't bother to repeat the speech about investigating a death. 'I'm happy to just sign out the key and find my own way,' she told him. 'I know you're a busy man. But of course, if it's too late now, I can come back tomorrow morning.' *During* your damned degree ceremony.

The bursar caved with alacrity. He had the sad man on reception bring the cleaner's sub-master key from a locked cabinet on the wall behind him. 'This will open all the doors in that corridor,' Ellis told her. 'But obviously I'll need to be told if you intend to go into any other rooms. There are privacy implications.'

'I'm only interested in that one room,' said Kennedy. 'Thank you.'

Ellis turned away, but Kennedy detained him with a touch on his arm. He turned back, wearing an aggrieved expression.

'Mr Ellis, there was one other thing I wanted to ask you about before you go. Professor Barlow was a member of an online group or society of some kind. The Ravellers. Do you know anything about that?'

'A little,' Ellis admitted, grudgingly. 'Not my field, as I said before, but yes. I know what they do.'

'Which is?'

'They translate documents. Very old, very difficult documents. Badly preserved codices, decontextualised fragments, that sort of thing. Some of them, like Stuart, are professionals in the field, but I think a lot of people in the group are just interested hobbyists. It's a place where they exchange ideas, suggest hypotheses and get feedback. Stuart used to joke that when the CIA found out how good the Ravellers were, they'd either recruit them all or have them assassinated.'

Kennedy didn't get the joke. In answer to her blank expression, Ellis elaborated. 'Code-breaking, you see. Some of the early codices are so badly damaged, you're trying to make out the whole message from about a third of the characters. You have to use X-rays, fibre analysis, all sorts of things, to guess at what's missing.'

'Where does the name come from?' Kennedy asked. 'The Ravellers?'

It was Ellis's turn to look blank now. 'I have no idea. Ravel isn't actually a verb, is it? Just a back formation from "unravel". To knit things together? To combine small pieces into bigger meanings? Or perhaps it's a technical term. I really couldn't say.'

'Do you know who any of the other members of the group are or how I could contact them?'

The bursar's interest, not huge to start with, was visibly waning. 'You'd have to get in touch with whoever runs the forum, I suppose,' he said. 'I don't think it would be too hard.' Another thought struck him and he raised his eyebrows. 'Of course, that's assuming the server and the moderators are based here in the UK,' he mused. 'It might be harder if they were in the United States, say, or somewhere in Europe. There'd be jurisdictional problems, wouldn't there?'

'Possibly. Thank you, Mr Ellis, you've been a great help.'

She took the key and headed for the stairs. Behind her, she heard the sad man's woes being added to in low but ferocious tones. Clearly, the bursar felt that this could have been handled without his personal intervention.

Barlow's study was exactly as she remembered it, except that it was later in the day and the sunlight was shining through the slatted blinds at a shallower angle. She stood in the doorway, trying to recall what it was she'd seen earlier, what had stood out from its surroundings enough to register on her subconscious. It was a line, she decided, a line out of place, and lower than her eye level. It didn't seem to be there now, but maybe that was because of the changed light.

She picked up the framed newspaper article in both hands, glazed side facing outwards. Catching the light from the window, she reflected it round the room, a moving spotlight that stood in for the sunlight of that morning.

It took a while, but she got there in the end. One of the floor tiles was standing proud of its neighbours, creating a shadow along its trailing edge. As though it had been lifted and put back, but hadn't settled into exactly the same position as before.

Kennedy knelt down. Sliding her fingernails under the edge of the tile, she lifted it gently. Underneath, lying unprotected on the dusty floorboards, was a rectangle of slightly glossy card. At the top the single word: *Here?* Blue biro, scrawled, double underlined. And then at lower right corner, several sets of characters written more neatly and carefully in black fineliner.

P52

P75

NH II-1, III-1, IV-1

Eg2

B66, 75

C45

Turning the card over, she saw that it was a photograph.

It showed a building, from a distance: a factory, or more likely a massive warehouse of some kind. A grey-painted concrete wall reared up six storeys or more from the cracked asphalt of a weed-choked parking lot. A few small windows near the top, but otherwise an unbroken surface. A small strip of road visible at one corner of the photo. A chainlink fence that looked reasonably intact, but plenty of evidence of ruin elsewhere: the garbage piled up against the fence, the weeds squeezing up between the paving slabs, and at one edge of the photo the abandoned hulk of a car, its tyreless wheels up on bricks. The whole image was blurred and the angle was a little off: a picture taken very sloppily, or maybe very quickly, by someone in a car or a train. It looked like the test photo you'd take to bring the counter on your camera from zero to one at the start of a new reel of film. But who used film these days?

Kennedy flipped the card again to look at the figures on the back. A code of some kind? It couldn't be a very long message, if so. Unless the figures referred to passages in a book, a pre-arranged code key, something like that. Or maybe they made up a combination for a digital lock or a password to unlock a file. She had no way of knowing without some other clue to point her in the right direction.

She tagged and bagged the photo, and scribbled a brief note to herself in her evidence pad about where she'd found it. Then she lifted up the adjacent tiles to make sure she wasn't missing an obvious trick. Nothing there.

She hadn't intended to do a thorough search of the room, only to scratch an itch, but all the same she found herself checking out other likely hiding places: behind the pictures on the walls, the backs of desk drawers, the undersides of furniture. Nothing else appeared, and the sheer volume of papers and books defeated her. Someone needed to look at this stuff with an informed eye, and the someone wasn't her.

Her inner paranoiac was now fully awake, though, and in light of the intruder at the Barlows' cottage, Kennedy thought to check the door this time. The lock was a standard five-pin, built into the doorknob. There were light scratch marks around the keyhole, and way too much play in the lock itself. Someone had picked it part-way with a tension tool and then turned the whole cylinder with a plug-spinner to make it open.

There was an upside and a downside to that. On the one hand, whoever had broken in here hadn't found the hidden photo.

On the other, there was no telling what they *had* taken.

12

Chris Harper hated routine and repetitive tasks, and hated even more that he was good at them. Once he'd made initial calls to everyone on the London History Forum list, without turning up another corpse, he got on to the other two items on Kennedy's things-to-do list.

Michael Brand was no longer staying at the Pride Court, the desk clerk regretted to inform him. Brand had left several weeks ago, checking out on the thirtieth of June. Three days after Barlow and Hurt had died, two days after Devani. Barlow's sister had been right, then: Brand was in London through that whole time, while his fellow Ravellers were dying in colourful and ambiguous ways up and down the country. Then he'd waited a few days before shooting off to pastures new. Maybe he'd come to warn Barlow; or to bring him something, or take something from him. Maybe he knew the killer. Maybe he *was* the killer. Somehow, none of those hypotheses quite fitted with him hanging around in a cheap London hotel for two days after the shit hit the fan.

'Did he leave a home address on file?' Harper asked. The clerk became coy, but only until Harper mentioned an ongoing investigation. Then he volunteered without demur an address in Gijon, Spain, and a phone number to go with it.

Harper thanked him, hung up and dialled the number. He got

the one-note whine that means no connection has been established, then a click and an irritatingly patrician voice cut in: 'Sorry. Your number has not been recognised. Sorry. Your number has not—'

Harper hit the Spanish electoral rolls via the Interpol database and entered the Gijon address: 12, Campo del Jardin. The three names attached to it were Jorge Ignacio Argiz, Rosa Isabella Argiz and Marta Pacheco. No Michael Brand, and the phone number listed was different from the one that Brand had given. Harper called it, got Jorge Argiz on the first try. Did Jorge know a Michael Brand? Jorge's English was good enough to assure the detective that he did not.

Harper put Brand to one side and started to zero in on the Ravellers.

The very first thing an internet search turned up was their online forum, Ravellers.org, whose respectable and glossy front page hid hundreds of pages of gibberish about variant readings and disputed identifications. Readings and identifications of what? There didn't seem to be any way of telling. Threads on the forum typically had titles such as 'Pigment spread link variant 1-100, NH papyri 2.2.1 – 3.4.6', 'PH 1071 imaged in infra-red spectrum – using 1000nm filter!' and 'Challenged zayin in DSS 9P1, line 14, position 12'. Harper might as well have been reading Sanskrit. Some of the posts certainly contained Sanskrit, and weren't even apologetic about it.

There was a CONTACT US option on the menu bar, but the email address it linked to was in the defunct Freeserve domain, which probably meant that it hadn't been changed in years and no longer led to an active server. Harper sent a message anyway, but didn't trust it to get to anyone – and he couldn't post anything on the forum without joining the group, which seemed like a long way to go about things.

He went back to the search results and refined the parameters, searching for the intersection of 'Ravellers' with 'Barlow'. The first couple of items were obviously bot-based catch-alls. *Read Ravellers Barlow stories and see Ravellers Barlow photos and videos!* The third, though, was a short post on a different message board, announcing an award given to a Dr Sarah Opie for services to scholarship. Among the many follow-on posts on the thread was one from Stuart Barlow that read, 'Well deserved, Sarah!' The post was about eighteen months old. The item had come up in Harper's list because Dr Opie had listed membership of the Ravellers among her interests and credits – and she was on staff at the University of Bedfordshire, not in their history faculty (which didn't seem to exist) but in the school of computer science and technology.

Harper dialled the university's switchboard and asked to speak to Dr Opie. When the receptionist asked him to leave a message, he identified himself and explained that this was in connection with a murder inquiry. One short flurry later, he was talking to Dr Opie herself.

'I'm really sorry to bother you,' he started off, 'but I'm part of the team investigating the death of Professor Stuart Barlow. I understand that you belong to an organisation of which he was also a member. An organisation called the Ravellers.'

There was a long pause on the other end of the line. Harper was about to speak again when Dr Opie finally answered him – with a question. 'Who are you?' Her voice, which sounded younger than he'd expected, was also brittle with strain and distrust.

He'd already told her, but he said it again. 'My name is Christopher Harper. I'm a detective constable with the Serious and Organised Crime Agency of the London Metropolitan—'

'How do I know that?' She shot the question in before he'd even finished with the formalities.

'You hang up and check,' Harper suggested. Given the mounting body count, her paranoia seemed reasonable. 'Call New Scotland Yard, ask for Ops, and then for Detective Division. Use my name, and say I asked you to call. I'll still be here, and we can talk.'

He was expecting the line to go dead, but it didn't. He could hear the distant half-noises that go with someone moving, breathing, just being there.

'You said this is about Stuart.'

'Well, not just that. A couple of other things, too.'

'What things?'

Harper hesitated. *I'm building a list of dead historians. Do you know any?* That sounded like a loaded question, even inside his head. 'Look,' he said, 'why don't you hang up and call me back? I think you'll feel better talking about this if you know it's not a crank call.'

'I want to know what this is about,' the voice on the other end of the line said, the tension screwed up by half a notch or so.

Harper took a deep breath. Back when he wore uniform, which was right up until a year ago, he'd envied the detectives their cachet, the easy and natural authority they wore. But maybe it was a trick you had to learn. 'It's about a pattern of suspicious deaths,' he said, and then added the lame amendment, 'Potentially. Potentially suspicious.'

He heard a sound like a hollow knock – as though the phone had fallen out of her hand and hit the floor, or bumped into something as she turned.

'Hello?' Harper said. 'Are you still there?'

'What deaths? Tell me. What deaths?'

'Stuart Barlow. Catherine Hurt. Samir Devani.'

Opie let out a disconcerting moan.

'Oh God. They weren't ... they weren't accidents?'

'Wait,' said Harper. 'You knew them all? Dr Opie, this is important. How did you know them?'

The only answer was the click and burr of the phone being hung up. He waited, irresolute, for a minute and a half. If he called her switchboard again, his phone would be tied up while they patched the call through to her faculty building, and then to her extension. If she was calling him back, rather than just ending the call, he'd be shutting her out.

Just as he gave up and reached for the phone, it rang. He picked up. 'External call for you,' the comms clerk said. 'A Dr Opie.'

'Go ahead,' said Harper. 'Put her through.'

The noise of the despatch room gave way to the silence of another space.

'Dr Opie?'

'Yes.'

'How did you know those three people?'

He knew what the answer would be, which went some way to explain the prickle of déjà vu he felt as she said it. 'They were Ravellers. They were all in the group. And ...'

He waited. Nothing came. 'And?'

'They were working on the same translation.'

13

Tillman surfaced in Calais, where he booked a passage on a cross-Channel ferry to Dover. But of course, he would: the shortest sea route, the smallest window within which he would be enclosed and vulnerable. Still, Kuutma didn't take anything for granted. He kept his anchors in place all along the northern coastline, and his mole in the offices of the SNCF on full alert, until he had visual confirmation of Tillman boarding the ferry.

Even then Kuutma moved methodically and meticulously. It was the last sailing of the day, leaving harbour at 11.40 p.m., but the Calais ferry terminal was still crowded. The Messengers – three of them again, as in Bucharest and Paris – boarded last and remained near the exits, which they watched until the bow doors closed and the vessel began to back out of its berth.

Kuutma stood at the quayside, watching. Would Tillman appear on deck at the last moment, claiming he'd left something behind and had to disembark after all? Was this to be another double or triple bluff?

It seemed not. No last-minute alarums came, no diversionary scuffles or panics, no false starts. The ferry left without incident, with Tillman on board. Tillman, and the three who were to kill him. Kuutma made the sign of the noose as it departed, calling for the hanged man's blessing on his Messengers.

Belatedly but fervently, he yearned to be with them. Again, he found himself thinking unprofitable thoughts. Picking apart his own thought processes, fruitlessly and even dangerously. It did not do to be divided from oneself in this way. He was prepared to admit, now that it was all but done, that he hated Tillman and had waited too long to move against the mercenary because he doubted the purity of his own motives. He wouldn't make that mistake again.

There was nobody left to make it for.

Tillman watched the coast of France recede, with mixed feelings.

Kartoyev had confirmed a lot he already knew, had provided a few new clues and crucially had given him a fix on his next destination. He sensed for the first time that he was closing in on Michael Brand. That where he'd once chased a name, and then a phantom, now he was in pursuit of a man, who could almost be glimpsed running ahead of him.

On the other hand, he had fresh anomalies to consider. The drugs, for one. He'd never found a link before now between Brand and the drugs trade. He'd run covert ops in Colombia, and he was aware, in a general way, of how that trade was plied. Brand's movements across the globe were not the movements of a salesman or a purchaser. An enforcer, possibly, but what was he enforcing? And why, if he was in the drugs business, would he travel so far to source ingredients that were readily available in most countries? The former Soviet Union was not Brand's base, Tillman felt sure of that. His stays there were too short and too narrowly focused on a few specific contacts.

A smokescreen, then. Brand bought his chemicals in Ingushetia because he didn't want to leave a trail that led any closer to his real base of operations. And he refused Kartoyev's offer of refined methamphetamine, presumably because he wanted to mix his own. And he was about to mix a batch that was larger by factors of ten than his usual batch.

File that one for future thought. Tillman had more urgent things to think about right now.

In his journey westwards across Europe, he had become aware as never before that he was hunted as well as hunter. In Bucharest it had been pure luck that delivered him. Walking in Mătăsari, a place where everyone keeps one eye over their shoulder, he'd read from the reaction of a man he passed in the street that he might be being followed. He didn't look back, but tested the theory by walking through a crowded street market, where his tailgunners had closed in out of sheer necessity. He'd tacked from stall to stall in random patterns, memorising the faces around him, and after half an hour had isolated one as a definite tail, another two as probable. Once he knew he was marked, it had simply been a case of choosing the best moment to shake them off. But he had no clue as to who they were or what they wanted.

In Paris he was ready for them. Expecting to be found, hair-trigger for any whiff of pursuit or surveillance, he was able to turn the tables on his shadowy followers and tail one of them back to base. But he had little to show for it. The house they'd been using out on the Périphérique had been unfurnished, apart from three bed rolls lying side by side on a bare wooden floor. These men were ascetics, clearly. Like the early Christian saints who spent years in the wilderness, mortifying their flesh. It troubled Tillman to think that the people chasing him were capable of such humourless and stern dedication. It troubled him, even, to find that they were so many. He had no idea why an organisation of this size and this degree of organisation would kidnap women and children from London streets.

But perhaps *chasing* was too strong a term. It was possible that they only wanted to see how far Tillman had got. Whether he was moving in the right direction at last, or still going round in circles. He wished, now that it was too late, that he'd gone on through Belgium and the Netherlands, tried harder to make a false trail. But at the end of the day, there were only so many ways to get to Britain from mainland Europe, if you didn't want to take a plane. With even moderate resources, it was possible to keep watch on all of them.

And he had to go to Britain. He'd stayed in Paris long enough to contact some former friends and acquaintances in the private security business. Many of them were still active in that amphibian, quasi-legal world, and they had been able to give him some very interesting and very current nuggets of information about Michael Brand. For thirteen years the bastard had stayed below the water line. Now he'd breached, and Tillman had to be there. There just wasn't any other option.

Tillman turned from the rail and made his way through the light sprinkling of passengers on the deck towards the double doors that led back inside. As he did so, he checked his watch. It was only a ninety-minute crossing, and he noted with approval that twenty of those minutes had already gone.

In the lounge area it was much more crowded. Families sat in inward-looking groups, their territory marked with handbags and rucksacks. They mostly looked either grim or tired, but happier families had been reproduced on the walls behind them in giant photographic prints, maintaining some kind of a karmic balance. In the absence of any free seats, people were sitting with their backs against a bulkhead, while others were propping up the bar that ran down the right-hand side of the room. A single barman stood serving draught Stella Artois from a single pump. The adjacent Guinness pump had been marked OUT OF ORDER. Further on, the bar gave way seamlessly to a food counter where people queued for baguettes and chips. The air smelled of stale beer and old frying fat.

Tillman didn't feel hungry, and preferred whisky to lager. He looked at the optics of Bell's, Grant's and Johnny Walker lined up behind the bar, all perfectly drinkable. But in the army he had only drunk when he wanted oblivion, and these days he didn't often afford himself such a luxury. He felt tempted for a second or two, slowed his stride, then dismissed the idea and walked on. Later, when he got to London, he might find a bar and reacquaint himself with that momentary chemical caress. For now, he preferred to stay awake and alert.

He was looking for a place to sit that fulfilled his usual criteria: a view of all exits, a wall at his back and something nearby like a wall or a counter that would block a sightline at need. In this crowded room, he knew that wouldn't be possible. It was also, he was aware, faintly ridiculous to apply criteria like that in a setting where any attack would be hampered by the instant panic stampede it would trigger, and where the assassin would have no ready escape even if the attack succeeded. The people who had followed him in Bucharest and Paris had still done nothing to suggest they wanted to harm him. All they'd done, both times, was to tail him.

So was this paranoia? The carrying of his usual caution over the edge of the abyss at last into mania and psychosis? Or had he responded to some cue he hadn't even consciously processed? Normally he trusted his instincts, but he'd been pushing himself hard for a long time. He felt a weight of weariness fall on him, so abruptly it was like a physical thing. With it came a revulsion against the crush of humanity all around – the babble of voices sounding like an externalisation of some confusion or plurality in his own heart and soul.

Tillman pushed on to the far end of the lounge and out into

a much smaller lobby area with fruit machines on one side and toilets on the other. He dug into his holdall for one of the bags of loose currency he carried – one that held some euro coins. He found Mr Snow, the unicorn, and tucked the fluffy, vacant, sickly sweet thing into the pocket of his jeans by one front paw. It dangled there, an ineffectual mascot, as Tillman fed forty or fifty euros into the one-armed bandit. Pulling the levers and pressing the buttons at random ate away at the time without using up any of his attention, allowing him to watch the flow of those who passed and those who loitered. They passed and loitered with perfect conviction. No anomalies, no warning bells. But then, there hadn't been any in Bucharest, either. He wasn't going to stay the distance if he underestimated his enemies.

When Tillman finally ran out of coins, he checked his watch. They had to be already more than halfway over by this time. He went back into the lounge, stood in line and bought a coffee, but once again the noise and the claustrophobic press overwhelmed him. He walked out to the lobby before he'd taken more than two sips of the bland muck.

Not that many places left to go. He decided to spend the last half-hour of the crossing on deck, but he felt the tiredness catching up on him. In the absence of caffeine, he could at least splash some cold water in his face. He went through the door bearing the stylised man whose arms were thrown out from his sides like those of a gunslinger walking into a duel.

The restroom was a windowless twenty-by-twenty cube with urinals along one wall, sinks opposite, and three cubicles at the back. He stepped across a floor awash with water, which had slopped over from a sink that had been filled with toilet paper in lieu of a plug. A single flickering neon strip lit the depressing scene.

He draped his jacket over a condom machine, dropping his

holdall at his feet, and ran the cold tap for a long time before finally accepting that the water wouldn't run cold. Tepid as it was, he splashed it on his face anyway, then hit the hand drier and lowered his head into its jet of air. The door at his back sighed as it opened, sighed again as it closed.

When he straightened up, they were there. Two of them, side by side, already coming at him. Two suited men, startlingly handsome, clean cut and serious-looking. The kind who might knock on your door to ask if you'd found Jesus or whether they could count on your vote for the Conservative candidate. Tillman had time only to take in their uncanny synchronisation – something that had to be born out of endless drilling under the same trainer or commander. Then they raised their hands and the short blades they held flashed, one high one low, as they intersected the light from the neon strip overhead.

Tillman hooked his jacket off the condom machine with his left hand and whirled it in the air in front of him, retreating into the ten feet of space that the room allowed him. Behind that moving screen he hooked the squat, heavy Mateba Unica from its customary resting place, tucked into the back of his belt, and in the same movement thumbed the safety.

The two men seemed to anticipate him. Even as he brought the gun up, one of them half-turned away and kicked back against the turn: a perfect *yoko geri*. Tillman saw it coming, but the man moved so inhumanly fast that seeing it didn't help him. The guy's heel smacked into the inside of Tillman's wrist before he could pull it away, knocking the gun from his grip. It clattered across the floor. Both knives came up in slashing feints, one aimed at Tillman's heart and the other at his face. Caught out of position, he faked right and whipped the jacket down like a flail so that it wrapped around the wrist of the man on his left. The other man's blade cut across his upper arm in a broad, deep slash, but he ignored the pain. Wrenching on the jacket brought the man within reach and Tillman headbutted him in the face, then – since he didn't go down – circled behind him to use him as a shield and snatch a moment's respite.

Again the two men moved and reacted in frictionless unison. The one tangled up in the jacket dropped into a crouch and the other leaned over him, launching another slashing attack. Tillman bent backwards from the knees like a contestant in a limbo competition, just about staying out of the blade's reach.

The attacker jumped over his kneeling comrade and advanced again, the knife flicking back and forth at the level of Tillman's stomach. Tillman instinctively lowered his hand to block a possible disembowelling thrust: the instinct almost killed him. The knife came up inside his guard, moving around his block as effortlessly as if it wasn't there. Flinching aside, he felt as well as heard the air part as it passed by his face.

The other man was back on his feet now, moving in behind the first, and things were likely to go from bad to worse. Tillman weighed the odds. Karate skills didn't impress him overmuch: both men were slighter in build than him, and even the knives didn't count for so very much in the restricted space of the restroom. What made the situation impossible was the two-for-one deal and the men's appalling speed. All things being equal, he was probably going to be dead inside the next ten seconds.

Tillman's only hope was to change the odds. Reaching over his head, he drove his fist into the exact centre of the neon tube.

In the absence of windows, the fluorescent strip was the only light in the room. As the glass crunched against Tillman's bare knuckles, the restroom was plunged into absolute darkness.

Tillman dropped to the ground and rolled. He groped for the gun, whose location he held in his memory. Nothing.

The splash of feet in spilled water. Something moving to his right. He kicked, made contact, rolled again. This time his fingertips brushed the familiar cold metal of the Unica. He found the grip, raised it and came upright firing in a wide arc: once, twice, three times, spaced to quarter the room.

It was a calculated risk. Firing blind revealed his location. In the perfect dark, nothing would be easier than throwing one of those wickedly sharp knives directly at the muzzle flash. But the Unica was loaded with .454 Casull, exceeding even the stopping power of the Magnum cartridge. Even if his attackers were both wearing Kevlar under those elegant suits, at this range it would make no difference. A single hit would take them out for the duration.

With the gun at head height, moving in a figure of eight, Tillman backed toward the door. His near-photographic memory came to his aid again, and after only three steps he felt the blunt bar of the door handle prodding the small of his back.

Another movement, this time to his left. Tillman fired in that direction – leaving a single bullet in the Unica's cylinder – and kicked the door open behind him. A wedge of light invaded the room, as did the incongruous tinkling conversation of the fruit machines in the alcove opposite. Both men had been advancing on Tillman in the dark. One was clutching his arm, indicating a glancing impact from that last bullet. The other threw himself on Tillman, jabbing the knife at him in a straight stab.

Without that fortuitous light, Tillman would have taken the thrust full in the throat. Forewarned at the last moment, his *krav maga* training, acquired in his mercenary days from a wily old bastard named Vincent Less, kicked in automatically. As the two of them fell out into the corridor, he used his right hand, still gripping the gun, to turn the blow aside, then caught the man's wrist with his free hand and twisted so that he dropped the knife. Bringing his gun hand back inside the man's guard, he clubbed him in the face with the butt of the Unica to complete the move. He staggered free as the man fell, then he clambered to his feet, turned and ran. One of his opponents was down, the other at least hurt, but he had only the one round left – and win or lose, he couldn't afford to stay for any kind of official investigation.

Tillman headed away from the lounge. He figured the shots must have been heard and the panicked crowd there would probably be impassable. Slowing to a quick walk, he turned the first bend in the corridor and immediately hit another crowd surging out of the duty-free shop. Clearly the sound of the ruckus had penetrated there, too, but it didn't look like anyone knew where the shots had come from. Nobody had quite made their mind up which way to run. Tillman pushed his way through the skittish mob as quickly as he could. Right now, the biggest danger to them was proximity to him.

He found a stairway, went up it and came out on to the deserted upper deck. Immediately a woman came out through another door at the deck's further end. She stopped when she saw him and stared at him in something that might have been perplexity or concern.

'Go back inside!' he called out to her. He went to the rail and looked out. Still a fair few miles from the Dover shore, but the ship had become non-viable so he really had no other choice. If he stayed here, he'd be questioned, and if he was questioned, he'd be arrested – for the unlicensed firearm, if nothing else.

He'd left most of the documentation he had with him in the jacket, which was back in the restroom. That meant trouble, too, since he was travelling under his own name this time. But it was trouble that could be postponed. He slipped his shoes off and kicked them away.

The pain that flared in his side took him completely by surprise. A blunt concussion that flowered suddenly into a chrysanthemum burst of pure agony. Turning, he saw the woman walking towards him, drawing a second knife from her hip and balancing it in her hand. The hilt of her first weapon now protruded from his thigh, where it had buried itself all the way to the guard.

The woman was beautiful, and very similar in features to the men in the washroom: pale-skinned, dark-eyed and dark-haired, with a solemnity in her face like the solemnity of a child in a classroom told to stand up and recite.

There was nothing he could do to prevent the second throw. She had already drawn her hand back, and as he raised the gun he knew he couldn't aim and fire in the time he had. He tracked her arm anyway and squeezed the trigger as she let go. The knife was invisibly fast except for the small part of its trajectory where the light from a security lamp lit it up in incongruous gold.

His bullet hit the blade and sent it whispering away over his head. It was much more luck than judgement, and Tillman knew he couldn't do it again in a million years, even if his gun hadn't been empty.

He vaulted on to the rail and jumped. A third knife flew over his shoulder, very close, and accompanied him on his wild, parabolic leap. The main deck at this point jutted twelve feet further out than the upper one. The knife made the distance comfortably, Tillman by inches.

The cold water closed over him, and he kept on falling, through a denser, colder and altogether more hostile medium. Thirty feet down he slowed, stopped, began to rise again.

With some effort, his leg already stiffening, he somersaulted in the water and swam further down. There were no directions in the midnight-black of the water, so he couldn't be sure where he was in relation to the ferry. Staying down as long as he could was the best way to get some distance from it.

When his breath began to give out he stopped swimming and let himself rise. At this moment, his lungs empty and screaming for air, he glimpsed something falling away from him into the depths below, where he couldn't now follow it. Something pure white, which picked up the unsteady, murky gleam of the ferry's stern lamp and flashed like the wing of a bird.

It was Mr Snow.

Tillman broke the surface a long way behind the ferry. He saw no figures on the deck looking or pointing back towards him. The night would hide him, and the assassins would hardly report that he'd jumped. There probably wouldn't be a search. The intensely cold water would lessen the bleeding from his wounds, and he was unlikely to miss the south coast of England, given how big a target it was.

He also had an answer to his question, at last. The people who'd been following really did want him dead. Perhaps that meant Michael Brand was afraid of him. He hoped so.

But he couldn't hope to find Mr Snow in the dark and the biting cold of the water. He needed every ounce of his strength if he was going to survive to make the shore. 'I'm sorry,' Tillman muttered, as the waves rocked and pawed him. Not to the toy, but to the daughter he'd lost so many years before. He felt as though he'd broken faith with Grace, in some way. And as though he'd lost a link that he really couldn't afford to lose.

Survival. It was all that mattered now. He used the ferry's wake to orient himself towards the north and the shore that was still ten miles distant.

14

When Kennedy called in from Prince Regent's to check on Harper's progress, he told her – with pardonable smugness – that he'd found a link between the three dead academics. It was spectacular news, but it shrank in the telling, as Kennedy kept coming up with other questions that he should have asked Sarah Opie while he had her on the line: were the three dead Ravellers only in direct contact through the website or did they know each other from elsewhere? How long had their shared project been going on, and who knew about it? Was anyone else collaborating with them, who wasn't at the London History Forum? She wasn't giving him a bollocking: it was just the way she operated, as he knew even from their brief acquaintance. She was putting things together in her mind, figuring out what they had, and what they needed.

'I thought some of this could wait until we go to see her,' Harper said, chagrined. 'I mean, this is the breakthrough, right? We've got the link. If we've got the link, we must be really close to getting a motive. But I knew we'd need a full statement, and I didn't want to put ideas into her head in advance.'

'You did good, Harper. But tell me what this thing is that they were translating.'

'The Rotgut Codex,' Harper said. 'It's sort of a standing joke on the Ravellers board, apparently. Most people think it's fake. But Barlow had a new take on it, Dr Opie said, something that came out of his research on those early Christians. The Acrostics.'

'Gnostics.'

'Or whoever. So it all comes back to Barlow. He started trying to translate this Rotgut thing and he brought the other two on board.'

'Just the other two? I mean, there's nobody else involved? Nobody who needs to be warned that someone might want to kill them?'

Harper was on firmer ground here. 'No other collaborators. Barlow did approach one other guy, because he's a big expert on all these early documents. Emil Gassan, his name is – works up in Scotland somewhere. But he refused point blank to have anything to do with Barlow. Told him to sod off, essentially.'

'What about Opie herself? How does she know all this?'

'Postings on the forum?' Harper said, but he made it into a question. 'Okay, I admit that was just a guess. I asked her a couple of times, straight out, but she managed to give me a body swerve both times. She's a friend of Barlow's. Well, he knew her anyway, because he posted on this message board when she got a big prize of some kind. But she said she wasn't part of this. Very definitely. Nothing to do with the project. She said that twice.'

'And yet she knew what the project was all about?' Kennedy asked.

Harper began to feel that the subtext here was that he was an idiot and couldn't debrief a suspect. 'It's not like it was a secret,' he reminded Kennedy, trying not to sound truculent. 'This woman is active on the Raveller site, so I didn't think there was anything unusual about her being in the know. Anyway, you can ask her yourself. I should set up a meeting, right?'

He looked at his watch as he said it. It was after six, which meant that they probably wouldn't catch Opie on campus now. Harper would have to get her home number or her mobile and try to reach her on the fly. Opie wouldn't be happy. Her mood had darkened in the course of Harper's very tentative questioning. She'd been afraid, and shaken, as anyone might be to learn that three people they knew well could all have been victims of the same killer. Her answers had become more and more terse and monosyllabic, not because she was refusing to cooperate, Harper suspected, but because she was having trouble even getting her mind to touch this stuff. Physical trauma induces clinical shock. Psychological trauma gums up the wheels of thought so they won't turn – which was the real reason why he hadn't pushed Opie too hard for further details. He'd been afraid he might be pushing her towards some sort of mental crisis that he wouldn't be able – at long distance – to talk her down from.

'Not tonight,' Kennedy said, to his relief. 'I think the next step is to go back to the DCI. When he gave this to us, he thought he was kicking it into the long grass. He needs to know what it's turned into, so he can make a decision about resources.'

Harper was scandalised. 'You mean give it to a different team? No bleeding way, Sarge. This is *my* serial killer. Ours, I mean. And I've got a name for him.'

'Harper, I don't even want to—'

'The History Man. You have to think about these things, Kennedy. If you want big headlines, you've got to give the media something they can get their teeth into. I can't wait for that first press conference.'

'That's nice, Harper. But if there's a press conference, there's a good chance we won't be on it.'

'I'll be on it if it bloody kills me.'

Her sigh rustled down the line. The sigh of a mother with a wayward kid. 'They probably won't want to sound any fanfares about any of this because of the screw-up over the Barlow investigation first time around. If they do throw a media-fest, you can bet that Summerhill will be at the mike himself. Maybe we'll get to sit there and look solemn. Have you written up everything you've got?'

'Pretty much,' Harper lied. He only had the indecipherable scribble he'd jotted down as he went along. He'd typed nothing and filed nothing as of yet.

'Leave it on my desk. I'll add my own stuff to it and drop it into Summerhill's tray tonight. In the morning we go see him, get him to call it. If a major witness interview is still pending, it forces his hand: he won't want to hold things up in ways that might show on the file. Let me have that other guy's number, though, the one in Scotland who said no to Barlow. I'll call him now – dot the i's and cross the t's.'

'Okay.' Harper recited the number he'd been given for Emil Gassan, so that Kennedy could take it down. He felt uneasy. 'You don't really think Summerhill will move us off this, do you?'

'Not you, maybe. He's definitely going to put a different case officer on it, though.'

'Why?'

'Because if it stops being time-wasting bullshit, it stops being my special property. On second thoughts, don't leave your notes on my desk. Send me the file and I'll print the whole lot off in one go.' Kennedy didn't say it, but he knew she was thinking about Combes and his posse. They wouldn't scruple to pick up the stuff on Kennedy's desk and read it over, whether out of mischief or just idle curiosity. If they saw something they wanted, they'd go all-out to get it, and suddenly he and Kennedy would be squeezed on two fronts. That was how Harper thought of it anyway: as though this multiple murder (triple slaying sounded even better) was a rosy apple that had fallen into his lap, proving the universal law, which he hoped would some day be named after him, that great detectives magically call forth cases worthy of their uncanny abilities.

After Kennedy had hung up, he realised that he'd forgotten to tell her about Michael Brand giving a false name and address. Dr Opie's revelations had washed that little nugget clean out of his mind. Maybe Kennedy would have been more impressed if he'd led with the news that they might actually have a suspect. Well, she'd get it from the case notes, and then she could tell him what questions he should have asked the Spanish guy while he had him on the phone.

He typed up the notes – another tedious job he had a mildly embarrassing flair for – and started getting his stuff together to leave. But he hadn't logged off. Stanwick ambled over and began to read the open file over his shoulder. Harper turned the monitor to an oblique angle, away from him.

'Jesus, I was only looking,' Stanwick grumbled. 'Anyway, I thought your case was a turd that wouldn't flush. That's why they gave it to you and Calamity Jane. So where's the big secret?'

'The killer's someone in the division,' Harper said. 'Could be the Super. Could even be you.'

Stanwick stared at him, nonplussed. 'Is that supposed to mean something?'

'Yeah,' said Harper. He reached down and pulled the plug on the computer with the file still open. 'It's supposed to mean mind your own damned business.'

He walked away, expecting a hand on his shoulder, expecting the big man to haul him round and plant one in his face. But

Stanwick only whistled, the dipping-then-rising note that signifies surprise. If he hadn't made a good impression earlier, refusing to join in the trashing of Kennedy's reputation, that whistle clearly said that Harper had put himself into a file drawer now. One that everybody else in the division was going to be using as a urinal.

Harper truly didn't care. He was ambitious, in a general way, but more for experience than for career rewards. He wanted to see and do extraordinary things. The uniformed branch had been too small for him, and maybe Detective Division would turn out the same. He just wanted it to be a wild ride.

After Harper left, the early evening currents swept a few more people through the bear pit, but mostly this was ebb tide. The DCs and DSs trickled away one by one or in small knots until, by the time Kennedy got there at around eight, the great room was empty. She didn't mind that one bit.

It took her a while to write up the day's work. It wasn't that she'd covered a vast amount of ground: the findings, sensational though they were, could be condensed into a few explosive paragraphs. She was just covering her back. Even though the screw-ups on this case predated her involvement, that wouldn't offer much protection if a head had to roll. And with three overlooked murders instead of one, a decapitation for the sake of morale was looking like less and less of a longshot.

So she made sure the case notes were immaculate. She and Harper had adhered punctiliously to every rule and protocol, had been unfailingly courteous and endlessly explanatory to witnesses, had paused in their diligent, by-the-book slogging only to keep full and simultaneous notes on everything they were doing. In short, they were saints of policework.

Reading through Harper's notes, she discovered the Michael

Brand bombshell and swore aloud. A false address? An invented phone number? Christ. Why hadn't Harper put that to Opie, and asked her what Brand had to say for himself on the Ravellers forum? Was he still posting there? Did the site moderators hold any contact information on him? If Brand was lying about his address, there was no telling what else he might have lied about – and Rosalind Barlow had said that her brother met with Brand on the night before he died. This could be their man, or else a potentially vital witness, and he had a three-week head-start on them already.

What did that leave? It left the Scottish guy. Emil Gassan. She called him on the number that Harper had given her, but found it was just the university switchboard. She was told that Dr Gassan had left for the evening, and got the desk clerk – after the usual foofarah of identification – to release the doctor's personal contact numbers to her. She tried him on his home phone, where she got no answer, and on his mobile, which was switched off. Out of options, she left her own contact information on his voice-mail, along with a message saying that she wanted very much to talk to him in connection with a pending investigation. She made a mental note to try the home and mobile numbers again later.

Troubled and preoccupied, she printed up Harper's notes and added them to her own. She hated this game of catch-up – the sense of being hamstrung by the bad policework of other officers. They were going to be three weeks too late for everything, all the way down the line. She forwarded the notes to Summerhill as an email attachment, then made the short walk up the corridor to his secretary's desk and placed the hard copy, along with the rest of the case file, on top of his in-tray where he'd see it the next morning.

Done. There was nothing to keep her from going home now. No good reason to put it off any longer.

She collected her coat from the bear pit, noticing as she did so that the steel rat-trap had gone from her waste bin. Whoever brought it in to intimidate her must have wanted it back. Or maybe it would turn up in her file cabinet next, or her locker.

Compared with what awaited her now, those petty provocations shrank to their proper proportions.

15

It was ten o'clock before Kennedy got back to her flat at the cheaper end of Pimlico, and she got there in time to hear Izzy talking dirty in front of her father for the fourth time in a row. That meant she had to apologise to Izzy while simultaneously being pissed off with her. It was the kind of bitter-sour cocktail that left Kennedy bilious.

Izzy lived in the flat upstairs and was able to combine looking after Kennedy's father – and the kids of their downstairs neighbour – with her regular job. But her regular job was being the receiving end of a sex phone line, and her shift started at nine most nights. If Kennedy came home late, Izzy just whipped her phone out and clocked on – and Peter got to hear a-hundred-and-some variants on 'Would you like to, babe, would you like to stick it in me?'

Izzy seemed to cope with this a lot better than Kennedy did. It didn't inhibit her at all to have the old man listening to her perform. It even kept her up to the mark, she said, trying to elicit some slight flicker of a reaction from Peter. She knew that her boss sometimes monitored the calls to make sure that his girls were pulling their weight while the customers, as it were, pulled theirs. She didn't want to get a reprimand for the quality of her smut, and raising a ripple in Peter's almost Zen-like calm gave her a target to aim for.

Kennedy found this disturbing on a lot of levels, and her feelings were complicated still further by the fact that she found Izzy insanely attractive. The woman was a petite brunette with a tiny waist and a huge butt, which was close to Kennedy's perfect type. But because of the convenience of the dad-sitting arrangement, and because Izzy was almost ten years younger than her, she'd never felt able to make a pass.

Every time she had to hear Izzy conducting phone sex with lonely self-abusers, she experienced a bittersweet surge of arousal and frustration.

But it wasn't as though she had much of a choice. The truth of it was that the intermittent supervision her father had always needed was becoming more and more continuous now. Kennedy apologised profusely to her neighbour. Izzy waved the words away, the phone still jammed to her ear even though she was between performances.

'He's already eaten,' she said, as she pocketed the little sheaf of notes that Kennedy had given her. 'Spaghetti Bolognese, because I was cooking it anyway, for the little monsters downstairs. Only I didn't give him any spaghetti because he can't handle it. So he's just had meat sauce. Maybe you'd better see if he wants toast or something for supper.'

Kennedy walked Izzy to the door, listening with half an ear to the status report: Peter's eating and drinking through the day, Peter's mood, Peter's incontinence pants. Izzy always considered the information dump as part of the contract, so Kennedy had to listen to it, or at least stand there while Izzy recited.

Finally Izzy left, and Kennedy went to check on Peter for herself. He had the lights out and the TV on – a Channel 4 documentary on the latest immunisation scare – and was sitting in front of it, watching it for the most part, although his gaze also wandered around the walls and floor quite a lot. He was dressed in trousers and a shirt, but only because Izzy had a phobia of old men wandering around in their pyjamas: she would have chosen the clothes for him and helped him to dress. Peter's white hair looked wild, his chiselled face all inconstant shadows in the TV's rippling spotlight, like speeded up footage of clouds scudding over a mountain.

'Hi, Dad,' Kennedy said.

Peter looked in her direction and nodded. 'Welcome home,' he said, vaguely. He rarely called her by name, and when he did he only had a one in four chance of getting it right. He called her Heather about as often as he called her Janet (her mother), Chrissie (her sister) or Jeannine (her niece). Occasionally he called her Steve (her older brother), even though nobody in the family had seen Steve since he turned eighteen and walked out the door.

Kennedy put the light on and Peter blinked a couple of times, troubled by the sudden glare. 'You want some toast, Dad?' she asked him. 'A cup of tea? Maybe a biscuit?'

'I'll wait for dinner,' Peter said, and returned his attention to the TV. She fixed him a couple of rounds of toasted rye anyway, and brought them in to him. He wouldn't remember having said no, and he could definitely use the carbs if all he'd had to eat was a bowl of spaghetti sauce. She put the toast on a tray in front of him, along with a cup of instant coffee, and retreated to her bedroom, which had a TV set and a sound system and a desk. It was like the whole of the rest of the place was a granny flat and this one room was her territory. It was smaller than some of the rooms she'd lived in as a student, but it pretty much had all she needed – which at this point in her life sounded a lot more like an indictment than any kind of a boast.

But she felt bad about leaving Peter alone, after being out all evening. It was ridiculous, she knew. The phantom figure of her sister stood at her ear, delivering a phantom lecture. 'After what that bastard put us all through . . . ' She had no defence: it was true. Peter had been a truly awful husband and father, was infinitely more bearable in his current condition, a placeholder for a personality that had gone AWOL. His cruelties, his failings, had shaped her, but so had his example and his expectations. In the long run, none of it mattered. It came down to whether you could walk away, and clearly she couldn't.

So she took her own coffee back into the living room and sat through the rest of the programme with her father. When it finished and the ads came up, she turned the TV off. 'So how was your day?' she asked him.

'Pretty good,' he said. 'Pretty good.' He never gave any other answer.

Kennedy told him about her murder investigation in a reasonable amount of detail. Peter listened quietly, nodding or murmuring an 'oh' from time to time, but when she stopped he didn't offer any comments or questions. He just stared at her, waiting to see if there was any more to come. Well, she hadn't expected a reaction. She just felt a compulsion – intermittently, and up to a point – to treat him as a human being, since there was nobody else around who was prepared to do that for him any more.

She went over to the stereo and put some music on: the Legendary Gypsy Queens and Kings, singing *Sounds from a Bygone Age*. Kennedy's mother, Janet, whose claims to gypsy blood Peter had always declared to be utter nonsense, had listened to nothing but Fanfare Ciocărlia through the year of her final illness. Peter scorned this while she lived, as he scorned most things his wife did and the basis on which she did them, but when she died he cried, for only the second time in his life as far as Kennedy knew. And then he took to playing the album himself, late in the evening or in the early hours of the morning, in hypnotised silence. And then he started buying Balkan gypsy music in wholesale amounts. Kennedy had no idea whether he enjoyed it or not. She suspected, though, that sometimes, if they hit him at the right time and from the right angle, those albums could function for Peter as a sort of sound construct of his dead wife. The music had the power – intermittently anyway – to change him, both while it was playing and for a little while after it stopped.

Tonight it seemed to work. Peter's eyes swam into a clearer focus as the skirling fiddle and bombastic accordion clashed with each other for domination of the tune. She only played three tracks, because clarity was a double-edged sword. If he remembered that Janet was dead, his mood would shift into something darker and more unpredictable, and he probably wouldn't sleep that night.

'You look tired, Heather,' Peter said to Kennedy, while the last notes of 'Sirba' were still hanging in the air. 'You're working too hard. You should be a little more selfish. Look after yourself more.'

'Like you always did,' she countered. The bantering tone was wholly assumed. It was more painful than pleasant to hear him talk like himself again. It made her miss him, but it made her hate him, too, as it partially reconstructed him – took him some of the way back to being someone who was responsible for what he did, and could be hated.

'I worked for you,' Peter mumbled. 'You and the kids. What are you working for?'

It was a good question, even if the way he phrased it seemed to confuse her with her mother. She gave a glib answer. 'The public good.'

Peter snorted. 'Right, right. The public will thank you the

way it always does, sweetheart. The way it did me.' He tapped his chest on the *me*. It had been his characteristic gesture once, as though the words *I* and *me* needed an extra assist when they referred to Peter Kennedy.

'You do what you know how to do,' she said. A better answer, and Peter accepted it with a laugh and a nod. His eyes were changing again, the light in them softening as his mind slipped off the little island of awareness into the sea of fuzz and static in which it usually floated.

Involuntarily, Kennedy raised her hand and waved goodbye to him.

'Piss off, Dad,' she said, gently, and she blinked in quick staccato, half a dozen times, determined that the tear wouldn't fall.

From her own room, later, Kennedy tried Emil Gassan again. This time she got lucky: someone picked up on the home number. He had a high-pitched, querulous voice, and his accent was pure RP rather than Scots. 'Emil Gassan,' he said.

'Dr Gassan, my name is Heather Kennedy. I'm a detective sergeant with the London Metropolitan Police.'

'The police?' Gassan immediately sounded both alarmed and slightly indignant. 'I don't understand.'

'I'm investigating the death of a former colleague of yours – Professor Stuart Barlow.'

'I still don't understand.'

'It's possible that there might be something suspect about his death. Particularly in light of the coincidental deaths of two other academics with whom Professor Barlow had dealings.'

'Are you suggesting that Barlow was murdered? I thought he fell downstairs!'

'I'm not suggesting anything at this stage, Dr Gassan. Just

138

gathering information. I wonder if you have a little time to talk to me about Professor Barlow's translation project.'

'Barlow? Barlow's project? Good god, you don't mean the Rotgut?'

'Yes. The Rotgut.'

'Well, I'd hardly dignify that asinine proposal with the term "project", Sergeant ... ' He waited for the prompt.

'Kennedy.'

'And for that matter, I'd hesitate to call Stuart Barlow a colleague. He's barely set his name to paper in the last two decades, did you know that? He floats wild hypotheses on his, what do you call it, Ravellers forum, but a few emails here and there don't amount to serious scholarship. And as for the idea that anything new could be discovered about the Rotgut Codex at this stage ... well, better minds than Barlow's have foundered on that rock.' The last statement was accompanied by a sour, supercilious laugh.

'So when he approached you,' Kennedy said, 'and asked if you wanted to be part of his team ... '

'I said no. Emphatically. I didn't have the time to waste.'

Kennedy chanced her arm. The entire case seemed to hinge on things way outside her comfort zone, and this guy's arrogance had to be based on at least some degree of knowledge. 'Do you have the time to explain to me exactly what the Rotgut is, Dr Gassan? I've heard various accounts now, but I'm still not clear.'

'Well, read my book. *Palaeographic Texts: Substance and Substrate*. Leeds University Press, 2004. It's available on Amazon. I can send you the ISBN number, if you like.'

'I'm no expert, Dr Gassan. I'd probably get lost in the details. And while I've got your ear, so to speak.'

There was a slightly charged silence at the other end of the line. 'What was it you wanted to know?' Gassan demanded at last. 'I don't have time to give you a thorough grounding in palaeography, Sergeant Kennedy. Not from a standing start. And even for an introduction, I'd normally expect to charge.'

'I wish I could afford you,' Kennedy said. 'But really, I don't want to know much. Just what you think Professor Barlow was trying to do, and why it might have mattered – to him or to anyone else in your field. Obviously, from your standpoint, he was making some elementary mistakes. I just wish I had the context to understand where he was going wrong because right now I'm floundering in the dark.'

Another hesitation. Had she gone overboard with the implied flattery? Presumably Gassan wasn't a fool, whatever he sounded like.

Fool or not, he took the bait. 'To explain the Rotgut, I'll need to explain a few basics about Biblical scholarship.'

'Whatever it takes.'

'A quick run-through then. Because really, I have other things I need to attend to.'

'A quick run-through would be great. Is it okay if I record this? I'd like my colleagues to have the benefit, too.'

'So long as I'm credited,' Gassan said, warily.

'Absolutely.'

'Very well, Sergeant. How much do you know about the Bible?'

16

TRANSCRIPT OF STATEMENT TAKEN FROM DR EMIL GASSAN, 23 JULY INSTANT, COMMENCING 10.53PM.

EMIL GASSAN: Very well, Sergeant. How much do you know about the Bible?

DS KENNEDY: Not a whole lot, I suppose. I know there are two testaments.

EG: There are indeed. And you know, of course, that the New Testament was written a lot later.

DSK: Of course.

EG: How much later?

DSK: Oh. Must be at least a thousand years, right? The New Testament is written right after the events it describes – right after Jesus died. The other stuff is ... well, back when the Pharaohs were around.

EG: Some of it is, yes. But it took a long time to put the Bible together – to get it the way we've got it now. Some of that material dates from the thirteenth century BC, so you're right, it's very, very old. Before Rome. Before Athens. Almost before Mycenae, even. But other parts of it were written a thousand years later. The Dead Sea Scrolls,

141

which are our oldest surviving copies of some key sections of the Old Testament, date back to only a century before Christ. And it kept changing. What was included – what counted as the word of God – was different from generation to generation.

DSK: Is all this relevant to the Rotgut Codex?

EG: Oh, I'm barely getting started, Sergeant Kennedy. So the Old Testament was a thousand years in the making, more or less. The New Testament was the same in some ways, different in others. It took its time to settle down into the form we know now, but the actual writing happened relatively quickly. Most of the key texts are already written by the end of the second century. That is the prevalent theory. Now, how many gospels are there?

DSK: Four?

EG: Thank you for playing. The correct answer is closer to sixty.

DSK: Umm ... Matthew, Mark, Luke, John ...

EG: Thomas, Nicodemus, Joseph, Mary, Philip, Matthias, Bartholomew ... And I'm just talking about the books that call themselves gospels. The word doesn't really mean that much, at the end of the day. To a police officer, perhaps it means, um, a witness statement. A witness statement from someone who saw amazing events.

DSK: That's an interesting analogy.

EG: Thank you. Perhaps I'll use it again. All told, there are close to a hundred other books that have been included in the Bible at different times, or by different churches, but don't make the cut any more.

	Although some of them still do make the cut, in some of the other schools of Christianity. The Greek and Slavonic Orthodox faiths, for example, have a very different bible from the Catholic Church. There are a lot of extra books in there.
DSK:	You're talking about the Apocrypha. Apocryphal books.
EG:	Well, yes. Yes, I am. Partly. But I'm also saying that one man's Apocrypha is another man's orthodoxy. The argument about what was really the holy word, and what wasn't, went on well into the Middle Ages. And it's hard to tell who won. The different churches took away their own texts, and each of them said they had the right one. The books that are usually called Apocrypha are the ones that nobody wanted. But even they sometimes got promoted – or vice versa, books that used to be part of the Bible got kicked out. Like the Book of the Shepherd of Hermas. The early church fathers put it right after the Acts of the Apostles. Now, scarcely anyone even remembers what it was.
DSK:	So is the Rotgut Codex an Apocryphal book? Something that dropped out of the Bible?
EG:	You're determined to get to the punchline, aren't you, Sergeant Kennedy? Straining at the leash. But I'm afraid we're not quite there yet. In the early Christian church, this whole question – what came from God, what came from man – was literally a matter of life and death. They fought over it. They killed each other to decide who had the better version of the truth. And I mean murders, as well as

143

executions and martyrdoms. Arius of Alexandria was poisoned, and died in agony, because he attacked the doctrine of the holy trinity. And many of the religious texts that we've got from that time are really polemics. They say 'Don't believe that, believe this', and 'Stay away from the people who say such and such.' You've heard of Irenaeus?

DSK: No, I'm afraid not. Oh, wait. Stuart Barlow's sister . . . she said Barlow was studying him at one point.

EG: Stuart studied everything at one point or another. Bishop Irenaeus of Lugdunum – and later, in due course, Saint Irenaeus. He lived around the close of the second century after Christ, in what was then still called Gaul. And he wrote a very influential work called the *Adversus Haereses*. It was, essentially, an attack on deviant faiths – a list of what good Christians were and were not allowed to read. Most of the writings he attacked belonged to what we now call the Gnostic tradition.

DSK: Another of Stuart Barlow's pet subjects.

EG: I refer you to my previous comment.

DSK: And you're saying that the Rotgut Codex ties into the Gnostic tradition in some way?

EG: Oh yes.

DSK: Please go on, Dr Gassan.

EG: Irenaeus's *Adversus Haereses* is very much an early Christian public safety announcement. It tells the faithful what to avoid. It talks about all these ideas that were floating around – survivals, some of them, from earlier ages, but shoehorned now into the Christ-religion – which in the good bishop's

144

view were really unexploded bombs. He warns his flock about supposed holy men who were actually strangers with sweets in their pockets and wicked intentions. And he was particularly keen to attack the Gnostic movements, which were almost like secret societies within Christianity – mystery religions, passing on arcane knowledge about Christ's life and teachings. Knowledge that sometimes went directly against the teachings of the orthodox churches.

DSK: So is the Rotgut one of the things that Irenaeus attacks?

EG: [laughs] Not exactly.

DSK: Okay, I'm missing something there, obviously.

EG: The Rotgut Codex dates from the fifteenth century, Sergeant. It's called that because a Portuguese sea captain traded a barrel of rum for it. It's a translation – in English – of a gospel.

DSK: An Apocryphal gospel?

EG: Not in the slightest. It's the Gospel of John. The whole of the Gospel of John, not very well translated but very close to what we have. But then at the end, and this is what makes it fascinating – and controversial – there's something else. A few verses of a different gospel. And this one is very Apocryphal because we've never found it. It never turns up elsewhere. Seven verses of a different gospel, which starts with some very peculiar statements. Do you know what a codex is, Sergeant?

DSK: I found out very recently. The first books, right?

EG: Exactly. But they were only like books in that they were aggregations of pages that had been folded and stitched together. Unlike modern books, they often threw together several texts that had not the slightest connection to each other. People at that time didn't really have the concept of a book as a single text between a single set of covers. Codices didn't even have covers. Just pages, bound together. And if you got to the end of what you were writing before you got to the end of your page, very often you'd just start right in on something else.

DSK: Which is what the Rotgut does.

EG: Which is exactly what the Rotgut does. The extra verses at the end are not from John. They're not from any gospel we know. But Judas Iscariot figures prominently in them, and Irenaeus talks about a Gospel of Judas that was current in his time – a gospel that he thought contained very evil teachings indeed.

DSK: So you're saying, after the Gospel of John, the Rotgut has a small sample of this other gospel? The Gospel of Judas.

EG: Well, possibly. Possibly the Gospel of Judas. Certainly a gospel in which Christ speaks to Judas alone, and in secret.

DSK: So the Rotgut . . .

EG: Well, we don't know. We don't know. The Rotgut at least appears to be a translation of a codex – a book that has the Gospel of John followed by the Gospel of Judas. But if that's the case, then the original – the actual codex, written in Aramaic, from which this partial English translation has been taken – has never been found or at least never positively identified.

DSK:	That's something of a let-down.
EG:	Isn't it? Captain De Veroese should have kept his rum. What he bought was very much a pig in a poke.
DSK:	Wait. Maybe I'm not understanding you after all, Dr Gassan. I thought that what Barlow was doing was putting together a new translation of the Rotgut Codex.
EG:	No. It couldn't have been that. The Rotgut is already a translation. It's written in English. Quite bad English, but English, all the same.
DSK:	Then what was it that Barlow was proposing to do with it?
EG:	I'm afraid you'd have to ask him that.
DSK:	He didn't tell you what he had in mind? When he spoke to you about all this?
EG:	He said he had a new approach. That there might be more to the Rotgut than anyone had ever imagined. But he wasn't prepared to tell me any more unless I agreed to come on board, and I had no intention whatsoever of doing that.
DSK:	Would you be willing to speculate?
EG:	Certainly. I speculate that whatever it was, it was a complete and utter waste of time. Had he told me that he intended to shed new light on Christ's life and works by means of a close examination of the lyrics of the musical *Jesus Christ, Superstar*, I would have had – if anything – slightly more interest in the enterprise. Is there anything else I can do for you, Sergeant Kennedy?
DSK:	Doctor, you've done more than enough. Thank you.
EG:	You're very welcome. Goodnight.

17

Kennedy slept, and dreamed of Judas. He wasn't very happy. He sat in a field, underneath a bare tree from which a knotted rope hung, so she knew what moment this was. The moment before his suicide. He seemed preoccupied, though, with counting the money in his hand.

At a certain point, he noticed she was there. He glanced up, met her gaze with sad, dark eyes, and showed the coins to her. Thirty pieces of silver.

'I know,' Kennedy said. 'I know it's serious.'

It was a line from a Smiths song, and she felt inclined to apologise for it. But Judas was hanging from the tree now, dangling slowly to and fro like the world's ugliest wind chime.

The moment had passed.

18

It took Tillman a long time to get himself together and on-track again after he finally crawled up on to the beach at Folkestone. Drenched, freezing, weak from exhaustion and loss of blood, he knew he couldn't afford the luxury of checking in to a hospital. He had to keep moving, if he wanted to stay alive. Otherwise he'd succumb to hypothermia, and shock.

He was lucky in one respect. Folkestone at three in the morning was a relatively easy place to go shopping. He broke into a chemist's for bandages and sulfadine, and raided the plastic bags dumped outside a charity shop for a change of clothes. A gents' toilet next to a caravan park became his dressing room and his operating theatre.

The wounds in his shoulder and thigh were bleeding way too freely, and the sulfadine didn't even slow the process down. Tillman suspected that the chill water, close enough to freezing to constrict his arteries, had saved his life. Something nasty – something coated on the knife blades presumably – was stopping his blood from coagulating. He made another break-in, to a small convenience store, where he looked in vain for BIC lighters, settled in the end for Swan Vestas. He used a few of the matches to light a broken branch from someone's hedge of over-tall Douglas firs. Then he bit down on his wadded T-shirt as he cauterised the clean, straight-edged gashes with naked flame. The heady smell of the fir-tree resin mixed nauseatingly with that of his burning flesh. When it was done, he applied a whole lot more of the disinfectant salve with hands that trembled slightly, and dressed the wounds as best he could.

Getting to London was the next hurdle. At least he still had his wallet, which had been in his trouser pocket rather than in the jacket he had left behind on the ferry. Tillman stayed away from railway stations, knowing that he looked bad enough that someone might be tempted to call the police if he tried to buy a ticket. A night coach seemed like a better bet. He felt pretty sure Folkestone had a coach station, and the town was small enough that he found it without too much trouble. The first coach of the day was before sun-up. He bought a ticket from a tiny booth next to a colossal NCP car park, waited out of the reach of the street lights until he saw the driver get on board, and joined the small queue at the last possible moment. He excited no comment, but a few wary glances. He looked like an unusually well-built wino, and probably smelled like a fire in a pharmacy. Good. Nobody would want to meet his gaze, let alone talk to him. He could sleep, as far as his wounds would let him sleep.

At Victoria, things got a little easier. He ordered a huge fried breakfast from a café on Buckingham Palace Road whose proprietor was used to dealing with homeless guys from the adjacent hostels and didn't give a damn how Tillman looked or smelled. The food made him feel a lot better, and the fiery ache from the knife wounds began easing off just a little. Enough for him to function anyway, and to think clearly.

He had to set up a base, until he heard from Vermeulens. He had to find out what Michael Brand had been doing in London, and if he was still here. He had to be ready to move, and move fast, if there was anyone or anything for him to move against.

Tillman still owned the house in Kilburn where he'd lived with Rebecca and raised a family with her, but didn't even consider the possibility of going back there. Whoever had tried to kill him on the ferry had to know a lot about his current movements, which were complex and cryptic. So they'd also know everything there was to know about his past, which was transparent and obvious.

After visiting a storage facility at St Pancras, one of his many emergency stashes, he went by Underground out to Queen's Park. There he checked into a bed and breakfast. He paid with cash, showing as ID a fake passport in the name of Crowther – one of the last batch he'd bought from Insurance before she cut him off. It occurred to him to wonder whether the passport was safe now. Maybe not, for any purpose that would involve checking it against a database. The next time he took a plane – if he ever decided it was safe to do so – he should probably go shopping for some new identities first.

Laying out his few surviving possessions, and making a tally of the things that would have to be sourced and replaced in the next few days, he remembered the drowning of Mr Snow. The memory was like a fisherman's line with a great white shark clamped to the other end of it. Tillman hauled on it, felt the tension and quickly, desperately, turned his mind to other things.

He took off his clothes and the bandages, and had a cold shower. He didn't want to risk hot or even warm water on the burned skin of his barely closed wounds. He placed a call to Vermeulens, and left a message on the voicemail giving him the new cellphone number. It was a bright, sunny morning, but the thick curtains shut out most of the light. He lay down – on his stomach, which seemed less aggravating to his shoulder – and slept for eighteen hours straight.

What woke him was the phone. He groped for it, trying to

pull his thoughts together and dredge up a memory of where he was. 'Hey,' he croaked into the phone – a stop-gap until he found out who the hell was calling him.

'*Hoe gaat het met jou*, Leo?'

'Benny.'

'Yes, it's me. You went off the radar for a while. I called you on your usual number, but the man who answered I didn't know. He said he was a friend. I chose to assume that he was not.'

His phone had been in the pocket of his jacket. The knife men and their Girl Friday must have taken it. They would have checked for a phone book or list of memorised numbers, but Tillman never kept one. So they were keeping the phone turned on, in the hope that friends or contacts of Leo might call him. It was a clumsy, opportunistic strategy, and it wasn't going to get them very far. Only half a dozen people had the number, and none except Vermeulens was likely to call Tillman without prior arrangement.

'No friend of mine,' Tillman confirmed.

'And yet he seemed very anxious to know that you were well. Or at least, if you were unwell, where he could visit you.'

Tillman laughed. 'Yeah. Flowers would have been forthcoming. Probably white lilies.'

'You're upsetting people, Leo. I know this because rumours are circulating about you that seem unlikely to be true.'

'MacTeale.'

'And other things. You're dealing in drugs now, apparently, but also your partners in these deals have twice been arrested in sting operations. You walk, each time. So clearly you've decided that selling out your own people is a lucrative sideline.'

'I'm not dealing drugs, Benny. Or snitching.'

'Of course not. You never had that much of a work ethic. But

152

rumours like these cost money, Leo. Someone wants to cut you off from comfort and supply. From your friends.'

'From oxygen, too. I just got off a ferry where they tried to carve me up like a turkey. Professional job.'

'Professional,' Vermeulens agreed. 'Very. That was, in fact, my point. That they are professionals and they are well connected, with access both to money and to channels. You should watch yourself.'

'Is that why you called?'

'No, Leo. That is not why I called. Mostly, although we're friends, I don't fret about your well-being so much that I call you to tell you to wear a scarf in the cold winter evenings. And anyway, it's probably summer where you are.'

'How do you know where I am, Benny?' He heard the edge of paranoia in his own voice, the unfocused fear underneath the aggression. Something had changed in Tillman's mind, in his world. He experienced it as a change in gradient, as though the flat ground had become a slope that he stood on, so that he needed to shift his balance from one second to the next to keep his footing.

'The phone, Leo. Your new number is a UK number. Most likely that means you're back in Britain, but you notice that I'm not asking. In the meantime, and let me come to the point here, there is Michael Brand.'

Tillman sat up. 'What about Michael Brand?'

'He has been indiscreet. Very.'

'What does that mean?'

'He's wanted for murder, Leo. For many murders. I think your luck may finally have changed.'

19

The next morning they waited outside Summerhill's office for a good forty-five minutes, but Summerhill didn't show. WPC Rawl, on despatch, said he was on his way but running late. Then a few minutes later, she amended that.

'He's been diverted. Had to go to Westminster first, to talk to some select committee. Funding and appropriations, something like that. He'll be at least an hour.'

Kennedy and Harper considered and conferred. The argument about leaving Opie pending so as to add urgency to the DCI's decision still held. Summerhill was more likely to keep them on the case if there was something that needed doing right there and then. On the other hand, debriefing Opie properly was something that *did* need doing, the sooner the better.

'Have you had breakfast?' Harper asked Kennedy.

'No,' she admitted. Breakfast was very rarely part of her routine.

'Well, let's grab something, then. Work up the questions while we eat, come back in half an hour. If he's not back, we head out.'

Kennedy agreed, suppressing a qualm of reluctance. Her working day tended to be a straight sprint. Eating, like everything else in ordinary life, was relegated to the margins.

But someone had recently reopened the Queen Anne Café and Business Centre on the corner of Broadway, a whimsical enterprise that Kennedy had always had a certain amount of time for. So she agreed, and they went.

The place was a lot more crowded than she'd expected, and talking about the details of the case seemed awkward in the presence of so many possible rubber-neckers. They tried various circumlocutions, but murder sounds like murder through any number of gauzy veils. They gave up around about the time when Harper's fried breakfast and Kennedy's toast and butter arrived.

'You know that breakfast is the most important meal of the day, right?' Harper said, eyeing Kennedy's monastic platter.

'For me, that would be dinner,' she replied.

'So what, with dinner you add an extra slice? A muffin? Strawberry jam?'

Kennedy considered telling him it was none of his business what she ate, but she looked at his face and saw that the joke was meant as an ice-breaker, nothing more. He still didn't know exactly how to talk to her, what basis their professional relationship was on. It hadn't even been twenty-four hours since she told him to press the ejector-seat button.

'Marmalade,' she said. 'With bits in.'

Harper whistled. 'With bits in. Now you're talking.'

He ate fast, and was a good way into his sausage, egg and bacon while Kennedy was still spreading butter.

'So did you always want to be a detective?' he asked, between forkfuls.

'Yeah,' Kennedy said. 'Always.' It wasn't the literal truth but close enough that it would do. She'd always wanted to be something that earned her father's approval, that took her out of the poisonous, perilous hinterland of his contempt. 'What about you?' she answered, instinctively turning the conversation away from that territory.

'What about me?'

'When did you decide this was the life for you?'

'Year seven,' Harper said, without hesitation.

The numbering system had changed since Kennedy's day. She had to do a mental translation. 'The first year of secondary school,' she said. 'You would have been twelve.'

Harper was polishing off his last piece of sausage, having used it to mop up some yolk from the fried egg. It occupied his full attention, although he seemed to be thinking, too, about the explanation he was about to give. 'I was a skinny little kid,' he said at last. 'And a bit of a dreamer. One of the quiet ones. I was pretty wet, to be honest. So wet you could have shot snipe off my back, as my mum used to say in her nastier moods. I got picked on in primary school, but nothing too bad. The teachers were there to see that it didn't get out of hand, and I used to hide behind their skirts. I had no shame.'

He pushed his empty plate away. 'Then I moved up to Burnt Hill – to comprehensive school. And it all went bad. Little mummy's boy, suddenly thrown right into the fiery furnace.' He grinned at Kennedy, as though inviting her to laugh at the image. 'The first time I saw a kid pull a knife in a fight, it was a real eye-opener. It was like ... there'd been a balance before and now there wasn't. The willingness of the kids around me to do harm – and their ability to do it – had escalated by about n per cent, where n is a really big number.

'But the system of control hadn't changed much at all. We were still being threatened with detentions, demerits, loss of privileges. Pint-sized Al Capones, malevolent little bastards with weasel minds and heavy weaponry, being told that if they didn't buck their ideas up they'd have to stay behind after class. I

156

realised right there and then what cops were for, and I started wanting to be one.'

He grinned at her again. 'And eight years later, my dream came true. Don't you love a story with a happy ending?'

Kennedy acknowledged the potted autobiography with a solemn nod. 'Okay,' she said. 'Thank you. I understand you a little better now, Harper. The strict disciplinarian keeping the naughty schoolchildren of the world at bay. Do uniforms figure in this fantasy at all?'

'I only just got out of uniform,' Harper reminded her. 'Uniforms aren't sexy for me. Plainclothes – that's where it's at, Kennedy.'

'Of course.' He was looking at her in a speculative way. She met that look squarely, a little irritated by it. 'What? What's on your mind?'

'You are. I'm wondering about something, and maybe you can explain it to me. You seem pretty focused on the job – and you seem to be pretty good at it. I've only known you for a day or so, and I've already got you clocked, more or less, as career police. I mean, this isn't even a little bit casual to you. You'd never describe it as "just a job". Am I wrong?'

'Is this relevant to anything?'

'Well, maybe not. I'm just asking because it would be a good thing to know. I mean, since we find ourselves working together.'

'It's not just a job. So what?'

Harper threw out his hands. 'So how do you find yourself in such a ridiculous mess? It's like you chose it. Like you wanted to be shoved out on your own, and hated. I mean, going your own way instead of backing up the rest of your unit. Briefing against other officers, in an official inquiry. That's a marked choice, isn't it?'

Kennedy went through several answers in her mind. Most involved telling Harper to shove it up his arse and work it in really deep. She finally settled for: 'The rest of my unit had just put four bullets into an unarmed man.'

'That's not the point, though, is it? Not really. I'm assuming that wasn't the point.'

'Why shouldn't it be? You think Marcus Dell doesn't matter because he was black and stoned?'

'Jesus.' Harper shrugged brusquely, as though the words had settled on his shoulder and he wanted to dislodge them. His tone became more serious. 'Listen, I put my name down for ARU as soon as I got my transfer into Detective Division. The shortlist is three years, I knew that. But I didn't even get short-listed because the psych tests are so sensitive – I mean, really hair-trigger. I didn't score quite high enough on impulse control. So I think it pretty much follows that anyone who did get their hand on a gun has proved their fitness to carry one. You hear what I'm saying, Kennedy? You put yourself into an elite group. Self-selecting. Top of the class.

'So once you're in a situation like that, I'm thinking your team is first and last and everything. Doesn't matter if this guy, Dell, was carrying or not. He *looked* like he was carrying, and he assaulted an officer. You don't second guess the luckless bastards who have to make that call, right? I would have said that was basic. So what am I not getting?'

Harper fell silent, staring at her expectantly. They could have sat there like that until the crack of doom. Kennedy didn't feel that she owed him an explanation, or care overmuch what he thought about her. But she did care about the false logic. She knew where it led.

'You have any idea how many kills the Met has to its name, Harper?' she asked him. 'Total. Going all the way back to 1829,

158

when they kicked out the Bow Street Runners and formed the modern service?'

Harper made a tutting sound. 'No. And neither do you.'

'Right. You're right. But I can tell you how many we bag in an average year. Shootings, I mean. Not accidents. Officers shooting to kill.'

Harper chewed it over, along with a stray piece of fried bread. 'Well, I'd be guessing, but I know it's a lot less than—'

'It's one.'

Harper's eyebrows did a dip and rise. He said nothing.

'Yeah,' said Kennedy. 'Some years it bumps to two, or God forbid three, but some years there aren't any. So on average, over the long haul, it's just the one.' She didn't say: *and last year, the one was me*. It didn't seem to need saying.

Harper nodded, accepting the figure, inviting Kennedy to get to the point.

'Across the whole of the country – and I'm counting in Wales and Scotland – the worst year so far this century was 2005. That was a bad one, all right. A shame and a scandal. Three times the body count of the previous year. That brought it up to six. Six shootings in a year. In the country. You got that, Harper? But you know, we can drop the bar a little lower. All deaths arising from civilian contact with police officers – beatings in remand cells, dodgy restraint techniques, high speed chases that go that little bit too far. What's the score now? Any guesses?'

'No,' Harper said. 'No guesses, Kennedy. But I'm sure you can tell me.'

'It's less than a hundred a year. A whole lot less. Most years, say sixty and you'll be close. There are cities in America – and not even particularly big cities –that have more deaths in police custody than our whole island. And I'll tell you why. It's because most cops aren't out there to score points or fight wars. They're

159

out there to do a job. A job that's hard. Blood, sweat and tears *hard*.'

'Okay.' Kennedy's tone had a hard enough edge to it that it would have taken a brave man to disagree. But Harper wasn't about to disagree in any case. 'That was sort of my point before it was your point,' he said. 'That the job is really tough and if you've been doing it for any length of time, you maybe deserve a bit of love and understanding. But you draw a different conclusion, obviously.'

'Not just a different conclusion, Harper. The opposite conclusion. If you're proud of those figures, or if you just think they mean anything, then you hold serving officers to a higher standard, not a lower one. Because the worst thing anyone can do is let things go by on the nod. Between the three of us, my team and me, we killed a man, when there was no good reason to. If you think we should get away with that, then sit back and watch those numbers climb and climb. Sit and watch accountability go out the window while brain-dead cowboys like Gates and Leakey go back into the division and get clapped on the back as though they took one for the team.'

She was talking a little too loudly by the time she'd finished, and a few people at other tables were shooting her nervous glances. 'All right,' Harper said. 'All right, Kennedy. Point taken. I guess that was what I wanted to hear. I guess I know where you're coming from now.'

'No, you don't,' she assured him, grimly. Because she'd left out the main point of the story. She hadn't particularly meant to. She just found, when she came to it, that it was the hardest part to put it into words.

But Harper was still looking at her, waiting for the punchline. So she gave it to him, without quite knowing why.

Before there was Kennedy, H., Det Sgt 4031, there was

160

Kennedy, P., Det Sgt 1117. He served twelve years in uniform and twenty-eight in Division. He got his ARU in 1993, although they didn't call it that back then, they called it Open Carry, because that was an American phrase that was getting some currency and it sounded pretty damn cool.

On the 27th of February, 1997, openly carrying, Detective Sergeant Peter Kennedy pursued an armed man, Johnny McElvoy, who was fleeing the scene of a gangland shootout. The chase led Kennedy into an alley, where, in the dark and thinking – as it turned out, wrongly – that he was walking into an ambush, he fired three rounds at a pregnant woman at a range of twenty feet.

Amazingly, the woman survived. But the bullet that passed through her uterus and mulched its contents also passed through her lower spine and left her paraplegic.

Kennedy was devastated. His friends, though, were supportive, and agreed between them a version of events that spared both him and the force a great deal of pain and embarrassment. McElvoy, they said, had taken up a defensive position in the alley and was firing on them. Kennedy had returned fire, and the woman, panicked, had run into the path of his bullet.

Kennedy got to this point in her account and just stopped. Harper was looking at her, clearly expecting more, but this was where it got complicated and ugly and harder to explain. 'They covered his back,' she summarised.

'I got that,' Harper said. 'But it was an accident, yeah? Just a horrible accident.'

'Harper, it was an accident that wrecked one life and aborted another.'

'So ... ?' He looked blank.

Kennedy was exasperated that he didn't get it. 'So rallying around your mates isn't the right response in a situation like that. If it was a reasonable mistake, the truth should be good enough. If it was a screw-up, then the truth has to come out and a copper has to lose his gun licence because he wasn't good enough to have it in the first place.'

Harper settled back in his chair, staring at her shrewdly. 'Okay,' he said. 'What's the bit you're leaving out?'

'I'm leaving nothing out,' Kennedy said.

'Yes, you are. I'll agree with you this far: what your dad did was terrible. It was *really* terrible. And I could see where that would leave a scar on you. But it didn't stop you from joining the force, or going out for detective, or applying for your ARU. So where's the scar, Kennedy? Which bit hurts?'

Kennedy didn't answer. She left a tenner to cover the breakfasts and the tip, and they walked back to the yard. She was silent as they walked, and so was Harper. He seemed to have that interrogator's knack of making a silence push against you, until you felt like you needed to do something to fill it.

'Okay,' Kennedy said at last. And she told him what was, for her, the worst thing. The thing that, even after all this time, she couldn't describe in a level voice. How Peter Kennedy had lined up his wife and two kids and schooled them in the fine detail of the lie, in case anyone – a friend at school, a journalist, someone they met in Sainsbury's – should ever ask. Because God forbid there should be a crack big enough for a stranger to pry a crowbar into and overturn the rock under which he was now hiding. Heather and Steve and little Chrissie, along with their mother, had to parrot back to Sergeant Peter Kennedy the exact sequence of events, in the right order, again and again, and when they got it wrong he shouted at them in a fury that came undiluted from the panic in his soul, and when they got it right he hugged them with fervent love.

'It pretty much wrecked us, as a family,' Kennedy said. Over the hump now, she could at least do the summing up dispassionately. 'We had that big lie sitting in between us, then, all the damn time. You couldn't talk around it, so you didn't talk at all. What was saved, Harper? He never got past sergeant, because whatever the docket said, everyone knew what had happened. Everyone could see the monkey on his back. He started drinking like a maniac, and I think that brought his Alzheimer's on. The stress – well, maybe it didn't cause my mother's cancer, but it seemed to make her give in to it a whole lot quicker. And none of us feel anything for each other any more. I haven't seen my brother for ten years. I see Chrissie once in a blue moon. We … we stopped working, and we fell apart. Game over.'

'And your dad's dead?'

Kennedy thought about the shambling set of mannerisms she shared her flat with. 'Yeah,' she said. 'My dad is dead.'

'So. Did you become a lesbian to get even with him?'

Kennedy stiffened, stopped, turned to face Harper, ready to tear a number of thin strips off his facetious little ego. But Harper was grinning and he threw up his hands in surrender.

'Trying to lighten the tone,' he said.

'Idiot.'

'No, really. Sigmund Freud said—'

'I'm probably going to get my gun licence back at some point, Harper. Bear that in mind.'

He nodded, still grinning, and bailed out of the joke right there.

Summerhill still hadn't shown. Rawl said he hadn't even gone into the committee room yet.

Kennedy called it. They'd head out to Luton and be back by lunchtime. Probably they'd still return before Summerhill surfaced. She went to retrieve the case file, so they could add in Opie's statement if she said anything pertinent, and to leave a handwritten note for Summerhill explaining what they were doing. In the meantime, she asked Harper to shoot out an Interpol trawl for Michael Brand. You never knew your luck, after all.

The car they'd been driving the day before was unavailable for some reason, so they signed out another one from the pool and found it, after a short search, in the Caxton Street garage: a bottle-green Volvo S60, in good condition apart from a deep scratch down the full length of the driver's side where somebody had keyed it. Opening the doors released a miasma of stale smoke, which made Harper swear and Kennedy wince. But it wasn't worth the trouble of going back inside and working through two more sets of paperwork.

They'd missed the worst of the rush hour by the time they hit the M1, but it was still slow going. Harper was all for mounting the roof light and turning on the siren. Having lost so much of the morning already, Kennedy didn't see the point.

Unlike Prince Regent's College, Park Square still seemed to be swarming with purposefully moving students despite the time of year, and the car park was pretty much full. They circled the asphalt twice, just ahead of a white Bedford van that was doing exactly the same thing, before Harper pulled into a faculty space on which the word RESERVED had been blazoned in big yellow letters. The van nosed past them and Heather caught a brief glimpse of its driver: a man in early middle age, strikingly handsome in an austere, patrician way. His black hair was tightly frizzed and short, as sleek as though it had been anointed with oil. His face, though, looked as pale as the face of a Greek statue, and his gaze as she briefly met it gave her an unwelcome jolt of recognition. It was like the look her father got in his eyes when he was drifting off into the inner landscapes of his dementia. A look that never quite made it as far as the outside world, or else went clear past it. Unnerved, she looked away.

20

From the main gate, they were directed to the computer science faculty, which was on the far side of a ragged, bleached expanse of lawn, and then up to a lab on the third floor where a hundred students were working silently on a hundred new, gleaming machines. No, *silently* was the wrong word. The room was filled with a susurrus of fingers tapping on soft-touch keyboards, like the clucking of a hundred birds in covert. Sarah Opie was sitting at a workstation that looked no different from any of the others, except that it faced them and was attached by a hanging cable to a huge LCD screen above her head. The screen was switched off.

Dr Opie looked younger than Harper had been expecting: younger, and a lot more attractive, with strawberry blonde hair worn shoulder-length and lightly tousled. She had to be in her mid-twenties, young enough that the doctorate must be a very recent achievement. Young enough that the students in the room, who she was presumably teaching or supervising in some way, looked more like her contemporaries than her charges. She'd tried to distinguish herself from them by going for a formal look, but the dark-blue pinstriped two-piece she had on came across almost like fancy dress – the outfit of a sexy secretary strippergram.

Opie was expecting them. She stood and went without a word into an inner office whose glass frontage formed the rear wall of the main lab. She waited with her hand on the doorknob until they joined her, then closed the door. Some of the students had glanced up from their work when the detectives arrived and were still covertly watching now. Dr Opie turned her back on them to face the two officers, her arms stiffly folded.

Her glance went to Harper first. 'I've told you everything I know,' she said, quietly.

'This is Detective Sergeant Kennedy,' he said. 'She's in charge of the case, and she'd like to hear the story, too. I've also got some follow-up questions from our talk yesterday. I hope that's okay.'

The set of Opie's face indicated that it probably wasn't, but she moved her head in what was almost a nod and a moment later sat down in one of the two chairs in the office. Kennedy took the other, leaving Harper to lean precariously against one of the aluminium uprights that separated the floor-to-ceiling panes of glass.

'So we've got three fatalities,' Kennedy said, as soon as she'd set up her voice recorder and got Opie's permission to use it. 'Stuart Barlow. Catherine Hurt. Samir Devani. They're all interested in history – or at least, in old documents – and they're members of this group of yours, that likes to discuss that stuff. Now, you say that they were all working on one particular project?'

Dr Opie frowned a little impatiently. She seemed to feel that this was ground that had already been covered.

'Yes,' was all she said.

'And the project was something that they discussed on the message board? On your online forum?' Kennedy pursued.

'Yes.'

166

'Which is a historical forum. But you're not a historian, obviously.'

'No.'

This time Kennedy waited, staring at Opie in silent expectation. Harper knew what she was doing, and was careful not to jump into the gap. Closed questions were good because they were focused, but if you weren't careful, and if the witness wasn't the loquacious type, you could fall into a pattern of closed question/one-word answer – and then you could end up chasing your own tail. The silence stretched for a few seconds, but in the end it had its intended effect.

'It's a hobby for me,' Sarah Opie said. 'I did classics at school, and I'm pretty good at Ancient Greek. People think that's a bit weird, for an IT specialist, but I love languages. And I'm good at them. I had a Jewish boyfriend once, who taught me some Hebrew, and I worked backward from that to Aramaic. It fascinates me, with Aramaic and Ancient Greek, how the character sets are almost the same as for the modern languages but sometimes there's been a phonic shift, so that the same sign designates very different sounds. Of course, in some cases we don't even know how the living language actually sounded. The dry versus nasal pronunciation of mu plus pi – you know, where does that come in? You've got ancient texts and modern speakers, and it's not easy to—'

'Can you tell us what you know about Stuart Barlow's Rotgut project,' Kennedy interrupted. Harper almost grinned. Having coaxed Opie to move beyond monosyllables, the sergeant was now having to rein her in again. Always a feast or a famine.

'Professor Barlow came on to the board to ask for collaborators,' Opie told them. 'That was how it all started. He said he wanted to look at the Rotgut again from a new angle, and he asked if anybody had an appetite for that. That was the title of the thread: "Does anyone have any appetite for a new look at the Rotgut?"'

'And this was when?'

Opie shook her head, but answered anyway. 'Two years ago at least. Maybe three. I'd have to go back and look at the threads. They're all still available on the site.'

'So who responded?' Harper asked.

Opie's voice trembled just a little as she reeled off the names. 'Cath. Catherine Hurt. Sam Devani. Stuart went after Emil Gassan because he's so good on New Testament Aramaic, but Gassan didn't want to know.'

'Why was that?'

'He thought Stuart sort of lacked the academic credentials. Well, the whole team, really. He didn't want to be associated with them.'

'So it was just those three,' Kennedy said. 'Barlow. Hurt. Devani.'

'Yes. Just those three.'

'Nobody else you've forgotten?'

Opie let her irritation show. 'No. Nobody.'

'What about Michael Brand?'

'Michael Brand ...' She repeated the name with no particular emphasis. 'No. He was never part of this.'

'But you know him?'

'Not really. I think I've seen his name come up on the board once or twice. He's never been part of any discussion that I was in. And I only turn up on the board, not at the symposia. I'm not a historian, obviously – so I couldn't get funded to go to a history conference, and I couldn't afford to do it out of my own salary.'

'That's unusual, isn't it?' Kennedy pursued. 'That you could be part of the same message board group and not know each other?'

Opie shrugged. 'Not really. How many registered members has the Ravellers board got? Last time I checked the counter, it was up over two hundred. There's a counter on the front page so you can see when someone new joins – and a thread where they introduce themselves. They don't all post regularly. I don't. Not unless I've got an actual project on the go. I'd say I know maybe twenty or thirty of them well, and I could tell you the names of twenty more besides. Their screen names, I mean.'

'You say "when you've got a project",' Harper began, but Kennedy clearly wasn't interested in getting Dr Opie to talk about herself. She wanted to know about Stuart Barlow's group and what they were doing. She rode over Harper's question, which annoyed him a little – but she was ranking officer, and she had the right to take the lead in the questioning. 'Did Professor Barlow ever talk to you about exactly what it was he was trying to do?' she asked now. 'What he meant by his new approach?'

'Well, yes,' Opie said, looking puzzled. 'Of course he did.'

'Why of course?'

'Stuart and I were pretty good friends. I said I didn't go to any of the conferences, and that's true – but when the conferences were in London, sometimes I'd get a train down there and meet one or two of the people I knew after the sessions were over on the Friday or the Saturday. We'd go for a few drinks, maybe for dinner. I met Cath that way, and Stuart, too. He was really funny – like the cartoon of an absent-minded professor in a TV show. But he was one of the most intelligent people I ever met. I think that was why he never published. He found it hard to settle on one thing. He'd have an amazing idea, but then while he was working on it he'd have another amazing idea and just leave the first thing unfinished. He talked like that, too.' She smiled, probably remembering some specific conversation, but then got serious again almost at once. 'So, you know, there's no way he wouldn't at least mention something this big to me. He probably told me about it before he told anyone else.'

'So you can sum up the project for us,' Kennedy said, pulling Opie back on track again. 'I think that might be useful at this stage.'

Opie looked – maybe a little longingly – out through the window at her class. Some of them were still shooting the occasional glance in the direction of the inner office, but for the most part they were working quietly. No riots in progress. They could all be surfing porn or playing minesweeper, but they were doing it discreetly.

'Okay,' Opie said, looking resigned. 'Stuart said he wanted to use a brute force approach.'

'Which means?'

'Well, I'm not sure whether he knew what it meant when he said it, but what it came down to, in the end, was crunching the numbers. Digitising the Rotgut and then interrogating it using a really high-end software array that practically had to be written from scratch. That was why Stuart particularly wanted to have IT support. You see, he thought the best way to find the source document for the Rotgut was to—'

'Wait a minute,' Harper blurted. 'Say that again. He wanted?'

Opie blinked, startled. 'He wanted IT support. Because what he had in mind was going to involve hundreds of hours of—'

'Does that mean you?' Harper demanded, interrupting again. 'Does IT support mean you?'

'Of course it means me. I wrote the software and ran it. How else do you think I know about all this?'

'But you said you weren't in the team!' Kennedy exclaimed, coming to her feet.

Dr Opie still looked mystified, but now she also looked scared and defensive. 'I wasn't,' she said, involuntarily pushing her chair a little back from Kennedy, who was standing over her, evidently a little too close. 'I was only doing search runs and filter runs for them. Support. Stuart, Cath and Sam were the team. They were the ones going to write the monograph, if it ever got to be published. I mean, you know, if they found what they were hoping to find. Stuart just asked me to do tech support, and I said yes. That doesn't make me—'

'What it makes you,' Kennedy snapped, cutting Opie off, 'is a target. If someone is killing the members of this group, why should they draw a distinction between you and the other three? You say you were only helping them out – but you talked to them, worked with them. From the outside, doesn't it look like you were on the team?'

Opie shook her head, firmly at first, but the conviction drained away in three easy stages.

Shake to the left – you're crazy in some very well-progressed ways.

Shake to the right – but then, there are a lot of people dead already.

Shake to the left – and you're saying ... oh dear.

She let loose an incredulous and slightly tortured-sounding laugh. Harper felt for her. Incredulity seemed like a reasonable response. If you live in the rarefied air of arcane theories and academic quibbles, you probably get to feel as though there's at least a tower or two of good, clean ivory between you and the red, bleeding business of the world. But now the History Man was in town, and the walls were coming down. Just for a moment, he felt guilty about the part of himself that was enjoying this.

'I'm not,' Opie said again. 'I'm not on the team.' But it was a weak protest now. An appeal to a non-existent court of natural justice.

'Tech support,' Kennedy said, reminding her of her own words. 'Professor Barlow wanted you to help him. Who else would know that? Did you talk about it on the board?'

'Of course I did.' Opie stood up herself now, confronting Kennedy for a moment or two with her fists clenching and unclenching in unfocused but strong emotion. 'Of course I did. It wasn't a secret. All I did was run the programs. I didn't even read the print-outs. They didn't mean anything to me.'

Kennedy opened her mouth, but changed her mind and closed it again. She turned to Harper, looking a question at him. He nodded. The specifics didn't matter. What she was asking him was whether this party needed to change venues, and the answer had to be yes. They could be wrong about everything else: the accidents that had killed Hurt and Devani could just be accidents, and the break-ins at Barlow's cottage and his office at Prince Regent's amazing coincidences. The disappearing Michael Brand – Harper suddenly remembered that he still hadn't mentioned any of that to Kennedy – could be a complete innocent who was just absent-minded about his address. It made no difference. They had only one priority here, and only one way to take it. They had reason to believe a witness was in immediate, physical danger. They had to bring her in.

'Should I move the car around to the entrance?' Harper asked Kennedy.

'Yes,' Kennedy said. 'Thanks, Chris. Do that.' Then she held up her hand – stop – and turned back to Opie. 'Is there a back entrance?' she asked.

'What?' Opie asked. She didn't seem to see where this was going.

'To this block. Is there another way out?'

172

'Only the fire escape.'

To Harper again: 'We'll go that way, and we'll go together. Dr Opie, we're taking you into protective custody. Please collect any things you need to take with you right now. Obviously we'll send someone round to your house later to pick up anything else you'd like to have – but it may be some time before you go back there yourself.'

'I'm in the middle of a lesson,' Opie pointed out, as though that was still an issue.

'Dismiss the class,' Kennedy said. 'Or tell them to keep working unsupervised. Presumably they can be trusted to do that?'

'Yes, but—'

'We'll explain to your employers – to the college authorities – that this was out of your hands. That it was our decision. And I'm sure they'll find someone to cover your work while you're away.'

Opie still looked unhappy, and she carried on arguing right up to the point where Kennedy picked up her handbag and placed it in her hands. Somehow that both galvanised and silenced her. She collected a few items from the desk – a flashdrive, a purse and a few thick whiteboard markers – and dropped them into the bag. Then she gave Kennedy a reproachful, bewildered look, which perhaps was intended for God or Nemesis, and took a step towards the door. Almost immediately she yelped as if stung and went back quickly to the desk. She turned a few papers over, rummaged through the contents of a red plastic in-tray, and at last came up with a single folded sheet of yellow paper. 'Password,' she said to Harper and Kennedy. 'For my files. I change it every week.'

'You write your password down?' Harper asked, slightly scandalised.

'Of course not,' Opie snapped, nettled by the implied disapproval. 'But I keep a mnemonic in case I forget it.'

She went through into the main workroom. Harper and Kennedy followed.

The students all looked up from their work, knowing that something out of the ordinary was going down and curious to see what it was going to be. 'We're winding the lesson up a little early,' Dr Opie said. 'Any of you who want to carry on working can do so, up until twelve-thirty. And the due date for the database assignment stays the same, so please do use the time sensibly. I'll see you all next week.'

The students all turned back to their screens, but it was clear from their brisk movements and sweeping up of stray belongings that most were packing up. Kennedy hustled Opie towards the door, keen to get to it before the general exodus began. Harper brought up the rear, the narrow aisle between desks obliging them to stay in single file. They had to step over bags and books left in the aisle, so progress was slower than it might have been.

Abruptly, Kennedy stopped. She turned to look at Harper, or maybe past him, her expression a puzzled frown.

'Wait,' she said. 'Those men looked—'

There was a sound like the scrape of a chair being pushed back. Something moved at Harper's elbow. He turned and found himself staring into the face of a man maybe ten years older than he was, dark-haired and pale-skinned, dressed in a loose white shirt and light tan suit, their coarse fabric making them look hand-woven. The man was standing, had just come to his feet. He had an expression on his face of strange, detached calm, but the pupils of his eyes were enormous. Drugs, Harper thought: he has to be on something.

He put a hand on the man's shoulder to make him sit down again. The man took Harper's hand at the wrist, his grip like the inflexible bite of a handcuff, and twisted it suddenly, unexpectedly.

Harper gasped and buckled at the knees as pain lanced up his arm.

He heard Kennedy shout, but didn't catch the words. He struck out clumsily, with his left hand, and made contact, but the punch caught the man on the shoulder rather than the point of the jaw. The grip on Harper's arm stayed as tight as before as the man returned the punch, catching Harper full in the stomach, forcing the breath out of him in an explosive grunt.

He found it hard to take an in-breath, to replace that lost air. The man let go of his arm, and to his own surprise Harper sprawled backwards, knocking over a computer on the desk behind him. He heard screams, and he could understand why. The man who'd just hit him was weeping, and his tears were dark red.

More screams. Harper tried to right himself, but his legs felt wobbly and didn't want to take his weight. The man with the bleeding eyes, red runnels in his cheeks, stared at him for a moment longer – a stare of total contempt – before turning away.

Over the screams, Harper certainly couldn't have heard the blood pattering to the ground between his feet. But he caught sight of one of the drops as it fell. He touched his stomach and felt the sticky wetness there, insinuating and terrible. He looked at his red fingers, and an incredulous laugh forced its way out of his throat.

The universe shrank to that redness. It was as hot as hell and tasted of iron.

21

Kennedy's first and only warning was that doubled sense of déjà vu.

She walked past the man, feeling only a vague prickle of recognition. When she walked past him a second time, the memory clicked into place. He was the man she'd seen in the car park below, in the white Bedford van. But now there were two of him.

She stopped, forcing Harper to stop too, and turned. Almost instantly, she realised that her initial impression had been wrong. There were differences in the physiques of the two men, one being a little taller, a little bulkier than the other. A disparity in their ages – ten years, at least – and in their faces, too, or at least in their expressions. What looked like slightly tripped-out calm in the face of the thinner man metamorphosed on the other's broader features into a scarily robotic blankness. They were mostly alike in their complexion and the colour of their hair – and in the weirdness of their bearing, that wide-eyed stare that took in the whole world while barely acknowledging its presence.

Harper was looking at her expectantly, and she opened her mouth to say something, but hesitated, trying to frame in her mind a warning against a threat she wasn't even sure was there.

The second man, the one nearest to them, pushed his chair back and rose, the sound of the chair legs on the floor making Harper turn his head to look at him. After that, things happened so quickly they seemed to be pictures in a stroboscopic slide show, each impressing itself on Kennedy's mind as a still image.

Harper was touching the man on the shoulder.

The man's arm was out, connecting with Harper's stomach.

Metal flashed, then didn't because it was sheathed: sheathed in flesh.

Harper fell against a desk.

At some point in this flicker-book series, Kennedy yelled to the room at large, 'Down! Everybody down!' and stepped in to help Harper as he pitched over on to the floor. She aimed the simplest of karate punches at the man, the only one she'd ever practised: palm up, knuckles of the index and middle fingers forward, punching from the hip while advancing the same leg.

She didn't even come close to touching him. The man leaned aside from the punch and stepped in closer to her, moving with terrifying, near-impossible speed while not seeming to be in any special hurry. For an instant Kennedy was staring into his face, and she realised that he was crying: red tears, like blood, running down his face. For some reason, the sight made her stomach lurch, and that instinctive revulsion saved her. She leaned back as though from some atavistic fear of contamination. The knife the man had used on Harper, its stubby blade obscenely crimsoned and trailing beads of blood like spray, parted the air in front of her chest and then, at the end of its arc, bit into her shoulder. The blade was so sharp that her shirt and jacket, the flesh and sinew beneath, didn't even seem to slow it down.

Screams rose around her, sustained beyond all reason as though a rock star had entered a room full of teenaged fans. The man was off balance momentarily, and Kennedy kicked from the direction in which he was already moving, catching him way down on the leg. He lurched, his centre of gravity momentarily outside his base, and she clubbed him with her closed fist on the side of his jaw as he went down.

His twin – his twin who looked so very different from him, and yet so eerily alike – was standing behind him, at much the same angle to Kennedy. The effect was of peeling one layer of skin from an onion and finding the same structures, the same textures repeated underneath. But the second man had his arm out horizontally, straight from the shoulder, pointing at her. Not with an accusing finger, but with a long-barrelled handgun. His eyes, staring at her steadily over that matt steel barrel, were pale blue shot with red.

Kennedy had never before frozen up at the sight of a gun. Guns were familiar things to her: tools, dangerous but useful, and answerable to her will. In other people's hands, they were to be feared, but she knew how to read a shooter's body language and to get her dodging in early. You couldn't move out of a bullet's path once it was fired, but you had a reasonable window before then. Half a second between that tug on the trigger and the arrival of the payload: at the beginning of the half-second, the shooter committed himself. The interim was negotiable territory.

This time was different. Seeing the gun, Kennedy felt a sudden absence of will, a draining of thought. She stood still, not because she was frozen in place but because she couldn't make herself decide to move.

'Da b'koshta,' the man said.

He fired three times, so quickly the sounds of the three shots seemed to overlap. Kennedy flinched and stiffened, expecting the arrival of death, expecting it to pass through her like a wind through corn.

Sarah Opie danced a short, brutal jig as the bullets all went home, and didn't start to fall until the third had hit her.

The sound came later, mooching on to the scene like lazy thunder after the lightning had already gone by. Too late, much too late, Kennedy threw herself forward. The gun turned in a swift flick of motion to point at her head, but this time her punch was quicker and better aimed, and she knocked it aside. Stepping inside the man's guard, she tried to lock her leg behind his and throw him, but the cramped space worked against her. She collided with the projecting edge of a desk and stumbled. Something caught her on her left temple and slammed her down. She hit the floor hard, random flashes of light and dark superseding each other in front of her eyes.

She tried to move, to lever herself up off the floor. As her sight came back in patches, the angles and the colours sickeningly wrong, she found herself staring into the eyes of Dr Opie. The woman's lips, as white as her face, moved seemingly without sound, and her fingers trembled as they scratched at the tiled floor.

There was a lull in the screaming, and Kennedy heard, with dreamlike clarity, a small fragment of what Opie was saying. 'A dove ... a dove got ... '

Occulted light warned Kennedy and made her flick her gaze upwards. The man with the gun loomed over her, then drew back his foot and kicked her hard in the chest. Pain expanded from a point in the middle of her ribcage like a synaesthetic firework. The kick lifted her and dropped her down again. She had no breath left, her flickering awareness rebuilt around the astonishing pain as though around a bulky, solid object.

With unhurried but precise movements, the murderer – the *assassin*, because that was what he was – helped his fallen colleague to his feet. The two stepped over Kennedy, out of her line

179

of sight, and she heard their steps receding. Or perhaps she only felt the vibrations through her cheek as she lay on her side on the floor. The screaming had resumed with full vigour and volume, so it was hard for any other sound to get a purchase on the saturated air. And maybe, if she ever managed to suck in another breath around the bolus of agony in her chest, she'd add her own voice to the chorus.

She rolled over on to her back and then – laboriously, fighting nausea and the numb buoyancy of encroaching unconsciousness – struggled to her feet. She was taking oxygen in tiny sips and it hurt like swallowing half-chewed barbed wire.

A few students hadn't been quick enough to get to the door and so had just pressed themselves into the corners of the room in terror as the hideous pantomime unfolded. 'Call the police,' Kennedy told them. The words came out wrong, or maybe it was just that she was hearing them wrong. Her tongue felt too big for her mouth, and her body swayed as though it couldn't find the vertical.

She set off at a run anyway. The killers would be heading for the van. There was still time to stop them, or at least to get the goddamned licence plate.

She almost fell on the stairs, moving too quickly to keep her balance. Her balance was gone, in any case. Time was moving in a pizzicato rhythm, moments pinched out on taut strings to the irregular beat of her pulse. Blood soaked her sleeve, so dark it was more black than red. In the foyer, students stepped back in alarm from this drunken madwoman with a bloodied, swollen face. Kennedy hit the double doors, wrestled with them, staggered through into daylight.

She saw the van immediately. It was a few feet taller than the compact cars that filled every other space in the lot. She saw one of the men climbing into the driver's seat. The other had opened the door on the passenger side, about to get in, but had turned to look at a security guard who, Kennedy guessed, had offered him some challenge. The man's hand moved to his jacket. The guard was angry-faced, overweight, oblivious and about to die.

'Police!' Kennedy yelled. Or something that shared vowel sounds with that word. 'You're under arrest!'

The assassin turned to glance at her as she walked out on to the asphalt, among the parked cars, into a narrow avenue that contained nothing else but her and him. He stared at Kennedy, momentarily inactive as though he required a context in which to understand her, the guard temporarily forgotten, which was something at least. Kennedy strode towards him and he completed the movement he'd already begun, reaching into his jacket to remove what was ready to hand there. But it wasn't the gun, which was what she'd been expecting. It was the knife. Incongruous relief flooded her. The knife might kill her, but it wouldn't annul her the way a cross annuls a vampire. It didn't even look particularly formidable, though she knew by now what it could do. It had a bizarre, asymmetrical shape, bulging out at one side. She kept on walking, as the security guard backed off with a muttered 'Oh shit.'

The assassin's arm unfolded, the movement abstract and perfect, the knife aligning precisely with her gaze, so that its slender blade became invisible.

'You're under arrest,' Kennedy said again, with a fair bit more conviction this time even though it was getting harder to talk. 'And you will lower that weapon or I swear to God I will take it away from you and peel you like a piece of fruit.'

'Da b'koshta,' the man said. The exact same sequence of sounds he'd made inside the lab. He drew his arm back and Kennedy tensed like a goalkeeper facing a penalty kick, already deciding which way to jump. If he missed her, she'd have a window of a second or so and she meant to use it.

There was a crisp, hollow boom that seemed to come from all directions at once and the knife exploded in the assassin's hand like a steel firework. But he didn't cry out: didn't make a sound, in fact. He pressed his hand to his chest, the fingers curled strangely, and turned to gaze off to Kennedy's left. The second shot thudded into his chest, visible because his light-coloured jacket developed suddenly a poppy-bright circle of red.

The shooter came into sight now, from the direction of the gates, running and firing at the same time. A bullet shattered one of the rear windows of the van, another hit nothing that Kennedy could see.

The assassin moved, diving – or maybe it was falling – into the vehicle through the already open passenger door. The engine snarled, sputtered, snarled.

The newcomer – a big man, bigger and more solid even than the heavier of the two killers – was a scant few feet away from the van when it slammed into reverse, forcing him to jump aside. It shot across the narrow aisle, punched into the back of another parked car, then veered around in a wide, drunken arc towards the gate.

The newcomer took careful aim and squeezed off two more shots. The first went nowhere. The second blew off one end of the Bedford's rear bumper but missed the tyre. The van crashed through the closed barrier – the attendant at the gate ducking and flinching as jagged fragments spun end-over-end through the air – and was gone. The shooter lowered the gun, which looked like some outlandish kind of revolver, and turned to Kennedy.

Sandy-haired and rough-hewn, well over six feet tall, with big shoulders and ham-like hands, the man was built for bar fights and hard labour. He was hard to reconcile with that pinpoint shooting. There was something in his face, though: a grim stoicism that seemed to look inward as well as out, as though the man's physical body was a stopper in the wall of an interior dam. Kennedy could imagine brave men flinching from that stare.

But the man's washed-out blue eyes weren't looking into Kennedy's. He was focused on her wound, which he indicated with a brusque nod of the head.

'Get it looked at quick,' he said. The voice, a soft burr, didn't go with the hatchet hardness of the face. 'Really. Right now.'

And then he took off after the van. The security guard at the gate screwed his courage up and stepped into the man's path, but stepped right back out of it again when he didn't slow. Another instant and the shooter was gone, too. As though the whole thing had been a hallucination. As though she were asleep and dreaming this somewhere, maybe as she sat outside Summerhill's office with Harper whistling tunelessly at her side.

Harper.

She staggered back inside and up the stairs. The stairwell and the corridor were full of milling people, most of whom got out of her way quickly when they saw the blood. She still had her badge in her hand and she flashed it whenever necessary to avoid having to speak. Her ears were full of a sickening, monotone hum like the sound you get when you bring a microphone too close to its own loudspeaker.

The crowd was thickest right outside the IT lab, mostly students who'd fled from the violence, now creeping back to peer at the aftermath. But she saw a fair few men in suits who had added themselves to the fringes and were vainly trying to restore calm by requesting it at high volume. Kennedy grabbed one of these and shouted into his face: 'Dial 999. Get an ambulance.

Get the police, and an ambulance.' The man, who was bald and florid, stared stupidly at her bruised face, at her badge, at her face again, until she sent him on his way with a push. Her voice had thickened even more, her jaw grating agonisingly with each word, but only a congenital idiot would have failed to get the message from her tone.

Harper lay where he'd fallen, and he looked to be in a bad way. He was barely conscious, clutching his stomach from which blood welled and flowed in unfeasible amounts.

Kennedy knelt beside him, then slumped into a sitting position, resting her back against a fallen desk, as the last of her strength drained away. Harper turned his head to stare at her speechlessly.

'Hang in there, Harper,' she said. It was just a slurry of sound.

Faced with that inarticulacy, Kennedy did something that amazed her even in the midst of so much else that was amazing. She raised Harper's head, awkwardly but carefully, and cradled it in her lap, stroking his hair and his white, sweat-slick forehead until his eyes finally closed.

They told her later that it shouldn't have been a life-threatening wound. Deep as it was, it had missed all the major organs and – by a scant half-inch – the celiac artery. Harper might have been at risk, later, of peritonitis, as with any wound to the body cavity, but with immediate abdominal surgery and broad-spectrum antibiotics he ought to have made a full recovery.

He died in her arms, his blood a never-ending fountain.

PART TWO

DOVECOTE

22

Six days passed in a fog.

The wound to Kennedy's shoulder had been mended with a great many stitches, but it seeped first blood and then clear fluid for the first three of those days. There was an anti-coagulant on the knife blade, the doctors told her. It was the only explanation. That was why Harper had died so quickly from a wound he ought to have survived. They hadn't identified the substance so far, and therefore it was all but impossible to neutralise. All they could do was wait until it left her system, keeping her on a plasma drip and changing the dressings on the wound every few hours.

The lower half of her face had puffed up and become swollen to the point where talking was impossible until the fourth day, but she found the grotesque, lopsided aspect it gave her a lot harder to bear than the pain, dulled as it was with morphine. Most of the damage had been done by that final kick, which had cracked two of her ribs. The doctors had taped them up, running the tape from her sternum all the way around to her spine. It felt like being in a corset that she couldn't take off or loosen.

Lying in the hospital bed, trying to think through the painkiller-fuzz, she brooded on the gaps in her memory – not of the fight, but of its aftermath. She remembered sitting with her back against the fallen desk, Harper's head in her lap. His hand on the wound and her hand on his hand, pressing down, slowing the bleeding. They might have been that way for hours or only for a few minutes. The students had all fled, so the only company they'd had was Sarah Opie's corpse, whose stare was not so much reproachful as incredulous.

She remembered talking to Harper and him talking back. But when she thought about what he'd said, she realised it wasn't even his voice but her father's. *What do you want to be a cop for? Haven't we given enough?*

'What counts as enough, Dad?' she muttered, her voice made unintelligible by her swollen jaw.

Yeah, keep talking back to me, Heather. Make me come over there.

Then there was another gap.

And then someone was prising her hand from Harper's stomach, where it was no longer needed, and she couldn't unclench her fist because she had held it so tightly and for so long in the one position.

'He's a detective,' she told the paramedics. 'We're both detectives.' Her voice, forced out of the side of her mouth, sounded like the voice of a bellows, of Victor Frankenstein's hunchbacked assistant. 'Call it in.'

'Can you stand?' someone asked her. 'Can you walk?'

She must have done both. She remembered stepping into the ambulance, sitting upright on the gurney, staring at Harper's body as they laid it down opposite her in an opaque, unlovely plastic envelope thirty-six inches wide by ninety long.

Another gap. She was staring down into Harper's face. Someone must have unzipped the body bag.

A voice said, 'Oh. Hey. You're not supposed to.'

Harper looked troubled, his eyes tight shut, his forehead creased, as if he were trying to remember something.

She stroked his cheek. His skin was too cool, with a waxy unresponsiveness.

I'm sorry, she told him, without speaking. *I'm sorry, Chris.*

And then, although she had no idea whether or not it was true, *I'll get them.*

On the seventh day, God rested. Kennedy wasn't God: she returned to her labours, and to the incident committee.

It was chaired by DCI Summerhill, who wore the face of a hanging judge but kept the questions softball for the first half-hour or so as he took her through the contents of the case file. Once he'd established for the benefit of the HR officer, Brooks, and the IPCC observer, a hard-nosed old battle-axe named Anne Ladbroke, that this was a case potentially involving at least three homicides, he moved in – with clinical and detached animosity – for the kill.

'Why did you and Constable Harper go into this without support?' he asked. 'It must have been apparent that Dr Opie was at risk.'

'No, sir,' Kennedy said. 'It wasn't apparent at all.' Her jaw still ached when she spoke, but she had a lot to say and she wasn't going to let that stop her. 'The three people known to have died had all been directly involved in Stuart Barlow's research project on the Rotgut Codex. Dr Opie had expressly denied any connection to that project. It was only in questioning her that we realised she was a member of Barlow's team – something that she herself, as you've heard on the tape, continued to deny.'

The room, basically a storeroom, was hot, without air conditioning. With every breath she was ingesting the sharp tang of toner cartridges. Talking about these things brought them back vividly, but with overlays of the time she'd spent remembering them in her hospital bed. After a while, all memories must metastasise in this way, until you were mainly recalling the emotions that accompanied each successive revisit and revision.

'Only in questioning her ...' Summerhill mused. 'Something that you could have done on the previous afternoon. Why did you wait?'

Kennedy looked into his expressionless eyes. 'For the same reason, sir,' she said. 'There seemed no reason to move quickly because Dr Opie had been identified as a useful witness, not as a potential victim. If she'd been more open with Constable Harper – if she'd told him that she was providing software and technical support for Barlow and his people – we would have come to a different conclusion and moved faster.'

'So the fault lies partly with Constable Harper's interview technique,' Summerhill summarised, with envenomed casualness. 'Still, as the case officer, you have to take some responsibility for that.'

The IPCC woman scribbled a note to herself.

Yeah, keep pushing me, you bastard. Back me into the corner and see where you get bitten.

'I don't accept that there were any shortcomings with Detective Harper's questioning of Dr Opie,' she said, and then after a slight pause, 'sir. As you're aware – as you were aware when you gave it to me – this case came down to Division as a mislabelled homicide. The investigation was reopened after the autopsy results failed to support the initial presumption of accidental death. Subsequently, we found evidence of a burglary and a stalking incident, both pertinent to the case. Both incidents had been reported, but neither had been attached to the case file. This accumulation of errors made it harder for us to identify a pattern in what we were seeing. In spite of this, Detective Harper succeeded in unearthing the other two suspicious deaths and in linking them to that of Professor Barlow. This in a single day. By any standards, his handling of the case was exemplary.'

Summerhill made a show of examining the accumulated papers in front of him, then looked at her again. 'Perhaps you just have lower standards than the rest of us, Sergeant.'

'Perhaps so, sir,' Kennedy answered, without inflection.

'At Park Square,' Summerhill said, returning to his perusal of the documents, 'you ascertained that Dr Opie was a potential victim, but still failed to call for back-up.'

'We decided to bring her in ourselves. We considered that time was of the essence.'

'And that therefore, standard operating protocols were negotiable.'

Kennedy thought before replying. 'Your earlier questions were about unreasonable delay, sir,' she said, meeting Summerhill's gaze. 'Are you now saying that in bringing Dr Opie into protective custody, I didn't delay long enough? If so, please remember that her murderers were already in the building. Back-up couldn't have reached us before they did unless it teleported. We thought we were short on time, and my God, we were right.'

'You could have remained in Dr Opie's office,' Brooks mused. 'With the door locked.'

'With the door locked?' Kennedy echoed, deadpan.

'Yes.'

'The walls were made of glass, and the killers had guns.' *Have you even read the file, you pole-climbing bitch?*

'Still,' Summerhill broke in, briskly, 'we can safely assume there were other offices in that building whose walls were more solid. Hindsight is always perfect, Sergeant Kennedy, but we're talking about your decision-making – which, ultimately, led to a situation where a fellow officer and a civilian informant both died.'

191

There was a heavy silence. Kennedy waited it out. Summerhill seemed to have run out of inspiration now, and Kennedy read that as a bad sign. It showed just how thin a veneer he was painting over his desire to be rid of her.

Brooks stepped into the breach again. 'There was a further altercation,' she said. 'A further encounter, I mean. You followed the two men – the murderers – out into the car park.'

'Yes.'

'Where a third shooter appeared. And apparently wounded one of his own people.'

'I don't think they were his people. He was acting against them, not with them.'

'Or else he was a very bad shot.'

'He shot a knife right out of the hand of one of those mopes. Hit him again before he could get back into the getaway vehicle, and then hit the vehicle itself while it was in motion. I'd have to say he was pretty good.'

Brooks acknowledged this answer only with a rustle and gathering of papers. 'And he was left behind, when the van drove away?'

'Yes. Briefly. Then he pursued it.'

'Did you attempt an arrest, Sergeant?'

Kennedy bit back her first answer, and her second. 'As you'll see from my report,' she said at last, 'I'd already tried to arrest the killers. The third man's intervention came at that point, when they were turning on me and were about to attack me for a second time. Furthermore, I was unarmed. An unarmed officer, acting alone, is not required to accost an armed assailant if there's no reasonable expectation that she can bring him down.' *Especially when he's probably just saved her life.*

'So we come back to the absence of back-up.'

'I suppose we do.'

'Your description of the third man is very sketchy.'

'I must have been distracted by my broken ribs and the incised wound to my shoulder.'

Brooks raised her eyebrows in innocent amazement: the blameless victim of drive-by sarcasm.

'Your tone isn't helping you, Sergeant,' Summerhill said.

'I imagine not.' She was running out of patience. Fortunately, they seemed to be running out of questions.

But the DCI had saved the best for last.

'Let's come back to the events in the IT lab,' he said. 'Specifically, the shooting of Dr Opie. DC Harper was already wounded at this point, yes?'

Kennedy nodded warily. 'Yes.'

'But the knife man – the one who'd attacked first him and then you – was down.'

'That's right.'

'When the second man produced the gun and aimed at Dr Opie, where were you in relation to the two of them?'

She could see where this catechism was leading her, but she had no way to deflect it. 'I was between them,' she admitted.

'Distance, what, about ten feet from the shooter?'

'More or less.'

'Which? More, or less?'

'Less, probably. Eight or nine feet.'

'A couple of steps, then. And the gun was aimed past you at someone else. In your assessment, was there a possibility there for you to step in and try to disarm the shooter before he fired?'

Kennedy remembered that moment of frozen horror, the draining away of her ability to think and move and act. It had been rooted in another memory: of Marcus Dell lurching towards her, locking his hands around her throat, and then of her own G22 kicking against the palm of her hand as she sent the .40 round on its short, eventful journey through Dell's thoracic cavity.

Some things hurt too much already to lay them open still further with a lie. 'It happened very fast,' she said, aware of the slight hesitation, the tremor in her voice. 'Maybe ... maybe I hesitated, for a second. It's hard to remember. But the shooter was very quick. Very professional.'

'He fired three times. That must have taken a few seconds.'

'I suppose so.'

'But there wasn't sufficient time for you to intervene?'

'I've said I don't remember.'

Summerhill began to collect up the papers and slip them back into the case file. 'Well,' he said, 'we'll consider our recommendations. Please make yourself available to us for the rest of the day. We'll give you a decision before you leave this evening.'

It was too sudden, and Kennedy's mind was still too full of images that defied and accused her. She'd been waiting for this moment, but when it came she wasn't ready. 'Is that it?' she demanded, her voice sounding stupid and sullen in her own ears.

'For now, yes,' Summerhill said. 'You may want to speak to Human Resources, if you've got any questions about how this procedure works. Mrs Brooks will be available throughout the day.'

It was now or never: the hour of the knife. 'Actually, sir,' Kennedy said, 'I'd like to speak to you. In private.'

Caught in the act of closing the case file and, with it, her career, the DCI looked up again, surprised. 'I think we have all the information we need, Sergeant,' he said.

'This is information that relates to the conduct of the case,' Kennedy persisted, her voice level and courteous. 'However, it's of a sensitive nature and can only be discussed with case officers.'

Summerhill's face went through a range of emotions, all behind a slightly slipping mask of professional indifference. 'Very well,' he said at last, 'we'll discuss it in my office. And then,' he added, addressing Brooks and Ladbroke, 'I'll rejoin you.'

With his office door closed on the world, Summerhill sank into a chair, but pointedly did not invite Kennedy to take the other. She sat down anyway.

'What do you want to tell me?' he demanded.

'I've got gypsy blood,' Kennedy said, her voice still far from steady.

Summerhill stared at her in faint bewilderment. 'What?'

'Straight up, Jimmy. I can tell your fortune. A couple of months from now, maybe three, I see you emptying out those desk drawers and walking off into the sunset. And it's raining. It's raining really hard.'

Summerhill's expression indicated that this was still nonsense to him. 'You said you had information pertinent to the case,' he reminded her, coldly.

'Pertinent to the conduct of the case,' she corrected. 'Yes. I do. It's in your inbox already, where it's been for a week. On the departmental mail server, too, and God knows where else. Central Support keeps copies of everything, right? So it's all over the place, if anyone wants to look. Header: "Stuart Barlow case file". Go ahead and look.'

Summerhill did, found her email of a week before, and shrugged. 'So?'

'So check the dateline. That was the night before we went to Luton to see Sarah Opie. It was right there waiting for you when you clocked in the next day. Only you clocked in late. I know that because we waited for you for well over an hour before we finally gave up and went to interview the witness.'

Summerhill made a brusque gesture: *get to the point.*

'Did you even read the email, Jimmy? I told you the case had blown up into something really scary. I suggested that you should review the size of the case team and the scope of the investigation. I asked you to make a ruling – urgently – on immediate priorities.'

'All of which,' Summerhill said, 'makes no difference to the facts. You went in without back-up and a civilian died. So did your fellow officer, who was new to the job and taking his cue from you.'

Kennedy nodded. 'Yes,' she said, grimly. 'He did. He died in my arms, Jimmy. I'm not likely to forget that. But I thought your first question back there was why we waited so long. It doesn't seem to have occurred to you that we waited for you.'

Summerhill was already shaking his head. 'No, no, Sergeant. I'm sorry. That won't do. I was absent because I was at Westminster, on divisional business. And in my absence, you're required to go through another senior officer.'

This was as far as Kennedy had taken it in her mind. The rest was just a guess, and she was either right or wrong. She thought of Harper lying across her lap, bleeding out. The horror of that moment, still fresh, acted like a plumb line, keeping her level and composed in this one.

'Maybe,' she allowed. 'Maybe you were at Westminster. But that's about the fifth or sixth time I've heard that select committee story, and one of those times was in January, before Parliament even came back from recess. You used to have a booze problem, didn't you, Jimmy? A couple of reprimands, almost a disciplinary hearing once, or so the story goes. I'm out of the loop now, for obvious reasons, but I don't think a problem like that just goes away. So my theory is that WPC Rawl has two big crosses to bear around here: a general brief to cover up for you when you come in late, and a complete lack of imagination.'

She paused again. This was where the roof would fall in, if it was going to. It seemed a long time before Summerhill spoke. When he did, his voice was a lot more controlled than she'd been hoping for and a lot more aggressive: turning full on to the salvo, not wallowing and waiting for another broadside.

'Detective Sergeant,' he said, 'you seem to think that you can take the heat off yourself by attacking me. Let me repeat, in case you didn't hear me the first time: an officer is dead because of your actions. Attempting to blackmail me can't possibly affect—'

'I'll bring you down too,' Kennedy said. Summerhill carried on speaking over her, so she couldn't be sure that he'd heard her, but most of the message was in her face and her tone.

'—the decision of an independent tribunal of which I'm only—'

'If Rawl was covering for you, I will sink you.'

'—one member. The decision comes from all of us.'

'Then give me a Viking funeral,' Kennedy said, her throat tight. 'Go ahead. Because that's all I've got. But I swear to God, Jimmy, if you shit-can me, or even if you just try to keep me off this case, I'll get my lawyer to shout it from the rooftops that Harper died because you were too drunk to show up for work. If I'm right, if you weren't called to the Commons that day and you've got no MPs to vouch for you, then Rawl's entry in the day book will be enough to prove you lied. They will crucify you. And that won't bring Chris Harper back from the dead but it will mean a little bit of justice has been mixed in with the usual bullshit.'

They'd both ended up on their feet, facing each other, and he ran out of words before she did. 'Let me know, either way,' she muttered, suddenly disgusted with him and with herself.

She left Summerhill's office without looking back, went to the bear pit to wait it out, but the atmosphere there was palpable. They all knew about the review, and they all knew what it was for. She'd gotten a detective killed. She'd gone from being someone they hated to something they wanted to disavow. No eyes met hers.

She wasn't even sure that she could have met her own eyes right then, if there'd been a mirror handy. She knew, objectively, that Harper had already taken his wound when she froze in front of the gun. Moving quicker wouldn't have saved him, but it might have saved Sarah Opie.

She'd been through it in her mind so many times now, the memories had stripped threads and came together in the wrong sequence, from the wrong angles, jumbled and incomprehensible. She endured them anyway.

23

Kuutma was a long way from London when he took the call from Abidan's team. In fact, he was in Moscow, patching up communications networks that had been damaged by Tillman's murder of Kartoyev. He was standing in the antechamber of the Russian business minister, a hall half the size of a football stadium, travelling under his customary identity and waiting to find out whether he would be seen.

When Abidan told him about the mysterious shooter who had appeared only just too late to sabotage the mission, Kuutma knew at once from the description – the height, the build, the hair that was either the lightest of light browns or else pale red, and of course the accuracy of the shooting – that the man was Tillman. His concerns had proved only too well justified: Tillman had taken his time but he had been heading for London ever since Kartoyev's death, and now he had picked up on the connection between Michael Brand and the recent deaths.

The problem was built into the very charter of the Messengers because it was the way they worked, and had always worked, and must continue to work until the thirty centuries were done (and it was getting late, already; the count could be argued, but the count was close). They took the drug, *kelalit*, and it gave them the blessings of strength and speed. It was a sacrament.

Also, a neurotoxin, and in the end it either killed them or drove them mad. So Kuutma was constantly engaged in training new Messengers and had endless trouble finding team leaders of sufficient experience.

Mistakes had been made in the handling of the Rotgut project, just as mistakes had been made in the handling of Flight 124. Loose ends had been left untied, opportunities had been missed, convoluted methods used where simple ones were available. It fell to Kuutma, now, to manage these situations and to bring them to happy outcomes.

Being an honest man, he acknowledged, too, his own errors of judgement. Tillman still lived: Kuutma had to bear the responsibility for that disastrous circumstance and he had to put it right.

He could almost make the argument for going in himself at this point. But the strength of his desire to do so had to be taken as a warning that he must not: his emotions were involved, and therefore he couldn't trust his judgement.

But Abidan's team was depleted now. Hirah had been shot in the chest and in the hand. Both wounds had already partially healed, another side effect of kelalit, but in this, as in everything else, the drug both gave and took away. The chest wound was fine, but the bones and muscles in the hand had become twisted as they healed and set into an unnatural position. The hand was useless.

Kuutma pondered, and reached a decision. 'You must take Hirah back to Ginat'Dania,' he told Abidan. 'He needs to rest and to be with his family. The injury done to him – to his soul, as well as his flesh – will heal faster there.'

Abidan looked dismayed. 'But *Tannanu*,' he said, 'the mission ...'

'I know, Abidan. There's work still to be done. A lot of work, perhaps, now that this Tillman is involved.'

'Tillman?'

'The man who shot Hirah. That was who it was.'

Abidan's tone expressed shock and perhaps alarm. 'But Tillman – Leo Tillman – was the man who—'

'Abidan.' Kuutma silenced his Messenger with that gentle rebuke.

'Yes, *Tannanu*?'

'Go back to Ginat'Dania. Take your team with you. I have another team in that country now. They pursued Tillman from France and will welcome another chance to engage with him.'

'May I ask, *Tannanu*, what team is this?' Abidan was cautious, but unhappy. It hurt to be taken out of the line, as Kuutma well understood.

'Mariam Danat's team. Mariam herself, Ezei and Cephas. Go well, Abidan, and be proud of what you've done.'

He switched off his phone and stared at the wall facing him. It was adorned with a painting of Napoleon's retreat from Moscow as imagined by a Soviet painter, whose signature at the bottom of the canvas was illegible. In the painting, Napoleon slumped in his saddle, staring hollow-eyed at an endless corridor of swirling snow. Behind him, a line of defeated, dying French soldiers stretched into infinity, all wearing variations on the same expression: the humiliation of the conqueror magnified and duplicated magically, as in a hall of mirrors.

Kuutma thought about seeing that expression on Tillman's face.

'*Will he forget you?*'

'*Never.*'

'*Then he's a fool.*'

'*Yes. And you should be afraid of him. He's far, far too stupid to know when he's lost, or when to surrender. He'll ignore that note. He won't stop coming. He'll look into your eyes, some day, Kuutma, and one of you will blink.*'

201

Mariam's team. He'd brief them personally. And although he wouldn't go to London himself, he'd watch over their shoulder and steer them; not directly at Tillman because the Rotgut situation was the problem that demanded an immediate resolution. But clearly, Tillman had put himself on a collision course with Rotgut.

One way or another, whatever momentum he had accumulated and whatever resources he brought, he would be destroyed by that collision.

24

It was a partial victory, and if Kennedy had had anything left to lose in the department, it would have been a pyrrhic one. Whereas Summerhill had been content before to leave her to her own devices and to the not-so-tender mercies of the bear pit, now he was on her case in a much more committed, much less casual way.

The incident committee gave her a clean bill of health, and they kept her on the case, but there was no question now of a mere sergeant heading it up. Summerhill had already appointed himself as case officer, which meant she'd be working directly under him. Right in his gunsights, every hour of the day.

Rather than just replacing Harper, he'd widened the case team to five, not counting himself. The other sergeant, to rub her nose in her failure as thoroughly as possible, was Josh Combes. Three constables rounded out the roster, and she knew them all. Stanwick was Combes's lap-dog, pure and simple; McAliskey was competent but ground-hugging, and had failed sergeant twice; Cummings was his own man, good at everything except sharing.

Kennedy printed out a hard copy of the case file and took it home with her that evening. After a long, hot bath she sat down on the sofa in a robe, her wet hair wrapped in a towel, to read it. The file wasn't much thicker than she had left it the week before. The next briefing meeting – or shout, as they tended to be called in Division – was at nine the following morning. Summerhill would be looking to trip her up if he could, and everybody else there would enjoy the show.

Her father came and looked over her shoulder as she read, which was kind of unusual. He never picked up a book any more, or even a magazine. His attention span just wasn't long enough to last out the average sentence. But the week she'd been away had left him unsettled. Her sister, Chrissie, had stepped in (with very bad grace) to look after him. She'd taken him down to her own place in Somerset, where nothing was where he remembered it being, and where he had last claim on the TV after her cricket-obsessed husband and teenage daughter. It must have been pretty miserable for him. Although if Alzheimer's had an upside, it was that past miseries presumably stopped being real as soon as you forgot them.

'Murder case, Dad,' she said, deadpan. 'Multiple. Multiple and then some. Four civilians dead and one cop.'

She thought he might react to that – to the death of an officer – but he didn't seem to hear her. He wasn't trying to read the file, either. He was just standing close to her, watching her intently. Maybe he'd missed her and was reassuring himself that she was back. Whatever it was, she didn't like it much.

'Swiss rolls in the kitchen, Dad,' she said. He liked the little mini-rolls, the ones that came individually packed in foil, and his response to the phrase was Pavlovian. He shuffled off to look for them, leaving Kennedy to immerse herself in the file.

The working assumption on all three of the original deaths – Barlow's, Hurt's and Devani's – was now murder. The car that had run Catherine Hurt down had been found by chance, abandoned a hundred miles away in Burnley, having (as it transpired) been stolen only a few streets from where Hurt was killed. It stank of disinfectant and proved to be clinically devoid of fingerprints or fibres. CCTV footage showed the journey north, but wouldn't resolve far enough to show anything of the driver.

The clothes fibres she and Harper had found at Prince Regent's had correlated exactly with what Barlow was wearing at the time of his death, so the hypothesis of him having been dragged up the staircase unconscious looked robust.

From ballistics reports, the gun that had killed Sarah Opie was a Sig-Sauer P226, a popular gun with armies and police forces around the world. The ammunition had been bought in Germany as part of a large shipment originally intended for the Israeli Defence Force. As far as could be determined, the container in which it had been shipped from Lübeck to Haifa had gone astray somewhere and was never unloaded.

Emil Gassan had now been placed in protective custody. When he'd heard about the events at Park Square, he hadn't even protested much – although he seemed to be in shock at the thought that Stuart Barlow's work had inspired something beyond mild contempt.

Some gesture had been made towards mounting a search for Michael Brand, but he hadn't been found. He'd paid by cash at the Pride Court Hotel, had shown a fake photo ID identifying him as a lecturer at the University of Asturias in Gijon, where – of course – nobody had ever heard of him. Combes now had an alert out on him, but so far he hadn't surfaced. Descriptions of the two men who killed Dr Opie and Chris Harper, and of the third man who appeared from nowhere in the Park Square car park to tackle them, had likewise been circulated: no takers.

Footprints. Number plates. Roadblocks. Searches. No fingerprints or clear sightings. Like trying to clutch at ghosts, but she couldn't fault Summerhill's methods. He seemed to be doing everything he could do, everything she'd be doing in his place.

The phone rang, breaking a train of thought that was going round in a tight, unavailing circle. She picked up, hooked the receiver absently under her jaw: it was probably going to be someone from Division, with some bullshit coming out of the incident committee.

'Kennedy,' she said, shortly.

'Good name,' said a male voice. 'Any Irish in the family?'

It was a voice she knew, without being able to place it immediately. It was also a voice that made her come upright, sending some of the papers from the case file sliding from her lap on to the sofa and the floor.

'Who is this?' she asked. The answer came into her head even as the man told her.

'We met at the Park Square campus. A week ago. I was the one who wasn't trying to kill you.'

A pause, while she thought about how the hell to answer that. *Go for the obvious.* 'What do you want?'

No pause at his end. 'To talk.'

'About what?'

'The case.'

'What case?'

The man breathed out loudly, sounding annoyed or impatient, she couldn't tell. 'I was a good Catholic boy,' he said. 'But nobody's asked me to recite the catechism in a long time. I'm pretty much up to speed on what you've been doing, Detective. That's why I was at Park Square in the first place, watching you try to make an unarmed arrest on two stone killers. I know about Barlow's murder, and I know it's part of a pattern – although you haven't managed to sort out a motive yet or a link between the victims besides the obvious one that they all knew each other. I know that you've been in a firestorm because your partner died, and I know you're not running the show any more. But I'm guessing you know more about what's been happening than any of these other guys who jumped on board last week. Plus I like to think we've broken the ice already, so it seemed to make sense to call you first.'

It was Kennedy's turn to breathe hard. 'Look,' she said, 'I'm grateful for what you did. It got me out of a tight spot. But with respect, all I know about you is that you can handle a gun and you don't bother with a warning shot or a challenge. That could make you a lot of things, and cop isn't one of them.'

'I'm not a cop. Got some good friends who are, though, and a lot more who used to be.'

'So you're what? Somebody's hired security?'

'No.'

'Military?'

'Not exactly.'

'Corporate muscle of some kind?'

'We're getting into that catechism territory again. If we're going to talk, the phone's not the best way to do it.'

'No? Where, then?'

'There's a café up by the Tube station. Costella's. I'll be there in five minutes. Gone in about seven.'

'That doesn't give me much time, does it?'

'No, it doesn't. Specifically, it doesn't give you the time to set up any surprises for me. Seriously, Detective, we could do each other some sizeable favours, but I'm not asking you to trust me and I'm not stupid enough to trust you. Wait for me outside the café, be alone, and bring your cellphone. We'll take it from there.'

She heard a click and the line went dead.

Kennedy considered her options, but she was hauling on

jeans and a sweater, street shoes, as she did it. Nothing she could do about her hair, which was only half-dry and as wild as a haystack. She corralled it into a baseball cap and ran upstairs to Izzy's.

Izzy was on the phone, unsurprisingly. 'Well, I *like* them big,' she said, looking at Kennedy but talking to whoever was on the other end of the line. 'I like them *very* big. Tell me you're touching it now, lover.' Kennedy held up both hands, fingers spread. Ten minutes. Izzy shook her head violently but Kennedy already had a twenty-pound note in her hand. Izzy changed her mind mid-shake, snatched the note and waved to Kennedy to *go, go go*.

Kennedy went.

25

Kennedy got to the Costella Café around about the end of the seventh minute. The place was empty – it was small enough so that there wasn't anywhere someone could sit without being visible from the street – and nobody was waiting outside to meet her. She turned a slow circle on the pavement, scanning everyone in sight, but none of them looked remotely like the brick shithouse of a man who she'd met so briefly the week before.

Her mobile rang just as she was completing the circuit.

'Kennedy.'

'I know. I can see you. Walk to the end of the street. There's a church. Go inside. Buy a candle and light it.'

'You being a nice Catholic boy.'

'Oh, I was lying about that. The candle's just to give me time to walk around the building a couple of times – see if anyone's following you.'

'I'm not trying to set you up. If I were, I'd do it with a wire, not with a tail.'

'Assuming you had a wire lying around the house, sure. Actually, I'm giving you the benefit of the doubt on that one, Detective. The people I'm worried about right now aren't the people on your team.'

Kennedy walked to the church – a nondescript modern building in yellow brick – and did as she'd been told to do. Lighting the votive candle and putting it into the wire rack in the side aisle felt like a meaningless act – she'd never believed in any god, or any other kind of free-floating power – but she found herself, to her own surprise, slightly queasy about going through the motions. Harper's death was too recent, too fresh in her mind. This pantomime of devotion felt in bad taste, somehow – like a joke at his expense, or her own.

With the candle in place, she turned around, half-expecting to find that the big man had appeared soundlessly behind her, but she stood alone in the church.

Kennedy waited, feeling a little ridiculous. Her phone didn't ring again and nobody showed. After five minutes, she went outside by the same door she'd entered. The big man was leaning against the wall just beside the door, hands thrust deep into the pockets of a black donkey jacket. Right then he looked less like an avenging angel than a brickie or a navvy, innocuous for all his bulk. His weathered face revealed nothing. 'All right,' he said to her. 'We seem to be alone.'

'Great,' Kennedy said. 'What now?'

'A drink,' the big man said. 'In a very noisy pub.'

The Crown and Anchor on Surrey Street was heaving, so it fitted the bill just fine. The drink turned out to be whisky and water, which the big man – who'd introduced himself as Tillman – bought for her without asking. She didn't touch it, but then he didn't touch his, either. It seemed to be just a bit of protective camouflage. So was the noise, Tillman explained.

'You can't do much about phase grid microphones,' he said. 'Or lip readers, for that matter. But neither of them is going to have an easy time of it in a place like this. You need clear air to aim through or a clear line of sight.'

'So you still think I'm being followed?' Kennedy asked him, half impressed and half bemused. Whatever else he might be, it was clear that this man was serious about watching his back.

Tillman shook his head. 'No. I'm pretty certain you're not. They weren't after you in Luton, were they? They wanted the computer woman – the last one on the list. I was the only one following you – because I thought you were following someone else. Someone I've been after for a long time.'

Kennedy gave Tillman a narrow look. 'You said Sarah Opie was the last one on the list. Whose list? And how would you know?'

'Just an inference,' Tillman said. 'You haven't gone chasing after anyone else, so you don't think anyone else is in danger. I'm not saying you're right. I'm just saying you seem to think it's over for now. That there won't be any more killing.'

Tillman watched her expectantly, waiting for her to confirm or deny. She did neither, just met the stare and left the ball in his court.

'So what's it about?' he asked her at last. 'Barlow was the first – or the first you found. They were working together on something. And it got them killed. That's the working hypothesis.'

'That sound you hear,' Kennedy told him, coldly, 'is me not talking. You've got the advantage, Tillman. You're telling me things you shouldn't know about my own case – things we haven't told the public or anyone outside the division. I'm not saying a word until you tell me how you know those things. I'm certainly not going to assume that since you're already halfway down the slipway I should tow you the rest of the distance.'

Tillman nodded tersely, conceding the point. 'Okay,' he said. 'That's fair. Michael Brand.'

'What about him?'

'You're looking for him. So am I. The difference is that you've been looking for him for about ten days. I've been looking for him for thirteen years. Did you ever do that thing people do in movies, of stretching a hair across your door or wedging a matchstick in the jamb so you can tell if anyone's been in your room while you were out?'

'Not so far,' Kennedy said. 'I might try and get into the habit.'

'I've been doing it for years, Detective. All sorts of hairs, and matchsticks, wedges of cardboard, tin cans and bits of string. My own little network, stretching backwards and forwards and all over the place, just to let me know when Michael Brand pops up. I've got friends, and friends of friends, in odd little oases around the world, watching the information as it flashes by on the superhighway. Bits of viral code in online databases. Old-fashioned cuttings services in a couple of dozen countries where computers are still a bit of an oddity or where I just want that extra bit of assurance. Michael Brand is an obsession with me, you see. He doesn't get out much, but when he does I want to know about it. So when he turned up in your investigation, I turned up too. That's the short answer.'

Kennedy was nonplussed. Not very much about the speech had sounded sane, even though Tillman delivered it in a calm and reasonable tone of voice. She didn't reply. After a moment or two, by way of a distraction, she picked up her whisky and took a sip. It wasn't nice at all, but it beat staring at Tillman in the way you stare at the nutter on the bus.

He laughed, a little ruefully, as if he'd read her expression in any case. 'Okay,' he said. 'Maybe that needs a little context. You see, I lost my wife and kids, a few years back.'

'I'm sorry,' Kennedy said – the automatic, meaningless response. 'How did they . . . '

'How did they die? They didn't. I just lost them. I came home

212

one night and they weren't there. The house had been cleaned out, from top to bottom. Thirteen years ago. I'm still looking.'

He sketched it out for her. The official stonewalling; the police's refusal to mount an investigation; his grief and fear and confusion; his fruitless searching and skirmishing; and his realisation at last that he needed a different approach entirely if he was ever going to get beyond square one.

As she listened, Kennedy assumed, at first, that Tillman was like any man still in love with a partner who's outgrown him. But his absolute conviction began to get to her. Thirteen years is a long time to spend in denial, and for that matter a long time to play hide and seek with three kids. A woman alone could hide easily enough. A woman with three children would have to register them with doctors, dentists, school boards, care services of all shapes and descriptions. They'd be a cluster, distinctive and easy to find. Unless they were dead, of course. She didn't mention this possibility, but again Tillman seemed to anticipate her thoughts.

'She left a note,' he said. 'Asking me not to follow. And there was a sort of logic ... no, I mean a sort of signature, in the things that were taken. I said the house was cleaned out, but it wasn't quite like that. A few things were left behind: a few little things, that didn't matter. Books. Toys. Clothes. But that was the point. All the things that were left were things that didn't matter. Things that the kids wouldn't miss. The favourite books, the favourite toys, the clothes they liked to wear, and that still fitted them okay, all those things were taken. It was Rebecca's choice, and she got it exactly right, except for ... ' His voice tailed off.

'Except for what?'

'Nothing. Nothing important.'

Kennedy shrugged. 'Okay. But then, where does that leave you, Tillman? It means she went of her own free will, right?'

'No,' he said, bluntly. 'It means she knew they were going to be alive and they were going to be together. She took all the things they'd need, for a life somewhere else. But I don't believe – I can't make myself believe – that a life without me was what she wanted. And even if it was possible to be wrong about that, Detective, I'd still want to find her and ask her why. And I'd still want to find my kids again. But I'm not wrong. Rebecca went because she didn't have a choice. And she left me a note telling me not to look for her because she didn't think I'd ever be able to find her or bring her back from where she was going. She was trying to spare me at least some of the pain.'

He stopped, watching her closely. It seemed to be important to him that she should accept all this on his bare word. Kennedy ducked the issue.

'Michael Brand,' she reminded him.

Tillman nodded reluctant approval. It was the right question, as far as it went, sticking to the business of why they were here. Why they were talking at all. 'Rebecca saw him,' he said. 'She arranged to meet him – or the other way around, more likely. He called and asked her to come and see him. At a Holiday Inn about five minutes' walk from the house, where he was registered as a guest. It was the same day they left.

'And she went. She met him. The desk clerk knew Brand by sight – a guy in his thirties, he said, with a shaved head and a really hard look about him, like he might be police or ex-army. I showed the clerk a photo of Rebecca, and he remembered seeing her with Brand. I don't know what happened between them; what he told her. But whatever it was, they left together. Went back home, I guess, where Rebecca started packing. That was the last time I saw her. Saw any of them.'

Tillman's tone stayed level through this recitation. Kennedy couldn't guess what effort that cost him. If he was still searching thirteen years later, these events he was describing were, collectively, an open wound that had subsumed his whole life. She knew, too, as Tillman had to know, that even if he was right on every count, it didn't mean that his family were still alive right now, or were still alive an hour after they left the house. It only meant that Rebecca had believed they would be. He could be chasing a ghost: four ghosts, or five if you counted Brand.

And obviously, once you started thinking about it, Brand was the weakest point in the whole house of cards.

'It can't be the same man,' she said. 'Your Michael Brand, our Michael Brand ...'

'Why not?'

'Well, why should they be? Your Michael Brand has hole-in-corner meetings with married women in cheap hotels. My Michael Brand lies his way on to academic message boards, pops up at history seminars like ...' she groped for a simile '... the comet before a plague. He presides over mass murder, then disappears. They don't have a whole lot in common, Tillman. And it can't be that unusual a name. Seriously, what are the odds that your man is our man?'

Tillman was swirling the whisky in his glass, but still hadn't tasted it. 'Give or take?' he asked her, calmly. 'I'd say a hundred per cent. Even on the basis of what you just said, there's the same MO working: he turns up, he signs into a hotel, he does what he's come to do and then he disappears. Two very different mission statements, obviously, but that's how he operates, in both cases.'

'I still don't ...'

'Let me finish, Detective. Because I promise, you'll like my detective work. I started putting out my tin cans and strings for Michael Brand a long time ago. That means I've had a chance to do some things you haven't done. I've built up a scrapbook. A database, sort of, except that databases are on a computer

215

and I don't get on with computers. These are just notes I've taken, as I went along. Backs of old envelopes, kind of thing. A fact here, a fact there.'

He leaned towards her across the table, fixed her with an Ancient Mariner stare. 'It's not just the name. There are other things he doesn't change. If he gives a false address, it's always the same false address. Garden Street. Or Garden Road, Garden Crescent, Avenue, Mews, Terrace, whatever, but Garden something. Where did your Michael Brand say he lived?'

'Campo del Jardin,' Kennedy murmured. 'You could have got that straight out of the file.'

'I haven't read your file. But I would have bet good money on it. Anyway, there's more. I met one of Brand's contacts in Russia – sorry, the former Soviet Union – who told me the man I was chasing was coming to London. That was how I caught on to your investigation in the first place. But you're right, it could still have been a different Michael Brand. A total coincidence. So I turned over a few rocks and got the address of the hotel he'd been staying at.'

'The Pride Court. Bloomsbury.'

'Exactly. Did you go take a look at the room?'

'No,' Kennedy admitted. 'Not personally. One of my colleagues carried out a search.'

'Did one of your colleagues find anything?'

'Not to my certain knowledge.'

'No. Well, I did. I found this.' Tillman reached into his pocket, took out something small and bright, held between finger and thumb, and put it down on the table between them. It was a silver coin.

Kennedy just looked at it for a moment. It was like a sliver of her dream, made solid, and it unsettled her very deeply. She pulled herself together with an effort she hoped he couldn't see, reached out to pick it up – but then stopped and shot Tillman a look: *may I?* 'Sure,' he said. 'Go ahead. There are never any fingerprints on them. Never any spoor at all, anywhere, after Brand has cleaned out. Except for these.'

The coin looked old and worn: the only way you knew it was a coin at all was because it was a small, flat piece of metal bearing the outline of a human head. It was far from circular, far from regular in shape. The head had blurred to the point where you couldn't even tell if it was male or female, but there was a series of tiny bumps across the forehead that could have been some kind of head-dress, maybe a laurel wreath. She turned the coin over. The obverse was even harder to make out: a figure that could have been a bird with its wings folded, or maybe just a sheaf of wheat, and a few symbols that seemed to include a K and a P.

The anomaly struck her after she'd turned the coin over and over several times. Silver oxidised quickly and developed a black patina that was hard to remove. If this coin was so old, why was it so bright? It had to be a reproduction of some kind. But it was heavy enough to be solid metal.

'He left it inside the U-bend of the wash basin,' Tillman told her. 'Your colleague should have looked a little harder. Brand – my version, Brand one-point-zero – always leaves one of these things behind, in any place where he stays for longer than a day. He used to put them some place fairly obvious, like on top of the lintel of a door or behind the headboard of a bed. He still does, sometimes, but these days he usually shows a little more imagination.'

Kennedy shook her head. 'I don't get it,' she muttered. 'If he's going to the trouble of giving false addresses, why leave a calling card?'

'Why stick with the same name?' Tillman countered. 'That's the real question, and I don't know the answer. But he does. I used to think he was playing a game with me. Taunting me, maybe. Like, "I can make it as obvious as I like and you still won't ever catch up with me." But I don't think he knew until a couple of years back that I was even looking for him, and he was doing this all through that time. So it's something else. Something that will maybe make sense when we know what it is he's doing.'

What it is he's doing? Kennedy's common sense asserted itself in one last effort of rebellion. 'There's no kind of mission statement that could include kidnapping your family thirteen years ago and murdering four history teachers today.'

'Three history teachers. One IT lecturer.'

'Still and all. And I don't want to burst your bubble, Tillman, but there were two killers at Park Square. Not one. It's possible that neither of them was Michael Brand.'

'It's certain that neither of them was Michael Brand,' he said. 'I don't think he does his own killing.'

'Then what does he do?'

'I'll tell you. But not for free. I've given you a lot already. You share with me everything that comes up in your investigation – everything you've got so far and everything you get from now on – and I'll give you what I've got.'

Kennedy didn't even have to think about it. She shook her head. 'No.'

'Why not?'

'Because I'm a police detective, Tillman, and you're not anything. I'm really grateful that you stepped in when that guy was about to cut slices out of me, but I can't discuss active investigations with people who aren't on the case team. And more especially, people who aren't even on the force.'

Tillman stayed silent, studying her face. 'You're serious?' he asked her, finally.

'I'm serious.'

'Then I guess we're done.' He held out his hand for the coin. Kennedy held on to it.

'This is evidence,' she said. 'It's relevant to a murder investigation, and you don't have any right to keep it.'

'Give me the coin, Detective. This isn't a one-way street. I came here with an offer, you turned me down. We go back to where we were.'

She opened her handbag and dropped the coin inside.

'Kennedy—'

She cut him off. 'No. By rights, I should bring you in as a witness, if not a suspect. I'm not going to do that because I owe you, and because you've been through enough already that I'd feel bad about adding any more. But you don't get to keep this. Tillman, there's a line. I'm on one side of it and you're on the other. I have the right to hunt for criminals. It's my job. You don't. So what you did to that man – the one who was about to stab me – that makes you a criminal too.'

Tillman made an impatient gesture. 'You're talking technicalities,' he said. 'I thought you might be someone who could see past garbage like that.'

'No, I'm really, really not.' She thought it was important to explain to him, although it was so obvious and basic to her that it didn't even need saying. 'There are bad things I can do and not lose a second's sleep over them, but this isn't one of them. I can't share information with you, Tillman. Not and stay a cop myself. That puts me over a line. A line that still matters to me.'

It mattered a lot, she realised now. Her voice was shaking. Talking about these things had brought up in her mind the complex of emotions and anxieties that wound themselves around what she'd done to Marcus Dell. What Tillman had done to Harper's killer was different – and what her father had done, all those years ago, different again. But somehow the differences felt a little tenuous right then.

She stood up, and Tillman withdrew his hand. 'Okay,' he said. 'Keep the coin. I've got others. You'll have a hard time explaining where you got it, though, and an even harder time logging it as evidence. I'm sorry we couldn't do business, Sergeant Kennedy. If you change your mind, well, you've got my number on your mobile, now, haven't you? But don't call me up unless you decide to share. That was your last freebie.'

The look in his eyes as he said it was what stayed with her. It stayed because it was so much at odds with his words. He talked like a tough guy out of a movie. He looked like a man hanging on the ledge of a tall building as his fingers lose their grip, one by one, counting him down to disaster.

He walked away, leaving his whisky untouched.

Kennedy drained hers.

At home, after thanking Izzy and putting her dad to bed, Kennedy went back to the file. She panned its murky depths for an hour or so, without coming up with a single nugget of gold.

But there were things she could chase, all the same: three of them, all told.

There were Dr Opie's last words, as she lay dying. Kennedy had mentioned them in her report, but they didn't seem to lead anywhere and the reference had been ignored. It was difficult to see what anyone could do with it anyway.

There was the photo she'd found in Barlow's office. A photo of a ruined building in a nondescript, anonymous place, with some meaningless strings of characters on the back. Barlow had hidden it; his killer, or maybe someone else, had searched both his home and his office but not found it. Or else – not so good, but it had to be considered – had found it and put it back because it was irrelevant.

And there was the knife.

It took her a long while to get to sleep. She kept thinking about Tillman's haunted eyes just before he walked away, and about his journey: a thirteen-year trek through the wilderness that couldn't possibly lead him to a land of milk and honey. In abduction cases, most detectives counted in three-day blocks. The first three days were fifty-fifty: the supposed victim was about as likely to turn up alive as dead. Every three days after that doubled the odds against alive.

Did Tillman really believe in his crazy quest or was he using it to distract himself from the near-certainty that his wife and kids were dead?

Either way, she suspected, it was only the hunt that kept him going. Like a shark, he'd die if he ever came to a standstill.

26

The morning shout was one of the things that try men's souls. Women's souls, too, for that matter. Summerhill began it by closing one line of inquiry completely.

'As you know,' he said, 'we brought in all of Professor Barlow's computers – the two at the college and the one at his home – on warrant. We gave them to the IT forensic support team to see what they could squeeze out, but they came up empty. There's nothing on the machines at all. No files, no emails, no pictures, not even an internet cache. Someone's done a clean system install over whatever was there, on all three of them.

'Barlow had a couple of external hard drives and they're empty, too. Half a dozen recordable discs, which turned out to be blank, not even formatted. That's all there was. We're going over the paper records at the moment, but there doesn't seem to be anything there that's new, or relevant.'

Kennedy thought about the break-ins at Barlow's office and at the bungalow. Maybe that was all they'd been for: not a fishing expedition but a wipe-clean. If the ITF data hounds, who could not just get blood out of a stone but give you a choice of blood types, had come up empty-handed, then this was professional work. Most people thought that clicking DELETE got rid of a file, whereas in fact it just added a flag to it, allowing it to be overwritten later. Whoever had killed Barlow had been a lot more thorough.

'What about the other victims?' she asked. 'Did we requisition their files and papers as well? I mean, if we're assuming that the motive relates to Barlow's Rotgut project in some way ...'

Combes was sighing and shaking his head, but it was Summerhill who cut her off. 'We're emphatically not assuming that, Sergeant,' he said. 'At least, if the project provides a motive, our best guess is that it was in an indirect way. The project was what brought the victims together – although, even then, there seems to have been an existing relationship through the Ravellers message board. Once assembled, Barlow's team got itself into something that drew the attention of a very professional and well organised crew of killers. Possibly they bought some document or artefact on the black market and accidentally trod on the toes of the criminal cartel they bought from. There are any number of scenarios that might explain this pattern of deaths, and very few of them bear directly on the contents of Barlow's research. People don't generally become murder victims because of an academic disagreement.'

'But if we at least knew—'

'We're not ruling any of this out.' Summerhill's tone was sharper this time: *stop rocking the boat*, he was saying, *when you should be grateful you're even in it*. 'Of course we searched the other victims' computers. Opie's particularly, since all her files had been backed up to the college server and we were able to go back a long way. We didn't find any correspondence with Barlow or any references to his name. We also failed to locate any files or folders that referenced the Rotgut Codex, or the project, or anyone else connected to it. Obviously there are other search parameters that could be applied, but we didn't want to get too deep in among the trees at this stage. You'd be talking, at a conservative estimate, about thousands of pages of material, tens of thousands of emails, possibly millions of words. Until we've got a compass to steer by, trying to read every single word didn't seem to offer much of a way forward.'

Summerhill looked away from Kennedy, caught Combes's eye. 'Let's hear what you've all been up to,' he said. 'Josh, start us off.'

Combes brought them up to date on the search for the elusive Michael Brand. He'd put out a query to major hotel chains in the UK and Spain to see whether the man had ever checked in anywhere else under that name. He'd also mailed out a verbal description and photofit, both provided by the desk clerk at the Pride Court: a middle-aged man, bald, above average height, with brown eyes and pale skin, his accent foreign but hard to pin down.

It wasn't a lot to go on and there hadn't been any ping-backs yet. In the meantime, Combes had also requisitioned searches of airline, train and ferry operational databases, to see if he could map Brand's movements prior to his arrival at the Pride Court, and after. A parallel search of prison and police records had already come in negative. There was no Michael Brand anywhere in the known universe who had a criminal record and made a possible match to their own man by age or description.

Combes was now working through the other members of the Ravellers forum to see whether any of them had met Brand or had any private correspondence with him.

Stanwick and McAliskey had been taking corroborative statements from the students who had witnessed Sarah Opie's death. They'd also gone over camera footage from the college's security system, hoping to find some film of the two murderers either in the computer lab or on their way to it. Their luck was out.

The cameras saved on to disc, and the relevant disc had developed a formatting error, which meant that it could not be accessed. They'd found a technician who might be able to extract some usable data from the disc, but it was turning out to be a slow process. In the meantime, they'd put out identikit images both to the other regional forces and on *Crimewatch* programmes, and were asking anyone who'd seen the two men to call a dedicated helpline. Half a dozen PCs from the uniformed branch were sorting through the hundreds of calls that had come in already.

Cummings had picked up the slack on Samir Devani's death, the only one that could still conceivably have been an accident. By dismantling and examining the components of the fatal computer, he had been able to rule that prospect out, more or less. The power cable had come loose inside the machine and then somehow bent back on itself to touch the casing. The angle was an acute one, and the wire had had to be threaded through the heat sink of the motherboard to keep it in place, so that when the computer was turned on at the wall socket the handsome retro-styled metal casing went live. Now Cummings was trying to determine who had had unsupervised access to the machine in the sixteen hours between its last use and the fateful throwing of that switch.

Summerhill heard all of them out, interpolating questions and suggestions. He kept it fast, kept up a sense of urgency and purpose. Then he paused when he got to Kennedy.

'Anything from your end, Detective Sergeant?' he asked, with suspicious mildness. Nothing had been assigned to her, and she'd only been out of hospital a day. Maybe that glint in the DCI's eye was kindled by the expectation of a 'no'.

'I want to follow up on the murder weapon,' Kennedy said. 'I mean, the other murder weapon. We've got all this intel on the gun, but nothing on the knife that killed Harper. I think it's worth—'

'Wide, three-inch blade,' Combes said. 'Very sharp. Probably angled at the tip. Is there anything else you want?' He talked over his shoulder, without looking at her.

'I think it's worth following up,' Kennedy went on, still talking to Summerhill. 'This Michael Brand had a foreign accent, according to witness statements, and in Luton the assailant with the gun spoke to me in what I'm fairly certain was a foreign language. Maybe all three men are from the same region – the same country. The knife was of a very odd design. It's just possible that it's geographically specific. If it is, we might end up with enough data for a shout-out to another force.'

Summerhill looked unimpressed, but he didn't dismiss the idea out of hand. 'Did you see the knife clearly enough?' he asked. 'Really? Clearly enough to recognise it again if you saw it?'

Kennedy nodded at the flip-chart in the corner of the room, with some marker pens left over from somebody else's meeting. 'Do you mind?'

'Go ahead.'

She crossed to the board, took a pen and began to draw what she'd seen. Behind her, someone muttered, 'Can you tell what it is yet?' and someone else laughed. She ignored them, trying to remember the exact shape of that weird, ugly blade. It had only been as long as the knife's handle, and thicker, and it was asymmetrical, flaring out at the top on one side like one half of the head of a mushroom. It looked clumsy and unfit for purpose, but it had been as sharp as a razor and it had done for Chris Harper on a single pass.

She put the pen back and turned to face the rest of the team. 'Like that,' she said, going back to her seat.

They stared at it. 'Okay,' McAliskey said, laconically. 'It's distinctive.'

'Could be a smoothing knife for plaster,' Cummings observed. 'Or a cake slice. Doesn't look much like a murder weapon, though.'

'I'd like to talk to someone at the Royal Armouries,' Kennedy said to Summerhill. 'Unless you need me for anything else. I'd also like to go back over the Ravellers message board archives and see if there's any information there about what Barlow was trying to do with his Rotgut project.'

'There isn't,' said Combes. 'We already went through that stuff. Barlow didn't put anything up on the boards except that first call for volunteers. Nobody got to hear what he wanted them to volunteer for except the people he chose to be his team, and, oops, we just ran out of them, didn't we?'

'That's enough, Sergeant Combes,' Summerhill growled. 'Yes. Fine. You do that, Kennedy. The URLs and access codes are in the case file.'

'I'd also like to talk to Ros Barlow again.'

'The professor's sister? Why?'

'Because the professor talked to her about Michael Brand, and Michael Brand now seems to be central to the case – whether you think of him as a witness or as a suspect.' She was uncomfortably aware as she made this proviso that it was a smokescreen. After talking to Tillman, she was definitely thinking of Brand as the villain of the piece. She'd need to watch that. 'Also, if Barlow was keeping the project close to his chest as far as the forum was concerned, it's at least worth asking if he talked about it at home.'

Summerhill nodded, but looked to Combes. 'Follow that up, Josh,' he said, and Combes nodded, scribbling a note to himself.

'She already knows me,' Kennedy pointed out, trying not to lose her temper.

'Let's not get territorial, Sergeant Kennedy.' Summerhill clasped his hands together as though about to lead the group in a prayer, then opened them again, palms up. 'Call me if you get anything. Otherwise, case notes on my desk for six. What are you waiting for, gentlemen? Peerages?'

They folded up their tents and scattered. So Summerhill was keeping her on the farm, Kennedy reflected as she walked back to the bear pit. Or trying to anyway. But he couldn't tell her not to leave the building. He could only assign all the promising leads to other people.

Which just meant she had to turn up some other leads.

Her call to the Royal Armouries was answered by an intern, who left her on hold for a long time and then put her through to a Ms Carol Savundra – the acquisitions manager for the collections. Savundra was perfunctory: her tone said that she had a full in-tray, a short fuse and zero time or patience for unusual requests that came in via unorthodox channels. Kennedy didn't have high hopes, but she described the knife anyway.

'Nothing springs to mind,' Savundra said.

'Well, can I fax you a sketch of the blade? It might spark an association – or you could circulate it around your colleagues.'

'By all means,' said Savundra, but she didn't volunteer the number until Kennedy asked for it, and was vague as to when she might be able to get back in touch. 'To be honest, antiquities are a smaller and smaller part of what we do.'

'This knife was used in a recent murder.'

'Really? Well, go ahead and send it in. Perhaps once I see it I'll have a flash of inspiration.'

Kennedy drew the knife again, on an A4 sheet, and faxed it over.

Next she tried Sheffield Knives, where she spoke to a Mr Lapoterre, their principal design engineer. He was a lot friendlier, but had never heard of anything remotely resembling what Kennedy described. He called her back as soon as he got the fax, but only to confirm that he was clueless. 'We do a lot of knives with asymmetrical blades,' he said, 'but that's a new one on me.'

'It doesn't remind you of knives produced in a particular part of the world?' Kennedy coaxed, a little desperate.

'It doesn't remind me of anything at all. It's like – if you found the skeleton of a bird, you'd know it was a bird because the bones would be in the right places for a bird's bones. This isn't anything. It doesn't fit any category I've got a name for. Sorry.'

Kennedy hoped for better from the British Knife Collectors' Guild and the US Office of Strategic Services, which included knife procurement for the American army in its online boast-list, but neither was of any help.

Discouraged, she turned to her other job for the day: the old message board threads of the Ravellers, which other people had trawled before her without result. Kennedy logged on to the forum and used the access code to get into the archived directories. Immediately she saw the scale of the task and realised that – however categorical Combes had sounded – he hadn't been through this stuff. There were seven thousand pages of it, or rather seven thousand threads, each of which just ran on until it stopped. There had to be tens of thousands of posts. Probably a couple of months' work just to read through it all once.

Maybe you could sort it in some way. The site had no search engine, but she knew how to make the department's bespoke engine, which had been written by MoD wonks, search a specific domain. Barlow's nom de forum was written on the file under the access codes: BARLOW PRCL, his surname and his college ident.

Evidently the Ravellers didn't have so many members that they needed to get tricky and postmodern with their IDs.

A first pass showed her that Barlow had posted comments on two hundred and eighteen threads, seventy one of them threads he'd started. She directed her attention to those, first of all.

Immediately she ran into the same problem that Harper had complained about. The subject headers, which in theory stated the theme of each thread, were so arcane that in most cases they provided no clue at all to their possible contents.

AWMC Catal-Hyuk omit/revise?
Medial sigma misallocations by period stat 905
Greensmith 2B won't fly
Proposed sub-fold matches for Branche Codex in M1102

She clicked on a few threads at random. In the older ones, as she might have expected, the Dead Sea Scrolls got a lot of mentions. Barlow picked fights with existing readings, proposed counter-readings of his own, was shouted down or applauded or condescended to.

Then the Scrolls faded out of the picture by degrees, and other things trickled in, the focus still on translation and textual interpretation, but the texts now mostly New Testament – odd fragments of gospels identified by strings of letters and numbers. Barlow's views often seemed to be controversial, but Kennedy couldn't tell why because the arguments were too abstruse and the in-jokes too thick on the ground.

Eventually, she found the thread she was looking for. The header, as Opie had already told her, was: *Does anyone have any appetite for a new look at the Rotgut?* Under that heading, a couple of terse sentences: *I'm thinking of coming at the Rotgut Codex from a new angle – for fun, and for a book I'm writing, not for funding. Hard slog, endless data crunching, possible fame and fortune. Anyone interested?*

It sparked a short chain of comments, most of them pugnacious or derisive. Why go back to the Rotgut? And without funding? Barlow couldn't be serious. There was nothing new to find there, and the codex probably wasn't even a translation, just a mash-up. The positive responses came from HURT LDM and DEVANI [field left blank]. Nothing from Sarah Opie. Barlow promised to get in touch with his collaborators by phone, and the thread petered out after a few more unsympathetic heckles from other forum members. Then, much later – almost two years later, according to the header, and only three months before Barlow's death – another reply appeared, from BRAND UAS. *Very excited by what you've achieved so far. Would love to talk, and maybe get you over a hump.*

After that, nothing.

After that, fatal falls down darkened stairwells, electrified computers, hit-and-run drivers and daggers drawn in daylight.

So how did Barlow reply to Brand? Kennedy wondered. He didn't respond on the thread itself, even to ask for a contact number. Maybe he accessed Brand's profile and picked up his contact information from there. She tried and found there was none. Brand's profile was just a name, nothing else.

UAS, she discovered in an on-site registry, meant University of Asturias, Spain. But if Barlow had gone by that route, he'd have found out at once that Brand was a fraud. Presumably, trusting that nobody would be on a historical forum except historians, he hadn't bothered to do that.

A private message, then. Private messages had a different access code, but the moderator of the Ravellers board had provided that, too. Kennedy opened the archive in a different window, found that the data was stored by member ID. Under Barlow's name, a couple of dozen messages, but not to any member of the project team.

There was a message to Sarah Opie, a little later than the correspondence with the other three team members: *Sarah, you remember the conversation we had at the Founders' dinner? Do you think it would be possible to do what I was asking for, using your own system, or your work machines? Call me, and let's discuss.*

And one message to Michael Brand, dated on the same day as his forum post: *Mr Brand, you intrigue me. I know Devani talked to you at FBF, but I also know he didn't tell you anything. How did you hear about us? Please don't reply through the forum. I'd rather dampen speculation on this than inflame it. My college extension is 3274.*

Nothing after that. Nothing that seemed to relate to the ongoing project anyway. On an impulse, she searched through the other Ravellers' private messages to see if anyone mentioned the Rotgut Codex there. Probably she was in technical breach of the search warrant, but it would only matter if she turned anything up, and she didn't. The Rotgut wasn't a hot topic. Nobody was gossiping about Barlow's big project or speculating about what it was for. Nobody seemed to give a damn. Of the message headers she could actually understand, most seemed to relate to money – research grants, departmental budgets, per diems, bursaries, bids to the Lottery fund, capital allocations, loose change found behind sofa cushions. Nobody had enough and nobody knew where the next pay cheque was coming from.

It was tough all over, except for Stuart Barlow and his little band of irregulars: they'd been doing it for fun. And they were dead.

The day passed in this almost directionless searching, grindingly slow and inert. One of the breaks in routine occurred when Kennedy went over to Harper's desk to clear it of any case-related paperwork that might still be there. Underneath a stack of unrelated intra-departmental rubbish, she found the Interpol data requests he'd filled in on Michael Brand. These were the originals, kept because what had been sent out were faxes. Looking them over, Kennedy found that Harper had made an elementary mistake. He'd only asked to be copied on cases in which Michael Brand had been linked as a suspect or listed as a potential witness. There was a huge middle ground in which Brand's name might have come up in other people's testimony, and she wanted to see those listings too. She sent an amended request – the same form, with a few boxes ticked. Because it was the same form, she didn't need to bounce it back up to Summerhill for authorisation, but she added her own signature and ID at the bottom and – with a brief ache of unhappiness – crossed out Harper's.

She made a few more knife-related calls, with nothing more to show for it, and walked out of Division on the dot of five – the first time in seven years that she'd done so.

Izzy was amazed to see her turn up at the flat before six: almost indignant. 'You're never back this early,' she said, gathering up her things. 'What, weren't there any crimes today?'

'I'm Serious Crimes,' Kennedy said. 'There were crimes today, but they were funny ones.'

As always, they walked to the door together. 'Well, he's in a rotten mood,' Izzy reported. 'He was crying earlier and listening to that bloody awful twang-twang-twang music. He was talking about your mum.'

Kennedy was surprised and disconcerted. 'What did he say about her?'

'He said he was sorry. "Sorry, Caroline. Sorry I ever hurt you." Stuff like that.'

Kennedy would have said she was beyond feeling anything for her father now beyond the mixture of pained affection and half-healed-over resentment that she was so used to. This hurt: it came right on the heels of too much other stuff that made the wound feel raw. She drew in her breath and Izzy realised that she'd somehow put her foot in it.

'What?' she said, distressed. 'I'm sorry, Heather. What did I say?'

Kennedy shook her head. 'I'm fine,' she said. 'It's just ...' But there was too much to explain from a standing start. 'My mother's name was Janet,' she muttered.

'Yeah? So who was Caroline? His bit on the side?'

'No. Just a woman he killed. Goodnight, Izzy.'

She closed the door.

27

They had no shout the next morning. Summerhill was in the building but kept to himself, and the other detectives scattered early and without consultation. Kennedy was left to cool her heels in the bear pit, and service her knife experts once again – without any joy.

Nothing had come in from Interpol, but she could access their online archives and see if there was anything among the older, written-off cases where no interdepartmental clearances would be necessary.

Interpol's digital records service had an overly complicated user interface that required you to fill out a whole raft of often irrelevant data parameters before you could start to interrogate the system. But Kennedy had plenty of time on her hands and was feeling bloody-minded enough to hack her way through the digital deadwood to get to the sap within.

And there was some sap, once she got there. Michael Brands had been involved in petty larceny and date rape, but their ages and descriptions were worlds away from the Michael Brand she was looking for. But ten years ago, in Upstate New York, and then seven years ago, in New Zealand, South Island, there were missing persons cases that tripped the Michael Brand search field.

Kennedy drew down what was available on both cases, and was amazed and appalled by what she found.

The New York case: a woman, Tamara Kelly, and her three children, all reported missing by the woman's husband, Arthur Shawcross, a sales rep for a stationery company. He came home from a week on the road to find the house stripped, his wife and kids vanished into thin air. The day before, a call had been made to the house from a number Shawcross didn't recognise. It turned out to be registered to a Michael Brand, but subsequent investigation failed to turn up the man himself.

New Zealand: Erwin Gaskell, a carpenter and cabinet-maker, had been away from home for two days, visiting his mother, who was recovering from a heart op. He came home to find the house a burned-out shell. His wife, Salome, and their three children, were gone. Because of the fire, and the suspicion of arson, residents at a nearby motel had been questioned. One of them, Michael Brand, had not been questioned because he had never returned to his room to retrieve the few belongings he had left there. He'd been seen talking to Salome Gaskell on the day she disappeared – or at least, someone answering to his description had been seen. It was a pretty circumstantial description, too: the bald head and the dark eyes stayed in people's minds.

Woman and three kids, every time. What the hell did that mean? For one thing, that Tillman might be less crazy than he looked. For another, that Michael Brand was in the women and kids business on a hitherto unsuspected scale.

Sex slavery? But why go for whole families, in every case? And why always for families with that exact configuration? Also, why would the women agree to see and talk to Brand, as Rebecca Tillman had and as it seemed each of the other women had, too? What line was he selling them?

Serial murder? Was Brand a psychopath, recreating some

primal moment in his own past? That sounded ridiculous, if he was the same Brand who was able to call up a phalanx of assassins to take out Stuart Barlow and his luckless team.

At that point, momentarily out of ideas and suffering badly from cabin fever, Kennedy just started to improvise wildly. She did a repeat of her knife trawl, calling up museums and archives and reading down the phone to them the strings of letters and numbers from Barlow's carefully hidden photograph.

P52

P75

NH II-1, III-1, IV-1

Eg2

B66, 75

C45

Nobody admitted to any knowledge as to what they might mean.

Kennedy switched tack, using online search engines. But it was useless because random alphanumeric strings turned up everywhere – in the serial numbers of products and components, the identifying plates of cars and trains, the makes and model numbers of everything under the sun. There was just no viable way to narrow down the search.

She decided, while she was at it, to check everybody else's case notes on the departmental database, to see what if anything had been added to the sum total of their knowledge. Her log-in didn't work.

She looked around. None of the other case officers had returned yet, but McAliskey had left his machine switched on and logged in – a disciplinary offence, if anyone had cared to report it. Kennedy crossed to his desk and opened the file from there.

What she saw made her swear at the screen, eyes wide with amazement.

She wasn't given to storming but her progress from the bear pit to the DCI's office could fairly be called a serious squall. Rawl seemed amazed to see her.

'He's ... he's not taking any—' she began.

'I'll just be a moment,' Kennedy said, already striding past her.

Summerhill was on the phone. He looked up as she entered, but made no other response. 'Yes,' he said. 'Yes, sir. I'm aware of that. We'll do our best. Thank you. You too.'

He put down the phone and looked across the desk at her, shrugging with his eyebrows to invite her to speak.

'You cut me out of the case file,' she said.

'Not exactly.'

'My password doesn't work. What counts as exactly?'

'It's an administrative hiccup, Heather. Nothing more. When you're the subject of a committee of inquiry, all your operational files have to be scrutinised by HR and the IPCC. That inevitably means your security is compromised. All passwords are deactivated and all access codes are revised. You'll get a new password in a day or so.'

'And in the meantime, you turn me into the lady who comes round with the goddamned tea.'

'I don't know what you—'

Kennedy slapped the print-out down on his desk and he looked at it for a moment before realising what it was: a page from Combes's notes from the day before, added into the file with a date stamp of 7.30 p.m.

'Combes saw Ros Barlow yesterday afternoon and she told him to go piss over a five-bar gate,' Kennedy summarised.

Summerhill nodded. 'Yes. Well. Your suggestion of asking her if her brother had ever talked about his work was worth following up. But she proved less than cooperative.'

'Jimmy, she asked for *me*.'

'I'm aware of that.'

'She refused to talk to Combes and she specifically asked for me. When were you thinking of telling me?'

He met her stare, unapologetic. 'If you read the rest of Sergeant Combes's notes, you'll see that he didn't feel Rosalind Barlow had anything further to add to the testimony she'd already given. He recommended against a follow-up visit.'

'Screw that!' Kennedy exploded. 'She asked for me. Do you think that meant she had nothing to say or do you think it meant she thought Combes was a jumped-up little cartoon prick-and-balls with a squeaky voice and she preferred to talk to a human being?'

'Kennedy, I'd advise you to moderate your language. I'm not prepared to overlook outbursts against fellow officers.'

Kennedy shrugged helplessly. 'For the love of Christ,' she said, her voice strained, 'am I on this case or am I in the toilet? If you refuse to give me anything substantial to do, Jimmy, what's the point of my being here?'

Summerhill seemed to perk up at this, as though he'd seen it coming a long way out and felt glad it was finally here. 'Are you requesting a transfer?' he asked. He pushed his chair away from the desk back towards the filing cabinet behind it – which Kennedy knew contained run-off copies of all divisional paperwork, including the PD-012 form that she'd advised Harper to fill in with respect to herself. *Officer requesting transfer because of personal factors affecting work effectiveness.*

She laughed.

'No,' she said, and Summerhill's hand, half-lifted, fell into his lap. 'Sorry to disappoint you, Jimmy. I'm not asking for a transfer. I thought we already had this discussion, and I thought we understood each other, but that was just me being naive, wasn't it? No, you carry on. And in the meantime, get Rawl to cut me a temporary password. You can keep me on a leash if you like, but do not try to hood me as well.'

She stood, and he shot her a look full of suspicion and dislike. 'You're not to speak to Ros Barlow, Heather,' he told her. 'That's not a productive use of your time, and her hostility to this office and this investigation makes her an unreliable witness.'

'I think it makes her a soulmate, but you're the boss.'

'Try to remember that.'

'If I forget, I'm sure you'll remind me.'

She left quickly, so that if the urge to punch something overwhelmed her self-control, Summerhill's face wouldn't be so temptingly close to hand.

At her desk again, she thought it through.

Summerhill was determined to keep her at the margins of things. Probably, in his own way, he felt absolutely at ease about doing so: she'd had her chance with the case and proved at Park Square that she couldn't handle it, leaving an officer dead on the ground. Her last-ditch play after the incident committee met had got her back on to the team, but the DCI was telling her in his own charmless way that this was as far as she was going to get.

That left her with three options.

She could shut up and watch the world go by from the comfort of her desk. In which case, she might as well be dead.

She could dust off her earlier ultimatum and try to twist Summerhill's arm a little further. But she hadn't been bluffing the first time around, and this time she would be. She had just that little bit more to lose now that she had her job back.

Or ...

She took out her mobile, slid it open and thumbed through the call log. She found Tillman's number easily enough: it was the only one she didn't recognise at once. She keyed CALL BACK.

'Hello?'

'Tillman.'

'Sergeant Kennedy.' He didn't sound surprised, but there was an edge of anticipation in his voice; an implied question.

'This isn't an all-or-nothing deal, is it?'

'I don't know what you mean. We pool information, that's all. I'm not asking you to work with me – just to tell me what you know. Let's agree on one rule, though: no lies, even by omission. No holding things back to get an edge.'

'And you'll do the same for me?'

'You've got my word.'

'Okay.' She shifted to McAliskey's desk, where the case file was still open. 'I've got something for you, first off. A freebie because I feel like I owe you one.' She told him about the other two women – names, places, dates and times. She could hear him scribbling the details down, probably so he could check them with his own contacts. He didn't react to the news, though, or not in any way that she could read over the phone.

'Okay,' she said. 'Got all that?'

'Yes,' Tillman said. 'What now?'

'Twenty questions. You go first.'

For an hour, he grilled her about the case. She started with Stuart Barlow, went on to the other known victims: cause of death, the Ravellers connection, Barlow's secret project (which as a pretext for multiple homicides sounded just as ridiculous as it always had), the unknown stalker and the shape of the investigation so far. Tillman asked focused and circumstantial questions at every stage. The sort of questions a cop would ask. What had made them decide that Barlow's death was murder? Had the killers left any fingerprints or DNA traces at any of the

241

crime scenes? Failing that, had they found any physical evidence at all that proved the link, or were they just working from the fact of a suspicious cluster of deaths? Kennedy gave him what answers she could, and admitted her ignorance wherever she had nothing to offer. When Tillman had run out of questions – or at least, had fallen silent – she interjected some additional points of her own.

'We're still working in the dark when it comes to motive, but I'm thinking it's significant that Barlow and his team felt the need to be so secretive about what they'd found – what they were looking for, even.'

'Significant how?'

'I have no idea. But there's an overlap between legitimate historical research and treasure-hunting. You remember those big Anglo-Saxon finds last year – Viking gold, worth millions? It becomes treasure trove if you declare it. Finders and landowners get a reward, state gets the property. Suppose Barlow had stumbled on something like that? And then someone else found out what he had?'

'It works as a motive for murder,' Tillman allowed.

'You don't sound all that convinced.'

'Neither do you, Sergeant.'

'Heather. It's Heather, Tillman. Heather Kennedy. This isn't a cop talking to you right now. I took it as far as I could as a cop. You're talking to a concerned citizen.'

'Okay. Heather. I'm Leo.'

'I know. I looked you up. And you're right, I don't buy that this is just about money. That's a big, all-purpose motive, and people will do more or less anything to get it, but those people in Luton – they behaved more like soldiers than anything else. And they killed three people over the space of two days, in three different ways. They've got reach, and trained muscle.'

'Organised crime cartels can operate like armies.'

'Yeah, I'm sure. But correct me if I'm wrong, don't they also operate like businesses? Import-export, distribution, sales divisions, reliably sourced product and massive turnover. If it weren't for the fact that the things they're selling are illegal, they'd be in the Fortune Top 100. Would they be chasing stolen antiquities? I don't think so. It would be another kind of criminal. The kind who doesn't have worldwide infrastructure.'

'So where does that leave you?'

'It leaves me wondering about Michael Brand, Leo. That's one reason why I called you. I think maybe this case doesn't crack open by inductive logic, like something out of Sherlock Holmes. Maybe we need what you've got.'

'One reason? What's the other?'

'I'll get to that. Tell me about Michael Brand.'

'If you'll tell me one thing first.'

'Shoot.'

'I notice you don't have Brand pegged as Barlow's stalker. You refer to them as two different people. Why is that?'

'Oh, right.' She had to think before she answered. She'd made the assumption very early on, and it had been a while since she'd thought about it. 'It's mainly because Barlow already knew Brand online. At some point – not long before Barlow was murdered – they met. Obviously that gives us a connection, but why would Brand take the trouble to set up this fake persona of an interested academic, if he's going to follow Barlow around like a cheap gumshoe?'

'So it's two different approaches to the same problem,' Tillman said.

'Yeah,' Kennedy said. 'I think it's exactly that. We know someone's been turning over the victims' stuff – houses, offices, computer data. So they're looking for something and they keep coming up blank. Brand cosies up to Barlow. That's the softly-softly-catchee-monkey side of the equation. But he's got one of his people sitting on Barlow's ass in case they can find what they want by following him or frisking him.'

'And when both approaches fail, they kill everyone.'

'And go over their possessions with a fine-toothed comb.'

'Okay.' Tillman was silent for a while. Kennedy waited. Brand was the centre of everything for Tillman, had to be, because of what he'd told her the last time they met. She guessed he was about to touch again on the agonising knot that had become the centre of his life. So she was completely unprepared for what he finally said.

'Brand is a buyer.'

'He's a *what*?'

'Or a procurer, maybe. Someone who sources and obtains things on behalf of someone else.'

'What kind of things?'

'Anything. Everything. There's no pattern to it. Weapons and medicines are the two constants, but all kinds of other stuff mixed in with that. Computers and motherboards. Software. Machine tools. Electronic surveillance equipment. Timber. Vitamin supplements. And . . . in among all that . . .'

Kennedy filled the static-laced silence. 'Women with exactly three children.'

'Yes.'

'All right. So let's assume that what's happening now is part of the same pattern. Brand is trying to get his hands on something else – something that Barlow and his people found, or made, or just knew about. He moved in. He moved his people in. He sweet-talked Barlow, then killed him and ransacked his house. But he didn't find what he wanted because the team didn't leave yet. They're still looking.'

She heard nothing but Tillman's breathing for a few seconds. 'They're still looking,' he agreed. 'But your scenario doesn't work.'

'Why not?'

'Because they didn't try to talk to Sarah Opie, they just shot her down. I don't think this is procurement. I don't think it's business as usual. I think it's something else, and that makes me think maybe we've got a chance here. Brand is an expert at coming into a place out of nowhere, getting what he wants and then disappearing again. He never sticks around and he never leaves a trail. But it's, what, getting on for a couple of months now since Barlow was murdered? And Brand's people are still here. So the situation isn't entirely under his control. It's—'

Kennedy filled in the missing words again. 'Damage limitation.'

'I'm thinking. Yeah. Look, you said there was something else you wanted from me.'

She told him about the knife and her failed efforts to identify it. He sounded happy to engage with a discrete and concrete problem. He made her hang up so she could take a photograph of her own sketch and send it to him via the phone. Then he called her back.

'I met a knife like that just recently,' he said.

'Met it? Met it how?'

'Someone threw it at me.'

'Are you sure it was the same kind?'

'I had to cauterise the wound by setting fire to myself to stop it from bleeding.'

'Okay,' Kennedy admitted. 'It was the same.'

'It never occurred to me to chase the knife itself,' Tillman said, sounding maybe a little unhealthily animated. 'You see? This is why it's better to have two minds on the problem.'

245

Kennedy laughed in spite of herself. 'But we're both clueless,' she pointed out.

'Agreed. But I know someone. An engineer.'

'An engineer? Tillman, my point is that the weapon's origin might—'

'He knows a lot about weapons. He's a real oddball. His name is Partridge. Let me talk to him and get back to you.'

Tillman hung up, and Kennedy gathered her things. Right then, she felt a sort of weird kinship with the mysterious Michael Brand. If he was involved in damage limitation, trying to corral a difficult, messy, intractable situation back under control, then so was she: compensating and correcting for other people's mistakes, and her own; trying to find the one safe course through a minefield she had helped to lay. Then again, there might not even be a safe course.

But she knew where she had to start.

28

'I don't mean to be difficult,' Ros Barlow said. 'I just have a low tolerance for bullshit. Your colleague kept lying to me. And he wouldn't stop, even when I asked him to point blank. So I told him to leave.'

She cut a Danish pastry into slices, spaced them out on the plate with what Kennedy considered an obsessive-compulsive level of care. The plate bore the logo of the restaurant where they'd agreed to meet, in the City, a hundred yards or so from the Gherkin building where Ros worked: *Caravaggio*. It was an unfortunate choice, in several ways: the price was one, the unwelcome reminder of knife fights another.

'I don't think Sergeant Combes would have told you any outright lies,' Kennedy answered, scrupulously. 'But perhaps he didn't give you the full picture.'

Ros snorted. 'He didn't even give me the preliminary sketches. He came in with a lot of self-important blather about how the investigation was a lot wider now than it had been, and it was really important that he went over my earlier statements to make sure I hadn't missed out anything ... what was the word he used? ... anything material. But when I asked what had happened to change things, he wouldn't give a straight answer. I said I thought you were leading the case, and he laughed and said no. Just no – but as though he could say a lot more if he wanted to. I asked what no meant, and he tried to slap me down like a schoolgirl: that wasn't really my concern, and he was there to go over my statements, and he only had a limited amount of time, and – this was the one that did it – if I cared about catching my brother's murderer, I'd do as I was told and let him do his job. So then I dug my heels in.'

Kennedy nodded. It wasn't unpleasant at all to imagine that scene. 'It's true about the investigation getting wider,' she said, choosing her words carefully. She told Ros about the other deaths – most of them anyway. She found herself skirting around what had happened to Harper. Ros had read about it in the papers, though, and knew the rough shape of what Kennedy was leaving out.

'Were you there?' she asked. 'When the other man died? This Constable Harper?'

'I was there,' Kennedy said. 'Yes. Sarah Opie was the last member of your brother's project team left alive. We didn't know that when we got there, but it became clear as we talked. We decided to take her into protective custody, but we'd left it too late. They got her, too.'

'Right in front of you,' said Ros, looking at her searchingly.

'Right in front of me,' Kennedy agreed. She knew this was sympathy, not accusation, but it was still hard to keep her voice level, her emotions locked down. Ros seemed to see the strain she was under. She didn't say any more about Harper.

'Why go after Dr Opie just then?' she asked instead. 'After so long a wait, I mean? I thought the other deaths were all ...' She hesitated, leaving a gap for Kennedy to insert the technical term.

'Clustered? Yes, they were. And I think the answer is that she died because we went to see her. It can't have been a coincidence that the killers were there at the same time as us. They were watching us – either to figure out how much we knew or to fill the spaces in what they knew.'

'Or both.'

'Yes. Or both.'

With admirable composure, Ros polished off half the Danish – three slices, each consumed in a mouthful, in the way people eat oysters, straight down. She touched the sticky tips of her fingers together.

'So there's more than one of them,' she said. 'Killers, plural, not one killer.'

'I saw two,' Kennedy told her. 'And there's a third man floating around in the background – the man your brother met as Michael Brand. We still don't know what his role is, but it's hard to believe it's entirely innocent.'

'And you don't know why they did it? Why they killed Stu, and all these other people?'

'Not yet, no.'

'Do you think they'll come after me now?'

'I don't know that either,' Kennedy admitted, frankly. 'But I don't think so. They didn't come after you the last time we talked. If we're right, and your brother's research project is the key factor, the real link between the victims, then the only way you'd be at risk is if they thought you knew something. And for the moment, they seem to have decided that you don't. Of course, we still don't really have any idea what they're trying to achieve – what their motive is. Until we know that, we can't quantify the risk in any meaningful way.'

Ros considered this for a number of seconds, in silence.

'Fine,' she said at last. 'I'll take my chances. I want these bastards hanging by their heels. What do you want to know?'

'Anything you can tell me. Anything about your brother's work.'

'Stu didn't talk about his work. But you know your bully-boy colleague took his computer.'

Yes,' Kennedy said. 'There's nothing there.'

'Nothing relevant, you mean?' Ros asked.

'The hard drive has been wiped clean.'

Ros's eyebrows rose. 'Then why are you still wondering about the motive?' she demanded. 'They're trying to kill off the book. They have to be.'

'That's still not an explanation, Ros. Not unless we know why. You said yourself there was nothing in this book that mattered – no reputations at stake. The Rotgut has been around since the fifteenth century, right? And it's just another translation of a gospel that already existed in a lot of different versions.'

'Stu said that was the whole point,' Ros shot back.

'What do you mean?'

'That the Rotgut was so well worn, and so worthless. Why did Captain De Veroese give a full barrel of rum for something that wasn't ancient, wasn't unusual and wasn't rare?'

Kennedy shrugged. 'So what's the punchline?' she asked.

'I don't know,' Ros admitted, glumly. 'I just remember Stu saying that to someone he was having an argument with.'

'Who? Who was the someone?'

'He was talking on the phone. I have no idea who to. It was months ago. Most likely one of the others on the team.'

Kennedy chewed the conundrum over. 'It might be something about the document itself,' she speculated. 'Something besides what was written on it. The material it was made of, or the binding, or a hidden message that had been missed ... ' She fell silent, suddenly realising how little she knew about this document that had got five people killed that she knew of, and possibly a sixth. It was a thought that made her feel faintly ashamed.

'Ros, where is the Rotgut? The original, I mean?'

'The scriptorium at Avranches,' said Ros, promptly. 'Brittany. Or Normandy. Northern France anyway. But the British Library has a beautiful photographic copy: every page, in really high resolution. That was the one Stu used, most of the time. He only went to see the original twice.'

Kennedy decided to raise the other thing that was on her mind. 'I told you that your brother's computer had been wiped,' she said. 'Sarah Opie had all her files backed up on to her college's network, and they have been retrieved intact. But we found nothing relating to the project.'

'Could those files have been tampered with as well?' Ros asked.

'We don't think so. To remove every trace of a whole set of files from a large server, without leaving some sign that you'd been there ... it's possible, but it calls for a very high level of knowledge and skill. And if they could do that, the brute-force wipe they did on your brother's computer doesn't make any sense. They'd have tiptoed in and out both times.'

'What are you asking me, Sergeant Kennedy?'

'Well, I was thinking that your brother knew he was being followed and might have known that it was in connection with his research. Is it possible he had another hiding place, either at the cottage or in London, at Prince Regent's, where he could have kept hard copies or discs that relate to the project? If he had a secure stash like that, he might have told the others to erase everything they had in case their machines were compromised.'

'That's a lot of maybes,' Ros observed.

'I know. But is there somewhere?'

'If there is, he never shared it with me.'

Kennedy felt her spirits sink a little. She was down to her last shot – or rather, her last two shots. 'Okay,' she said, trying to sound neutral and detached. 'I'd like to bounce a couple of things off you. If they trigger any associations for you, I'd like to know what they are.'

'All right,' Ros said.

Kennedy took from her purse the photograph she'd found under the floor tile in Stuart Barlow's office. She'd transferred it to a clear evidence bag, with date, time and place written on a standard ID label at lower left: a half-hearted attempt to dress up its complete illegitimacy. She put it down on the table and pushed it across to Ros.

Ros stared at the image for a long time, but finally shook her head.

'No,' she said. 'Sorry. I've never seen this before. And I don't know where it was taken.'

'It looks like an abandoned factory of some kind,' Kennedy said. 'Or a warehouse. Do you know of your brother having any kind of a connection to a place like that, or having visited one?' When Ros shook her head again, Kennedy turned the photo over to show her the strings of characters on the other side. 'What about these? Ring any bells?'

'No,' said Ros. 'Sorry. What's the other thing?'

'The other thing is even more tenuous,' Kennedy admitted. 'As Dr Opie was dying, she said something that I didn't understand. She mentioned a dove.'

Ros looked up from the photo, which she still held and was continuing to study. 'A dove?'

'I only heard a few words. She said, "a dove, a dove got", and whatever followed that, I didn't manage to—'

She broke off. Ros was staring at her intently: a stare that seemed either nonplussed or suspicious.

'I'm going to assume this is for real,' said Ros, 'and not some weird joke. Because you don't strike me as the sort of person who plays weird jokes.'

'It was real,' Kennedy assured her. 'Why? Do you know what it was that she was trying to tell me?'

Ros nodded slowly. 'Not "a dove got". It was "Dovecote". Or maybe it was "at Dovecote".'

There was more. There had to be more. Kennedy didn't ask. She just waited and watched while Ros Barlow took a gulp of coffee.

She put the cup down again and it rattled against the saucer, as though her hand had been unsteady. 'Sorry,' Ros said. 'It just brought it all home to me again. We used to go there a lot when we were kids.' She fell silent for a moment, shook her head and looked squarely at Kennedy. 'My parents owned two properties,' she said. 'The cottage, and the farmhouse. It's called Dovecote Farm. It's down in Surrey, near Godalming. Just off the A3100, in fact, and you can't miss it because Dad had this horrendous sign put up. He was a great fan of the Goodyear blimp – so the D of Dovecote has a bird's wing coming out of it, like Hermes's helmet. Bloody ridiculous, but he thought it was wonderful.'

Kennedy said nothing for a moment. She didn't want the excitement to be audible in her voice. 'You said that Stu had gotten to be a little paranoid in the weeks before he died,' she said at last.

'Only, as it turns out, not paranoid enough,' Ros pointed out, bitterly.

Kennedy accepted the qualification with a grim nod. 'So it's at least possible that he held meetings at the farm, for the members of his team. If he thought he was being watched at the college, and if your house had been broken into . . .'

'It would make sense,' Ros agreed.

'Do you have a key to the farm?'

'I've got *all* the keys. Four of them. They're all on the same ring, in the kitchen drawer at home. I would have said nobody had been near them in years. Do you want to come out and collect one?'

Kennedy thought about this for what felt like a long time. 'Actually,' she said at last, with some reluctance, 'no, I don't. I really believe that Harper and I were followed to Luton, and we didn't see the people who were doing it. Let's take the worst-case scenario. If they're still watching what I'm up to, they know we're meeting up now. It seems insane to talk like this but you said yourself that your brother's paranoia wasn't enough to save him. Let's make sure you don't go the same way.'

Ros didn't exactly take this in her stride, but she seemed to accept the logic. 'All right,' she said, her tone almost matter-of-fact. 'What did you have in mind, then?' She handed the photo back across the table to Kennedy, and Kennedy returned it to her purse.

'Do you send stuff out by courier, when you're at work?' she asked, still rummaging in the purse and therefore not meeting Ros's gaze.

'All the time.'

'Take one of the copies of the key into work with you tomorrow. Put it in an envelope and send it to Isabella Haynes. She's my neighbour.'

'What's the address?'

'22, East Terrace, Pimlico. Flat 4,' Kennedy said. 'Two and two make four – do you think you can remember it without writing it down?'

'I work in investment banking, Sergeant Kennedy,' Ros told her, dryly. 'I have to remember currency rates to four decimal places, and they change every day. 22, East Terrace, flat 4.'

'In Pimlico.'

'In Pimlico. You can give me the postcode, if you like. I'm not going to forget it. Or get it confused with the flat number.'

Kennedy gave it to her, then put her credit card down on the table. Ros Barlow pushed it back to her. 'Go,' she said. 'You'll hear from me tomorrow. And I'll settle up here. All of this on one condition.'

'Go on,' said Kennedy. She was on her feet, putting her jacket on.

Ros stared up at her. 'Anything you find, tell me. When you can.'

She saw the unreconciled grief and guilt behind the other woman's eyes, wondered if that was what Ros saw when she looked at her.

'I'll do that,' she said. 'I promise.'

Back in the bear pit, Kennedy wrote up the meeting with Ros Barlow in full paranoid mode, but omitted any details that could imply either one of them had access to relevant information about the case.

You're learning, she told herself, with a sort of fatalistic satisfaction. Which meant, really, that she was going down the rabbit hole: accepting that she now moved in a world where unidentified cabals might be stalking her informants with a view to murdering them before they could tell her anything useful.

Anything useful about what? The answer – a bad medieval translation of a readily available Christian gospel – still made no sense whatsoever. But at the bottom of the rabbit hole, where bottles labelled DRINK ME could change your life for ever, you just rolled with things.

Her mobile, which she'd turned to mute during the conversation with Ros, vibrated in her pocket. She took it out and flipped it open.

'Kennedy.'

'Busy day?' Tillman asked.

'Busy. Not necessarily productive.'

'Maybe the best part comes last. I talked to Partridge – and he's found our knife.'

29

Kennedy spotted John Partridge at once because he was exactly as Tillman had described – and the polar opposite of what his cultured, diffident voice had led her to expect. He was a barrel-chested, florid-faced man who looked as though he could have stepped straight out of an advertisement for premium pork sausages. He wore a grey turtleneck sweater and cargo trousers rather than an apron, and carried a cellphone instead of a cleaver, but the image of a smiling butcher stayed with Kennedy as she threaded her way through the milling schoolchildren and Japanese tourists to join Partridge on the front steps of the British Museum, where he stood out like a monk in a massage parlour.

Kennedy crossed to him and stuck out a hand. 'Mr Partridge?'

'Sergeant Kénnedy?' he enquired, giving her the briefest and most gingerly of handshakes. 'It's good to meet you. Good to meet any friend of Leo's.'

'You're doing me the favour,' she reminded him. 'Where's the knife?'

Partridge smiled. 'It's close at hand,' he said. 'In Middle Eastern antiquities. Come.'

He led the way, and as Kennedy fell into step beside him began what turned out to be a long list of reasons why he wasn't the right person to ask about this. 'You must understand,' he said, 'that your little problem lies far outside my specialism, and doesn't touch on any field in which I'm even marginally competent. I'm actually a physicist.'

'Leo Tillman said you were an engineer.'

'A physicist by training. An engineer de facto, by profession. I studied at the Massachusetts Institute of Technology, in their materials science programme. So my comfort zone is, broadly speaking, the physical properties of objects and substances. Within that field, which is a great deal bigger than it sounds, I have a narrower specialism: ballistics. The past year of my life – more than a year, in fact – has been dedicated to the supposedly obsolete Lagrange ballistics equations, which relate to the pressure of expanding gases in the chamber of a gun after ignition of the primer. Really, I'm as innocent as a child when it comes to edged weapons.'

'And yet you solved my problem inside of a day,' Kennedy said, hoping not to be diverted on to the subject of obsolete equations. 'That's impressive.'

'Even more impressive than you know,' Partridge said, gleefully. 'This falls outside my discipline in so many ways, Sergeant Kennedy.' He turned to smile at her and to watch her reaction. 'It's not even a weapon.'

Kennedy frowned. Harper's messy, drawn-out death rose in her mind, against her will. 'I've seen what it can do,' she said, as neutrally as she could.

'Oh yes, it's dangerous,' Partridge agreed, still smiling. 'Deadly, even. But its significance lies in the fact that it was never meant to wound or to kill.'

'Explain,' Kennedy requested.

The smile widened by an inch or so. 'All in good time.'

Partridge paused in front of an open door. The sign beside it

258

read, ROOM 57: ANCIENT LEVANT. Through the door, Kennedy glimpsed a cabinet full of unpainted clay pots. It was what she had always associated the British Museum with as a child: and why she'd preferred both the Natural History and the Science Museums, and even the Victoria and Albert.

'The Levant,' Partridge said, with the slow precision of a lecture, 'is the area that today comprises Syria, the Lebanon, Jordan, Israel and the Occupied Territories adjacent to Israel.'

'So how long ago was it the Levant?' Kennedy asked. She was wondering whether this was a wild goose chase after all, and if so, how long it would take to disentangle herself from this well-meaning but somewhat irritating man.

'I'm not a historian,' Partridge reminded her. 'I think most of the exhibits here date from a period between eight thousand and five hundred years before the birth of Christ. Ideally, I'd have liked to show you a later example of your asymmetric blade, but to do that I'd have to take you to the Museumsinsel in Berlin. There are none here in the UK from the appropriate period.'

He stepped into the room, and again Kennedy followed. They walked past the pots, past stone slabs with bas-relief sculptures carved into them, before stopping in front of a cabinet full of metal tools.

'The second shelf,' Partridge said, but Kennedy had already seen it. In spite of herself, and in spite of knowing that Partridge didn't need any confirmation, she raised a hand and touched the glass, pointing. 'There,' she said. 'That one.'

In terms of physical condition, it was completely unlike the weapon that had sliced through her shoulder, had ended Harper's life. Age had eaten it. The discoloured surface had become pitted with verdigris to the point where you couldn't even tell what the original metal had been, the handle worn away to a slender spike. But the blade had the exact shape that stood out so clearly in her memory: very short, almost as wide as it was long, and with an asymmetric extension at the tip, rounded on top and hooked underneath.

Now that she saw it in cold blood, it looked a bit ridiculous. What was the point of such a piddling little knife? And what was the point of the rounded extrusion at its tip, where you'd expect it to narrow to a point? But something constricted in her chest as she stared at it, squeezed out her breath in a short huff. It wasn't fear: she had been afraid when the Park Square assassin had pointed the gun at her. This knife, though it had killed Harper and taken a tithe out of her, she only hated.

'What is it?' she asked Partridge. She was relieved to find that her voice was level, the emotion locked down inside her for later disposal 'It's a razor,' Partridge said. 'A man would use it to shave and sculpt his beard. That one is bronze, and as you can see from the accompanying notes it was found in a tomb at Semna. But the design is most commonly associated with a later era and a different part of the Middle East.'

He turned to face her, clasping his hands behind his back. 'During the Roman occupation of Israel-Palestine,' he said, 'the conquered Jews were forbidden to carry weapons. But you couldn't be arrested for carrying your shaving gear. Not at first, anyway. So freedom fighters took to walking abroad with razors like this in the sleeves of their robes. When they passed a Roman soldier or civil official, the razor could be put to immediate use and hidden again in the space of a few seconds. An assassin's tool, and a very effective one. The Roman term for a short-bladed knife was a *sica*, and so the insurrectionists who used these weapons came to be called *Sicarii*: knife-men.'

'But that was two thousand years ago,' Kennedy said.

'More or less,' Partridge agreed. 'And if you want to know anything further about your blade's historical context, I'm afraid

260

I won't be able to help. We've already exhausted my knowledge of that subject. But not – not quite – my knowledge of the object itself. Shall I tell you how I was able to recognise your blade, in the end? I mean, why it has something of a profile in contemporary weapons theory, despite its great antiquity?'

'Please,' Kennedy said.

'Because of its aerodynamic properties. It belongs to a class of bladed objects that can be thrown at a target and hit it without spinning end over end. The modern flying knife is the most famous example. That was designed by a Spanish engineer, Paco Tovar, who wanted to avoid the annoying habit most knives have of occasionally hitting the target handle-first. His knife uses longitudinal spin to impart stability and is thrown in very much the same way as a cricket ball. The *sica* doesn't spin longitudinally, and was never designed to be thrown, so it's a little mysterious why it should be so steady in flight. It turns out to depend on the blade's unorthodox shape. I attended a symposium on the subject when the flying knife was first displayed, in Müncheberg in 2002. I was standing in for a colleague, and had a dreadful time, since my knowledge of knives is minuscule, and my interest in them substantially less.'

'Well, I'm grateful that it stayed in your mind, despite that,' Kennedy said, sincerely. 'Mr Partridge, are you saying that this property – the flying straight – is fairly rare?'

'In bladed and edged weapons, yes,' said Partridge. 'There's usually a requirement in such things for the grip to be thick enough to fit the hand comfortably and to allow easy carrying and use, while the blade typically needs to be thinner and lighter. The imbalance normally imparts spin.'

'So would that be reason enough for people still to use knives like this?'

Partridge pursed his lips as he considered the suggestion.

'Possibly,' he allowed. 'But I'd assume that the flying knife does the same job a lot better – as do the half-dozen or so variants that have appeared since.'

'But they're all fairly recent?'

The old man nodded. 'Within the last ten years.'

'Thank you, Mr Partridge. That's really useful.'

'It's been my inestimable pleasure,' he told her, inclining his head in a slight bow.

Kennedy left him still looking at the knives, his brow furrowed in concentration.

She met up with Tillman at the City of London cemetery, where she found him sitting with his back to a tomb and with a gun – the same weird-looking thing he'd used at Park Square – in his lap. He was watching a funeral in progress way over at the cemetery's further end, closest to the gates. From where he was sitting, on a slight rise, he had a panoramic view.

'Do you mind putting that thing away?' Kennedy asked.

Tillman favoured her with a brief, slightly unnerving grin. 'As the actress said to the bishop.'

He made no move to holster the gun, which she now realised he was cleaning. She leaned against the tomb and watched him work. 'You're in a good mood,' she commented, dourly.

'I am.' He was jabbing a bore brush into the barrel of the gun with fastidious care. A small tub of Hoppe's No. 9 solvent was open beside him on the grass, and the pungent smell of amyl acetate hung heavy in the air. 'I feel pretty good about all this, Sergeant.'

'About the deaths, specifically, or just the general mayhem?'

Tillman laughed – a rich, throaty chuckle that had a slightly ragged edge to it, as if he were forcing it beyond its natural limits. 'About where we've got to. You have to understand: I've been looking for Michael Brand for a long time now. Longer than you've been a detective, maybe. And in all that time I've never felt as close to finding him as I do now. We met at the perfect time. What you know and what I know – it dovetails, pretty near perfectly. We're in a good place.'

He slid a wadded rag into each of the gun's six chambers in turn, with minute attention. 'A good place,' he murmured again, more to himself than to her.

'I'm glad you think so,' Kennedy said. In spite of herself, the peculiar revolver – like a lopsided six-gun – had caught her interest. She'd finally figured out what it was about it that looked so strange, and she was trying hard not to ask. She didn't want to show any interest in the damn thing. But he caught the glance and offered the gun to her to look at.

'I'm good, thanks,' she said. And then, in spite of herself, 'The barrel's lined up with the bottom of the cylinder. What the hell is that about?'

'Mateba Unica Number 6,' Tillman said. He opened up the cylinder to show her, sliding it up and to the left. 'Yeah, the cylinder is mounted above the barrel. Means there's very little recoil and most of what there is pushes straight back at you, rather than up and back. There's no muzzle flip to speak of.'

'I've never seen anything like it.'

'It's the only automatic revolver in production. Webley-Fosbery hung in there for a time, but its hour passed. Mateba still makes the Unica because enough people out there want that combination: fantastic accuracy with a real heavy round.'

'I'll take your word for it.'

'You should. I know whereof I speak. I'm only a medium good shot, but with this thing in my hand, I tend to hit what I aim at.'

She remembered the knife at Park Square that he had shot out of the killer's hand. Hard to argue with that.

She sat down beside him. 'So,' she said, 'you got the lecture about the knife?'

'Partridge filled me in. It's kind of interesting, isn't it? Your murder victims were looking at a really old gospel and these killers use a really old knife. Same point of origin: Judea-Samaria, first century AD.'

'It's interesting, yes. I don't know where it gets us, exactly.'

'Neither do I. I'm relying on your keen detective skills to piece it all together so it makes sense.'

'This isn't funny, Tillman.'

'I'm not laughing. This would be the wrong place to make a joke. But I mean it when I say we're close to something.' He sat silent for a moment, working the action of the gun to make sure the cleaning fluid got into every small crevice. 'The truth is ...' he said, thoughtfully. Another pause made her look around, stare at his face. It was blank, meditative. 'This – all of it, your case – came at the right time for me,' he went on. 'I was about ready to give up. I hadn't told myself that but I was losing momentum. Then I got a lead on this, from a guy way over on the far side of Europe, and I came here, I met you ...'

'There's no such thing as destiny, Tillman,' Kennedy told him, alarmed by his tone.

He looked up at her, shook his head. 'No. I know that. No plan. No providence. "No fate but what we make." Still. I'm glad we're on this. I'm glad we're on it together.'

Kennedy looked away. She didn't like to be reminded of how thin a line her de facto partner was walking. It made her own situation look that bit more desperate.

'Listen,' she said, 'I've got a possible lead on Barlow's project.' She told Tillman about the suggestive absence of any

Rotgut files on Sarah Opie's computer, and about Dovecote Farm. But she stopped short of actually naming the place.

'Sounds worth a look anyway,' he said. 'You want to do it tonight?'

'No. Barlow's sister is sending a key tomorrow morning. And I want you to stay clear until we've worked it as a possible crime scene. If you go in first, any evidence will be contaminated – and you might leave behind some evidence of your own. I don't want the rest of the case team to get you in their sights by accident.'

Tillman didn't seem convinced. 'What evidence?' he asked her. 'What crime scene? You're going in on the assumption that the thin white dukes don't even know about this place, right?'

'I'm hoping they don't.'

'So there's nothing to contaminate.'

'If I'm right, that's true. But we don't really have any idea what we might be walking into. And since that's the case, I want to walk into it first. Alone.'

He stood and faced her, his expression serious. 'The deal is that we share all the information we get,' he reminded her. 'It only works if we keep to that.'

'I swear to God,' Kennedy said, 'whatever we find, I'll pass it right along to you. I just want to do a book pass.'

'A what?'

'A pass. By the book. Means go in really carefully and disturb nothing. It may be that nothing's all I'll find. In which case, I come out again and I was never there. Because the other factor in all this is Ros Barlow. If these ... whoever they are get the impression that she knows anything, they might close her down the same way they did Sarah Opie.'

'Put her in protective custody, then. The way you did with that other guy – Emil what's-his-name.'

'Gassan. Emil Gassan. I'd do that if I could. But I'm not the captain of this ship. I'm more like Roger the cabin boy. I've been told to stay in Division and count case-relevant paper clips.'

Tillman looked at her shrewdly. 'So you need me as much as I need you,' he said.

'If that makes you feel good, Tillman, then yes. I need you. And I'm going to need you a lot more if we get a solid lead out of this. Which is why I want you to stay out of it and keep your powder dry until I've given the place a once-over.'

He nodded, apparently satisfied. 'Okay,' he said. 'I trust you.'

'You do?' Kennedy was puzzled. 'Why?'

'I'm a good judge of character. I'm an especially good judge of the characters of sergeants. I was one myself for a dog's age – and I knew dozens more. The bastards were easy to tell from the saints.'

'What about the ones in-between?'

'There weren't that many. Other ranks have their grey areas. Sergeants are polarised.' He'd been watching her closely throughout this conversation, but now he looked off towards the cemetery gates, where the last of the mourners had finally trickled away and the sextons had finished their work.

'If you want to pay your respects,' he said, 'now would be the time.'

'My respects?' She followed his gaze. 'Why? Whose funeral was that?'

'Sarah Opie. Would have been sooner, I guess, but your people couldn't release the body until they'd done the autopsy.'

She had a momentary feeling of disorientation – of being pulled out of normal time, like Scrooge; visiting the way-stations of her life so far, with Tillman as the spirit of screw-ups past. 'What were you doing at Sarah Opie's funeral?' she demanded.

'I wasn't at the funeral. I was watching it from way over here. Just in case.'

'In case what?'

'In case our untanned friends decided to do a stake-out here. For me, or for you, or for anyone else they might have missed. I did a pretty extensive recon before, and another one during. Nobody showed.'

Kennedy had no answer to that. And she could think of nothing she wanted to say to Sarah Opie's grave. In this thing, at least, she belonged to the school that views actions as speaking louder than words.

30

The next morning seemed long. Kennedy spent most of it in the bear pit, reviewing the case notes and finding little that was new or significant in them.

The one area where she did make a little progress was in cross-checking the witness statements from Park Square, as taken down and collated by Stanwick and McAliskey. The first time around, she'd missed the account they'd obtained from Phyllis Church, a desk clerk at the car rental agency who had rented the white Bedford van to Sarah Opie's killers. (That had been yet another promising lead that went nowhere: the men had used extremely good fake ID, identifying them as Portuguese wine merchants in London for a trade show.)

Church's description of the two men was broadly in keeping with everybody else's. She remembered their tightly curled black hair and pale complexions, had wondered if they were related, since they shared these striking features. But she also said that one of them must have been injured because he'd been bleeding.

Kennedy read the account three times, absently highlighting different words as she chewed it over.

It was the younger one. He wiped his eye. Then, when I was photocopying his passport for the file, I looked at him and I thought he was crying. But it was blood. He had blood coming out of his eye. Only a little bit. As though he was crying, like I said, but blood instead of tears. It was a bit creepy, really. Then he saw me looking at him and he turned round, so I couldn't see any more. And the other one said something to him in Spanish. Well, I suppose it was Spanish anyway. I don't speak it. And the younger one went outside to wait. I didn't see him again after that.

The words stirred an echo, made Kennedy's memory dredge up an image of the man who had killed Harper. It was true: there had been red tears running down his cheeks. In the chaos and horror of that moment, she'd forgotten it until now. It could so easily have been a trick of the light. But no. When the other man turned to face her, to aim at her, his eyes had been blood-shot too. The pale face and reddened orbs had given him the look of a dissipated saint, drunk on communion wine.

She did some research on congenital conditions and drug side effects. *Bloodshot eyes; bleeding eyes; bleeding tear ducts; weeping blood; ocular lesions.* These and many variations on them told her nothing beyond the obvious. Almost anything could rupture the tiny capillaries in the eye, from a strong cough or sneeze to high blood pressure, diabetes or blunt force trauma. Changes in external air pressure could do it, too, but any phys-ical exertion would be enough in itself, even in people who had good overall fitness.

Weeping blood was something else again. It had a name, haemolacria, but that just described the symptom. The actual phenomenon seemed to be much rarer – and more often asso-ciated with statues of Christ or the Virgin Mary than with medical conditions. A cancerous tumour in the tear duct could bring it on. So could certain rare forms of conjunctivitis. Kennedy decided to rule out for the moment the possibility that the Park Square killers could both simultaneously have been suf-fering from one of those conditions.

A long article on a fringe medical website discussed the spontaneous occurrence of blood-enriched tears in the adherents of ecstatic religions during rituals where gods were called down into them. It turned out, though, that there were no authenticated instances. The article leaned heavily on anecdotal sources from the Caribbean in the nineteenth century: voodoo bokors claiming to have Baron Samedi or Maître Carrefour riding them, and producing bloody tears and bloody sweat by way of a clinching argument. Stage magic, most likely. Another dead end.

She called Ralph Prentice in the police morgue, an old not-quite-friend with whom she hadn't spoken since the shooting of Marcus Dell and the subsequent loss of her ARU licence. He made no reference to either of those things, though he must certainly have heard.

'I was looking for your help on something,' Kennedy said.

'Go for it,' Prentice invited her. 'You know I'm a goldmine of useless information. And the three stiffs on my table this morning are all a good deal less attractive than you.'

'I got lucky, huh?' Kennedy said.

'Oh yeah. I had a real looker in yesterday.'

'Leaving your sex life out of this, Prentice, do you know anything that could make people weep tears with blood in them?'

'Oestrus,' Prentice said, promptly.

It was completely irrelevant, but momentarily stopped Kennedy in her tracks. 'What?'

'Oestrus. Ovulation. Some women do it every month. If you're aiming to get pregnant, it's sometimes a pretty reliable marker.'

'"Some women"?'

'It's pretty damn rare. Maybe two or three in a million.'

'Okay, what about men?'

'Not so much. I'd imagine you could get an infection of the

tear duct itself that would lacerate the inner surface and cause a little blood leakage. In fact, I'm sure conjunctivitis can bring it on – although just plain old bloodshot eyes are the more usual symptom there.'

'Two men at the same time. The two men who killed Chris Harper last week.'

'Ah.' A long silence on the other end of the line. 'Well,' Prentice said at last, 'leaving aside the scenario where one of them gets an eye infection and passes it on to the other by reckless, close-up winking, two possibilities spring to mind.'

'Which are?'

'Drugs. Stress. Possibly some combination of the two.'

'What drugs, exactly?'

'No drugs I've ever heard of,' the pathologist admitted. 'But that doesn't mean it ain't so, Kennedy. I've got a formulary sitting behind me on the shelf that lists twenty-three thousand pharmaceutical delights – with a good thousand of them coming online in the last twelve months.'

'Is there a list of possible side effects?'

'Always. That's one of the things the book is for. It lets doctors see if there are any contra-indications for a particular patient. Like you wouldn't prescribe venlafaxine to someone who already had high blood pressure because it would make their heart explode.'

'Got you. Well, could you do a search for me, Prentice? See which drugs list haemolacria as a—'

'Twenty-three thousand different compounds, Heather. I already told you that, remember? Sorry, but there aren't enough hours in the day, or days in the week. And I have my own job to do here.'

She adopted a tone of contrition. 'Understood. I'm sorry, Ralph, I wasn't thinking. But there'd be online formularies, right? Places where you could just run this stuff through a search engine?'

'Bound to be,' Prentice admitted. 'But you have to understand, those lists of side effects run to three or four pages sometimes. Any condition that manifested in the trials, even if it only showed up in one patient, has to be put in there. So you're probably going to find that you get a hundred or so drugs where the literature cites blood in bodily secretions as a possible concomitant. I honestly wouldn't bother, unless you've got some other way of narrowing it down.'

Kennedy thanked him and hung up. She went online anyway, found an internet drugs database run by a hospital trust in New York State as a service to local hypochondriacs, and did the search. But Prentice had overestimated: only seventeen drugs listed haemolacria as a rare but known side effect. All were derivatives of methamphetamine, apparently designed to treat either attention-deficit disorder or exogenous obesity.

Around about this time, Stanwick walked into the bear pit, followed a few seconds later by Combes. Kennedy had no real enthusiasm for their company, and they clearly felt the same about her, but as she was waiting for Izzy to come by with the key to Dovecote Farm, she didn't want to leave her desk. She saved the drug list and closed the file, devoted some time to updating the case file with what she'd found out from John Partridge about the knife.

Her phone rang, and she picked up.

'Hey.' Tillman's voice.

'Hey,' she said. 'Can we talk later?'

'I'd rather we talked now. Before you leave.'

'What about?'

'That perennial David Bowie favourite, *The Thin White Duke*.'

She hesitated, torn. 'Where are you?'

'St James's Park. Your side.'

'I'll see you there.'

She grabbed her coat and walked.

She strode the length of Birdcage Walk without seeing Tillman; and the only birds she saw were pigeons working the tourists there. The mayor's office considered the birds enemies of the state and hired Harris hawks from private aviaries to chase them from Trafalgar Square, where their excrement caused an estimated eight million pounds of damage every year. The pigeons just moved a mile or so south and waited for the heat to die down.

But the heat was on full force right then. The sunlight hit the ground, the trees in the park, the back of Kennedy's neck, like a rain of tiny hammers. Bright sunlight always seemed somehow out of place in London: something the mayor's office would no doubt control if it could.

When she got to the corner of Great George Street, and the massive grey fascia of the Churchill Museum, Kennedy stopped. There were a lot more people here, and it occurred to her that any one of them could be someone assigned to her as a watcher: a friend or associate of the men who had killed Chris Harper. She realised then that she had been unconsciously scanning every face that passed her, looking for that tell-tale combination of features – the pale skin and black hair – that the Park Square killers had shared. A young couple walked by, their heads leaning inward, the man murmuring something into the woman's ear, too low for anyone outside their charmed circle to overhear. *Target acquired*, perhaps. A hawk-faced man in shirtsleeves who moved purposefully towards her turned out to be clearing a way for a crocodile of children heading towards the museum.

Kennedy stood at the junction of the two roads, hemmed in by towering neo-classical arcades like the barred sides of a sheep pen. The sunlight on her back felt like a hand pushing her, herding her. She thought of Opie, dancing jerkily as her body absorbed the kinetic energy of three bullets; Harper bleeding out in her lap; the moment of her fatal hesitation as the gun was pointed at her.

This was no way to live. No way to think. She saw her future foreshadowed in the poisoned filaments of fear and uncertainty that turned inside her mind, in the subtle shadow that had come between her and the world: a possible future anyway. She could see herself declining into a more profound uselessness even than her father's, a paralysis like death.

She turned around. Tillman stood leaning against a lamp post a few feet away, watching her with bleak patience. She crossed to him.

'Okay,' he said, without preamble. 'Two nights ago, I check into a fleabag B&B in Queen's Park. It looked clean enough, but last night I go back there and it's already picked up an infestation.'

'Wait. You mean there were—'

'Two charming young men, scarily close to identical, waiting for me to come home. Pale skin, black hair. The same two I met on the ferry, I think. They almost killed me back then, and they'd definitely have killed me last night if I'd walked into their line of sight. And when I tried to double around behind them instead, they melted like snow in the Sahara.'

Kennedy absorbed this news in silence, while Tillman stared at her, waiting for a response.

'The identical features,' she said at last. 'I think it's kind of an optical illusion. They've got a way of moving, and a cast of expression, that's sort of a signature. It makes you ignore obvious differences of age and build.'

'Screw the family resemblance,' Tillman said, without heat but with a grim emphasis. 'Sergeant, they're up on my comms.

That means they're up on yours, too. If you've told anyone about this farmhouse, or put it into your case file, or taken a call from Ros Barlow where she told you the key was coming, I'd lay a pound to a punch in the throat they know where the place is by now and they're there before you.'

'I haven't told anybody,' Kennedy said.

'Or written it, anywhere? Don't you have to do that when there's a break in the case?'

'Yeah, but I haven't. Nobody knows except us, Leo. And I'm keeping it that way.'

'I want to come with you.'

'No. We've been over this. First pass is just me. Then I'll leak you the address.'

'Okay.' He said it with huge reluctance. 'You'll need my new number. I switched, just in case.'

He gave it to her and she wrote it on the inside of her wrist.

'You could be getting in over your head, Kennedy,' he told her.

She walked away without answering. She'd been in over her head ever since Harper died, and she knew that Tillman had been in far deeper, for a whole lot longer. The question now was whether either of them would make it back to the surface before their lungs gave out.

In the bear pit, a FedEx package was sitting dead centre on Kennedy's desk. Izzy had arrived in her absence and handed it in at the street desk with a note for her. It read, GOT A PACKAGE FOR YOU, BABE. GOT A BIG, BIG PACKAGE. YOU WANT TO FEEL IT? DO YOU? DO YOU? – LOTS OF LOVE, I. Kennedy blushed furiously – partly at the thought of Combes or one of the other assholes around her reading the note, but mostly at the thought of calling up the sex line that Izzy worked on and talking dirty to her.

275

She pulled her mind out of the gutter with an effort. Combes and Stanwick, still working on something together off in the far corner, didn't look towards Kennedy or seem to notice her. But even if they'd sneaked a look at the package, they wouldn't have found any mention of Ros Barlow on the address label. It identified the sender as Berryman Sumpter, Investment Consultants.

Kennedy opened the package, reached inside. The tips of her fingers touched cool metal. She took out the key – an old, solid-looking Chubb whose brash golden sheen had faded to a dull mid-brown. Then she ripped off the address label, just to be sure, and put it in her jacket pocket before dropping the envelope into the waste bin.

There was one more thing she needed. She left the bear pit and went downstairs to the basement, where the evidence lockers were. The constable on duty was someone she didn't know: a uniform whose name tag was obscured by the headphones draped around his neck. She'd seen the guy hastily pull the headphones into that neutral position as she came down the stairs. He was so fresh out of training he sat up straight as she approached, like a kid in school. A copy of *Empire* sat before him on the desk, open.

'Sarah Opie,' Kennedy said, writing it in the day book as she spoke. 'Case number fourteen-triple-eight-seventy.' She showed ID and the constable opened up the door in the counter to let her through, then took out the metal bootlocker box with the requisite number and put it on the big central table for her. For a while he watched her sifting through the contents of a dead woman's pockets.

Kennedy got out her notebook, made some annotations. The desk constable's attention moved gradually but inexorably back to a review of a Korean martial arts movie.

Fourteen-eight-seven-eight-sixty was Marcus Dell. Kennedy

could see the bootlocker on a lower shelf, at the same height as her knees. She eased it out a little way, peered in. This was where her life had begun to go off the rails. Like Pandora's box, this one contained all the evils in Kennedy's world. Or at least it was their source.

She opened it anyway. Doing so without signing the day book was a serious offence, carrying a mandatory written warning, but the desk constable was absorbed in his magazine and seemed to have forgotten her existence. She knelt down and stared in at Marcus Dell's effects. She put her hand in and picked up the ruined phone that had brought about his death. Tagged and bagged, inviolate behind cold polythene, its relationship to the world was ended.

Kennedy reached a decision, an accommodation with herself.

'Okay,' she said, a few moments later. The clerk looked up and found that she had already put all the various envelopes and packages back into the bootlocker. He came over and counted them cursorily, then checked a little more carefully to make sure that all the numbers matched those on the docket. All present and correct. He nodded, locked the box and put it back in its place on the shelf.

'Did you find what you wanted?' he asked her. Kennedy nodded. 'Yes. I did. Thanks.'

The clerk let Kennedy out again and she walked back to the stairs. Combes was leaning against the wall halfway up, waiting for her – at the turn so that she didn't know he was there until she almost walked right into him. He gave her a hard, unfriendly look, and he didn't bother with small talk.

'Tell me what you're up to, Sergeant,' he said, with heavy and sarcastic emphasis. 'Or I'll make you wish you'd never been bloody born.'

31

Kennedy kept her face perfectly inexpressive as she came to a dead stop in front of Combes. In the narrow stairwell, he made a pretty effective roadblock. She decided to let him speak first. Maybe he'd run loose enough at the mouth to tell her what he already knew, and she could decide from that how much more – if anything – she needed to tell him.

Combes seemed more than happy to make the running. 'You came down here to look through some logged evidence,' he said.

'So?'

'So if it's related to the Rotgut killings, I'm entitled to ask you what it is you're looking at and why.'

'The Rotgut killings?' she repeated. 'Is that what we're calling them now?'

'I'm serious. You're meant to be working on the knife, and the message board stuff. If you've got new information, or a new angle on what we've already got, you should have logged it in the case file and copied it to the team.'

'Nothing new,' Kennedy said. 'Nothing substantial anyway. I wanted to check through the Park Square stuff.'

'Yeah?' Combes didn't even bother to hide his aggressive scepticism. 'On a whim? Nothing to do with that package you just got?'

'I don't do anything on a whim, Combes. I'm not sure what package you're talking about – or why you think it's your business.'

Combes had been holding the FedEx envelope behind his back the whole time, she realised now. He brought it out and brandished it in front of her face. 'I'm talking about this package,' he said. 'You remember it now?'

Kennedy's gaze flicked from the crumpled FedEx envelope to Combes's eager-beaver face. 'Very curious behaviour,' she said. 'Going through my rubbish.'

Combes was unabashed. 'Berryman Sumpter,' he said. 'The brokerage firm where Ros Barlow works. I had to go see her at the office, Kennedy. You didn't think I'd remember two days later?'

'I didn't think it was your business,' Kennedy told him. 'I still don't.'

'You didn't log this in the case file.'

'Which might be taken to imply that it's not relevant to the case.'

'But you did tear the label off, so nobody could search through your waste bin and make the connection.'

He had her there. 'I'm entitled to do whatever I want with private correspondence,' she temporised.

'And what you did was to come charging straight down here to collect something from stored evidence. That's a hell of a coincidence.'

'No, Combes. That's one thing following another thing. And since the second thing was me working, and this is where I work, it's not that big a coincidence at all, is it?'

He didn't rise to the bait, and his expression was still a gloating half-smile. 'You're on to something, and whatever Ros Barlow sent you plays right into it.'

'You mean, what Berryman Sumpter sent me.'

'Oh yeah,' he sneered. 'Sorry. That was just a message from your brokers, then? New investment portfolio, something like that?'

'Something like that.'

'Except it wasn't a portfolio at all. It wasn't papers. It was something small and solid, like a flash drive.'

'Right,' Kennedy said. 'But we're not playing twenty questions, are we? You want to let me past?'

Combes didn't move. 'Nah, not yet. What did you look at in the evidence? And if you tell me it's none of my business, I'm walking straight to the DCI's office.'

Kennedy really didn't want that to happen. The truth – or selected extracts – seemed the best bet, seeing as Combes could just go on down and check the day book. 'I was looking at the things we got out of Opie's pockets,' she told him.

'Yeah? Why, exactly?'

'In case there was anything we missed. Anything that might give us a clue to what she was doing on Barlow's team.'

'Just going through her pockets. At random. That's bravura police work.'

'Well, I aspire to be as good as you some day.'

'I read what you put into the file after you met with Barlow's sister,' Combes growled, more or less ignoring what she'd said. 'It didn't say anything about her sending you a package.'

'No,' Kennedy agreed. 'It didn't.' She could see no point in trying to conceal any longer the fact that Ros was the sender. It would be ridiculously easy to check. 'Barlow remembered something she hadn't said, sent me a note.'

'By courier? Through a third party?' Combes's voice dripped with scorn. 'Piss off, Kennedy. I'm not an idiot. And I already told you, I was watching you open that thing: there was no note in there. So come clean or I'll go to the DCI and tell him you're playing fast and loose with the reporting rules. Maybe the evidence rules, too, since you're down here. You want to tell me what you got out of the lockers?'

Kennedy showed him instead. She opened her notebook to the page and held it out to him. He took it from her and read: three lines of butchered poetry.

Oh what can ail thee, knight at arms
Alone and palely loitering the sedge has withered
From the lake and no birds are singing.

'I don't get it,' Combes said, giving it back. 'What the hell is it?'

'When we told Opie we were taking her into protective custody, she took a sheet of paper from her desk. It was the last thing she did as we were leaving. She said it contained a mnemonic for her password – a password that protected her files. And that was what she had written on it.'

Combes shook his head. 'The stuff on the college network wasn't locked,' he said. 'We didn't need a password to get to it.'

'Then she must have been referring to some other files, mustn't she?'

'We checked all her—' Combes stopped abruptly as Kennedy held up the key.

'Barlow inherited a farmhouse from his parents,' she said. 'It's called Dovecote. Dovecote Farm. Opie's dying words weren't "a dove got". They were "at Dovecote".'

Combes stared hard at the key. Kennedy could see him making mental connections. 'Okay,' he said. 'So you're thinking what, that Barlow was using the farm as a spare office? That the files on his Rotgut project might be down there?'

'Yes.'

'Why?'

'Leaving aside Opie's famous last words? Because they weren't anywhere else, Combes. And because the killers did system wipes on Barlow's computer, but they were still ready and waiting – and watching – when we went to Opie. There's something they don't want us to see and they can't be sure we won't find it. So maybe it's still out there, and maybe Barlow stashed it at Dovecote Farm. Or Opie did.'

Combes shot her a look of open contempt. 'And you thought you'd sneak off and find it by yourself, yeah?' he said. 'Blindside the team and grab the glory?'

Kennedy lost her patience. 'Sarah Opie died for talking to us, you idiot,' she yelled. 'I wanted to make sure that didn't happen to Ros Barlow. And as far as the rest of the team goes, you drove me into a damned lay-by and parked me. I didn't have any other choice – except to sit upstairs at that desk and watch the sodding world go by.'

She'd leaned forward as she spoke, without particularly meaning to: her face was an inch from Combes's, and he blinked rapidly a few times in the face of her point-blank fury. Then there was a pause for what must have been thought. Finally he nodded.

'Something in that,' he admitted. 'A lay-by is exactly where you are. But it's what you asked for. Even before you got Harper killed, it's what you were asking for.'

Kennedy didn't bother to argue the point.

'Look, it's just a drive down to Surrey,' she said. 'And I'm not asking you to go with me. If I'm wrong, what do we lose?'

'I don't lose anything,' Combes said, holding his hand out, palm up. 'Give me the key.'

'What?' Kennedy really hadn't seen this coming, although knowing Combes as she did, she probably ought to have done.

'How we're going to work it,' Combes said, 'is like this. I'm going to go down there and check this out. You're going to go back upstairs and write up that package from Ros Barlow. Your log entry from yesterday is already in the system, yeah? Okay, so you'll have to say that Barlow thought about the farm after she got home last night, and sent the key over unsolicited – to Division, I mean. Don't mention it was to you.

'The fact is, Kennedy, this does look like a solid lead – only it's me that's going to run with it. I'm screwing you over the same way you screwed over John Gates and Hal Leakey. If you don't like it, complain to Summerhill. Only bear in mind that if you do, he'll probably want to know what you were doing going out to see Barlow in the first place after he'd told you to keep clear.'

Since she didn't offer him the key, he tried to take it from between her fingers. She slapped his hand away, hard.

'It's not negotiable, Kennedy.'

She folded her arms, putting the key well out of reach. 'You're right,' she said. 'It isn't. I promised Ros I'd keep this low profile. I'm happy to cut you in, if that's what it takes. But we go under the radar. If we find something, fine. Then we come back, we open it to the team, and we decide how we're going to play it. Until then, nobody hears word one about this. Nobody else dies on my watch, Combes.'

He let out a loud, pissed-off sigh, rubbing the back of his neck as he stared at her hard: a stare that said, 'What the hell am I going to do with you?' Kennedy felt a strong urge to bring her knee up into his crotch, but realised with regret that this might not be the best time. Particularly as they were now deep into a mutually incriminating discussion as to the best way to falsify the case file. 'Fine,' he said. 'Then we do this. We go down there together – but we tell Stanwick before we go. He doesn't write it up, but he knows where we are in case this goes tits-up on us.'

Kennedy pondered this – particularly the 'we' and the 'together'. It stuck in her throat like a fishbone, but there seemed no way of cutting Combes out now that he knew about the farmhouse and the key. And it seemed as though, in his own patronising way, he was trying to do the right thing. The plural pronoun couldn't have been any easier for him than it was for her.

'All right,' she said at last. 'I agree. But Stanwick has to keep it quiet. If he goes to Summerhill as soon as we're out the door, he gets a brownie point, we get to stand in the corner and Ros Barlow maybe gets her throat cut or a bullet in the head. Are you sure you can get him to keep his mouth shut?'

'Stanwick wouldn't fart without my blessing,' Combes assured her. 'He's a total arse-licker. Don't tell me you didn't notice.'

Combes led the way back up the stairs. Kennedy was tempted to ask why he employed the same tactics with Summerhill that he despised in Stanwick, but she didn't want to endanger the precarious understanding they seemed to have reached.

Stanwick was still in the bear pit, as it turned out working his way through another list of European hotels that might once have welcomed Michael Brand as a guest. He had his phone to his ear and was in the middle of a loud and probably bilingual conversation.

'Well, is there anybody there who can speak ... No, is there anybody there who speaks English a little better than ... What? No, I know you can speak English, sir, but your accent ... If I could speak with ...'

Combes made a hang-up-the-phone gesture. Stanwick only hesitated for a moment. Then he dropped the handset back into its cradle and made an obscene gesture. 'Screw it,' he said. 'There's no way this guy uses the same name twice.'

'You might get lucky,' Combes said, consolingly. 'Listen, Stanwick, Kennedy got a lead from Barlow's sister. She needs someone to go check it out with her.'

Kennedy wouldn't have gone so far as to say she needed Combes, but she looked out of the window and kept her own counsel as he explained to Stanwick about Dovecote Farm. Stanwick really seemed not to get it. He obviously felt that if Combes was going to drive down to Surrey in pursuit of a lead, the privilege of riding shotgun belonged to him. He didn't say that: it was just implicit in the way he kept asking – with only slight variations in wording – what he should say if anyone asked him about this, given that he didn't really know anything about it.

'Nothing,' Kennedy said, breaking in at last. 'You say nothing. It's not in the file yet, Stanwick, okay? It doesn't exist yet. That's the point.'

'And if it turns out to be nothing,' Combes agreed, in a more emollient tone, 'then it never did exist. No harm, no foul. But if there's something to it, then we all share the glory. Equal split, twenty-five per cent each.'

'Three times twenty-five is only seventy-five,' Stanwick objected.

Combes shrugged. 'DCI gets his cut, obviously. Look, Stanwick, we just need an anchor here, that's all. If everything goes okay, we're back before the end of the afternoon and nobody's the wiser. Then we write it up so it happens in real time, take the treasure to Jimmy. Everybody's happy. But if we hit trouble, if we go off the grid for any reason, you know where we are.'

'Yeah, but *how* do I know?' Stanwick said. 'How does this not come back on me?'

'Note on the desk,' said Kennedy, writing it as she spoke on the top sheet of his scribble pad. 'Keep it in your pocket. Find it if someone tries to call us and we don't answer.' She gave

Stanwick the note, which read, *Dovecote Farm. Following up information from civilian informant.* 'Okay? So you're off the hook whatever happens.'

'But nothing is going to happen,' Combes added. 'And most likely there's nothing down there in the first place. We've just got to tick it off.'

Stanwick gave in finally, managing to get his puppy dog stares of reproach under some degree of control, and they hit the road. They took Combes's car, a smoke-grey Vectra V6, and he held open the passenger door for her with cold courtesy. Kennedy ignored it and climbed into the back seat.

'Fine,' Combes said.

'For the first few miles,' Kennedy told him. 'I don't care how stupid it looks. I'm trying to be invisible on this.' She lay down across the back seat, and drew her mac – brought along for the purpose – over herself. If anyone was watching the street ramp, she'd look like nothing much: a payload of old laundry or a rolled tarp in the back of the car.

Combes started the V6 and eased it into motion. Kennedy closed her eyes and willed herself into immobility. She found that she didn't mind the cramped conditions, but lying down across the back seat stirred potent memories. It gave her the feeling of being a child again, surrendering to a journey defined by omnipotent others. She sat up after ten minutes or so, and when Combes stopped for a longer-than-usual red light she took the opportunity to switch into the front passenger seat.

Kennedy would have bet money that Combes would turn out to be the boy-racer type she so despised, but in fact he was a reasonably safe driver, staying just above the speed limit most of the time and not using the siren at all, even on a couple of occasions when she might have been tempted herself. Maybe he was on his best behaviour on her account.

They didn't talk much until they got out of the city. Combes gave most of his attention to manoeuvring through the traffic, and when it thinned out seemed to be taken up with his own thoughts. Kennedy was more than happy to leave him there. She checked the rear-view once or twice a minute, making sure there were no vehicles hanging in their wake, following them south.

Once they hit the A3, Combes took a glance at the petrol gauge, flicked it with his thumbnail. 'That moron Stanwick left the tank three-quarters empty,' he said. 'I'm going to have to fill up.'

'Fine,' Kennedy said. 'I'll see if I can pick us up an ordnance survey map. Ros wrote some directions, but they're a bit vague.'

They drove on in silence for a while and then Combes pulled in at a service station that called itself Travellers' Haven: big words for a breezeblock shack and three petrol pumps. While Combes filled up, she went to the small pay kiosk and asked if they sold maps. The adolescent on the other side of the counter shook his head rapidly, wide-eyed, as if she'd asked whether he had any kiddie porn or hard drugs.

She bought some chewing gum and headed back to the car. When she was almost there, Combes hung up the pump and stared at his two hands, raised in front of his face. 'Can you get this?' he asked. 'I'm drenched here. Damn thing leaked.'

Kennedy went back to the kiosk and handed her credit card across the counter. 'Number three,' she said. She was tapping in her PIN when the sound of the car engine coughing to life made her stop and turn round again. Combes was pulling out of the forecourt, back into the traffic, already moving fast.

'Son of a bitch!' Kennedy yelled.

She started to run, but then slowed and stopped again immediately. There was no way she could catch up to him: the car was almost out of sight already.

Combes had had time to think it out and he'd decided that he didn't need the key to the door at Dovecote – just the address, which she'd already given him. And he didn't need her. He knew she couldn't complain at being cut out of the action: the only way to drop any heat on him was to draw it down on herself, too. She couldn't even call anyone in Division and ask for a rescue.

With that realisation came another.

Tillman.

She dialled the new number – the one she'd jotted down on her wrist. Tillman didn't pick up and there was no voicemail option, but as Kennedy was pacing backwards and forwards on the narrow forecourt, trying to come up with a plan B, he rang her back. 'Sorry,' he said. 'I was working on something. What's up? Are you at the farm yet?'

'Nowhere near.' She told him about Combes's double-cross, steeling herself for some bitingly sarcastic put-down. She knew how stupid she'd been – first of all letting Combes drive and then falling in with his half-arsed stitch-up like a trained puppy. But Tillman took it in his stride.

'You want to leave him to it?' he asked.

'Do I *what*?'

'Well, he's in your team, right? Anything he gets, he'll pass on to you. Maybe the best bet is to let him get on with it. We can always go back and have a skirmish around later, if we think he's missed anything.'

'No.' Kennedy had the decency to feel ashamed, considering how ready she'd been to cut Tillman out of this find, but she knew she was better at reading a scene than Combes was on the best day of his life, and the thought of him getting to open up the Dovecote treasure chest by himself was more than she could bear. 'We can't stop Combes from getting there first, but I really want to get the measure of this place now, while it's fresh. And the way things are in the department, I wouldn't get the clearance to come out here once it's reported in. This might be my only chance.'

Again, Tillman didn't waste any time arguing the point. 'Okay. I'll grab a car and come out and get you. Where are you?'

She told him where to find the Travellers' Haven, and he hung up with a curt 'See you soon.'

She had ample time to wonder, as she waited, what he meant by grabbing a car. Forty minutes later, when he turned up in a fourteen-wheeler, caparisoned in bright green and yellow livery, she had her answer.

They were driving down to Dovecote Farm in a stolen truck.

32

About forty minutes after Kennedy and Combes left, the phone on Kennedy's desk in the bear pit started to ring.

Stanwick was still in the room, along with McAliskey and a few DCs, who were busy with their own stuff. They all ignored the phone, and it cut off after a while as the call diverted to Kennedy's voicemail. Then it rang again. This procedure was repeated five or six times.

Nobody else seemed to be keen to take a message, but it occurred to Stanwick that it might be Kennedy herself calling in. Maybe they needed a third man after all or they wanted him to call in forensic or IT support. Maybe they just wanted to check the address or needed him to get some kind of clearance from the DCI.

Finally, he picked up.

'Hello?'

A cultured, slightly foreign-sounding voice said, 'I need to speak with Sergeant Kennedy, please.'

'And you are?'

'Whitehall exchange. Sergeant Kennedy can verify the number, and my ID: alpha zebra seventeen.'

Stanwick was impressed. Whitehall exchange meant MI5, most likely, although it could also be one of the parliamentary intelligence liaisons making an enquiry on behalf of a government committee or quango. It could even be Downing Street. However you cut it, it was serious.

'Sergeant Kennedy is away from her desk,' Stanwick said. 'I'm DC Peter Stanwick. Can I help?'

'I don't think so. Is Sergeant Kennedy working a case right now?'

'Yes, she is.'

'The Barlow murder.'

'Umm ... I'm not really at liberty to answer that, sir.'

'If it's the Barlow murder, there's nothing in the case file to indicate where she's gone or what she's doing.'

Stanwick was even more impressed now. Whoever he was talking to, the guy had stratospheric clearance: real-time access to case files was a privilege given to very few people outside of Division. You more or less had to be God or a close personal friend of his. Suddenly Stanwick's own position – right in the Whitehall line of fire – was starting to look a little invidious.

'It's ... something that just came up,' he said. 'Suddenly. She and DS Combes decided to check it out right away, and I'm ... I'm updating the case file now.'

'Please do so,' the other man said, curtly. 'It's possible that Sergeant Kennedy and Sergeant ... Combes, did you say? ... are walking into an operation we already have set up. That would be far from desirable and we'd want to do our best to head them off if there's still time.'

'I'll make the entry right now,' Stanwick promised. 'The refresh might take five minutes or so, but—'

'I'm not concerned about the refresh. Thank you for your assistance, DC Stanwick. We'll refer to the file – and I hope it won't be necessary to call again.'

Stanwick hoped that too, very fervently. He cursed Combes

for putting him in this stupid position, and himself for agreeing to be the fig leaf on their balls-out privateering. He updated the file to indicate that they were at Dovecote Farm, near Godalming, Surrey, pursuant to a suggestion made by Rosalind Barlow in a couriered package delivered at 11.20 a.m. After a moment's hesitation, he timelined the entry at 1.43 p.m. Bastards already had him, if they wanted him. But he was far from the epicentre of whatever shitstorm was coming, and if he kept his head down he might not even get wet.

Kuutma put the phone down and thought.

It was very fortunate that he'd had his people set up a visual feed from the Detective Division at New Scotland Yard, which included in its field of vision the desk at which the *rhaka*, Kennedy, spent most of her time. When she disappeared from the feed, but failed to emerge from the building (the followers assigned to her would have reported contact), his suspicions were aroused. He had waited for almost three quarters of an hour – she could be elsewhere in the building, even though the rest of the inquiry team had all been accounted for – but finally he'd reached a decision and made the call. He was devoutly grateful that he had.

He called Mariam and gave her the glad tidings. Her failure to make a kill on her previous deployment, against Tillman on the ferry, had left her distressed and ashamed, and her team demoralised. It was part of Kuutma's duty to consider the heft and the sharpness of the tools he used, and to whet them, wherever he could, against the rough edges of the world.

This would be good for them. They would take it for a blessing, which it was.

33

'It's here,' Kennedy said. 'The next left. Look, there's the sign.'

Even in the gathering dusk, it was impossible to miss the sign. About three miles out from the last village they'd come through, it looked exactly as Ros Barlow had described it: the golden wing rising from the 'D' of Dovecote in a ridiculous, melodramatic flourish, reducing the whole effect to bathos. The squat, thatched building and scatter of tumbledown barns beyond couldn't live up to that bombastic declaration. You needed the god Hermes descending out of a clear sky, maybe on wires.

The gravel drive in front of the farmhouse was far too short for the truck. Combes's grey Vauxhall Vectra was immediately visible, parked right out in front of the building in defiance of good search protocols and common sense. With the driveway blocked, Tillman swung to the right and drove over waist-high weeds to a broad open space to the right of the main building, where he rolled to a halt. Kennedy looked around for Combes, but it seemed that he was still inside. That meant he'd found something: he'd had at least a half-hour's start on them and had probably made better time on the roads. So whatever else it was, it seemed unlikely that Dovecote Farm was a dead end.

Fighting down her excitement, Kennedy got out of the cab. She scanned the ground. Apart from the gravel bed, the whole space around and between the farmhouse and its satellite buildings had become overgrown with weeds and scrub: no way to tell if tyre prints or footprints lay under there, although if the weather had been wetter she might have knelt down, parted the weeds and taken a look.

The farmhouse and the overgrown fields around it were absolutely silent. And there were no other houses or farm buildings in sight. Dovecote itself had half a dozen derelict-looking barns and outhouses, which crowded close around the main building like conspirators. If Barlow had set up this site as a secret base camp for his Rotgut project, he'd chosen his ground well. He'd also left no trace behind him: to judge by appearances, they – and Combes, of course – might be the first people to come here in ten years or more.

The farmhouse looked both dilapidated and deserted. All the windows but one had crude particle board shutters nailed over them. The one that was visible was broken. The wood of the window frames was scabrous with peeling paint, and a decorative porch roof over the front door had fallen in on itself like a dropsied stomach.

Tillman stepped down out of the truck on the driver's side, and, like Kennedy, stayed still for a moment or two. Where she checked the ground for sign, he scanned the outhouse buildings, presumably looking for any signs of life. He gave her a look, shrugged, shook his head very slightly and headed for the door. Kennedy fell in behind him.

The door looked undisturbed, but only at first glance. After a silent moment, Tillman pointed to what Kennedy had already seen for herself: the splintering of the jamb over an area of about three or four inches, just underneath the level of the lock plate. Someone had levered the door open with a crowbar or perhaps a car jack, and then pulled it to again.

Kennedy pushed the door with her foot. It opened a few inches with an audible creak.

Tillman grunted non-committally. 'Are you going to introduce us or should I wait in the truck?'

'Come on in. We're so far from the operations manual at this point, I don't think it matters all that much. We'll be sharing whatever we find, whether Combes likes it or not – and he's got as much reason as me to keep quiet about the details.'

She nudged the door with her foot a second time, pushed it open as far as it would go. The interior of the house was completely dark even on this bright day, the doorway in front a solid black rectangle.

'Combes!' she called.

No answer, and no echo: the darkness swallowed the sound absolutely.

Stepping over the threshold, Kennedy breathed in a sharp, musty smell as thick as incense. The smell of damp, working on paper and fabric at leisure in the dark. Unsettlingly, her shoulders brushed against unyielding substance to left and right – as though the space she was stepping into were somewhat narrower than the doorway itself. A tunnel rather than a hallway.

She called Combes's name again, louder this time. Again, the sound felt oddly flat and muffled.

Kennedy groped beside the door, hoping to find a light switch. Her fingers touched something soft and cool and ragged-edged. When it rustled, she recognised it as paper, and now that her eyes began to adjust a little to the dark she could see it, too: paper stacked in a rough and ready way to shoulder height, just inside the door.

She found the light switch immediately above the stack and pressed it, and light from a bare bulb flooded the scene before them. Poised there, Kennedy and Tillman stared.

'What the hell?' Tillman murmured.

It wasn't a single stack of paper, it was just the only one that didn't reach all the way from floor to ceiling. They were looking into a hallway that extended about ten feet, with two doors each to left and right and another at the end. Paper lined the walls, piled up in profusion, leaving a space between barely wide enough for one person to walk through. In places, clearly, it would be necessary to turn or lean inwards so as not to disturb the stacks. They looked precarious, but none had fallen over. Probably the fact that they were braced against the ceiling as well as the floor, and packed in very tightly, helped there.

In the one room that they could see, at the end of the hallway, more paper had been piled up, in haphazard blocks like the layers of a badly made stepped pyramid. It looked like someone had been filling the room with paper, to begin with in a methodical way, but had finally taken to putting it down wherever was closest and easiest.

Kennedy took the top sheet from the nearest stack – the one that only came up to her shoulder. It was printed with alphanumeric gibberish: letters and numbers, the letters all capitals, in a sans serif font. They filled the page completely, set out in an unbroken block from right to left, with three-quarter-inch borders. No breaks and no indentations: nothing to indicate whether this was a free-standing document or a single page of a much longer one.

Kennedy showed the sheet to Tillman. He scanned it briefly, then looked across at her.

'I was hoping we might find a floppy disk,' she said.

Tillman laughed: a bark of incredulous amusement.

Kennedy went in first, angling her body sideways so as not to touch the encroaching towers of paper. The air felt stiflingly warm, heavy with that sour tang, and she had the uneasy feeling of entering an organic space – of being swallowed or of being born in reverse. The thought of seeming nervous or flustered in the face of Tillman's stolid calm was an unpleasant one. She shoved her presentiments firmly down into her hind-brain and locked them in.

'You made a good call,' he said behind her. 'I'm guessing this is Stuart Barlow's research project right here.'

'I don't know,' Kennedy murmured. 'I don't see anything that looks like a gospel yet.' *Or anything that looks like that bastard, Combes.*

They moved on, slowly and warily. Bare floorboards creaked beneath their feet, and the smell got ever stronger as they left the daylight behind. The first doorway to the left showed them another room full of paper. The first to the right was the same, the second empty apart from a half-full bag of cement and a few lengths of two-by-four on the floor. The last door on the left led through to a sort of hallway, where a flight of narrow, steep wooden stairs led upward. Two more closed doors opening directly off this narrow space, behind the stairwell, turned out to be locked.

Tillman motioned Kennedy aside and kicked the doors open, without much difficulty: a single kick to each, at waist height. One was yet another paper store, the other a kitchen. Kennedy was interested in the kitchen. She went inside and looked around. A kettle next to the sink, when she flicked up the lid, still had a little water in it. A teapot next to it was brimful of feathery grey mould.

By this time, Tillman had found the fridge. He threw the door open, winced and covered his face with a hand. 'Take a look at this,' he called to Kennedy. She came and peered around his shoulder. The fridge was full of corruption: green milk, white-spotted cheese, apples whose fresh red faces had fallen in on brown plague sores.

297

'How long to get this bad?' he asked her. 'Couple of months?'

'Maybe less,' Kennedy muttered. 'Feel how warm it is in here, Tillman. We're six weeks out from Barlow's death now. He could have been coming here regularly right up until he was killed.'

And if he did, she thought, that means he was better than me at shaking his tail. I took death with me to Park Square. This amateur managed to keep his big secret in spite of everything – and his killers still hadn't found it.

That thought brought another in its train. If Combes had been here, why had these doors still been locked? It didn't read right. Unless he was still here somewhere – had found something so engrossing that he hadn't finished his search or heard their arrival.

'Nothing else down here,' Tillman said. 'Let's take a look upstairs.'

'Give me a second,' Kennedy told him.

She went back to the door, stepped outside and took a good look around – a one-hundred-and-eighty-degree sweep. Nothing and nobody in sight, and the silence was still unbroken apart from the cawing of a crow, softened by distance.

She went back inside, closing the door. Tillman stood watching her expectantly from the other end of the passage. She nodded to him and he headed up the stairs.

Bringing up the rear, Kennedy made sure to look behind every door and in the corners of the paper storerooms where someone or something might have hidden behind the uneven stacks. She found nothing. But at the top of the stairs, they struck gold.

They struck paper, too, of course: more murdered forests reduced to cubic yards of print-out, the same meaningless strings of letters and numbers on every sheet that Kennedy picked up and examined. But when they turned on the light in the largest bedroom, which did not contain a bed, among the stacks of A4 was another stack, of grey plastic slabs bearing the Hewlett-Packard logo.

'Looks like a hi-fi tower,' Tillman grunted.

'Servers,' Kennedy said. 'They use rigs like this to render 3D effects for movies. Somebody needed a lot of processing power.'

She pointed to a trestle table over by the room's only window. A monitor and keyboard sat there, connected by a thicket of wire cables to the server stack. From the servers, the wires arced away across the floor to a bank of adaptors, where they lost themselves in intricate cross-connections some of which terminated at wall sockets while others ran on out of the room. At least one rose vertically to disappear through a trapdoor in the ceiling. There hadn't been enough power points in this one room, obviously, to handle the traffic. Even with three- and four-way adaptors, it had been necessary to call on the sockets in other rooms. A tarpaulin to one side of the trestle table had been thrown hastily over another rampart of irregular but squared-off shapes: more computer components, maybe, that hadn't yet been called into service or had been replaced as inadequate.

This was the room that had the single unboarded window, but thick sack cloth had been draped over it, hanging asymmetrically from a row of nails. Whoever had been working here seemed to have been caught in a contradiction – wanting the possibility of light but wanting to avoid being distracted by the scenic view on the other side of the glass: or, perhaps, to avoid being seen from outside.

There was more paper on the desk. Only a dozen sheets or so: quite modest in comparison to the rest of the house. Also a stack-pack of CD-R discs, still in its shrinkwrapping.

Kennedy crossed to the table and turned the computer on.

She was rewarded by the faint humming and clicking noises of start-up, sounding fainter still as the barricades and escarpments of paper swallowed the sound.

She turned her attention to the paper on the desk. She was expecting the same endless streams of alphanumerics, but what she saw drew an exclamation from her – a monosyllable that made Tillman pick up the second sheet to see what she was seeing.

The text on the paper was still completely unformatted: a logorrhoeic stream that ran uninterrupted from top to bottom of the paper. The only difference – the realisation that had made Kennedy swear aloud – was that these were actual words.

ANDJESUSGAVEUNTOHIMTHEBLESSINGOFHISHANDSTHATHEWITHHE
LDFROMALLOTHERSEVENTHOSEWHOFOLLOWEDHIMANDHESAIDUN
TOHIMIAMCALLEDSAVIOURYETWHOWILLSAVEMELORDISCARIOTANS
WEREDHIMIFITBETHYWILLISWEARTHATIWILLSERVETHEEINANYWISE
ANDJESUSSAIDUNTOISCARIOTYOUWILLBETHELOWESTANDTHEHIGHE
STTHEALPHAANDTHEOMEGATHENWERETHEOTHERSANGRYTHATHE

The squared-off, bolded capitals and the absence of spaces and line breaks made the stream of words read like a drunkard's bellowed rant. The bottom of the page cut it off mid-word: the sudden, bathetic silence when the ranter realises that his meaning has escaped him, and shuffles off into the night.

The computer had booted up by this time, into a mode that didn't look like any interface Kennedy had ever seen. Folder icons were displayed in white on a black background, each with a header label: SYSTEM, BIOS, SECURITY, DEVICES, PROGRAMS, PROJECTS.

Kennedy sat down at the table. The tubular steel chair had a wobble, so she had to lean forward to keep it steady. She clicked

300

PROJECTS and the display disappeared, to be replaced by another list. It contained only two items: PARENT DIRECTORY and ROTGUT.

She clicked ROTGUT.

A box popped up, red-bordered. PASSWORD, it demanded.

Kennedy opened her handbag and took out her notebook. She turned to the last page, where she'd copied down the words from Sarah Opie's paper.

Oh what can ail thee, knight at arms
Alone and palely loitering the sedge has withered
From the lake and no birds are singing.

She typed in the number 2, then in quick succession 4334624. She hit return, and nothing happened except that the PASSWORD box flashed once and emptied itself again.

'What was that?' Tillman asked.

'I took these words down from a sheet of paper Sarah Opie had on her when she died,' Kennedy said. 'She told me it was a mnemonic for her computer password. It's from a Keats poem. "La Belle Dame Sans Merci." And it actually goes: "Oh what can ail thee, knight at arms / Alone and palely loitering? / The sedge has withered from the lake / And no birds sing."

'She played about with the line breaks, so that she'd be left with exactly eight words on a line. Messed with the wording a bit, too.'

'So you're thinking an eight-digit password,' Tillman said.

'Yeah. And I just tried the first line – assuming that Opie was just taking the number of letters in each word.'

She tried the second and third lines, too. Nothing: the box filled up each time and refreshed when she hit return, appearing empty and with the same silent demand.

'Initial letters,' Tillman suggested.

Kennedy tried that without success. Then she tried both sequences – numbers of letters and initials – in reverse. The box blinked at her, inscrutably, and refused to yield. She swore softly.

'It's got to be something obvious,' Tillman pointed out. 'It's no use as a mnemonic if she had to think about it too much.'

Kennedy chewed her lower lip, thinking furiously. Something obvious, but not initial letters or length of words.

Why three sequences of eight words, rather than just one? The blocks of eight indicated an eight-digit key, but maybe the three lines were significant, too. She took every third word and entered the letter totals.

can – knight – alone – loitering – has – the – no – singing
3-6-5-9-3-3-2-7

The computer chuntered industriously to itself for a few moments, then the screen went completely blank, before filling up again with a list of what were presumably file names:

ROTGUT RAW 1, 1–7

ROTGUT RAW 2, 8–10

ROTGUT RAW 3, 11–14a

ROTGUT RAW 4, 14b–17

ROTGUT PARTIAL 1, 1–7

ROTGUT PARTIAL 2, 8–10

ROTGUT PARTIAL 3, 11–14a

ROTGUT PARTIAL 4, 14b–17

ROTGUT FULL 1, 1–7

ROTGUT FULL 2, 8–10

ROTGUT FULL 3, 11–14a

ROTGUT FULL 4, 14b–17

Kennedy clicked on the first file: ROTGUT RAW 1, 1–7. The screen blinked, there was another rattle of dry, chitinous sounds from the hard drive, and then she was looking at a different list.

Dalath 2 actuals

Waw 3 actuals 1 spaced

Semkath 2 actuals 2 spaced

He exact

Resh exact
Mim 1 actual 1 spaced
Tau exact

She used the scroll bar on the right of the screen to see how much of this stuff there was. It went on through what looked like several hundred items.

She closed the file, opened one of the PARTIALS. This file was a whole lot busier.

He fai	dun [refer 7]	chall	whe [refer 4]	can [6,7,2] came
sai	sun	crall		
lai				

that [refer 21]	wil [into?] [refer 3]	that	[21,4,6] he had [insert 2]
	til	the t	
	nil	what	

given [refer 5] to them	in	get [hsem?]	ant	where [they?]
	on	bet	ane	there
	an			

saw the	sol [refer 18]	their	sand [let?]	him [refer 33]
	fol	tier	s and	gim
		dier	t end	lim

'Any idea?' Kennedy asked Tillman, nodding at the monitor.

Tillman had been reading over her shoulder. 'Translation,' he suggested.

'The file label said partial,' Kennedy offered back. 'And all these lists of words are places where they're not sure – where they're listing possible alternatives. They were working their way through a document, translating as they went.'

303

'The Rotgut.'

'Must be. No, wait. The Rotgut is already a translation, isn't it? I mean, the actual Rotgut manuscript is already in English. Nobody knows what the source document was, or what language it was in, so that wouldn't work.'

Kennedy picked up the top sheet of paper again and ran her gaze across the surface of the hectic verbal torrent.

THENLETNOTTHYSERVANTGTOILINVAINLORDORWITHOUTREWARD
THEREWARDISHALLGIVEUNTOTHEEWILLBEGREATERTHANANYHAVE
KNOWNANDGREATERTHANTHOUCANSTFRAMEINWORDSTHENHELE
DHIMFROMTHATPLACEINTOANOTHERPLACEFROMWHICHALLTHING
SINHEAVENANDINEARTHWEREVISIBLEIHAVEGIVENTHEEARTHUNTOA
DAMANDHISSEEDWHATSHALLIGIVETHEEMOSTFAITHFULANDMOSTU
NCOMPLAININGISHALLMAKETHEEHATEDANDREVILEDBUTTHENISHA

Downstairs, tens of thousands of pages of random characters: upstairs, a few scant sheets of real words. No formatting, no punctuation, no spaces, but still, an actual narrative of some kind with a distinctly biblical flavour.

'It was a code,' Kennedy said, wonderingly. 'And they broke it.'

She turned to stare at Tillman. He was looking at her in silence, waiting for more. And the pieces of it were all in her mind, now, but it was still hard for her to make out the final shape – like trying to figure out what a jigsaw might show by looking at the reverse face, the face that bore no image.

'Barlow gave evidence in a court case,' she said. 'Years back. A ring of counterfeiters, selling fake documents that were meant to be from one of the big biblical finds – Nag Hammadi.'

'So?'

'He was the expert witness. They called him in to look – look hard – at the real documents and the fake ones, so he could testify which was which and prove that someone was putting dodgy gospels on the market. It was a really big thing for him. He had newspaper cuttings framed and put up on the wall of his office.'

She looked at the screen again. At the list of maybe-Aramaic characters. Actuals. Spaces. Exacts. 'Hundreds of scholars and historians must have looked at those things. Maybe thousands. But Barlow was coming at them from a different angle. He was trying to catch them out – looking for things that didn't fit. And . . .'

That was as far as she could go. She had no idea what Barlow had found, but she felt sure that it had been the turning point. 'There was something wrong with the Nag Hammadi texts. Something you'd only see if you went in looking to catch a fraud in the first place.'

'But you said this was years ago,' Tillman pointed out. He'd picked up the pack of recordable discs and was turning it over in his hands, staring at it with unnecessary intensity.

Kennedy dredged her memory. 'Fifteen years,' she said.

'So if he found something then, why wait so long? What happened in-between?'

She didn't know, but she could see the shape of the thing she didn't know. It had a definite outline. 'He found something. Or he suspected something. He kept bouncing off it and coming at it again from a new angle. He goes away and looks at Old Testament texts – the Dead Sea Scrolls. For five years. Then he looks at the Gnostic sects. And finally he goes to see the Rotgut in Avranches. That was when it all came together. It's like . . . he had the key but he didn't know where the lock was.'

'I don't think I get it,' Tillman said.

'Leo, think about it. The Rotgut is a medieval translation of a document that already existed elsewhere. Nobody can figure out why this Portuguese sea captain bought it in the first place – why he'd ever think it was worth having. But Barlow goes to take a look at it and he sees ...'

Tillman scowled. 'What?'

'Something. Something nobody else saw. I'm sure I'm right. There was a code in the Rotgut. And Barlow knew enough by that time to see it for what it was.' She saw the hole in her own reasoning as she said it. 'But the Rotgut is just John's Gospel. Where do you hide a code in a copy of an existing document?'

Tillman didn't answer. He threw the pack of discs back down on the desk, but it hit the edge of the desktop and clattered to the floor, where it rolled away. Kennedy could see that he was angry, but she was slow to realise why. She plunged on, putting it all together while she had it clear in her mind.

'Maybe it wasn't in the words. Or maybe it's in the changes in the words. If you started from the King James version, or whatever version they had back then, but you messed with it and changed it around, you might end up with a code that someone could crack. Holy Christ, Leo. I'm right. I know I'm right. Barlow picked up on a coded message from centuries ago and built a team to crack the code.'

'Amazing,' Tillman said, flatly.

'Yeah, it is. It *is* amazing. But they needed a computer expert to do it. Three historians and a tech-head. It makes sense now. They were looking for some really subtle patterns in the text of the Rotgut, or somewhere else on the document. Patterns that you'd need some kind of statistical algorithm to nail down. Totally insane! But here's the question we've got to answer now.' She brandished the small sheaf of papers that had been lying on the desk. 'This information was hidden back in the Middle Ages. Why would anyone be prepared to kill for it now?'

It was at this point that she ground to a halt, seeing in Tillman's face that he didn't give a damn about the question or the answer. His expression looked as hard and set as if she'd driven her whole chain of reasoning into it with carpet tacks.

'What?' she asked him.

'None of this matters,' he said, tightly. 'None of it, Kennedy.'

'What do you mean?'

'It's not . . .' He seemed to struggle to find a word that was strong enough. '. . . relevant. This isn't even close to what I was looking for. I lost my family. I thought if Brand was killing these people, or arranging to have them killed, it was because they'd seen through him. That they'd dug up all his dirty little secrets.'

'I think they did, Leo. They found something that he wanted to keep—'

'This is ancient history.' Tillman all but spat the words out. His fists were clenched now and his face flushed red.

Kennedy absorbed the violence of that pronouncement, kept her own voice carefully neutral. 'The victims were all historians. I'd have to say that was on the cards.'

'It's not funny, Kennedy. Not to me.'

'Not to me, either. But you're wrong about one thing: it *is* relevant. It's the key to everything, somehow, and if we stick with it, I think we'll get all the answers we've been looking for.'

Tillman opened his mouth to reply but said nothing. Instead, he sniffed.

Kennedy was suddenly aware of a smell that had been riding under her conscious notice for a minute or more, masked by the stench of damp and dust.

Something was burning.

34

Although she was the only woman, and although it had been taught to her throughout her life that women should defer to men, Mariam was the team's leader. This hadn't even been something that anyone had to decide on, it was the outcome of a simple equation whose three inputs were the personalities of herself and the other two Messengers with whom she'd been partnered, Ezei and Cephas. Nobody who knew the three of them would have doubted for a second which way that calculation would come out.

So when Kuutma called, and Ezei answered, he passed the phone wordlessly to Mariam and she handled the rest of the conversation herself.

'Your hunt for Tillman,' Kuutma said. 'I believe you were successful. You found him again?'

Mariam kept her expression blank and calm because Ezei and Cephas were watching her, but she felt a sour-sweet wash of emotion rise in her. She was proud of what she'd managed to achieve but desperately miserable at how the operation had turned out. 'We backtracked from the call log on Tillman's phone,' she said. 'The one we took from him on the ferry. There was a number in the log that was registered to a name we knew – a man who fought alongside Tillman when he was in a mercenary cadre.

Benard Vermeulens. I spoke with Dovid's team, in Omdurman, and asked him to place a temporary tap on all numbers registered to Vermeulens. From that trace, we established that Vermeulens had called only one number in England in the last ten days. It was very easy to set up a GPS trace on that number.'

'You did well,' Kuutma said. 'But you haven't closed with him yet?'

Mariam's lips quirked. That was the only visible sign of what she was feeling but it was enough to make Ezei and Cephas glance at each other in unhappy solicitude. Ezei made the sign of the noose, a little raggedly. 'We tried,' she confessed. 'Two times, both last night. The first time, he saw our ambush and didn't walk into it.'

'And the second time?'

'The phone signal moved around very quickly for two hours, then was still. When we were able to zero its location, we went in. It was a sewer, in west London, but Tillman wasn't there. He'd dropped the phone into a storm drain. He must have realised that it was the means we were using to track him.'

Her confession was done. She waited for chastisement: for the *Tannanu*'s stern, concerned voice to tell her that he was disappointed in her performance and was recalling her and her team to Ginat'Dania.

'Tillman is a hard target,' Kuutma said instead. 'Your team is far from the only one to have been set back by him. Leave him to one side, for now. I need you for another task, which at the present time is more urgent.'

Mariam almost gasped aloud as relief made her let go of a breath she hadn't known she was holding. 'You know,' Kuutma told her, 'that we've been searching for written or digital records from the Rotgut affair. I believe, on the basis of new information, that the relevant files were kept in discrete and isolated form at a physical location, rather than at an internet node. I will give you an address. You will go to that address and destroy everything you find there that could conceivably contain information.'

Having escaped Kuutma's censure, Mariam was eager now to win his approval. '*Tannanu*,' she said, 'that would mean destroying everything.'

'Exactly, daughter. I'm pleased that you move so quickly to the point.'

'But to be sure of destroying everything, we'd need to examine the location carefully first – there could be writing engraved on walls that would not certainly be effaced by fire or even by an explosion. There could be a vault beneath the building that was sealed, and so on.'

'That you're raising these questions, Mariam, shows me that you see at once how complicated and exacting this task is. Yes, you must rule out all these things and make absolutely certain that no word or sign survives. Only so will we be safe.'

Mariam felt a fervent desire to thank Kuutma for giving her and her team this chance to prove themselves. They had failed so badly on the boat, even though it had seemed that they had the enemy Tillman at their mercy in an enclosed space with no obvious exits. And then they had failed again in London. To be given the opportunity – and so soon! – to redeem herself and her team from that taint was a wonderful thing. But she knew, too, that the *Tannanu* would not expect or welcome thanks. It was understood between them what was happening: the significance of the gift. She said nothing.

Kuutma gave her the address and she wrote it down. Ezei and Cephas read it wordlessly, over her shoulder, and exchanged a glance. There was no mistaking what this meant.

'I have it,' Mariam said, tersely. 'Are there any further orders?'

'Yes.' There was a short pause, as if Kuutma expected her to ask. Again, Mariam chose silence over unnecessary speech. 'The woman detective, Kennedy, will be there, along with a male colleague. Kill both of them, ideally in a way that prompts a minimum of further investigation. If their deaths could be taken to be an accident, that would be ideal. If there is evidence of violence, it must look like casual violence, with no trail that points forward or back from the event itself. We are too exposed in this already, Mariam. With Tillman still alive ...'

He let the sentence tail off. Mariam closed her eyes and mouthed an oath in which the number thirty figured prominently. Ezei, who could read lips, stifled a gasp, shocked at the blasphemy.

'I see the problem, *Tannanu*. Perhaps we can make it appear that the man violated and murdered the woman, and then killed himself out of shame.'

'A possibility, Mariam. Overly elaborate, perhaps, but a possibility. Remember, though, the sins that are forgiven you are very specifically defined. Do what seems best to you to do, and come to me afterwards. I'll hear your report in person.'

'I will, *Tannanu*. Where we have been, nothing will stand.'

'I believe this to be true. Goodbye.'

The line went dead and Mariam gave the phone back to Ezei. The two men were staring at her, excitement and anticipation making them stand very straight, like soldiers coming to attention. Mariam felt a surge of love for them and such a profound joy she almost laughed.

'We're on,' she said, simply. 'Cousins, we're on again. This very night.'

'This is wonderful,' Cephas said.

'Yes! Yes, it is.' Mariam went to the mini-bar in the hotel room they'd booked under a name that wasn't Brand (Kuutma

311

only bound himself to that convention, not his teams) and took out three hypodermic syringes along with three snap-in ampoules. She handed them out, trying to maintain a solemn face when all the while she felt as if she were giving out presents.

The ritual itself called for silence, so they opened the syringes, inserted the capsules and injected themselves without exchanging a word. Only the fervent glances the two men cast her showed that they shared Mariam's excitement.

The drug hit her system with its usual expanding slow-burn: a bubble waking in the centre of her being, then rushing outward until it filled her entirely and popped startlingly against the inside of her skin.

'*Beracha u kelala*,' Cephas murmured, shuddering as the pharmacon lit up his nervous system. It meant: *both the blessing and the curse*. The drug's more usual name, *kelalit*, recognised only the second part of this equation.

But when Mariam and her team descended on Dovecote Farm and delivered the final mercy upon Detective Sergeant Heather Kennedy, it was the blessing that would sit behind their eyes and hands.

The journey was quick and uneventful. They had no GPS, but Ezei had a great facility in map-reading and he led them unerringly.

They identified the farm at once from the prominent sign that faced out on to the road. Mariam drove on past the building, then took a narrow lane that led into woodland half a mile or so further on. Fortuitously, the lane bent back on itself, taking them around in an oxbow bend towards the rear of the property, so that by the time she found a secluded place in which to park, invisible from the road itself, they'd almost come back to where they started.

'What should we bring?' Ezei asked Mariam.

'*Sicae* and guns only,' she decided. 'We go in light and fast. Anything else we need, one of you will come back for.'

The grounds of Dovecote Farm were easy to find, and almost completely open at the back. Wooden posts held up a single strand of barbed wire: a purely symbolic fence, low enough for them to step right over.

They approached cautiously, but from a hundred yards out, and even in the gathering dusk, it was clear to their over-sensitised eyes that boards had been nailed over the windows of the farm. If their quarry was already in the building, there was no way they could be aware that the Messengers were approaching. And if they had yet to arrive, then so much the better.

All the same, Mariam was cautious. She didn't come in on a straight line but on a shallow diagonal, the two men following her lead without question, so that the closer they got to the farmhouse the more of its exterior and its outhouse buildings they could see.

They spotted the car when they were still some distance away. So Kennedy and her partner had already arrived and were inside. Using the language of gestures that all Messengers were taught, Mariam told Ezei and Cephas to split up so that they could approach the farm separately, from different angles. Silently and efficiently, they checked each of the outbuildings in turn. It was most likely that the police officers would be inside the farmhouse itself, but it was good to take nothing for granted. Mariam herself checked the car and found it locked and empty. Only when they had been over every inch of the ground did she call her team back to her, again with a gesture rather than a word.

The farmhouse had two doors, but a quick reconnaissance showed that the side door was screwed into its frame and would be hard to open quickly. Mariam stationed Cephas where he could see both doors and instructed him to shoot anyone who emerged. Then she and Ezei went to the front door.

They found it standing ajar. Damage to the jamb showed that the detectives had prized it open with a screwdriver or a crowbar. Mariam gestured to Ezei to walk behind her and to split off from her if the interior made it necessary. Then she pushed the door very lightly, widening the gap by a bare inch so that she could slide through. The warped, dried wood creaked, but the sound was low and wouldn't carry far.

The paper-walled maze that met their eyes came as something of a shock. They had grown up in an environment where books and pictures were few, so they had no referent for these head-high stacks of white sheets filled with inscrutable figures. They seemed faintly indecent. Mariam almost wanted to raise her hands and cover Ezei's eyes, even though he was older than her. He had always seemed to her to be someone who needed to be protected from the things of the profane world.

The paper aside, though, the interior layout of the farmhouse appeared to be very straightforward. They quickly ascertained that there was nobody on the ground floor – and just as quickly that someone was upstairs, moving around loudly and without precaution.

Mariam once again took point as they approached the stairs. So far their movements had been completely silent, but she could see that the boards of the stairs – as warped as the door – would creak under her feet no matter how she tried to distribute her weight. She unlaced her boots silently, slid them off her feet and signed to Ezei: hand upright, hand sloping forward, then a nod to the stairs.

He understood at once. Standing with the toes of his boots against the bottom step, he leaned forward carefully. He put out his hands, bracing one against the angle of stair and wall, the other against the angle of stair and banister. When he felt himself to be properly balanced, he nodded to Mariam. She stepped up on to his back, placed first one and then the other bare foot on his shoulders, and from there stepped up lightly on to the first landing. The wood beneath her shifted, with a slight creak of protest, but she was halfway up the stairs and could take the remainder in two strides.

Motioning to Ezei to stay where he was, she looked cautiously around the bend of the stairwell. She saw nobody, but the sounds were clearly coming from inside the room directly facing her at the top of the stairs. They were the sounds of purposeful movement. Someone inside the room was walking around, perhaps moving bulky objects.

She used the sounds as cover, moving when there was movement inside the room to mask any sounds she might make. In a few measured steps she was beside the door of the room – and by this time, she had reached some conclusions about whoever was inside it. One set of footsteps, heavy, distinctive and unvarying; no conversation. One person, probably a man, alone.

Where was the woman, then? That was a problem that she would need to solve, but a choice had to be made right now: to take down this man and then search for his partner, running the risk that she might be alerted by the sound of a struggle, or to wait and tackle both together.

Aim at the target that is in front of you, was a dictum that the *Tannanu* and her other teachers had drummed into her on many occasions. She felt confident in her own ability to kill or disable the man without giving him time to raise an alarm.

Reaching her decision, she stepped into the room. She was still moving as quietly as she could, but she knew that at such

315

a small distance even the movement of air might betray her. So her first priority was speed.

The man – stocky, broad-shouldered, probably outmassing her by as much as a half – was on the far side of the room, kneeling beside an electric extension into which he was inserting or trying to insert a number of plugs.

Out of the corner of his eye he saw Mariam coming towards him. He started to rise as she reached him, his mouth open on the first syllable of a greeting or a challenge.

Mariam kicked him in the throat. She hadn't put her boots back on, but she turned her foot to the side and made contact with her instep, the full weight of her body aligned behind her extended leg so that the force went from hip to knee to ankle and thence without mitigation into the unprotected flesh of the man's gullet.

The sound he made was no sound at all, but a muted vibration: his ruined voicebox pulsing momentarily against the flesh of her foot. Then she lowered that foot, raised the other, performed a half-pirouette and straddled him. It was easy: his rising motion had stopped and he had crashed back down on to his knees, hands raised to his throat, making no move to defend or to counterattack. Mariam pincered his head between her muscular legs and, reaching down, wrapped her forearms around his temples.

A half-twist from this position would have broken the man's neck easily, unless he knew it was coming and braced himself against it. Mariam applied a smaller degree of torsion but an equal amount of force, closing the man's airway without damaging any of his vertebrae. She was already assuming that it would be necessary to burn down the farmhouse, so any soft-tissue damage she inflicted would be disguised by the much greater damage done by the flames.

The man realised that he was dying, a few seconds too late

for the knowledge to do him any good. From this position, the only way he could reach her hands was to bend his arms back behind his own head. Most of his strength was lost in the awkward contortion, while hers was almost doubled by the *kelalit* she'd taken. The man writhed and strained under her, but she'd positioned herself well and he was unable to shift her balance or break free of the hold. His feet slammed against the bare boards, forcefully at first but then in a rapid diminuendo as his strength failed him.

When he was weak enough that she could afford to shift her weight a little, Mariam leaned forward to whisper into the man's ear. 'It's all right. It's all right. It's almost over.' Her English wasn't good, but she spoke slowly and carefully, and she was reasonably sure he understood her. It was a small gesture but important all the same. We dress our brutality in ritual to keep our own animal nature at a distance. Mariam was never more gentle or considerate than when she killed.

The man's last conscious movement was to fasten both of his hands around one of her ankles. It was a good idea, but again too late: he wasn't strong enough now to push against her leg and disturb her balance. The grip was ineffectual, the push feeble and short-lived.

Mariam maintained her hold for a full minute after the man stopped moving, then parted her legs to let him fall. Kneeling beside him, she felt his throat for a pulse. There was none. The man's face had gone hectic red and he fixed her with a reproachful, exophthalmic stare. She ignored it: the spirit didn't linger long enough to bear grudges, and the flesh was nothing.

She searched the rest of the upper floor quickly, finding no trace of the woman. By this time, she wasn't expecting to: if anyone had been within earshot, the frantic thrashing and kicking of the man as he died would have brought them at a run.

She went back down the stairs, less concerned now about the creaking floorboards, and found Ezei still waiting for her at the bottom. 'One man,' she rapped out, as she slipped her boots back on and laced them. 'Alone. Search again.'

Between them they combed every inch of the farmhouse, looking everywhere that a human body could possibly squeeze itself. Finally, Mariam satisfied herself that the woman wasn't on the premises. If she'd never arrived, that was fine. If she'd been there previously but had left, they might have a very narrow window in which to destroy these records – the other part of their assignment, and in fact the task that the *Tannanu* had mentioned first.

Mariam sent Ezei and Cephas back to the car to fetch some of their equipment, including the fire-starting kit. It included untraceable chemical accelerants and a flexible tube that she would use to breathe smoke into the lungs of the dead man. Most coroners wouldn't look further than that before pronouncing a verdict of death by fire.

Once the men had gone, she returned to the computer room. Their instructions were to destroy everything that was here, but she was aware that it was sometimes possible to retrieve information from computer discs and hard drives even when they'd been comprehensively damaged. Along with the fire-starting materials, Ezei and Cephas would bring the wipe-clean, a portable generator in a briefcase-sized box that produced a monstrously powerful AC magnetic field. A ten-second pass with the device at full charge would corrupt every file on the computer, so that even if anything was saved from the fire, it would be gibberish. Taking the computer away with them would be simpler, of course, but would expose them to the risk of being stopped and searched while they still had it in their possession. This was better.

Mariam wondered, though, what secret had been discovered in this house that she and her cousins were charged with deleting from the world's consciousness again. She crossed to the desk and picked up the top sheet from among the papers there. Reading it, she experienced a surge of mixed emotions. The words on the sheet were unexpectedly familiar: so familiar that she could have recited them from heart. But to see them in this place was momentarily disorienting, as though she had opened a door in a stranger's house and found her own bedroom behind it.

In that moment of strange suspension, a spotlight shone through the window and picked her out perfectly.

It was an illusion, of course. Even as her training made her freeze in place, the light swung past and was replaced by a second, moving in lockstep with the first. The sound of the engine and the crunch of tyres on gravel reached her at the same time. Headlights. The headlights of a car.

It was the woman, then. Or perhaps someone else. It didn't matter, either way: whoever it was had to die, and the task of destruction had to be completed. As soon as the lights passed by, Mariam moved to do what was necessary. Quickly, she dragged the body across the floor, to a stack of boxes that had been covered with a tarpaulin sheet. She manhandled it into position at the base of the stack and rearranged the tarpaulin to hide it from a casual glance.

Where were Ezei and Cephas? On their way back from the car by now, surely. They would have seen the headlights and they would know that the situation had changed. Hopefully they would stay in place and wait for her to contact them. Unfortunately, she couldn't leave or call them: not yet. She had to wait for her moment and she had to know who it was they were now dealing with.

She moved to the window and parted the folds of sacking very slightly. Below and to her left, a little way from the house, a large truck was now parked. As she watched, the doors of the cab opened. A woman and then a man got out. They were only silhouettes in the dusk, hard to make out even though, like her physical strength and speed, the keenness of her sight had been enhanced by the *kelalit*.

The two figures walked towards the door. Retreating from the window, Mariam considered her options and decided on the most direct and obvious. She would wait in the room and kill the two as they entered. She might have to break bones, but she would try not to. If there was visible damage to the bodies, that fire wouldn't hide, she might resort to the rape scenario she'd described to the *Tannanu*. Or she might drop the bodies from the window, so that it looked as though the damage had been sustained as the two tried to escape from the fire.

She walked silently to the door of the room. She could hear the two in the hall downstairs now: their voices, coming towards the stairs and then passing them. They were in the kitchen. She heard the man call the woman Kennedy, which came as no surprise at all. But the woman's answer caught her unprepared.

'Feel how warm it is in here, Tillman.'

Tillman.

Mariam's fists clenched involuntarily. The target they'd missed so many times. The man who'd first escaped from Ezei and Cephas, in the point-blank confines of the ferry's washroom, and then shot her knife out of the air. Who'd read their ambush from who knew what near-invisible clue, and escaped it. Who'd sent them down into a dank sewer in search of his abandoned phone. He was *here*. He was here with the woman.

Kelalit was known to heighten certain emotions. Part of the training of a Messenger included locking those emotions down into a manageable and containable part of the mind: you worked around them, refused to acknowledge them until, ignored, they lost the power to harm. That was what Mariam did then: she did not even look at the emotions that Tillman's name, Tillman's presence evoked. She folded those emotions in anaesthetic veils and pushed them down beneath the threshold of perception. At the same time, she conducted a rational appraisal of the situation. Tillman was a trained fighter and had survived an attack by her two cousins. There was a real chance that if she tried to take him here, even with the advantage of surprise, she might fail.

She heard footsteps on the stairs now: Tillman and the woman coming up. Moving as slowly as she dared, Mariam crossed the upper landing and stepped into the room opposite. It was possible that her enemies would go there first but it was unlikely. The computers were visible through the open doorway and would attract their attention. The logical thing to do would be to go and examine them immediately.

They passed within a few feet of her. She let them go by. Though her hands and feet prickled with the imminence of sudden, violent motion, she remained still.

The man and the woman went into the room, talking. 'Servers,' the woman said. 'They use rigs like this to render 3D effects for movies. Somebody needed a lot of processing power.'

They were ten feet away from Mariam now, then fifteen. If she moved, and they saw the movement, Tillman would have time to turn: possibly, to draw and aim. But the distance was so small, she couldn't miss with a thrown blade. She slid a *sica* from her belt and balanced it in her hand. She raised it, ready to throw – but only if the perfect window presented itself.

The woman passed between her and Tillman, blocking her

line of sight. Killing Kennedy would be easy, but would alert Tillman to Mariam's presence. If he were able to find cover in the room, and hold her off, everything might be compromised.

The moment passed. They both walked out of her line of sight, further into the room, heading no doubt for the desk.

Mariam left her hiding place and walked down the stairs. The voices from behind her were loud enough to mask the sounds her movements made, but she kept to the edges of the stair runners to minimise the risk that the old wood might speak and reveal her.

Only when she was in the hall did she acknowledge the slight tremor in her legs and in her hands: the small, almost insignificant component of that emotional surge that had been fear.

She walked out of the farmhouse and round to the rear, staying close to the wall. Once out of any possible line of sight, both from the bedroom window and from the road, she walked out boldly into the long grass. Ezei and Cephas rose in her way, not challenging her – they had recognised her even in the dark – but acknowledging and reporting to her.

'Tillman is there, as well as Kennedy,' she said.

Ezei blinked, startled. 'What should we do?'

'As we decided,' Mariam said. 'We burn the place. If they try to leave, we shoot them. If they stay in the building, we burn them. There are three of us and three faces to that building which have doors or windows. But if we work quickly enough, we'll trap them on the upper floor in any case, and doors and windows will be no use to them. Come on.'

Cephas nodded, and a second later Ezei did too. Mariam noticed the momentary hesitation and read it for what it was: an implied question. *If you saw them, why are they still alive?* She turned her back on her cousins and led the way to the building.

They had two drums of the accelerant, a clear chemical

compound that had no detectable by-products and virtually no smell – only a slight whiff of floral disinfectant – yet burned as quickly and as fiercely as kerosene. They started at the back of the building and worked their way to the door: Ezei and Mariam poured, anointing the piled-up papers, the walls and the floor. Cephas remained at the foot of the stairs until the last moment, his gun raised and ready.

Ezei had the incendiary flare – also unidentifiable from its breakdown products – that would ignite the blaze. He gave it to Mariam, who acknowledged the gesture of respect with a curt nod. His earlier hesitation was still fresh in her mind.

She pointed out to Ezei and Cephas the positions she'd assigned to them and they melted into the dark. There was nothing to be gained by waiting, and too much time lost already.

She tugged on the strip that kept the two chemical components of the flare apart. They merged and it sputtered into life in her hand. She threw it underarm down the hallway, where it bounced once before it settled.

There was a soft *whump*. Fierce light reared up like an angel in the narrow hallway, and hot, expanding air touched Mariam's cheek like the caress of an urgent lover. She closed the door gently and took up her station.

35

Someone had been burning flowers. The stairwell was a cauldron of seething air that stank of ruined blossoms: an inferno in a quiet summer meadow. Tillman wasn't an imaginative man, but images of sacrifice and massacred innocents rose in his mind anyway, too sudden to avoid. It was a smell you needed absolution from.

At his side, Kennedy swore. For a moment, she seemed rooted to the spot. Then she sank down on her knees. He thought she was praying, then realised she was searching. She came up with the pack of computer discs in her hand.

'There's no time,' Tillman told her.

'I'll bloody make time,' Kennedy snarled, tearing at the shrinkwrap plastic.

They didn't even have to shout: the fire wasn't loud yet, despite its fierceness. That was more unsettling even than the smell: this was a fire that got on with the job, with minimum fuss and maximum effect.

Tillman crossed to the door and stepped out into the heat, which was like pushing against a physical presence that filled the stairwell. He got as far as the angle of the stairs, beyond which a harsh actinic light, as much white as yellow, was writhing like a living thing. He cast a quick look around that corner, enough to tell him that there was no way through. The lower hall had become an oven, hot enough to render flesh from bone.

The windows, he thought. But there were boards nailed up over the windows. Except for the one in the computer room.

He ran back up the stairs and into the room. Kennedy was busy at the machine, hammering at the keyboard, feeding a disc into the drive. 'Kennedy!' he bellowed. 'Heather!' She didn't answer. 'We've got to *go*.'

'It's only the downstairs that's on fire,' Kennedy shouted over her shoulder. 'We've still got a couple of minutes.'

Tillman grabbed her arm, turned her around to face him. 'The smoke will kill us first,' he reminded her. 'You know that. Let's go.'

She hesitated for a second, then gave him a reluctant nod. 'Smash the window. I'll be right with you.'

He crossed to it quickly, looking around for something he could use to smash the glass out of its frame. Kennedy ejected the disc from the drive, snatched it up and stuffed it in her pocket.

Tillman went to the stack of computer servers and hefted the top one in his hands. Wires connected it to the others, but he shook and kicked them loose.

'That's evidence!' Kennedy yelled, anguished.

'It's going to be molten plastic inside of three minutes,' Tillman told her, tersely.

He struck the glass once, twice, three times. It smashed on the first impact: the other two were to clear the jagged shards from the corners of the frame so that they could climb through without slashing open an artery. He was leaning in for a fourth blow when something else hit the wood from the outside, slamming into the edge of the sash and making it explode into fragments inches from Tillman's face.

The whining report of a semi-automatic followed a second later. Tillman was already ducking back, acting on pure reflex. The second shot went past his ear, close enough for him to feel the wake of displaced air, and punched through the plaster of the ceiling, sending a shower of dust down on their heads.

Kennedy stared at the hole in the plaster and swore again. He thought she might be freezing on him: people did that in a crisis sometimes, even capable people, and the best thing to do in that situation was usually to punch them out. They were less trouble as a dead weight than as an active encumbrance.

But he was wrong. Kennedy was thinking it through. She cast a glance around the room, zeroed in on the blanket that was covering yet another pile of junk and snatched it up. That derailed her for a moment, since it revealed a fresh corpse lying on the floor, hidden by the blanket until now.

'You poor bastard,' Tillman heard Kennedy mutter. 'Should have ... oh Jesus, Combes! ...'

Her voice tailed off. She ran from the room, trailing the blanket behind her. Tillman followed, guessing what she was going to do. It wouldn't save them but it would buy them time.

He found her in the bathroom. She'd already started the taps running in the sink and in the bath, and she was trying to tear the blanket into strips. He took the hunting knife from his belt and offered it to her wordlessly. With the knife she quickly made a tear and ripped a ragged triangle from one corner of the blanket. Tillman took it from her and soaked it in the water filling the sink, while Kennedy cut loose a second strip of cloth for herself.

When the torn strips were thoroughly drenched, they tied them around their faces like bandanas. It would keep the smoke out for a few minutes and stave off monoxide poisoning. It gave them leeway. But leeway to do what?

The room was filling up with thick smoke now, on which motes of fire from the burning paper below floated like lanterns in a stream. The fire had got a lot louder now, too, roaring like a demon in the stairwell, making up for lost time. On top of the masks, that made it almost impossible to talk.

The stairwell was out.

Someone outside was waiting to kill them if they stuck their heads out of the windows.

What did that leave?

Kennedy tapped him on the arm, beckoned. He followed her, back into the computer room. She pointed upwards at the trapdoor, set into the ceiling. Tillman nodded vigorously, made a thumbs-up sign. *Okay, let's do it.*

They piled up unopened boxes of paper to make a step ladder. He boosted Kennedy up so she could first throw the trapdoor open – it wasn't locked, thank God – and then haul herself into the loft space above. He followed, climbing on to the precarious stack of boxes, then jumping and catching the edge of the trapdoor. The wood creaked loud enough to be heard over the buffeting roar of the flames, but it held. He got his elbows in and Kennedy hauled him the rest of the way over the edge.

The loft space was so full of dull grey smoke that it seemed like a solid thing, packed in there in cords and bundles. But when they moved, they left darker holes in the smoke that hung in their wake, tunnels of past time.

A skylight would have been too much to hope for, and in any case they didn't need one. The slates were of pre-war construction, probably nineteenth century, each hung on a single wooden pin in the traditional method, exquisitely balanced. But the spruce-wood laths were so old and worm-eaten that Tillman could dismantle them with his hands. Working together, they made a ragged hole and crawled out on to the sloping roof.

It was like climbing out of a hole in the ice of a pond. The area around the gap they'd made had been weakened so that it leaned inwards and clearly wouldn't bear their weight. They slid downwards from it towards the gutter, which also didn't look like a safe bet.

It became a lot less safe a second later, when one of the slates at the edge of the roof exploded into razor shards that tore at their faces. Tillman heard the *thup thup thup* of small arms fire: he could even identify the gun, within a reasonable margin of error. The light but sturdy Sig-226, probably in a double-action Kellerman version with two trigger reset points. The sort of gun a cop like Kennedy might have used in the days before .40 calibre became the word and the law.

Tillman backed away up the roof ridge, keeping his body as flat to the tiles as he could. Beside him, Kennedy was imitating his action: in fact, she'd started moving a second or so before him.

But there was no salvation on the roof ridge. They'd just be at the highest point when the roof collapsed, which couldn't be more than a couple of minutes away now. Assuming they didn't catch a bullet first, they'd plunge through the roof back into that furnace, and if they were lucky they'd break their necks in the fall.

That wasn't at all what Kennedy had in mind. She was looking off to Tillman's left, towards the rear of the building, and as he followed the line of her gaze he saw what she was looking at, or looking for: the nearest of the barns, maybe fifteen feet from the farmhouse and a yard or so higher. It faced the farmhouse full-on, and had a square hole in its front where a window had once been. Wooden shutters welded open by generations of lazy paint jobs stood to either side of the gap: landing guides for a short, unpowered flight.

Dangerous but not impossible.

Kennedy started to clamber upright on the ridge. Out of the corner of his eye, Tillman caught the movement from far below. He pulled her down again just as the bullets started punching through the tiles around them: heavy, slanting rain that brought a shower of shrapnel in its wake. He drew his Unica and returned fire, to buy them a little respite and to warn the shooters against pulling back too far from the walls of the farmhouse in search of a better shot.

'*Damn!*' Kennedy bellowed in rage and frustration 'This is total bloody overkill.'

Tillman emptied the Unica into the darkness below, then rolled on to his back to reload. He had two spare speedloaders, modified HKS 255s, both ready racked. After that he had nothing, not even loose ammunition. He emptied out the spent cartridges, slotted the speedloader and loaded the chambers with a quick twist of his wrist, all within a few seconds, but the virtuosity was an empty gesture. Firing into the dark, backlit by the flames that were starting to dance and weave between the gaps in the tiles, he knew he had little chance of hitting anything – of achieving anything beyond making himself an easier target. Maybe he could draw off the unseen assassins' fire while Kennedy made her run and jump for it.

And then they'd stroll over to the barn and pick her off at their leisure. He needed to come up with something better than that. Something that offered at least measurable odds on their surviving.

His gaze passed over the truck, then came back. Blow up the gas tank? It was a sign of how desperate he was that he considered it even for a second. Urban legend aside, it had been proved time and again that you couldn't make a petrol tank ignite by shooting at it. The bullet didn't generate enough heat,

329

and fuel-grade petrol wasn't unstable enough. Striking a spark off the metal of the tank itself might do it, but that was worse than a one-in-a-million chance, and there was no point gambling on those odds.

Which left one spectacularly stupid stunt: the sort of thing the phrase 'million-to-one chance' had been invented for.

Tillman groped in his pockets and found what he was looking for: the box of Swan Vestas he'd been carrying ever since Folkestone. Opening the cylinder of the Unica again, he tapped it against the heel of his hand and let a bullet slide out into his palm.

Kennedy was watching him, bewildered.

'Move towards the barn,' he told her. She didn't hear him through the mask, so he hauled it off and threw it away: the air was cleaner out here, and one way or another they probably weren't going to die from the smoke now. 'Move towards the barn,' he said again.

'They'll see me,' Kennedy pointed out.

'Doesn't matter. Move over there, as close as you can get, but don't jump until ... well, jump when they're looking elsewhere.'

'At what? What will they be looking at?'

'All the pretty lights,' Tillman muttered.

He turned his attention to the bullet. A .454 Casull, a round that had built on the Colt .45 casing and turned what was already a gun-range classic into a small masterpiece. Casull and Fullmer, the designers, were looking to make a handgun cartridge primarily for the biggest of big-game hunting, so they wanted to maximise power at point of impact – ideally, though, without breaking the arm of the shooter. So they'd married a rifle primer to a pistol cartridge, generating upwards of 60,000 cup when shot from a test barrel, and capable of accelerating a 230 grain bullet to 1800 feet per second.

For the low-recoil architecture of the Unica, it was the perfect round. Tillman stuck to the storefront standard most of the time, but occasionally rolled his own using the Hornady brass casing and a primer he'd gotten from an old Irish recipe. Consequently, he knew when he prised the bullet casing open with his teeth that it wouldn't explode and rip the lower half of his face off.

Kennedy was edging away from him along the roof, and the bullets had moved with her. She was pressed flat against the tiles, offering the smallest possible target, but a stray bullet was going to take her out sooner rather than later. Even a peripheral hit would probably send her sliding and tumbling down the slope of the roof, gathering momentum until she pitched right off at the bottom.

Right now she was probably wondering if Tillman was just using her as a decoy, aiming to make a run and jump himself off the opposite end of the roof ridge and trust to luck that he didn't break a leg or his spine when he landed.

Opening the Swan box, Tillman bit the heads off a couple of dozen matches. He chewed them up in his mouth, turning them into a thick paste, then let the foul, bitter mixture dribble from between his lips into the base of the bullet casing: a crude stew of red phosphorus and saliva. He resealed the casing, again using his teeth to bite around the edges of the base and crimp it into place. He bit down as hard as he could, until his teeth seemed likely to shatter under the applied pressure. Even then, there was a better than fifty per cent chance that the freakish, home-made thing would just explode in the barrel. But screw it, he was committed now.

Kennedy had gone as far as she could go: was pressed up tight against a broad chimney stack two-thirds of the way along the roof. It offered a little cover, at least, but it also blocked her passage unless she stood or knelt upright to edge around it. The shooters had followed her there and were more or less free now to choose their angle. They remained completely invisible in the perfect darkness below, but the muzzle flashes showed their positions each time they fired. Tillman could target the muzzle flashes, of course, but he knew, too, that only an idiot would be standing still while they fired.

Stick with plan A – where A stood for *absurd*.

He counted to three in his mind, then sat bolt upright. He took careful aim, even though he knew how well he must be showing up against the brightness of the fire at his back. A shot whucked past his shoulder, close enough to feel. A second smacked into the tiles between his legs.

Holding the out-breath, holding the target, he shut out the world and squeezed the trigger.

Instantly, the night turned into day: specifically, the *dies irae*, when God loses his patience and says enough is damned well enough.

36

It was endgame.

Tillman and the woman were effectively trapped in the building and the building was burning to the ground.

Mariam expected them to try the windows and was ready to push them back inside when they did. In fact, she felt almost certain she'd hit Tillman when he appeared at the bedroom window, where she was already aiming, and she would not have been surprised if they'd seen no more of either him or the woman.

It was Ezei who heard the sounds from the roof first. He whistled – two short notes, to get Mariam's attention – and pointed up. She saw the movement there, abstract at first and then suddenly resolving into the woman's head and shoulders. She fired and the woman ducked down out of sight.

Of course, out of sight was purely a matter of geometry. Mariam didn't need to tell Ezei and Cephas what to do. In synchrony with her, they stepped back from the walls of the house. Two figures were moving up on the roof now, but they blended in with their background for the most part: it was only when some part of one or other body broke above the line of the roof and was picked out against the glow of the licking flames that they could be seen. Mariam raised her gun on to that line and waited.

Twice something bulked briefly against the flames and she fired. The second time, shots were returned and she had to duck back in closer to the wall out of Tillman's line of sight.

She considered, for a moment, leaving it at that, allowing the two to burn to death in their own time, without further complications. But the roof wasn't completely isolated, and Tillman and Kennedy had seemed to be moving to the rear, from where it might be possible to jump across to the nearest of the outhouse buildings.

Mariam whistled and Ezei looked in her direction again. *To the back*, she signalled, and he took off at once. Quickly, she jogged along the front of the building until she could see Cephas on the other side. He looked round at her as she appeared and she gave him the same silent instruction.

She herself, Mariam decided, would stay at the front. It seemed impossible now that Tillman and Kennedy would duck back into the building, whose interior must be one undifferentiated mass of flame, and try to make it to the window again – but if they did, or even more inconceivably made a run for the door, then Mariam would be in place to shoot them down.

She watched approvingly as Ezei and Cephas circled, firing as they went. For a moment, she glimpsed the woman's shoulder and part of her back. Kennedy appeared to have gotten most of the way to the rear end of the roof ridge, where the abrupt vertical of a chimney stack stood in her way, providing a little cover so long as she didn't try to move past it. But if she stayed where she was, she had about a minute more before the roof collapsed, and in the meantime she stood out against the white-painted chimney every time she shifted her balance. Cephas took aim – but then suddenly shifted to fire at a different target, presumably Tillman. He squeezed off two shots.

The third shot came from the roof and Mariam *saw* it at the same time that she heard it: a luminous red streak in the air, drawing the shortest possible line between two points. The first point was Tillman. The second was the truck in which he had arrived.

The explosion was spectacularly sudden and agonisingly bright. Burning air washed over Mariam and slapped her off her feet. A buffeting thunderclap arrived so long afterwards that it seemed to belong to a different explosion altogether.

Groggy, she raised her head and blinked into the roiling smoke. Her ears were ringing, her eyes were blind and the hot air she breathed was a soup of overcooked petroleum. She tried to shout for Cephas and broke into jagged coughs that ripped her seared throat as though she were chewing on broken glass.

Then she saw a strange thing: a vision. The world had turned to black and white, and a man drawn in soot on grainy chalk was doing a ridiculous slapstick dance, his movements discontinuous and unconvincing. He fell down, as Charlie Chaplin was accustomed to fall down, with such energy in the fall that he rolled himself almost upright again, only to fall a second time.

It was Cephas. And it wasn't a dance or a comedic act. It was his death throes. The fire was all over him, clasping him like a lover, the burning petrol drenching his clothes and his skin, pulling the moisture from inside his body and turning it to vapour to fling it into the sky in a violent and terrible transubstantiation.

Mariam screamed, and the scream hurt so much that her mind almost shut down. She had to fight to stay conscious.

Her eyes streaming, she staggered to her feet. She saw Ezei running around the rear of the farmhouse, then stopping abruptly as he saw what she had seen: Cephas turned into an offering to God. 'Ezei!' she croaked, as she started towards him. She had to shape the sound with blistered lips. 'Ezei, don't—'

Don't go near him, was what she meant to say. *Don't step into the light, you'll only make yourself a target.* But Tillman's gun sounded even as she spoke, and the spectacular lighting allowed Mariam to see Ezei's fate with far too much clarity. The smoke beside his head rolled and reddened: some of that smoke was Ezei's blood and brains, exiting through a hole made by a heavy shell at close to medium range. He stumble-stepped to a halt, already dead, and fell heavily to the ground.

Mariam was running before she knew it, running for the barn, because that was what they'd do now. They'd jump and they'd be vulnerable when they jumped, vulnerable when they landed. She could still bring this home, she could still avenge, she could still finish the mission.

The closed barn doors hung off their hinges. She tugged and heaved until they opened, stepped back and then launched herself into the darkness inside in a tight vertical roll. She tensed as she unfolded, gun in one hand, *sica* blade in the other. If she saw him before he saw her, she'd use the knife. If it came to a shoot-out, she'd trust to the gun first and pray he lived long enough for her to get in close and slit his throat.

From outside came a soft thump, and then a second. They'd climbed *over* the barn, not into it.

Mariam screamed again – a profanity she wouldn't even have admitted that she knew. She ran outside, but the burning truck and the burning building and the air super-saturated with smoke seeled her eyes more effectively than any blindfold. There were running footsteps in the darkness beyond the painful light. She ran after them, firing in that direction until the clip emptied and the trigger locked.

Then she tripped on something in the dark and sprawled on the rough ground, tearing the skin of her palms. The breath was knocked out of her. Her chest felt like it had been ripped open, and the skin of her burned face was too tight on her skull, stretched like a death mask. She rolled over on her back in the long grass, spent. For a moment she felt she was dying. But the pain, which intensified with each breath, told her that she was still alive.

Through the agony, she began to glimpse the faint, uncertain outlines of a consolation. God wasn't done with her, yet. And she wasn't done with the monsters who had snuffed out the lives of her beloved cousins.

37

A moment came, in their running, when Tillman wondered what it was, exactly, that they were running from.

The shooters, obviously. But he'd laid out two of them, one with an exploding petrol tank, the other in a more conventional way, with a bullet. He'd tried to count, while he was up on the roof, and was almost certain that there could only be one or two more of them out there, in all.

But that meant one or two who'd actually fired: they could have reinforcements ready to hand and ways of bringing them to bear real quick. Maybe the scream they'd heard, after they jumped from the roof of the barn, was exactly that: a summons. It had sounded like a woman's voice. He wondered, inconsequentially, if it was the woman from the boat, who'd landed a knife into his thigh at thirty yards. That wasn't a woman to face in the dark, with an empty gun.

Better to run, then, and take stock later, rather than stay and fight what might be a premature last stand. Kennedy had the disc in her pockets: they'd gotten . . . something out of this, and it was something the pale assassins had swarmed to keep them away from. So it was worth having. It had to be.

Kennedy was keeping up with him, at first, and then suddenly she was outpacing him. His hip, still stiff from the knife wound, slowed him down. He put on an extra burst of speed, in spite of the pain, and caught up with her as they reached a shallow ditch that seemed to be the southern edge of the property line.

Negotiating the ditch, Tillman walked into a barbed wire fence, but it was only a single length of cable and it did minimal damage. He clambered over it and found himself on a dirt path that led back down towards the distant road on a steep angle. He looked back at Kennedy, who was struggling over the wire behind him. She either didn't see his offered hand or else chose to ignore it.

This was neutral ground: not Dovecote. They slowed at last, by silent consent deciding that they'd run far enough for now. Kennedy bent from the waist, hands gripping her knees, and gradually got her breath back under control. Tillman stayed upright, looking behind for pursuit: but they would already have heard any pursuit that wasn't made up of ninjas.

'Where now?' Kennedy asked, haltingly. 'We're ... in the middle of ... bloody nowhere, and you blew up the truck!'

'Felt like a good idea at the time,' Tillman said.

Kennedy laughed – a harsh sound that seemed torn out of her. 'Did the job,' she observed, grimly, and then, 'How? How did you do that?'

By the dumbest of dumb luck, was the answer. *The mere chance that I couldn't find a lighter to cauterise my wounds, back in Folkestone, and had to settle for matches; and a fun fact from a decades-ago chemistry lesson.* 'I turned a regular bullet into an incendiary,' he told her. 'The miracle ingredient was ground-up match-heads: they're mostly crystallised red phosphorus. Two-hundred-degree ignition point, more or less, which is about the same as the petrol in the tank – but you've only got to hit that temperature for a fraction of a second, say with impact friction, and then it sparks like crazy because it's a degraded form of white phosphorus, and that's a natural pyrophore.'

He wound down because that was as much as he knew, really. As a kid, he'd done it with BB pellets, anointing the noses of the tiny leaden slugs with gritty red slime and then waiting for them to dry: shooting at cans of lighter fluid at ten metres on a home-made range, then marvelling at the angel of light and heat that spread its wings suddenly above their tiny backyard.

Kennedy looked at him, in silence, for a long time, seeming about to speak but saying nothing. Tillman waited anyway, knowing that something was coming.

'That's two people dead,' she said.

'Sorry?'

'Two people dead. Extra-judicial killings. You killed them, Tillman.'

He shrugged, genuinely not sure what response she wanted from him. 'So?'

'So I'm meant to sodding arrest you. This is ... messed up. I'm not your moll, or your sidekick, or your ... anything else. We can't go on meeting like this.'

He breathed out slowly, his own equilibrium escaping him. It had been a wild night even by his sloppy standards, and the deaths, in memory, left him with no sense of triumph. 'No,' he agreed. 'We can't. Not for much longer. But the deal stands, Kennedy. Whatever you get from those discs or the papers ...'

'Yes? Whatever I get?'

'Well, I killed for it. So it's mine, too.'

She stared at him in silence again, and again he waited her out. This time there was no sequel. Whatever it was she wanted to say, she didn't manage to find the words for it. She walked on past him down the lane, heading towards the road. He respected her mood, allowed her a whole lot of distance all the way down.

38

What had happened at Dovecote Farm could not be hidden.

Kennedy called Division from the roadside, reporting the results of their search, Combes's death and her encounter with the killers. She left out nothing – except that in her account, she'd made her own way to the farm after being separated from Combes, and she'd been alone when she escaped from the blaze. About Tillman, she was silent.

Squad cars and ambulances, fire tenders and vans with flashing lights began to arrive within the next half-hour. They cordoned off the site, put out the flames still feeding fitfully on the remains of the farmhouse and the truck, and began the long, involved task of working the scene. Kennedy wished them joy of it.

Summerhill himself was almost the last to arrive. There could be any number of reasons for that, but one was certainly his backtracking through the files before he left Division, looking for the data trail that led to this pandemonium, making damn sure he hadn't given his blessing to it.

They exchanged words briefly. Kennedy played up her exhaustion and pain to keep Summerhill at bay and the paramedics mindful of their duties. She gave him the barest of bare-bones explanations, decisively derailed when she told him that one of the as yet unidentified bodies was that of Detective

Sergeant Combes: another man down. Summerhill didn't even ask if she'd managed to retrieve any of the physical evidence, so she didn't have to lie.

Temporary dressings were applied to her cuts and burns, and then she was spirited away to the Royal Surrey, the nearest hospital with an A & E department. Before she left, she asked Summerhill to send a black-and-white after her. If they were going to drug her – maybe put her under – she wanted to get her statement down first: there was no telling what she might forget under anaesthetic. Begrudgingly, Summerhill agreed. Apart from that, though, he ordered her to talk to nobody before she talked to him. 'Nobody, Kennedy. Not even a bloody priest.'

'I don't know any, Jimmy,' she croaked. 'Don't move in those kind of circles.'

In fact, her injuries were mostly superficial and nobody suggested putting her out. It was just topical analgesics, painkillers and an anaesthetic gel. They did suggest an intravenous drip, but Kennedy refused it, signing the prissy little form which said, effectively, that it was her look-out.

Twenty-five minutes later she walked out through the sliding doors of the A & E and found the squad car waiting on the tarmac. 'I need to go back to Division,' she told the slightly startled constable. 'New Scotland Yard. Now. There's some evidence that needs to be logged.'

The PC reached for his radio. Kennedy put a hand on his arm and he stopped.

'It's ATSA,' she said. 'No discussion on open channels. Sorry.'

The PC didn't argue or ask any questions: it was bullshit, of course, but the provisions of the Anti-Terrorism Security Act were a useful trump card, a shapeless bag of special powers invoked whenever anyone in Division wanted to jump a small hurdle without slowing down for explanations.

Or was it bullshit? Certainly she was up against a conspiracy that had better resources than she did and links to other countries.

Once they got back to Dacre Street, she let the PC go. He'd probably report in straight away, but only to his own super. She wasn't worried about word getting back to Summerhill any time soon.

In the bear pit, she made a copy of the disc. Then she dropped the original into an envelope and put it in the internal mail to Summerhill. She added a brief note explaining how the pain of her burns and the trauma of her narrow brushes with death had made her momentarily forget that she'd managed to save one small keepsake from the inferno.

She felt the absurdity of all this hole-in-corner intrigue. But she knew, too, that the next few days were going to be rough: rougher, even, than what had come before. Another man down, and once again the record would show that Kennedy had gone in without proper back-up. This time she'd also ignored chain of command and acted without any authorisation from her case officer. There was a real chance that the book, suspended in mid-air since the events at Park Square, would now be thrown full-force. If that happened – if she was embroiled in committees and hamstrung by inquiries – she wanted at least to be able to evaluate what she'd found, to stay involved in the investigation, as far as she could. She owed that much to Harper, and to herself.

She copied the disc one more time, for Tillman. While she was waiting for her creaky, ancient drive to finish the job, she checked her emails. Among them she found a reply from Quai Charles de Gaulle, Lyon. Interpol.

She scanned the email: 'Your request for information under the reciprocal arrangements set out in the UN Convention ... positive results recent enough to be relevant to your ... accompanying documents only to be circulated internally and by permission of ...'

There was an attachment. She clicked on it. And then stared at the screen for a minute without even blinking.

Then she picked up her phone and called Tillman's cell, the new number.

'Tillman.'

'Kennedy.' Considering what they'd been through a scant couple of hours before, he sounded pretty composed and matter-of-fact. She wondered where he was. In a transport café off the A3? A pub in Guildford? Back in the Smoke already, holed up in some rented room reading *Guns and Ammo*?

'Leo ...' she said, and got no further.

'Are you okay? What happened when your top brass arrived? I was watching that circus from about a half-mile off: really didn't feel like getting any closer.'

'I ... it was fine,' she foundered. 'It's fine so far. They can't convene a firing squad until they've checked their ammunition.'

'Let me know when it gets serious. I'll help any way I can.'

'Leo, listen. There's a message here from Interpol. They came back on my C52.'

'On your what?'

'Routine request. Information from other forces on pending cases. I asked them ... I asked them about Michael Brand.'

'And they came up positive?' The tenor of his voice changed instantly. 'Something new?'

'They forwarded a whole wad of stuff from America. PDFs of documents from local forces in Arizona, and from the FBI.' She swallowed, tried again. 'Leo, there are other ways into this. With what we've got from Dovecote, we can—'

He cut across her, reading her tension accurately, wanting her just to say it, whatever it was. 'Kennedy, ten words or less.'

'Michael Brand ...'

'Yes? Come on.'

'He went down in a plane crash just outside a town called Peason, in Arizona. He's dead, Leo. He died six weeks ago.'

PART THREE

124

39

The Colorado was a spent force these days. Extensively pillaged by Southern California via something known as the All-American Canal (what patriot wouldn't stand and salute for a watercourse that called itself that?), and by irrigation channels built to slake the thirst of Arizona farmlands, it mostly ran out of steam somewhere south of Yuma, lost its way in dry arroyos and never made it within a hundred miles of the ocean.

This much Kennedy learned from her cab driver, a chatty guy named John-Bird who claimed to be three-quarters Mojave Indian. He picked Kennedy up, as arranged, outside the main terminal at Laughlin Bullhead, which called itself an international airport but was accessible from London only via a stopover at Washington Dulles. It had been a fifteen-hour flight and Kennedy was ragged at the edges even before she got into the cab. The heat didn't help – local time was 11.50, and the sun was at its blinding zenith – although John-Bird cheerfully informed her that it was a dry heat and not nearly so debilitating as the wetter heats you got in less civilised parts of the world. He turned the air conditioning up a notch, which did nothing to the temperature but significantly increased the noise.

They caught the 68 and drove straight out of town, staying with the Colorado until they turned off east towards Kingman and distant Flagstaff. The river looked impressive enough to Kennedy, a meandering giant twice as wide as the Thames flowing between towering ramparts of orange rock. She couldn't see a single cloud from horizon to horizon.

'*Go south, go clockwise, veer left,*' John-Bird said. 'Know what that is? That's how to remember all the tributaries of the Colorado – the Gila River, the San Juan, Green River, the Colorado River Aqueduct, the … what's V, what's V? Okay, yeah, the Virgin River, and the Little River. 'S cute, huh? Sounds like directions, but it won't get you nowhere. It's just to remember.'

'Very useful,' Kennedy agreed, glumly. Peason was a forty-five minute drive away and John-Bird looked to be just getting into his stride. He was telling her now how the name of the river came from the fact that the water used to be coloured bright red with sediment – but these days all that stuff got filtered out by the Glen Canyon Dam, so it was the same colour as any other river. Cute, huh?

To get him off his speciality subject, she asked him about the plane crash. Yeah, it turned out, he was on the road that day, driving a fare from Grasshopper Junction, and he actually saw the plane come down. 'It was crazy sudden. Like, out of nowhere. Never seen nothing like it. But it was far enough away that it didn't make no sound, that I could hear. It was real quiet. That was what I couldn't forget, afterwards – that it came down out of the sky and there must have been, like, a huge explosion, but for me it was quiet like … you know, like when you've got the TV on with the volume turned right down. All those people dead, without a sound.'

He mused on this for a minute or so, which gave Kennedy a respite to look at the instructions the sheriff's office had sent her. But it was a short meditation, and soon she was being regaled by more fun facts about the south-west's favourite waterway. Not that John-Bird was limited to the Colorado: he knew all sorts of stuff about Lake Mead and Lake Mohave, too. He refused, though, to be drawn on the subject of Las Vegas Bay. 'Not a good place. Not a family place.' Spaced out from tiredness, and almost free-associating, Kennedy tried to imagine what a sleazy, non-family-friendly body of water would look like. Maybe there were illegal additives.

When they finally got to Peason, she made John-Bird wait while she dumped her bags at the hotel, an EconoLodge fitted out in fake hacienda style, so that he could take her straight on over to the sheriff's office. She knew she wasn't at her best, but she wanted to make contact and get things moving on that front. She might not have much lead time, so she should at least make the best use of what she had.

The sheriff's office was a single-storey building right on Peason's main street, next door to a realtor's that offered LUXURY APARTMENTS TWICE THE SQUARE FOOTAGE. John-Bird gave Kennedy a card. She solemnly put it in her purse, but promised herself that she'd only use it as a last resort.

She crossed the street and went on into the office, as John-Bird pulled past her with a final wave.

Inside, the place smelled of pot pourri – honey, wisteria, maybe rose petals – and the air conditioning was perfectly pitched. The formidable woman at the despatch desk, with bad skin, big hair and a face as flat and pugnacious as a bulldog's, looked like she might be responsible for keeping up the moral fibre of the place, and like she might take those responsibilities seriously. Beyond her desk, the room was bisected by a wooden dividing wall at waist height, into which a small gate had been set.

'Yes ma'am,' the bulldog said to Kennedy. 'How may I help you?'

Kennedy approached the desk and handed over the guarantors of her *bona fides*: a letter of introduction on London Metropolitan Police headed paper and a print-out of an email sent by someone named Webster Gayle, inviting her to come on over whenever she liked, he'd be only too happy to help out in any way he could.

'I'm from London,' she explained. 'I'm meant to be meeting up with Sheriff Gayle. I don't have an appointment as such, but I thought I'd let him know that I've arrived.'

The bulldog scanned both sheets with slow, imperturbable concentration. 'Oh yeah,' she said at last. 'Web said you'd be coming by. He thought it was tomorrow, but I guess it's today after all. Okay, why'n't you go ahead and take a seat, and I'll tell the sheriff you're here.'

Kennedy took the offered seat, while the bulldog tapped keys on a switchboard and murmured something into the intercom too low for her to hear. The sheriff's voice, by contrast, came through painfully loud. 'Thanks, Connie. Tell her to wait a minute, would you mind? I got to comb my hair and tuck my shirt inside my pants for a British lady. Is she pretty, at all? Or does she look like the Queen?'

The bulldog closed the channel and gave Kennedy an inscrutable look. 'He'll be right with you,' she said.

Kennedy sat down and waited, trying not to nod off. She drank a couple of glasses of water from the cooler, which was almost painfully cold and helped a lot. By the time she'd finished the second, a man the size of a Welsh dresser was lumbering towards her, unlatching the gate with huge, awkward-looking hands, one of which he held out to be shaken as he took the remaining space in two strides.

Kennedy pegged Gayle at once as the sort of big man who'd learned a kind of innate caution and delicacy from having to

352

deal all the time with a world several sizes too small for him. He didn't enfold her hand in his, he just touched her lightly on the palm and the backs of the knuckles with the tips of his own fingers, making a courteous nod stand in for an actual handshake.

'Webster Gayle,' he told her. 'County Sheriff. Always a pleasure to meet a fellow law enforcement officer, Sergeant – and your force has a great reputation.'

'Thank you, Sheriff,' Kennedy said. 'Listen, I only just got in and I'm more dead than alive. But if you've got some time tomorrow, I'd love to pick your brains about this business and maybe get your take on—'

'Tomorrow?' Gayle chewed on the word as though it was a dubious piece of gristle. 'Well, yeah, we could talk tomorrow. But I've got a window right now, and I'm aware that you've only got five days in your budget. If you're really too tired, then okay, let's let it rest and meet in the a.m. But if you think you can stay upright for another hour or so, then maybe we could at least go over the basics – what it is you want to do while you're out here and how we can facilitate that.'

'Of course.' Kennedy smiled and nodded. She was entirely dependent on this man's goodwill and she knew better than to pull back on the reins if he was ready to break into a trot. Besides, Gayle was right in saying that she didn't have much time: probably even less than he thought. 'By all means, let's get the ball rolling.'

Kennedy knew this interview had to come and she had a speech all prepared that she hoped she could deliver with the appropriate conviction despite the jet lag. The speech explained, with a fair amount of supporting documentation, exactly what crimes she was investigating, how they strayed into Gayle's jurisdiction, what international and inter-agency protocols could be invoked in support of her presence, and what level of support she wanted the County Sheriff's office to provide. In other words, she was ready to fill in the blanks from the official (or at least, official-looking) inter-force aid request and put precise limits on what otherwise might have looked like a blank cheque.

But it turned out that Webster Gayle, like John-Bird, had a pet subject on which he was only too happy to talk – and, mercifully, it was not the Colorado River but the fate of Coastal Airlines Flight 124. In his tiny office, which was really just a partitioned-off corner of the larger space with screens for walls, he got started before she'd even sat down.

'Human error,' he said to Kennedy. 'That was what they said, in the end. Human error.' His emphasis was heavy, almost sarcastic. 'I guess that's one of the things they come up with when they don't really know what all else they can say.'

'I thought it was the door,' said Kennedy. 'The door came open in the air and they lost cabin pressure.'

'That's right,' Gayle agreed. 'But the door mechanism was sound as a bell. So they don't really have an explanation as to why it blew. Human error is kind of the fallback position, is what I'm thinking. If nothing else went wrong, well, then the people must've gone wrong. That's easier than saying, "We just don't know", or maybe grounding the whole fleet while they check out the doors on every last plane, like the Australians did that time with their superjumbos. You know, when they had an engine blow? And hell, that didn't even kill nobody.'

Kennedy nodded politely. 'But it's all academic now, right? They closed the investigation when they found the flight recorder.'

'No, ma'am.' The sheriff was emphatic. 'They never did find that black box thing. They just stopped looking for it when it stopped signalling – which is something that's not supposed to happen, by the way. I read up on it. The battery's supposed to be good for three months, and you pretty much can't destroy it even if you've got a bomb. Makes sense, doesn't it? A plane falling out of the sky, that's kind of like a bomb, so it would have to stand up to ...'

He stopped abruptly and his face went blank. Kennedy thought he looked like he was remembering something very specific and very vivid, and trying not to.

'Did you see the crash, Sheriff Gayle?'

The big man pulled himself together. 'No, ma'am, I didn't. But I saw what it was like afterwards. The wreckage and such. Wasn't anything I'm going to forget in a hurry.' He drummed the table, thrown off track – either by the question or by his own disordered recollections. 'So the recorder,' he said at last, picking up the thread again, 'that's not gonna come to harm, and it's not going to stop sending unless it falls into a live volcano or something. And last time I checked, we don't have too many of those in Coconino County.

'So there's two mysteries, right there. How did the door come open and what happened to the box? Now I'm going to add a third one to that list. How many survivors were there?'

Kennedy blinked – running on empty and wondering how the conversation had gotten so quickly into *X-Files* territory.

'None, is what I heard,' she said.

'None is what they reported,' Gayle said, with something like relish. 'But then all this other stuff started happening.' He launched into a detailed summary of the post-mortem sightings, the walking dead of Flight 124, while Kennedy – deeply sceptical, and incapable of faking any kind of interest – did her best not to respond at all. When Gayle wound down, she groped for a non-committal comment.

'Well, I ... I guess that's a mystery of a different order,' she said. 'I mean, what happened on the flight, and what happened to the recorder afterwards – you could actually get an answer to those two things. But ghosts are, you know ... there's not ever going to be an explanation. People will believe they saw what they saw, but they won't ever be able to prove it. So there's no answer. It will just go down as one of those things.'

She was trying hard not to give offence: Gayle didn't take any but he dismissed the objection with an easy smile. 'Well, ma'am, I find that it's best in life to keep an open mind. Sometimes if a thing looks impossible, it's just because you're looking at it from the wrong angle.'

Damned jet lag. Kennedy really didn't feel up to this kind of brinkmanship. 'Well, like I said, my main focus is going to be on—'

'—the facts that relate to your investigation. I know that. But there again, what's relevant isn't always what seems to point in the right direction. I don't need to tell you that – you're a detective.' He was jocular and confiding, radiating a sort of proprietorial eagerness, and Kennedy realised why he'd agreed so readily to see her and help with the investigation: he'd been waiting for someone he could give this stuff to. She wondered, with glum fatalism, how far she'd have to humour him in his pet obsession to get answers to her own questions.

'Right,' she agreed, guardedly.

'Now I'm not saying you should give an ear to every crank theory that someone shoves your way. I just value an open mind, like I said, and I don't think you should straight away dismiss something just because it sounds stupid. Great things get invented on account of stupid questions, it seems to me. What if you put rat poison into someone's veins, 'stead of medicine? That's warfarin, in case you didn't know: stops lots of folks from dying of heart attacks. Or what if you close your eyes and try to see something with your ears? That's radar.

'So I went into this thinking there could be something to it, but not thinking for certain sure I knew what the something was. And then I talked it over with a good friend of mine, Mizz Eileen Moggs, who writes for our local paper and is the smartest person I know. And she said they always do this, after a disaster. She put it down to something called the *news cycle*: and the way that works is if they got to report a story but nothing happened since the last time they reported it, they just go ahead and make something up. Like, people want to keep hearing about this stuff, and that's a hunger that's got to be fed. You come across that notion?'

'Yes,' Kennedy said. 'I think your friend is right.'

Gayle seemed pleased by this response. He wagged a finger at her. 'Ah, but then I showed my friend all the stuff I collected up – all these bits and pieces I took off the internet and places like that – and she started in to thinking about it herself. And she said this time is different.'

'Different how, exactly?'

'Well, maybe you'll get to hear that answer from Eileen herself, Sergeant Kennedy. I'd really like to introduce the two of you, if the opportunity comes up.'

It was way past time, Kennedy decided, to start imposing her own agenda on all this. 'Well, that would be great,' she said. 'I'd be very happy to meet Miss ... Moggs? But as you know, I'm sort of on the clock here. And my main concern is to pursue some information pertaining to my murder inquiry.'

'Stuart Barlow and subsequent addendums. Yeah, I read the case files you forwarded. Something of a head-scratcher.'

'That's putting it mildly, Sheriff Gayle.'

'And you say our investigation into the plane crash might could help you out, in some way.'

'That's what I'm hoping, yes. One of the passengers on CA 124 was a man travelling under the name of Michael Brand.'

357

'That "under the name of" kind of implies it wasn't his actual given name. Is that the case?'

'We can't really say. We were totally failing to run him to ground in Europe when we learned that he'd died over here. We don't know much about him at all, except that he's got a career that goes back a fair few years and includes crimes other than murder.'

'Such as?'

'Kidnapping, maybe. Gun-running, maybe. Involvement in drug trafficking.'

'All maybe?'

'Mostly hearsay, and the source is a CI I can't even name. But the grounds for my being here relate entirely to the Barlow case. We think there's plenty in that case file to justify our concern and our approaching you with a request.'

Gayle scratched his chin – a pantomime of deep and weighty thought. 'Yeah, I guess I'd have to agree on that. Your multiple homicide has got to count as a good reason to knock on all the doors you can think of. We're pretty stretched here, but I think I can give you a couple of days at least.'

The implications of that took a second or so to sink in. 'A couple of days?' Kennedy repeated, inanely.

'After that I'll have to get back in here and do some desk stuff.'

'A couple of days of your own time? Sheriff, that's a lot more than I ever expected. Are you sure you can ...'

He was waving her silent, smiling a wide, self-deprecating smile. 'We're more than happy to do what we can, Sergeant. So tell me what you had in mind.'

Kennedy took a second to pull her thoughts together. She'd expected to meet indifference, if not outright hostility. Instead she'd found a friendly obsessive who wanted to be a part of her investigation because he hadn't been allowed to pursue it as his own. It was such a thoroughbred gift horse, she had to fight the urge to wrestle its mouth open and take a better look. 'Well, what I was hoping to do,' she told Gayle, 'first and foremost, was to find out whether anything came out of your investigations here that could throw light on Brand's origins or possible confederates. Like, for example, if any of his clothes or belongings were retrieved, and if so, whether they'd still be available for me or my colleagues to examine. And likewise, if any forensic data were available on the body itself, or if he filed an address with your civil aviation authority when he purchased his ticket. Anything like that.'

Gayle was nodding along to this list. 'I don't see how any of that would be a problem. I can tell you now there isn't much, but they did an autopsy, and there'd be photos and records pertaining to that. Clothes and belongings would have been logged into evidence – both the ones we could definitively match up with a particular body and the ones we had to give up on. Most of that stuff is up north of here, in a storage facility that we rent from Santa Claus.'

'From Santa Claus?' She'd have to watch this tendency to become a choric echo.

'The municipality of Santa Claus,' Gayle clarified. 'Sorry, Sergeant, that doesn't even raise a smile around here. Santa Claus is a town about ten miles out from Peason, just inside the county limits. A ghost town, these days. They got space to rent for next to nothing, and we got a space problem, so we use them for all kinds of overspill stuff. Okay, what else?'

'Depending on what I find – if I find anything – then maybe you'd be prepared to act as liaison. You know, talk with other US agencies or bodies, send information requests. I know that's a lot to ask, and if you prefer I can bounce through Interpol instead. It's just that I don't have any jurisdiction out here and it would be great to pick up a thread and just follow it, if we're lucky enough to turn up something worth following.'

'That'd have to be case-by-case,' Gayle told her, 'but we can probably lend you a deputy and a desktop, if it comes to it.'

'That's really kind, Sheriff Gayle. Thank you.'

'My pleasure. Now why don't I drop you at your hotel? I think I come near to talked your legs off and you probably need to get some rest after that flight.'

Kennedy made some token resistance and was overruled. Sheriff Gayle got up to leave and as she followed him out into the reception area, he counted off on his fingers the items on the agenda. 'So. Autopsy records. Victims' possessions. Paper trail. Would that be it for now?'

'That would be plenty for now, Sheriff.'

'We'll do it in the a.m. Connie, I'm going to drive Sergeant Kennedy out to her hotel. I'll be back in thirty.'

The bulldog looked at Kennedy and then at him. 'Okay,' she said, after slightly too long a pause. 'What shall I tell Eileen Moggs if she calls?'

Kennedy detected a sly intonation to the question, as though it was designed to catch the sheriff slightly off balance – to sucker-punch him. If it was, it didn't work. Gayle just shrugged. 'Tell her I'll call her back,' he said. 'I'll be seeing her later on anyway. Come on, Sergeant.'

Kennedy made one more token protest. 'I can take a cab ...'

'No, no. We aim to send you home with good memories of Arizona.'

Kennedy smiled and nodded, as he hustled her out the door. Privately, though, she thought that might be asking a lot.

At the hotel, Kennedy got herself in the mood for sleep by breaking out a bottle of Dos Equis from the room's mini-bar and soaking in a hot bath while she drank it. Perversely, it made her feel wired and restless rather than pushing her jet lag towards the edge of the catastrophe curve so that she could sleep.

There were still too many hours of daylight left, and nobody she knew in this place and nowhere particular to go. Even the *What's On in Peason?* magazine on the bedside table pretty much shrugged its shoulders, turned out its pockets and came back with the answer: *nothing*. She'd just missed the flower show, apparently, and the next cultural landmark was the Hardyville Days, over in Bullhead, which wasn't until October and seemed to lean heavily on the entertainment concept of ugly men in drag. She was planning to be long gone by then.

So what sort of innocent fun could she get up to in her hotel room?

She took out her laptop, actually her sister Chrissie's, logged on to the wi-fi network and accessed her email account. There were four items in the inbox, the first three from DCI Jimmy Summerhill, with the tone creeping up the scale from professional detachment to foam-flecked stridency. Into the wastebasket with those: she was paying for this connection by the hour after all.

She also had an email from Izzy, who had agreed to look after Kennedy's dad until Chrissie came to collect him at the week-end – assuming Kennedy wasn't already back by then.

You left so suddenly. Gonna miss you, while you're away. And, you know, hope nothing's wrong.

She started a reply but scrapped it; started another that went the same way.

Lots of things wrong, she eventually wrote. *But I'm still on the case. Maybe tell you about it over a drink some time?*

After that, and with no real hope at all of getting an answer, she sent an email to Leo Tillman – the latest in a series – telling him where she was and what she was doing. It was terse, but it covered the bases.

> Leo, as per last message I'm out in Arizona chasing the Michael Brand connection. No real news as yet, but I've made contact with local law enforcement and they're being really helpful. Hope to have a lot to report tomorrow. In the meantime, am attaching AGAIN the analysis Doctor Gassan gave me of the Dovecote Farm files. Maybe you've read them already, but if you haven't, you really should. This whole thing could maybe break wide open any time if we find the right crowbar – and everything suggests that Brand is it. Deal still stands. Let me know if you have anything to share.
> – Kennedy

She attached the files and hit SEND. She could think of nothing else to do with Tillman now, other than to keep pinging him and hope that in the end she got some faint echo back.

And now, since the files were there, she opened them again herself. She felt like she knew the contents by heart, but re-reading them kept it fresh – taking her back, every time, to her first and last face-to-face meeting with Emil Gassan, in the dismal, dilapidated safe house where they were keeping him until they certified his real life free from risk.

The one in which Gassan told her about the Judas tribe.

40

'So it is a gospel?' Kennedy demanded, bewildered.

'Yes.'

'I mean, the translated version is still a gospel? Barlow puts together a crack team, dedicates years of his time – sacrifices his life, in the end – to translate a gospel into another gospel?'

Emil Gassan shrugged, a little impatiently. They were sitting in a bare, bleak room: four tables, eight chairs, walls painted in the shade of dark green that exists nowhere outside of Victorian buildings that have become hospitals, police stations or lunatic asylums. A poster on the wall advocated safe sex with the aid of a cartoon unicorn wearing a condom on its horn. Gassan's right hand rested on a slender, black-covered notebook, as though he were about to swear an oath on it.

It was ten days after Dovecote: ten days after the fire, and Combes's death. Nine days and some odd hours, then, since she'd sent her own copy of the Dovecote disc to Gassan and asked him to put the files on there together into something that made sense. Gassan's haggling had been minimal: he'd wanted chocolate – Terry's Chocolate Oranges – some bottles of a good French Meursault, and the last three issues of Private Eye. Remind me that the world is still out there, he'd told her, essentially – and I'll solve your puzzle for you. Hearing the tremor of eagerness in his voice, she'd gotten the impression that she could have refused him on every count and he'd still have agreed.

'Yes, Sergeant,' Gassan said, with petulance in his voice. 'He translated a gospel into another gospel. But obviously I didn't manage to make myself clear. What Stuart has done is ... remarkable. Almost unbelievable, really. And if it weren't for the fact that the side effects would include my now being dead, instead of merely in Crewe, I could wish with all my heart that I'd said yes when he approached me. Also, if it weren't for the fear of those same side effects, I'd be running with this to every journal on my Rolodex, telling them to hold the front page into the foreseeable future. Not that I have access to my Rolodex, in this godforsaken place. Or a phone.'

As though complaining about the stringent security had made him aware of its temporary absence, Gassan got up, crossed to the door and opened it. A stolid constable sitting just outside nodded civilly at the professor, who closed the door again without a word.

'Perhaps it would be better to be dead,' Gassan murmured, as though to himself. 'Dead, and famous, and relevant. Is that preferable to an indefinite parenthesis? I don't know. I don't know.'

'Professor,' Kennedy said, 'I know this has been hard on you. But as you're aware, we're still pursuing the case. The more you can tell me, the better the chance that we can end this and get you back to your normal life.'

Gassan favoured her with a stare of utter contempt. 'That would be a huge consolation,' he said, acidly, 'if it weren't arrant, bloody nonsense. These people come and go as they please, and kill who they please. The only thing that's keeping me alive is that I said no to Barlow when it counted, and now they've got me marked down on their great stone tablets somewhere as being safe to ignore. God help me if they ever change their minds about that.'

'They're not omnipotent,' Kennedy said. The professor's fatalism angered her, even disgusted her a little, but she tried to keep her face and her tone neutral.

'They might as well be. Is anyone still alive who they wanted dead?'

'Me. I think they wanted me dead.' And Tillman, of course, but she wasn't about to bring Tillman into this conversation.

'With respect, they kill savants. People who know and understand. They only trouble with your sort when you accidentally step into their path.'

'Which I'm aiming to do again,' Kennedy answered, grimly. 'And I repeat, the more you can tell me, the better chance I'll have of finding them and bringing them to book.' She meant to stop there. It was cruelty that made her go on. She was nettled in spite of herself by the line Gassan drew between people who understood and dull, plodding coppers. 'The only alternative, professor, is for you to spend the rest of your life in places like this, hiding from a retribution that might not even be coming. Like Salman Rushdie or Roberto Saviano – except that they were hiding because they'd written something that made an impact on the world. You wouldn't even have that consolation.'

She broke off. Gassan was staring at her, half-aghast and half in wonder. She thought for a moment that he was going to storm out of the room, retire to his tents, as Tillman (with much better reason) had now done, and leave her to figure it all out for herself.

Instead, the professor nodded. And then, with impressive calmness, humility even, he came and sat down opposite her again.

'You're right,' he said. 'If I'm irrelevant, it's because I made myself irrelevant. I shouldn't complain. And I end up being part of the process in any event, don't I? The least I can do is act as Stuart Barlow's amanuensis, since I refused all the more glamorous roles available.

'Go on, Sergeant Kennedy, go on. Debrief me. Interrogate me. Bully and humble me. Beat me, even, if you want to. That would be novel, at least. Yes. Barlow translated a gospel into a gospel. After five hundred years of scholarship had failed to do as much.'

Kennedy let out a long breath. 'But this new gospel – the one he found when he decoded the Rotgut – it's one that wasn't known before?'

'Exactly. It's unique. An undiscovered gospel dating – probably – from the first century after Christ.'

'You can tell that? The Rotgut was medieval.'

'The Rotgut was itself just a translation, as you already know. When Stuart went looking for the source document, the original from which it was translated, he went straight to the earliest codices and the scrolls that immediately preceded them – to Nag Hammadi and the Rylands Papyri. And he applied a cypher key he'd already observed, in tiny, tantalising fragments, in the Dead Sea Scrolls. He had plenty to go on. In fact, his problem was that he was spoiled for choice. Here. Have you ever seen this before?'

He opened the notebook and flicked through a few pages, then turned it to face her. Kennedy found herself reading a short, itemised list.

P52
P75
NH II-1, III-1, IV-1
Eg2
B66, 75
C45

'Yes,' she said. 'It was written on the back of a photograph that Stuart Barlow hid under the floor in his office. What does it mean?'

Gassan closed the notebook again, as though he felt uncomfortable having someone else examine its contents, even though he'd promised her complete disclosure. 'All of these letters and numbers are shorthand,' he said, 'for specific scrolls and codices in specific locations. The prefix P indicates the Rylands Papyri. B stands for Bodmer and C for the Chester collection. NH, of course, is Nag Hammadi. I imagine you can guess what these specific documents all have in common. Or am I giving credit where none is due?'

Kennedy thought of the Rotgut. 'They're all early copies of John's Gospel,' she hazarded.

'Exactly. The Gospel of John, or in some cases the Apocryphon of John – a related text. Some are whole, some partial, some very fragmentary indeed. But they're all John. We don't know which of the scrolls that Barlow looked at turned out to be the Rotgut source, but we can infer that it was a copy of the Gospel of John – complete or almost complete – dating from the late first century or early second century of the Common Era.'

'And this is where I get lost,' Kennedy admitted. 'How do we get from the Gospel of John to this other text?'

'By means of a code, of course.' The answer was curt – stating the obvious. 'Which was the entire point of Barlow's work, and the core of his discovery.'

Kennedy was trying to think of a different way to frame the same question. She knew it was a code: what she needed to understand was the mechanics of it, the bread and butter stuff about what was being encoded as what. Gassan saw her hesitation and sighed.

'Very well,' he said. '*Ab initio*. Sergeant Kennedy, I believe I explained to you, when we first spoke, that a codex is a multi-part text.'

'You said that two or three separate books or documents could be bound together into a single codex,' she said.

'Exactly. The ancient world had no concept of the integrity or discreteness of the single message. Papyrus was scarce and costly to make, so you used what you had. If that meant making strange bedfellows – putting a Platonic dialogue next to a biblical tract – then you did it without a qualm. You probably wouldn't even start a clean page: you'd just go directly from one document to the next, writing them one after, or one beneath, another.

'So when scholars looked at the Rotgut, that was what they saw. The Rotgut has the whole of John's Gospel, then seven verses of a different gospel. It seemed natural to assume that someone had looked at an Aramaic codex and begun to translate it, starting at the beginning and going on until, for some reason, they were interrupted.'

'Okay.'

'But suppose those two texts – or the one text and the tiny fragment of the second – had been put together for a different reason? If you were solving an anagram, you might write the original version down so that you could cross off letters until you worked out the solution. "Has to pilfer", say, and then the answer, "a shoplifter". Or "a rope ends it", and the answer, "desperation". And similarly, someone faced with a coded message might write the cypher down first and the decoded message afterwards.'

'So the Gospel of John was the cypher?'

'A specific copy of the Gospel of John was the cypher. As I said, I haven't been able to determine which. Whoever wrote the Rotgut had found this version, this written copy of John, and had been told how the code worked or else had managed to work it out for himself. He – it was almost certainly a he – wrote out the surface meaning of the text and then began to decode the message, to write out the text hidden beneath. But he found it arduous: even knowing what he knew, he only succeeded in decoding seven verses before giving up. Or, just as likely, he switched to a different piece of paper. And since he neglected to write down the cypher key, the rest of the message was lost.'

'I get it,' said Kennedy.

'I'm so glad. And for centuries thereafter, that status quo remained unchanged. Until Stuart Barlow came along and – alerted by some clue or some leap of logic or intuition – started to take a really close look at the Nag Hammadi texts and these other early documents. He found the relevant version of John. And he found – on the papyrus itself – some sort of substitution code that depended on subtle, almost invisible variations on the standard letter shapes. He found a second message encoded in the same symbols: a buried gospel, lying beneath the obvious gospel.'

Gassan got up and crossed to the window. He looked out anxiously, although there was nothing to see: the window looked on to a light well that was interior to the building, a brick-sided shaft eight feet on a side. Kennedy waited a minute or two and then joined him. She knew how frustrated Gassan was at his enforced isolation – and underneath that, how terrified he was that by picking up the Rotgut project he'd become contaminated by its curse. Kennedy would have liked to reassure him, but the only comfort she could offer was a despairing one – that after Dovecote Farm had been wiped off the face of the earth, and Josh Combes became a burned offering, Michael Brand had vanished down whatever hole he normally inhabited. They might all be safe now simply because they offered him no credible threat.

She stared out with Gassan at nothing. 'So each letter, each symbol on the papyrus, was two letters?' she asked him.

'Essentially, yes. Each letter had a standard referent and a coded referent.' He didn't turn to look at her, but his tone, listless at first, picked up a little as he explained the technicalities. 'The code uses a combination of two features that are completely meta-textual. The first is the number of additional stylus strokes used to write the letters. For example the Aramaic letter "heh"' – he drew it in the condensation on the window – 'is typically drawn as a single stroke with an acute angle and a curve, and then a separate downstroke. Two movements of the brush or stylus, you see? But it's possible for a scribe to raise the marking tool from the papyrus twice in the course of making the complex stroke. Or once. Or he could do it as a single, continuous shape, without lifting the brush at all. That gives you three states of the letter. And then the simple stroke, similarly, could be one or two movements: the tool could be rested partway, leaving a slight thickening of the line. That gives six states – two times three.

'The other feature is the relative length of strokes within a letter, where the possible states are, to put it crudely, short, medium and long. In hch, the simple stroke is typically drawn down further by the scribe than the enfolding arms of the complex stroke on either side. But it could stop at the same level, or not come down so far, remaining above the arms. Now we have at the very least eighteen states of the letter: probably more, in that the encoding of comparative length probably also brings in comparative distance between one feature of the letter and another, or possibly between each letter and its neighbour.'

Kennedy thought about this slightly dizzying prospect, trying hard to get a handle on it.

'And each of those ... states, as you call them ...'

'Corresponds, within the cypher, to a different symbol. So this heh might then become gamal, or daleth, or zain. It would still be read as heh in the parent text, but it would stand as something else entirely in the decoded text.'

'Why would someone do this?' Kennedy asked. 'Isn't a gospel supposed to spread the word about your religion? If you have to hide it, then it loses most of its point, doesn't it?'

Gassan snorted through his nose. 'There are lots of steganographic texts – hidden messages – from that period, Sergeant. The early Christian sects were at war with each other, and often with their local governments as well. They had every reason to hide their messages away.'

'But hiding one Christian message behind another ... '

'... rather suggests that the Christians, or perhaps a specific group of Christians, were your target audience, doesn't it? With a code like this, you could disseminate your gospel and hide it at the same time. And your readers could carry the message from place to place without having to look over their shoulder. Anyone who examined the text would see only John's Gospel: canonical, unobjectionable.'

'Whereas the hidden message is a heresy?'

'It's safe to say, Sergeant, that the hidden message is heresy on the most breathtaking scale imaginable.'

'So what the hell is it?'

'You didn't read it?' Gassan turned from the window at last, to give Kennedy a stare of horrified indignation.

'I read some of the parts that had already been rendered into plain text. They didn't seem to be anything special – just Jesus talking to his disciples, most of the time. I couldn't find my way through the files – there were too many of them and they all seemed to be hundreds of pages long.'

Gassan hesitated: his disapproval at being asked for a précis fought against his desire to stand on a soapbox and hold forth. In the end, it was no contest.

'You're going after these people?' he asked. 'The people who killed Barlow and Catherine Hurt, and the others?'

'Yes.'

'Then I suppose you need to know what you'll be facing. You'll lose, though. I probably ought to make that clear up front.'

'Thanks, professor. For the vote of confidence, I mean.'

'Believe me, Sergeant, I wish it were otherwise. If you could beat them, I could go back to living a life worthy of the name. But then, of course, if you could beat them ...'

He walked back to the centre of the room, touched the cover of the black notebook, then the table, as if to reassure himself that both the words and the world were still where he'd left them.

'If I could beat them?'

He looked around at her, his eyes desolate. 'Well, then they wouldn't still be out there, would they? Not after all those centuries. If they were vulnerable on any conceivable level, someone would have beaten them already.'

41

Sheriff Gayle collected Kennedy from the front of the hotel at nine the next morning. The night before, when he had taken her back to the hotel, he'd used a police black-and-white. This morning, he was driving a car only a little smaller than a football pitch, its colour scheme two-tone, equally divided between sky blue and rust. In places there were actual holes in the bodywork.

Seeing her dubious expression, Gayle assured her earnestly that the car would get them to where they were going. 'Never let me down yet, Sergeant. If there was enough room at the cemetery, I think I'd aim to be buried in her.'

The scenery here was flatter and less dramatic than along the banks of the Colorado, but Kennedy experienced the same sense of colossal scale as they drove out of Peason along Interstate Highway 93. Distant mountains to their right piled up layer on layer, the stone audience in a planet-sized amphitheatre. To their left the horizon formed a single perfect curve. Highway 93 made the dividing line, a human act of ordering on a par with God's dividing the waters above from the waters beneath. For most of the journey, theirs was the only car on the road.

The town of Santa Claus, though, showed the bathos underlying human aspirations. At its height, Gayle had told her, the place had had a population of ten thousand: now it was a cluster of cutesy cottages from a Disney cartoon slowly being reclaimed by the desert. They'd been painted to look like gingerbread houses: red and white striped walls; candy-pink fascia boards; bright-green shutters with rounded tops, set permanently open. All was falling into ruin. A leprous Santa Claus leered from a porch whose railings hung askew like shattered ribs. Twin strips of abraded metal, joined by a few surviving railway sleepers, were visible here and there between the battered buildings: they seemed to have been built to serve a kiddie-sized red locomotive that now leaned against the side of a house, forever out of steam, its cow-catcher half-buried in the sand.

To either end of the street was an advertising billboard, perfectly well maintained. The southern one advertised computers, the northern one – on which the leper Santa fixed his hideous grin – incontinence pads. Just beyond this second sign, where Sheriff Gayle was pointing now, stood a small row of aluminum-frame sheds like scaled-down aircraft hangars.

'Third one's ours, Sergeant,' he said. ''Less you want to go tell Santa what you want for Christmas.'

'What every girl wants,' Kennedy said, joining in the joke. 'A pony and a Barbie doll. Peace on earth.'

'There you go,' Gayle said, leading the way. 'I think the old feller winked at you just then, so you probably got that to look forward to now. Okay, let's see what we've got here.'

He'd taken the heavy key ring from his belt and was sorting through it slowly and carefully. Finally he selected a big brass key with a hollow shank and inserted it into a keyhole that was perfectly circular. He didn't turn it, just pressed it in and then pulled it out again. There was a two-tone metallic sound: *tchik-clunk*. Gayle shoved the metal door sideways on its runners and they stepped into a dark space as hot as the inside of a furnace.

'There's an AC unit here,' Gayle said, fumbling with some switches on the wall just inside the door. 'You might want to give it a few minutes.'

'I'll be fine,' Kennedy said. As the lights flickered on, she moved out into the wide, undifferentiated space. It was just a single storeroom, with long metal shelf units dividing it up into aisles. At the nearer end she saw a desk with a couple of A4 folders on it, one blue and one red.

The shelves were full of boxes, no doubt bought en masse from the storage solutions company whose logo they all bore: EZ-STACK. Each box also had a number, and Gayle now flipped open the top folder on the desk, the blue one, to show her the master list.

He flicked over a page or two, found the Bs and ran his finger down the left-hand margin. 'Michael Brand, Michael Brand, Michael Brand,' he muttered. 'There you go. Box number 161.'

The boxes had been ranged sequentially, and every single one was in its proper place, so finding 161 was as simple as walking down the second aisle to the right spot and sliding it out. Gayle brought it back to the desk and set it down, nodding to Kennedy. 'Be my guest, Sergeant.' She slid the lid off the box and looked inside.

Each of the objects in the box had been separately bagged. Most were items of clothing: shirt, trousers, jacket, pants and socks. Sheathed in anodyne plastic, they looked – on first glance – like they'd just come back from the dry cleaner's. But the cleaner had done a really bad job, leaving red-black blood-stains here and there on pretty much everything.

In the bottom of the box, underneath the ruined clothes, she found a sparse sprawl of objects. A till receipt, also stained red-brown at one corner: it was for a newspaper and a pack of Big Red gum, paid for with cash at one of the Walden Books stands at LAX. A black plastic comb. A wallet, already emptied. A separate bag containing bills and coins that had been found in the wallet, to the total value of $89.67. An opened packet of paper tissues. A half-empty blister pack of cinnamon chewing gum, presumably the one described in the till receipt. And that was it: the total worldly goods of Michael Brand.

'No passport,' Kennedy remarked. She hadn't had high expectations, but felt a little deflated anyway.

'Stuff from the flight got scattered over a lot of ground, Sergeant – and this is a desert. Most likely it's still out there somewhere. Unless someone picked it up and handed it in at a local police station – or kept it as a souvenir, or sold it on. But his passport was scanned when he joined the flight. All that information's on record.'

'I know,' Kennedy said. 'I wasn't thinking of the passport itself, so much.'

'Baggage stub?'

'Yeah, that.'

'We already cross-referenced all that stuff, working off the flight manifests that Coastal sent us. Brand didn't bring a case on board. He had no stowed luggage at all.'

With Gayle's permission, Kennedy put on gloves and examined the disappointing haul. She turned the till receipt over, making sure the obverse was blank: no hidden messages or enigmatic lists. She rooted through the wallet, looking for slips of paper that had been missed, torn linings in which something might have been secreted, inscriptions or markings on the leather itself. There was nothing.

Someone had marked one of the dollar bills, though: three parallel lines drawn in red marker, running from top centre to bottom right. Someone had tried to cross out Ben Franklin's face and missed by a good half-inch or so. Kennedy puzzled over the note for a while, then gave it up.

'What about the unmatched stuff?' she asked Gayle.

'There's a whole lot of that,' he said. 'Boxes and boxes – takes up most of the last aisle. You'd be talking about a good six or seven thousand items. I don't think there's enough hours in the day for you to go over it all.'

'Do you have a list?'

'Most definitely we do. That's the second folder. The red one.'

Kennedy read through the list, looking for anything that stood out from the background. A number of things caught the eye for a moment, maybe a little longer: *part of glass unicorn; medallion with skull and marijuana leaf; dildo decorated with stars and stripes motif.* But how could she know what Michael Brand had been carrying or what it might have meant to him? More significantly, she noted three dozen or so cellphones whose owners hadn't been identified – but when she got to that page and looked up at Sheriff Gayle, he was shaking her head before she could even frame the question.

'I can't let you turn any of those on, Sergeant,' he said. 'It's not legal without a warrant, and there's no way I'd be able to get a warrant without showing probable cause – of which there ain't a shred, really, for any of these people. Not even for your Michael Brand, when you come right down to it.'

'No,' Kennedy agreed, reluctantly. 'A lot of this is more gut instinct than anything else.'

'And gut instinct is fine. I wouldn't hear a word said against it – but it limits my scope, if you see what I mean. There's things I can do and things I can't.'

Kennedy almost laughed. It could have been herself talking: herself before she met Tillman and waded into this mess so far she couldn't see dry land any longer. 'I totally understand, Sheriff,' was all she said, still holding the plastic evidence bag containing Michael Brand's cash. She held it up and showed it to Gayle. 'Listen, can I get a photocopy of this dollar bill here? The one with the red lines on it?'

'Surely. Let me sign it out and we can bring it into town with us now. Connie can copy it for you while we go on over to the morgue. Why, you reading something into those lines?'

'A code, maybe. The people we're dealing with seem to like codes. Might be nothing anyway. Most likely is. But I'd like to think about it.'

Gayle solemnly filled out a chitty, which he took from the top drawer in the desk, stamped holes in it with a tiny hole-punch (second drawer) and inserted into the evidence file. Then – just as the straining air-conditioning unit was starting to make some kind of an impact on the superheated air in the great hangar, they stepped back out into the desert.

42

'So who are the big villains, would you say, in the Bible?' Professor Gassan asked. He stood at the table as though at a lectern, even though there were only the two of them in the room. Old habits died hard: or maybe it was just a way of defining their relative status here.

Kennedy was in even less of a mood for a study session on the Bible than she'd been the first time they'd spoken. The gleam in the professor's eyes oppressed her spirit in much the way a snake's stare was supposed to paralyse a rabbit. But she suspected it might be the only way Gassan was prepared to give her what she needed to know – and the only way for him to keep functioning despite his fears and inner conflicts.

'Cain,' she hazarded. 'Judas. Pontius Pilate. Or did you mean tribes, like the ones who couldn't say "shibboleth"?'

'No, I meant individuals. And Cain and Judas were the two I was certain you'd mention. Most people would come up with those two names, I think. Most people, that is, outside of the Gnostic tradition. You've heard of the Gnostics, I assume?'

He looked at her hard, signalling that despite her impatience, he was coming to the point in his own way.

'Early Christian sect,' Kennedy said. 'Stuart Barlow's book –

379

the one that the Rotgut research grew out of – was meant to be a study of them.'

'Exactly. But let's say sects, plural. There were many, with some beliefs in common. The Gnostics were contrarians. Religious extremists. And they were already that long before Christ came along: he just gave them a new focus and a new momentum. They embraced the teachings of Jesus because Jesus was ready to stir up the hornets' nest. They must have felt they'd found a spiritual leader in their own image.

'The Gnostics started from the assumption that most of the Bible – all of the Bible really, as it had been handed down – was utter nonsense. The scribblings of people who really didn't understand the miracles they were attesting to. The word "Gnostic" comes from the Greek gnosis, which meant "knowledge". These sects believed that a hidden truth existed behind everything: behind the world and behind the word. When God spoke to man, as He did to Adam, and to Moses, and later to New Testament prophets like John the Baptist, He wasn't ever, at any point, handing down simple, univocal truths – because the universe isn't a simple place and the truth is a complex thing that has to be hidden from the eyes and ears of the vulgar.'

'When you say "hidden truth",' Kennedy asked, 'are you talking about codes? Is that the point here?'

Gassan raised an austere eyebrow at the interruption from the floor. A hectoring edge crept into his voice. 'The point, Sergeant Kennedy, is that your enemies – the people who killed your partner, and Stuart Barlow's team – don't share your world view. I'm trying to allow you to see them as they are, without the parallax errors you impose by your own values. No, I don't mean codes, as such. That's only a small part of what I mean. The Gnostics did use cyphers, and clearly the cypher that

Barlow found has to be read in that context. But these people saw the whole of the created world as one colossal hidden message: the will and word of God, expressed in other things. And they believed that most holy texts are just ... ham-fisted approximations of a message that the great mass of people are born without the capacity to understand.

'I'm telling you this because what I say next would sound strange without that preamble. In the Gnostic tradition, the heroes and villains of the Bible are not those you'd be most likely to recognise.'

'They think Jesus went over to the dark side of the Force?'

'No, the Gnostic tradition is very kind to Jesus. It's God they have a problem with.'

Kennedy smiled and shrugged: I'll bite.

'The Gnostic sects believed that the creator and ruler of our world, commonly worshipped as the ultimate god and source of all goodness, was actually a far lesser being – a flawed entity sometimes known as Laldabaoth. The real god is somewhere else, far above our perceptions and our plane of existence.'

'Wait,' Kennedy pleaded. 'If these Gnostics were renegade Christians, or renegade Jews, or whatever, then they had to believe that God made the world. It's right there in the Bible – even if you didn't manage to read past chapter one.'

'Certainly, a god made the world. But which one? Remember, these are people who pride themselves on reading between the lines – on finding the meanings that the ignorant miss. In their teachings, the ultimate God is a being of transcendent goodness and purity, who does not himself inhabit the universe of created things. Within that universe – our universe – there are beings of great power: beings who would be like ants compared with the ultimate God, but would still appear as gods to us. One of these beings, whatever you decide to call them, made the earth. And he's quite happy to claim our worship, even though, in the Gnostics' opinion, he doesn't deserve it.'

'Why not?'

'Why not what, Sergeant? Please frame your questions as complete sentences.'

Kennedy ground her teeth, not enjoying this at all. A trail of murdered men and women shouldn't lead to a schoolroom, especially one where you had to put your hand up before you could speak. 'Why does the god-who-made-the-world not deserve to be worshipped?' she asked, stonily.

'Because he did such a terrible job of it. Because he made evil, and sickness, poverty and hunger; the imperfect balance of the seasons which makes us die of too much heat or too much cold; flood and fire and pestilence and all the rest of it. Frankly, the Gnostics thought the world was a botched job and they weren't interested in clapping its creator on the shoulder and telling him how wonderful he was. They were looking up, past him, to the sphere of perfection beyond – which they called, some of them, sometimes, when they sullied it with a name at all, the realm of Barbelo.

'Read in this way, and with Yahweh seen – for the most part – as another name for the imperfect, the limited and limit-ing god of the fallen world, the Bible becomes a very different story. Those biblical figures who are paragons of obedience become fools and vectors of folly, to be shunned rather than revered. Adam is a coward who willingly takes the yoke. Eve is the brave soul who looks behind the curtain, plays outside the rules.'

'And is punished for her sins.'

'Oh, they're both punished, Sergeant. And so are their blame-less children, and their children's children, and so on. God – the lesser god, Laldabaoth – is a sadist and a psychopath: doing what you're told is no defence against his whimsical sense of justice. So the heroes of Genesis are disobedient Eve, the wise serpent who taught her, and Cain, her rebellious son. And when we get to Jesus, the moral perspective changes even more radically.'

'You said Jesus still got to be the hero.'

'Oh yes.'

'The son of god.'

'The son of ...?'

Kennedy breathed out heavily. 'The son of the big, pure god. Not the evil one.'

'Exactly, Sergeant. Jesus came from Barbelo, bringing his precious wisdom to the fallen world. And although he died for it, that too was part of the plan. Sounds a lot like the New Testament you already know and love, I imagine.'

'It's familiar,' Kennedy allowed.

'Well, don't get too comfortable. In 1983, in Geneva, a professional intermediary – not a fence, strictly speaking, but someone who knew fences and did a broadly similar job – offered for sale to interested bodies or institutions a document. A codex. A priceless antiquity. It was a lost gospel.'

'You told me once that there were hundreds of those things out there, professor.'

'Not like this one. This was the Gospel of Judas.'

'*The* Judas? Backstabbing Iscariot Judas? The man who betrayed the Messiah?'

'Or,' said Gassan, with something like a bravura flourish, 'the man who became the Messiah.'

He allowed a pause for effect that was probably longer than necessary. Kennedy waited him out, tired of the choric role that he'd allotted her. Eventually, with an austere sniff, like a man casting pearls before swine, the professor resumed. 'The Gospel of Judas, so called – the Codex Tchacos, to give it its official designation – is an appallingly damaged document. And most of that damage came when the idiot who'd dug it up, and his friends, agents and satraps, were hauling it around the world in an attempt to sell it and make their fortunes. They did everything that you're not supposed to do to a fragile papyrus, except possibly to wipe their backsides upon it. You might be forgiven for thinking that some of its interim custodians wanted to destroy rather than preserve it.

'So the Judas Gospel, as we have it – as we have it in the Codex Tchacos – is in a very fragmentary form. Only thirteen pages of the original thirty-one survived even in partial form, and the decay and disintegration were extreme. Still, enough remained to make it clear that the actual work must be an astounding document indeed.'

'Astounding in what way?' Kennedy demanded.

'It focuses on the relationship between Judas and Christ – and it portrays that relationship as unique and intense. In fact, the other eleven disciples feature mainly as comic relief. They understand nothing of Jesus's true mission on earth, and their misinterpretations cause Jesus to get somewhat snitty and sarcastic with them at several points. Judas, by contrast, gets it – gets the message without being told. He's a Gnostic: one of the many different sorts and varieties. He belongs to an already ancient cult that reads between the lines of the Bible. He knows that great truths must be hidden and he knows why. Consequently, it's to Judas that Jesus entrusts the most delicate part of his plan.'

'You mean Jesus actually wanted—'

'Yes, Sergeant. Jesus asks Judas to betray him. It was essential to his mission. He must suffer, and die, so that his message would never be lost. He must be attacked and destroyed by someone close to him and trusted by him: the power of that narrative was the means by which his teachings would be dispersed to the world. Judas was an active collaborator in Christ's thoroughly worked-out plan.'

'All right,' Kennedy said. 'I admit, that's novel. Arresting, even. But it's not something anyone would kill for, is it?'

'It was once. Irenaeus warned against the Judas Gospel explicitly in his *Adversus Haereses*, of which we've already spoken. Athanasius of Alexandria talked in rather more sinister terms about "cleansing the church of defilement" by texts like this. People did die for reading and disseminating the Judas Gospel. They died in large numbers, and they – by they, I mean the Gnostic churches, those who professed the faith of the serpent, Eve, Cain and Judas – ultimately disappeared from history.

'In the modern world, though ... well, the Judas Gospel in the truncated form of the Codex Tchacos has been in the public domain for several years now. The translation we have – partial translation, I mean, with holes you could drive a bus through – dates from 2006. Rodolphe Kasser and his people were the authors, and National Geographic helped with the funding. Nobody in that group, so far as I know, has been fired upon, stabbed through the heart or flung down a staircase.'

Gassan paused again and sat down with a gesture of resignation, giving up the charade. Maybe that reference to Stuart Barlow's death had soured the pleasure of showing off his erudition.

'So what's changed?' Kennedy asked, as Gassan stared at his hands, folded in his lap.

'The Rotgut text,' the professor said, in an entirely different tone of voice. 'It's an intact version of the Judas Gospel. Moreover, it has sleeve notes – instructions to whoever was carrying it as to what to do, and what not to do, with the message.'

'Go on,' Kennedy said, because it looked at that moment as if Gassan might come to the point and then shy away from it, unable or unwilling to elucidate the real mystery.

'Well, you see, Sergeant, if Jesus's plan was to die in agony on the cross, the disciple who understood his needs well enough to help with that plan was the greatest of all, and carried out a service to the Godhead that was infinitely precious. If Christ ransomed and redeemed us, it was through Judas's sacrifice that he was able to do so.'

'Judas's sacrifice?' Kennedy repeated, momentarily thrown. 'What did Judas sacrifice?'

Gassan shrugged as though the answer were obvious. 'The respect of his peers. The goodwill of all the world. The verdict of history. And his life, of course, but one imagines that was a relatively small part of the equation. Still, the death of Judas bears comparison with that of Christ. And in the complete gospel – in the Rotgut version, I mean, as translated by Barlow – Judas is offered a reward, in exchange for his faithful service.'

'Thirty pieces of silver?'

Gassan smiled faintly. 'No. That's a different gospel. Matthew, to be precise. But the figure thirty does appear, in a way that makes it seem likely that Matthew was referring to something specific when he chose that figure. Should I read you the text?'

Kennedy shrugged. 'Shoot.'

Gassan took up the notebook again. 'There's a digital version,' he said. 'A clean text, which I'll send to you. I imagine you'll want to read it in its entirety before you saddle up and go into battle again. I also sent a copy, with all of Barlow's notes and my own, to my solicitor, along with a letter telling him to publish after my death. I'll have nothing left to lose, then, will I? And I'll have earned the right to have my name added to the list of the gospel's discoverers, if I've already died for it.'

He found his place at last and read aloud, in a voice from which much of the tonal colour had drained away. 'Then Judas said unto Him, All will be done as you have laid it down, oh lord. And Jesus said, yes, even so, all will be done in that wise. And you will be reviled by them that know you not, yet afterward you will be raised up higher than them that hate you.

'And when shall I be raised, oh lord?

'Jesus said, from this moment in which I speak unto you thenceforward until the ending of the seed of Adam, they will execrate your name.

'But my Father has given dominion to the seed of Adam only for a certain time. And afterwards he will end them, that the world might be given unto you and yours.

'And Jesus gave unto Judas thirty silver pieces, saying, how many bronze prutahs have I given unto you? For so many years will the seed of Adam enjoy this world: for so many years will their lease endure. But afterward they will be cast down, and the world will belong to you and yours for ever.'

The professor looked up at Kennedy, perhaps expecting a question. The only one Kennedy could think of was pretty banal. 'What's the answer?' she asked. 'How many bronze whatevers?'

'Three thousand. There were a hundred prutahs in one shekel. Three thousand years, then the children of Judas get their turn in the big chair.'

'Guess we've still got a while, at least.'

Gassan frowned. 'Why do you say that, Sergeant?'

'Even if the gospel was written right after Christ died,' Kennedy said, with a shrug, 'it's only two thousand years.'

'True. Unfortunately, nobody in Judea in those days counted anything from Christ. In Judea and Samaria, where this text was presumably written, it was customary to count from the unification of the tribes, in 1012 BCE. Three thousand and twenty years ago, give or take. I hate to rain on your parade, but our lease is up.'

Kennedy closed her eyes, rubbed them with thumb and fore-finger. There was no headache yet, but she could feel the beginnings of one, forming like a thunderhead in the vaulted roof of her skull. 'Okay,' she said. 'So we got a chunk of the Gnostic Bible, and it was a big secret, once upon a time. I'm with you all the way, professor. But it still leaves me missing a piece, somewhere along the line. Nobody kills for a word. Or at least ... not a word this old.'

Gassan's depressed spirits flared up in sudden irritation, his arms flailing in truncated, awkward arcs. 'Oh, for God's sake, Sergeant. Everybody kills for words! What else is there to kill for? Money? Money is words from a government saying they'll give you gold. Laws are words from judges saying who gets to live free and who doesn't. Bibles ... Bibles are words from God saying do all the awful, awful things you want to do and you'll be forgiven anyway. It all comes down to words. And in every case, the people who kill for them are the ones who think they own them.'

He seemed to realise, suddenly, that his voice was too loud in the empty, echoing room – almost a shout. He turned away from her, embarrassed and still bristling. With a formless wave of his hand, he indicated the notebook.

'Read it,' he suggested. 'Read it all. Not just the gospel, but the words around the gospel – the messages that went with it. You need to see for yourself.'

43

The morgue was way over in Bullhead. It seemed that Peason kept nothing within its city limits: it was a sort of outsourced town.

Bullhead, though, was very different from Santa Claus: it was a small but busy urban hub, with an even busier morgue. Kennedy couldn't quite believe how busy, how many freezer rooms the place had and how many doors were marked full. Coming in through the parking lot, they had passed several windowless vans with massive freezer units attached, and Kennedy had clocked enough hours on enough different task forces to know them for what they were: mobile refrigeration units of the kind normally sent into disaster areas to put a lot of dead people on ice quickly and prevent the spread of epidemics.

'What's going on here?' she asked Gayle, as they stepped off the baking asphalt into the air-conditioned chill.

He didn't get what she meant, then he followed her gaze and grunted. He seemed about to speak, but a white-coated assistant who looked to be still in his teens was already heading in their direction, smiling a professional consultative smile he'd learned from his elders and smoothers. 'I'll tell you later,' Gayle muttered. 'It's kind of a taboo subject around here.'

They no longer had Brand's body on the premises, the assistant told them unnecessarily. He had been released for burial three weeks before, although in fact the state authorities had decided to cremate him, along with two other unclaimed bodies from the plane. Surely the sheriff's office was already aware?

'We didn't come to see the body, son,' Gayle broke in. 'Just the file.'

'The file is public access. It's available via—'

'Yeah, but that's just a summary. I mean the full file, with all the whistles and bells, photos and prints and what all. It's on my authority, and county's already approved it, but you're going to want to check in with your supervisor before you set us up, and we're happy to wait while you go ahead and do just that, long as it doesn't take more than two minutes out of my already over-full day.'

His script pulled out from under him, the lad scampered away without another word. Kennedy was impressed. Gayle's style, high on casual warmth and low on intimidation, but with an underlying steeliness to it that warned you not to mess with him, seemed to work like a charm. She felt glad she wasn't negotiating this maze by herself.

The assistant came back well inside of two minutes. He ushered them into a tiny windowless office, on the wall of which the original 'dangling kitten' motivational poster – *hang in there!* – had been pinned, with the overlay of a rifle sight zeroed on the kitten's head. Instead of the original legend, it was captioned with the words: *Hanging's too good for the little bastard.* Police morgues were entitled to police humour, which was always robust.

The assistant used his log-in and password to get them into the digital records, asked them – politely, and without ever managing to look Gayle entirely in the eye – to restrict themselves to the file they'd officially requested, and left them to it.

390

'You need me to stay here?' Gayle asked.

'No,' said Kennedy. 'Thanks, Sheriff. I can manage.'

'Okay. I got a phone call to make, and I guess I'll get a coffee along the way. You want me to bring you one back?'

Kennedy asked for milk, no sugar, and Gayle headed out. She turned to the file and immersed herself in its cold certainties.

Brand's corpse, like most of those that had fallen with the plane, presented with numerous abraded and crush injuries, friction artefacts and depressurisation traumas. The list ran to a page and a half, but could be summarised in four words: Brand was a mess. With such a spectacularly damaged body, it was almost meaningless to state a cause of death, although the usual conclusions, with the usual provisos, had been reached. The lining of Brand's lungs had been ripped when the cabin depressurised at speed. Oxygen concentrations in venous tissue suggested that trapped air had been forced through the lungs into the man's thoracic cavity, where the oxygen had formed bubbles in both major and minor blood vessels. The heart would have stopped in short order, but the brain would have been starved of blood in any case. Unconsciousness and death would have followed swiftly enough that it was almost impossible Brand was still alive when the plane hit the ground.

So much for the big picture. Smaller details were then sketched in lightly as observations and speculations, usually with no firm conclusions drawn. Abrasions to Brand's knuckles might indicate a physical altercation with another passenger, possibly in the panic of the initial forced descent. Broken fingernails and damage to the tissue of the fingertips on both hands was harder to explain: had he perhaps clawed at the frame of a window or door, trying to escape? It seemed likely, in any case, that Brand had been on his feet when the depressurisation occurred, because unsecured bodies collected more – and more widely distributed –

trauma artefacts than those that were fixed in one position. It could be stated with more confidence that he had not been wearing his seat belt: seated and belted passengers, without exception, had a pattern of bruising across the hips caused by sudden shifts in air speed pushing the body hard against the restraining belt. Brand didn't have those particular bruises.

He did have a lot of scars, though. Whoever had performed the autopsy had been punctilious in recording them. Bullet wounds, stab wounds, impact wounds, all remaining from previous brushes with death, all old enough to have mostly healed over. In one place, a newer stab wound had crossed the scar tissue from an older injury. This merited an exclamation mark from the coroner, who must have wondered exactly what kind of lifestyle Michael Brand had been enjoying. *Given his age, it was a most astonishing history of prior injuries. I can honestly say, I have never seen even in a career soldier at the end of his active service such a fascinating and varied collection.*

Given his age? Kennedy went back up to the head of the document and cross-referenced with the summary of Michael Brand's passport data included as an addendum. Then she went to the photographs.

There were several full-face shots, identical as far as Kennedy could see. They all showed a bloated face, the skin blotched and mottled from broken blood vessels. He could be any dead man, at any stage of life. But underneath the damage, how old was he? How much had Michael Brand lived, before he fell out of the sky like Icarus, imploding as he died?

Not long enough, was the answer. Or too long, depending how you looked at it.

The door was kicked open from the outside, slamming back against the wall. Kennedy was rising as she turned, hands flying into a defensive block.

It was Gayle: he had used his foot to open the door because he had a styrofoam cup of coffee in each hand.

'Sorry, Sergeant,' he said, staring at her with something like concern. 'I didn't mean to startle you. Don't know my own strength.'

Her heart pounding, she lowered her hands. When she took the coffee, she saw from the look on his face that he could feel the tremor in her fingers, but he maintained a casual tone as he asked her if she'd got what she wanted.

'I got . . . something,' she admitted.

'Glad to hear it. Something good?'

'I think I caught Michael Brand out in a lie. A big one, maybe. Could I have a few minutes longer?'

'We're not on the clock here,' Gayle said, easily. 'You go ahead. I'll watch the traffic go by.'

Kennedy finished her notes. She was doing it for form's sake now, and to let her breathing and heart rate return to normal, but her gaze caught on one small detail in the brain work. *Extensive damage to serotonergic neurons cannot be explained by or linked to other injuries, singly or in combination. Coupled with 5-HT depletion in the hippocampus, the nerve damage suggests prolonged and repeated exposure to a sympathomimetic drug such as methamphetamine, in extremely large doses.*

What makes people weep blood? Stress or drugs, Ralph Prentice had said. She believed she was seeing the drugs part of that equation. Michael Brand – and probably the pale assassins she'd met twice now – used some substance in the methamphetamine family, maybe to increase speed, strength and alertness. And it cost them: they took damage from it. As a cop, even one with very little formal narco training, she knew more than a little about what that damage might include. It was another fact for the file, abstract and useless for the moment, maybe relevant later.

She closed the Brand file and looked up. Despite his joke about watching the traffic, Gayle was actually looking at her, his expression thoughtful and maybe expectant.

He'd been the soul of professional discretion, but he had a right to expect her to share. Yet how could she explain the theory forming in her mind: particularly, how could she explain it to this bluff, friendly, uncomplicated man who seemed to embody a sort of homespun courtesy she imagined had disappeared from the world?

'I'm thinking crazy thoughts,' was what she said, almost apologetically.

Gayle shrugged with his eyebrows, acknowledging the proviso, inviting her to say more.

'I think Brand might be the answer to one of your questions. I think maybe he brought down the plane.'

Gayle looked at her in mild puzzlement. 'Why would you think that?'

Kennedy showed him what she'd found in the files: the evidence that Brand had been in a fight, and the damage to his fingertips – which he might have sustained in trying to pull the door open before the pressure seal broke. It was nothing much, when you thought about it, but Gayle nodded thoughtfully.

'Brand came on board late,' he told her. 'That was the call I just made – to the FAA. He bought his ticket when the plane was already boarding, got to the gate with a minute to spare. He was in a hurry to get to New York, that's for sure.'

'Or maybe not,' said Kennedy. 'Maybe he was just in a hurry to get on board that particular plane.'

'So he could sabotage it?'

Kennedy made a non-committal gesture. 'Possibly. Yes. I'm thinking yes.'

'Why?'

'It had come in from Mexico, right?'

'Mexico City.'

'How did they come in? What was the flight plan?'

'I have no idea, Sergeant. Mostly the airlines like to take the planes out over water if there's any to hand, so I guess it would have come up the Gulf and maybe clipped the south-western corner of the state before it turned west.'

'What's down there, Sheriff?'

'The desert. Then Tucson. Then more desert.'

Kennedy pondered.

'Could we find out,' she ventured at last, 'whether 124 filed a change in its flight plan at any point?'

'I guess we could. The FAA keeps all that stuff on record for twenty years, I seem to remember. Why? What's on your mind?'

What was on her mind sounded ridiculous even to Kennedy. She shook her head, meaning either *I don't know* or *I can't tell you*.

Either way, Gayle appeared to accept the head-shake as all the answer he was going to get for now. 'I'll call them from the car,' he said, dropping his coffee cup neatly into the waste bin. 'Let's move on out.'

On the way back to Peason, she remembered to ask again about the refrigeration trucks.

Grayle chewed on the question in silence for a while, as though thinking how best to answer it. 'Well, that's a thing that happens every summer,' he told her at last. 'We got a whole lot of illegals coming in from Mexico, across the border. Used to be it was only a problem in the southern parts of the state. You know, down around Tucson. But there's a lot more patrols out now, since the state legislature said we got to get tougher on this. So the coyotes – the people traffickers – they gotta stay further out from cities, further out from roads, and go through a lot more desert before they can do the hand-off. They'll cross the 8 and the 10, before they turn east. And that's a lot of desert. So every year, and specially in summer, there's a lot of them don't make it.'

'Jesus.' Kennedy was appalled. 'But if each of those trucks holds, what? Ten? A dozen bodies? That means—'

'Even this far north, we can get twenty or thirty in a bad month. Plus we take in some of the overspill from further south. It's hundreds, Sergeant. Maybe thousands. Thousands every year. Bodies wear down quick in the desert, get covered up with sand and dust. Get eaten, maybe. Get so you don't know if the bones are a year old or a couple of centuries. So don't nobody have a proper count of it.'

Kennedy said nothing, but something floated up to the surface of her mind: a quote that she'd read in a history textbook once. *Poor Mexico: so far from God, so close to the United States.*

'The only other place I've seen those trucks used . . .' she ventured at last.

'Was after an earthquake or something. A disaster. Sure. Well, this is our disaster, I guess. Arizona armageddon. Just happens to be in slow motion.'

The silence was somewhat hard to break after that. Giving up on light conversation, Gayle got Connie to place a second call to the FAA and patch him through. Obviously curious, the despatch clerk offered to call on Gayle's behalf and put whatever questions he needed answered. Gayle thanked her kindly but said he'd handle it himself, after which Connie maintained a sullen silence over the airwaves as she did as she was told.

But the call was a waste of time. There had been nothing anomalous about the flight plan of CA124 on the day of the disaster. It had come up along the line of the Gulf, as Gayle had guessed, and stayed west of Tucson, flying over Puerto Peñasco and then a whole lot of nothing until it veered off towards LA at Lake Havasu City.

Kennedy looked out of the car window at the desert through which the road wound like an electric cable: plugging Arizona into the world beyond, whose existence was otherwise so easy to forget. The smell of wild sage came in through the open window of the car, sweet and strong.

Why bring down a plane? Why move from one-at-a-time murder to hecatombs of dead stacked perilously in the freezer boxes of already overstrained mortuaries?

Assuming she was right at all, what made Flight 124 worth killing?

44

Kennedy flipped through the pages – what Gassan had called the full transcripts – with a gathering sense of unreality.

'There's . . .' she said, but the sentence she was trying to frame made no sense. She had to abandon it and start again. 'The gospel, it's . . . it stops being about Judas, here, and becomes . . .'

'It's a sort of meta-commentary,' Gassan agreed. He was standing over by the window again, as if hungry for the meagre light that was coming in there. The safe house had no windows at ground level and those higher up were kept shuttered whenever the security rating of the inmates seemed to warrant it. 'There are sections like this in the Old Testament. And in the Koran, too, I believe – instructions for how the sacred text itself is to be handled. To be complete, the message must include instructions designed to ensure its own survival. The recipe specifies not just the cake but the recipe for more recipes.'

'But . . .' Kennedy was struggling with unfamiliar concepts that she didn't even want to understand. 'The penalties that are written down here. You're not suggesting . . .'

Gassan laughed – a hollow, unnerving sound. 'I'm not suggesting anything. Think, though, about what happened when that American preacher, Jones or whatever his name was, threatened to burn a copy of the Koran at the site of the 9/11 attacks.

Islamists in Iraq bombed churches: dozens died. Some have posited that the inflexible interpretation of the word of God is the very essence of fundamentalism. The divine word, to the fanatic, is reified – it's a physical thing, a fact of existence, and since it's also the cornerstone of existence, it must be revered. There seems to be no rational limit to how far people with that mindset will go to avenge themselves on those they see as the enemies of the word.'

The professor turned his gaze on the sheaf of papers in Kennedy's hand. 'I presume,' he said, 'that you've reached the passage on page forty-one, commencing, "This testament shall not be read or known".'

Kennedy nodded, read aloud from the page. 'This testament shall not be read or known by any outside the kindred, or delivered to them in any wise. But if they come to know it, they shall be cut down ...'

Gassan took up the recitation. '... and their mouths stopped, and their days counted. For His bargain was not with them, but with us who bear our lives from Judas, from Cain, and from the serpent their father.' Gassan tailed off. The corners of his mouth quirked downwards, as if he were about to cry. 'That was their death sentence,' he murmured. 'Barlow worked out the answer and they killed him for it.'

Kennedy was aware of the anger building up inside her, powerful enough now to affect the rhythm of her breathing. She'd been struggling against it for some time, but without much effect because she didn't really understand where it had come from. Now she understood, but that did nothing, really, to help rein in her feelings. It was the same anger that Tillman must have felt. She'd gotten the wrong answer: this dry explanation and the nightmares she'd lived through seemed grotesquely, horribly mismatched.

'Gnostics,' she said, as though the word meant cobblers. 'You expect me to believe that Gnostics are out there killing people because their security was compromised. On a two-thousand-year-old *text*.'

Her tone was furiously sarcastic, but Gassan merely nodded. 'I doubt they call themselves Gnostics any more, Sergeant,' he observed, mildly. 'Assuming they ever did. Think of them as the Judas people. Although clearly, they claim a line of descent that runs back through Judas to the dawn of human time – and we must assume, there were proto-messages of theirs embedded in the Dead Sea Scrolls, which sent Stuart Barlow off on this tangent. I've wondered about that.'

'Seriously?' Kennedy laughed, and the laugh had a harsh, ugly ring to it. 'Did you wonder whether you were awake?'

'I've wondered,' Gassan repeated, 'when they speak of Cain and Judas, whether they had in mind a physical lineage that links them or something more spiritual. In a sense, anyone who rebels against Laldabaoth, the usurper god who represses and tyrannises, would be the spiritual successor of Cain, and of Judas: but "bear our lives from" suggests a more literal reading. A Judas tribe.'

'I repeat. A document from two thousand—'

'Your murders, Sergeant,' he cut across her, 'are very much of the here and now.'

'Exactly.' She threw up her hands. 'That's why I don't think they were committed by Gnostics.'

Gassan tilted his head a little to one side – a patronising and infuriating gesture, suggesting that he was listening to her arguments with minute care. 'Do you know,' he asked her, 'what Judas's name meant?'

'Judas? It's just another form of Judah, isn't it? "The lion"?'

'Judah didn't mean "lion", it meant "praise". The lion was

400

only his symbol. But I was talking about Judas's other name. Iscariot.'

'I have no idea,' Kennedy admitted.

'There are two theories. One is that it referred to a place: a town. Judas from Kerioth. The other is that it denoted his membership of a specific group. And this group, in turn, took their name from their favourite weapon ...'

Driving back into London later, Kennedy found herself turning over Gassan's next words again and again. Somewhere in those many repetitions, the idea of the Judas people crystallised, or – what was that other word the professor had used – reified for her: became something real that she now had to deal with.

'... their favourite weapon, which was a short knife – a sica. Judas Iscariot could have meant "Judas Sicarius". "Judas the knife-man". And you know what knife I mean, Sergeant Kennedy, because they used it on you, and on that poor man who worked with you. They have a sense of tradition, you see. Or possibly they see all of their battles as phases of the same battle, century after century.'

A lost tribe, then. Or, no, not lost, but hidden: an entire race that had retreated from the world and scuffed sand over their own footprints so that nobody would know they'd existed. But they came out of hiding whenever they had to. Not all of them, but some. Gassan's parting shot, as she was leaving, had made that clear.

'Page fifty-three, Sergeant. The Judas people send out two kinds of emissary into the world, to make contact with ordinary humanity: the Elohim and the Kelim, the Messengers and the Vessels. I don't know what the Vessels did, but it's pretty clear from the wording what the Messengers were for.

'"Send out your Elohim where there is need, that none shall trouble or persecute the people. Let those who would bring harm to the people be prevented, and their eyes sealed up, and the door of the grave closed upon them. They that do this thing are holy and righteous in God's sight.'"

'The Messengers were sanctified killers, Sergeant. And I think they still are. I think that's who you've been dealing with.'

'Son of a bitch,' Kennedy muttered.

Gassan nodded in sombre agreement. 'Remember that they trace their line back past grandfather Judas to great-great-great-grandfather Cain.

'Perhaps that's why they're so comfortable with murder. It's in their blood.'

45

Gayle dropped Kennedy off at the EconoLodge. He had duties to attend to elsewhere, he told her, so he'd have to leave her to her own devices for a while; but he'd check in with her later in the day, and be her chauffeur again if need be.

Up in her room, Kennedy powered up the laptop and sent another email to Tillman. Then for good measure she called him – knowing he wouldn't answer – and left a message on his voicemail.

'Leo, there's something I have to tell you. Something really important. It changes everything and it means your trail hasn't gone cold after all. Call me. Or else answer the email. Just do something to let me know you're listening and I'll tell you. But I'm not going to shout this out into the void and you know bloody well why. Call me. Please.'

She was planning to get down to some serious research after that, but she paced around the room for a good half an hour, unable to settle, finding pointless things to do with the few belongings she'd brought with her.

Finally she put through another call to Tillman's number. 'Me again,' she said. 'Leo, the Michael Brand who died on the plane was in his late twenties, which means he'd have been a kid when Rebecca went missing. There's no way he could have matched up to the description you got back then. It's a different man. I think it's always a different man. There probably never was a Michael Brand. It's just a name they use when they go out on this kind of job. They've got people they call "Messengers". Maybe all their Messengers are Michael Brand. For the love of Christ, would you just call me? And if you don't call me, then read my damned emails. I need you!'

That felt a little cathartic, at least. She went back to the laptop and got to work. First she called up a few maps of Arizona state. She found whole websites devoted to that one subject, offering every kind of map and chart – topographic, economic, physical and political. She also discovered a site that allowed her to switch between a simplified schematic map and satellite camera footage, which sucked her in for two whole hours. She followed the likely route of Flight 124, tracking along both arms of the California Gulf and then across the Mexican and Arizona desert as far north as Lake Havasu.

She wouldn't admit to herself exactly what it was she was looking for, but she found nothing: nothing out of the ordinary anyway. Nothing mysterious or unlabelled or controversial: nothing – say it! – that could be a secret enclave of crazed assassins hiding out from everybody in the middle of the wilderness. It was the wrong wilderness anyway, surely? Why would a group of religious refuseniks from ancient Judea be living in Arizona?

Maybe they liked the dry heat.

Or maybe they went where the power went. Maybe they'd lived in the Middle East for as long as the Middle East felt like the hub of something, then spilled west into Europe when Europe was a happening place, and decamped into the New World during the death throes of colonialism.

Is that what I'd do, Kennedy wondered, if I were a murderous madman who'd struck a special deal with God? All things considered, it was hard to tell.

She tried a different tack, using several search engines and meta-search engines to interrogate Southern Arizona directly. What were its biggest landmarks, its population centres, its most remote spaces and its anomalous microclimates?

She learned a lot, or at least surfed a lot of information, but got no real insights or inspirations. The terrain was harsh, parts of it were inaccessible, and nobody could say it was densely populated. With fifty or so people to the square mile, Arizona ranked thirty-third out of the fifty states of the Union – and most of those people were clustered in a few major population centres. But the state had good roads, it was on a whole lot of flight paths, and satellites looked down on it twenty-four hours a day.

Kennedy had been imagining a scenario. Flight 124 is winging its way up from Mexico City. Someone looks out of the window and sees something they weren't meant to see – something that points to the existence of the Judas tribe. An alarm bell rings somewhere, somehow, and Michael Brand – one of the Michael Brands – is despatched. He can't touch the plane while it's in mid-air, obviously, so the best he can do is to get to Los Angeles and board it during the stop-over, which he makes with inches to spare. Then he finds a way to bring the plane down, which with his unique combination of combat skills and frothing madness is a piece of rancid cake.

But the closer Kennedy looked at it now, the less she liked it. It all hinged on there being something to see: something big enough to be visible from 124's cruising altitude (about twenty-seven thousand feet, Gayle had ascertained), and not just visible but identifiable; and yet, at the same time, something that was presumably temporary, only there to be seen on this one occasion. Otherwise the skies over Southern Arizona and Mexico would be thick with falling planes like summer rain.

She couldn't, for the life of her, imagine what that something could be. And she couldn't, yet, come up with an alternative scenario. Finally, she came to the obvious conclusion that this wasn't something she could do from her hotel room.

When Gayle called at around three in the afternoon, she told him her plan. 'I want to go look at the area that the plane flew over. Some of it anyway.'

Gayle was surprised and clearly wary of the idea. 'That's a lot of ground,' he pointed out. 'Where were you thinking of starting?'

'I don't know. The state line, I guess. The Arizona part of the route is the most accessible from here.'

'Sure.' Gayle sounded far from convinced. 'Of course, the distance from Mexico City to LA is about fifteen hundred miles, give or take. Maybe sixteen. And only about a tenth of that is likely to be inside of Arizona. I don't know how much you're going to achieve.'

'Well, at least it will give me a sense of the lie of the land,' Kennedy said. 'How far apart these places are, and where they lie in relation to each other. It might spark some ideas.'

As she said it, she did the math in her mind: tried to anyway. Fifteen hundred miles, and at a height of twenty-seven thousand feet you'd probably have a field of vision that would be . . . the best she could manage to visualise was a triangle twenty-seven thousand feet on a side. You'd be seeing – seeing really clearly, right below you – an area that stretched for at least a mile on either side. So at a conservative estimate, she had three thousand square miles to search. It would take days just to cover that distance by road: and how much would she see from the road?

'I just don't want to sit here,' she said, glumly. 'And I can't think of anything better to do.'

There was a short silence while Gayle thought about this.

'Take the plane,' he said.

46

Kuutma was listening to music when Mariam's call came through. This was unusual because Kuutma hated music.

No, that wasn't true. But it was a refractory medium for him. He didn't understand its structures or its appeal. As a younger man, he'd listened to certain tunes with a kind of pleasure. He even remembered dancing once. All of this before he became a Messenger and left Ginat'Dania. After that, the course of his life had been irrevocably set, and somehow, music had slowly ceased to mean anything to him.

Perhaps it was an effect of the drug. *Kelalit* altered perception; or, more accurately, altered the interface between the user and the world. Reality became a dumb show, drenched in sepia and moving with the sluggishness of syrup. The mind was quicker, the movements surer: the overall sense was of heightened awareness, and yet paradoxically the things of which one was aware had been leached of much of their vividness, their 'thisness'. Sights, sounds, textures, tastes: all became flattened along one dimension, became – he could think of no clearer way to express it – schematics of themselves.

The ringing of the phone came, therefore, as a welcome distraction from the depressing enigma of the music.

'Hello,' Kuutma said.

'She's booked an airline ticket, *Tannanu*.' Mariam's voice sounded perfectly level, perfectly uninflected.

'Where to?' Kuutma asked.

'Mexico City. But I don't think the destination is the point. She's taking Flight 124.'

'Ah. Yes.' Kuutma considered. That was good, in a number of ways. It showed how little, even at this stage, the detective had managed to piece together. And it offered opportunities for finishing the job that had been left unfinished in England. And yet. And yet. This business had been badly handled at every stage. To act again now and leave more loose ends still dangling would not be acceptable.

That was why he hadn't ordered Mariam to move against Tillman. That was the only reason, he told himself yet again. There were no others. In any event, once Tillman returned to the rooming house in west London that had already been identified by Mariam's team, there had been no need to move. He had put himself in Kuutma's hands and Kuutma could order his death at any moment.

Kautma reminded himself that this removed the urgency from the situation: indeed, that it made surveillance more valuable and useful than immediate action. Kill Tillman now and perhaps some delayed action mechanism might be triggered: information released to others and a new danger opened up.

But Kuutma did not really believe this.

He had travelled to London. Taken the Underground, and then a bus, to the pitiful hole where Tillman now lodged. He had rented the adjacent room, and with infinitesimal care opened up a tiny hole in the wall, very close to the floor, using an exquisitely sharpened auger and taking several hours. Through the hole, he had inserted a pin-head spy camera on a micro-fibre lead.

What he had seen had given him considerable satisfaction.

'He won't stop coming. He'll look into your eyes, some day, Kuutma, and one of you will blink.'

'Rebecca, I do not think that it will be me.'

'But you don't know him, and I do.'

'I wish, dear cousin, that you had never had to know him. I rejoice that you don't have to know him any longer.'

'Ah, but I don't have to know anything any longer, Kuutma. That's why they sent you.'

Perhaps he should have killed Tillman then. Perhaps, at any rate, he should have left him as he was and interfered no further. He had not killed Tillman and he had not left: not immediately. He had done one thing more that might – that would – have consequences.

'What should I do, *Tannanu*?' Mariam's question dragged Kuutma out of his reverie, into which he should never have fallen.

Suppressing the memories, both old and recent, he turned various ideas in his mind and examined them for flaws. 'For now,' he said, 'do nothing. Let the woman go and let her return. Follow her, if she leaves the airport terminal in Mexico. Depending on where she goes, and who she sees, it might be necessary to move quickly, against a wider range of targets. For now, though, let them gather. It's good that they gather. It makes our task a great deal easier. You know, Mariam, the one great rule that we follow.'

'Do nothing that is not warranted,' Mariam quoted. 'Do everything that is needful.'

'And always – we must infer – be mindful of where our actions fall along that line.'

'I understand, *Tannanu*.'

'But you're grieving, Mariam, for your cousins. The hurt you feel ... if I know you at all, I would venture to say that it is more real to you, and bigger to you, than anything else in this world.'

'It is not bigger, or more real, than God, *Tannanu*.'

'Hence,' Kuutma answered, gently, 'I specified this world. You loved them. You fought with them and shared with them everything of yourself that was godly to share. What you've lost ... I know, believe me, how great it is.' When she didn't answer, he went on. 'If you wanted to go home now, there'd be no shame. Someone else could finish this and you could heal in the company of other loved ones.'

'*Tannanu*, forgive me.' Her voice had taken on a harshness now. 'If I flinched from this, because of some emotional pain, some imagined wound to my heart, how could I not be ashamed? When Ezei and Cephas gave everything, how could I weigh out what I give and say this is enough, or this is too much? You sent me out. Don't – I beg you – call me home again before my work is all done.'

He bowed his head, in a gesture of respect for her that she couldn't see and would never know about. '*Barthi*, I will not.'

There was a silence. 'What is that music?' Mariam asked, in a more subdued tone, as though her victory over him had exhausted her.

'The Rolling Stones,' he told her. 'A song called "Paint it Black".'

'Is the sound pleasant to you, *Tannanu*?'

Kuutma felt embarrassed. 'No. Of course not. It's a monstrous cacophony. I'm listening only to align my thoughts with those of my quarry. This is Tillman. Tillman's music. He's listened to it several times since the fire, and I wanted to understand what emotions it might give rise to.'

'Have you found an answer, *Tannanu*?'

Kuutma was on firmer ground here. 'Despair, *barthi*. He's feeling despair.'

411

47

Kennedy had feared that being on Flight 124 would feel eerie and unnerving, but after the first five or ten minutes it was just a flight. She took the window seat she'd specified when she booked, refused the complimentary drinks and pretzels, and settled in to watch the ground as it unrolled below her.

City, suburb, desert, desert, desert. A stone quarry, a small town, a dam and more desert. As the plane gained altitude, she became less and less able to distinguish individual features of the terrain. After a while, she could only tell built-up areas by their colour: sprawls of grey against the greater sprawls of tawny brown, turd brown and olive drab.

At twenty-seven thousand feet up, revelations were hard to come by.

She could see the coastline, obviously, and rivers stood out pretty clearly. Roads were harder but you could guess where they were sometimes, from the interruptions in the lines of mountains or where the area around them had been cleared. Was there a road, maybe, where a road shouldn't be? A road that serviced no obvious destination?

But that couldn't be it. Anything as permanent as that would be seen by the passengers of every flight that took this route. What she was looking for – what she needed – was something transitory: it would have been a one-off event. So the flight could give her a sense of the possible scale of the thing, but that was all. She was up here to play twenty questions, and she was still at the 'Is it bigger than a breadbox?' stage.

Roads, then, but not the traffic on the roads. Manmade structures, if they were very tall or reasonably extensive. Other planes: she saw several of those, passing by at leisurely speeds in the middle distance.

And lights. As evening came on, the landscape turned into a lattice, some areas lit up, others in profound darkness. Okay, that might be something: a light where no light should be? But of course, as it got darker, it got harder to see the salient features of the landscape, so you had less and less to orient yourself by. Who could say where a light shouldn't be or where it was in relation to anything else? The pilot would know. And the co-pilot. They'd have instruments to go by, as well as sight. Would Brand have downed a whole plane to kill the cabin crew?

She watched one of the lights below flashing on and off, with a fixed periodicity: visible for three seconds, dark for five. It was over towards the coast, so she guessed it was a lighthouse. Could 124 have seen and registered some other kind of beacon, lit to send a signal meant only for the Judas people? They loved their codes after all: maybe they spoke to each other across the darkness with flashing torches or those massive, slatted searchlights that RAF bomber command used back in the Second World War.

In the age of the mobile phone, that would be a really asinine thing to do, wouldn't it?

The plane began its descent into Mexico City – after the sparseness of the deep desert, a cluster of lights within lights as thick as enfolded galaxies – and Kennedy gave it up at last as a bad job.

She had almost three hours to kill before the return flight. She wandered the concourse like a grim ghost, finding most of the shops and cafés already closed for the night. Finally she found a bar, sat down and ordered a large margarita. When in Rome, she figured, you should at least make a token effort.

A woman at the other end of the bar was watching her, covertly and intermittently. She looked young; maybe pretty, too, but wearing way too much make-up. Not Kennedy's type exactly, because Kennedy preferred larger than life curves, but interesting all the same, with a slender and no doubt quite supple body. She was wearing very drab casuals: blouse and slacks in indeterminate earth colours, which she could have gotten away with if she'd had more of a tan but just looked muddy and off-white next to the clear, light skin of her arms.

Kennedy didn't feel the least bit horny, but she was as tense as hell and she considered, for the first time in a long time, the possible restorative effects of a quick tumble. As a first, exploratory step in that direction, she kept her gaze on the woman – so that the next time she shot Kennedy a furtive glance, their eyes met.

The effect wasn't what Kennedy was expecting. Without moving, the woman drew in on herself. Not like someone shy or withdrawn, but like someone tensing for a confrontation. Christ. Kennedy had obviously read her wrong. Maybe the woman had made her as a cop somehow. Maybe she had a thing against cops.

Kennedy was about to finish her drink and leave, but the woman beat her to it. She put her glass down, with a little more force than was necessary, beckoned the barman over and spoke with him for a few seconds before putting a wad of bills into his hands. The barman shrugged, counted, nodded. The woman left and Kennedy checked out her retreating bum with a vestigial twinge of regret.

414

She took her time with the margarita, allowing the alcohol to soothe her back from partial arousal to something close to calm, closer to resignation. She made a sign to the barman to bring her the tab and he shook his head.

'You're good, ma'am,' he said.

'I'm what?'

'You're good. The lady covered your drink. And she said to give you this.'

He put something down on the bar in front of Kennedy. It looked like a quarter until she picked it up and registered first its weight, then its irregular shape, finally the partially erased uncial letters around its edge. She had the twin of that coin in her wallet, given her by Tillman in the Crown and Anchor on Surrey Street.

She dropped the coin and sprinted out of the bar. She quartered the whole concourse at a quick jog-trot, hoping against hope that she might run into the woman again. There were few enough people around that she would have spotted her at once, but of course the woman wouldn't have left the coin if she'd intended to stay. Kennedy slowed to a walk at last, breathless from more than just the running, her heart pounding in her chest.

It had been ... what had it been? A taunt. A provocation. A promise. The woman at the bar was one of the people she was looking for: the Judas tribe. And she'd allowed herself to be seen, as if to say to Kennedy that it didn't matter how easy or how obvious they made it for her, she still wouldn't get there, still wouldn't put all the pieces together.

Or maybe, that it didn't even matter if she did.

Anger had swept through Kennedy like a hot wave, but now it broke, and she found herself strangely calm. Whoever the woman was, revealing herself like this had been a reckless thing to do: seen in the context of centuries or millennia of obsessive secrecy, it was an inexplicable mistake. Possibly she saw it as a show of strength, but it wasn't, couldn't be that. It was some emotion that she hadn't entirely been able to control, working through her and distorting her judgement. Kennedy remembered, suddenly, that she and Tillman had heard a woman's voice, screaming, on the night when Dovecote burned. Was it possible that this could be the same woman? That she'd followed Kennedy all the way across the Atlantic? Wildly unlikely: if they'd been so ready to kill her on that night of blood and fire, why hold back now?

Someone else, then. But someone who wanted her to know that she was known: that she was pursued, even as she continued with her own pursuit.

So the real confrontation wouldn't be long in coming. And now Kennedy was forewarned, so if she wasn't forearmed that was shame on her.

It was two in the morning when the shuttle flight landed at Bullhead, and after three when she got back to the hotel in Peason. John-Bird was her driver once again, but she forestalled his Colorado anecdotes by falling asleep instantly in the back of the cab. He kept right on talking anyway. Surfacing from her doze every now and again, Kennedy experienced the wash of words as bizarrely comforting: it felt good not to be alone right then. By way of thanks, she mumbled a 'really?' in response to whatever fluvial fact he was regaling her with, then promptly drifted off to sleep again.

Staggering up to her room, she intended to collapse face down on the bed and sleep some more, probably without even bothering to get undressed. But the red light on the bedside phone was flashing. She picked up the receiver and dialled 3 for voicemail, holding the handset jammed under her chin as she wrestled her shoes off her slightly swollen feet.

'Hey, Sergeant.' Webster Gayle's voice, hale and hearty and over-loud. 'I hope you got something out of your trip south of the border besides cheap tequila. Can't wait to hear how it went. Listen, we can't put this off any more. You got to talk to Moggs, so's you and her can put your heads together and reach critical mass. I promise I'll stand way back out of the blast radius. She's an early riser, so I thought we could do breakfast. I'll be waiting for you downstairs at seven-thirty. Sleep tight.'

One margarita, Kennedy reflected, wearily, as she rolled into bed and pulled the covers half-over her. One margarita, and nothing to look forward to but breakfast with ghosts. Not nearly tight enough.

48

It was clear to Kennedy inside of a minute that the relationship between Eileen Moggs and Webster Gayle went way beyond the professional. A minute or so after that, she could also tell that the man and the woman saw the relationship in different terms.

Sheriff Gayle was casual and matter-of-fact in introducing Moggs, calling her 'a very good friend of mine'. The phrase came from the lexicon of TV talk-show hosts and meant – in itself – as near to nothing as made no difference. But Moggs's smile as he said it seemed charged, momentarily, with both pride and pain. It asserted that the sheriff had no better friend; and it admitted, at the same time, that there was no better word for what she was to him.

The two women shook hands and sized each other up. 'Oh, you're a cop, all right,' Moggs said, with a chuckle.

'Got the look?' Kennedy asked, ruefully.

'In spades, darlin', and you can take that as a compliment. My papa was a cop and so are both of my brothers. Anyone who's got that set to their shoulders, I tend to think of them as being at the very least a kissing cousin.'

Which explains why you're dating the sheriff, Kennedy thought. She allowed Moggs to shoo her through a bead curtain into the kitchen, where waffles, eggs and bacon awaited her.

They were surprisingly good, as was the coffee and the orange juice – the latter, apparently, squeezed by hand using an old-fashioned crank-operated juicer that had pride of place on one of the countertops. Kennedy had been feeling physically and emotionally lagged, but the breakfast restored her, and her replies to Moggs's good-natured interrogation became steadily less monosyllabic.

So how long had Kennedy been in the Detective Division? Six years, give or take.

And had she always wanted to be a cop? Pretty much always. It was a family tradition ('Usually is,' Moggs agreed).

Was this her first visit to the States? No, second. Kennedy had spent a week in New York once, with a girlfriend – or girl friend, rather; one of many false moves in a relationship that had remained bafflingly platonic despite all the signs of developing into something more primal and fulfilling. Kennedy didn't mention the girl: she had no idea how Moggs and Gayle felt about homosexuality, and she didn't want to bring additional awkwardness into a situation that was already slopping over with the stuff.

'I went to London once,' Moggs confided. 'Had a really rotten time there. It was high summer and it didn't do anything but rain. Took the next month or so just to get dry again. Also, I had to point at the menus in restaurants because I discovered I couldn't speak the language – even though it's meant to be the *same* language!' She laughed uproariously at her own joke. Kennedy laughed along.

'So anyway,' Moggs said, just as suddenly serious. 'This murder investigation of yours ... Web won't talk to me about it because he doesn't want to abuse his position – me being a journalist and him being an officer of the law – but he said that you might want to talk about it, and if you did, he couldn't stop you. So I thought, hell, if I show you mine, you might be prepared to show me yours. What do you say?'

Kennedy decided to go for blunt honesty. 'I can't answer that until I know what yours is.' *And if it turns out to be ghosts, I'm probably going to have to throw your hospitality back in your face.*

Moggs conceded the point with a grin. 'That's true. That's very true. Listen, though. Web's a good man, isn't he? I mean, you only just met him and I bet you could tell that. He's so good, he thinks everyone else is good, too. That's kind of a weakness, in a cop.'

'Sitting right here!' Gayle protested.

'Shut up, Web,' Moggs told him, with affection. She kept her eyes on Kennedy the whole time and there was maybe a bit of a glint in them. 'But I'm a news hack, Sergeant, so I know most folks is dirty. I imagine you'd agree with that, right?'

'I'd say fifty-fifty,' Kennedy allowed, warily.

'Well,' said Moggs. 'I wouldn't. I'd say the odds are way longer than that. So here's how it works. Web gets a message from an out-of-towner, a fellow cop, and it's a request for help. And Web's first thought in that situation is, How can I help this person? Whereas my first thought is, What's the scam, here? What do I stand to lose? What does this look like if you walk around it a few times and poke it with a stick? You get me?'

Kennedy saw the question behind the question and knew beyond any shadow of a doubt that she'd been blown out of the water. 'Yes,' she said. 'I get you.'

'So while Web rolls out the red carpet for you and tells me all these amazing things about you – how smart you are, and how polite, and the amazing accent and everything – I can't help thinking, So who is this Sergeant Kennedy and what exactly is her angle? Because everyone's got an angle, right?'

'Yeah,' Kennedy said. 'I guess that's true.'

'And your angle is that you're not a cop any more. You got busted back down to civilian, or else you quit – depends who I ask. But you forgot to mention that to Web when you asked him to assist you in your investigation.'

Kennedy was surprised to find herself blushing. She knew it was just a matter of time before someone checked her credentials and found that they were no good. She hadn't expected the moment to be so painful when it came.

She turned to Gayle. 'I'm really sorry, Sheriff,' she said, meaning it. 'You must think I was using you pretty cynically, and maybe I was. But you wouldn't believe what I've done already to make this case. What I've lost. And I couldn't give it up. Even when it stopped being mine, when I stopped being police, I couldn't give it up.'

She stood, ready to leave either on her own or in his custody, but Gayle broke into a chuckle at her strained, solemn face.

'Sit down, Sergeant,' he told her. 'I don't see what you said as a lie, so much. I reckon there's some people are cops before they get a badge, and they go on being cops after they give the badge back. Or they never get a badge, like Moggs here, but still got the instincts and the way of looking at the world.'

'It's in the blood,' Moggs said, immodestly. 'Seriously, Ms Kennedy – I guess I shouldn't call you sergeant – I wasn't trying to rub your nose in any of this. I was just telling you that we know. We figured you out. But you don't have any jurisdiction over here anyway, and I know for a fact that you were working this case until your last day on the job. All you done wrong, in the world's eyes, is not to stop. And the other thing is, Web hasn't broken any rules in helping you. All of this is public domain stuff, as far as that goes. The County Sheriff can tell who he likes about a case in progress, if they ask.'

'Although he generally doesn't,' Gayle interjected. 'I wouldn't want you to think I'd be this indiscreet with anyone who just walked in off the street, Sergeant.'

'Hell,' said Moggs, 'the plain truth of it is, you're working on our very own favourite cabbage patch, and that's why we wanted to break bread with you, and that's why I want to share with you. So what do you say?'

She thrust out a hand. Still blushing, Kennedy took it – not in a formal shake but in a slap and thumb-lock that felt a lot more intense and reassuring.

'Come on through to the living room,' Moggs said. 'And I'll show you what I got.'

She led the way back through the curtain and across a narrow hall into the warm and welcoming space, full of soft furniture and sunset colours. A massive sofa wore a crocheted throw adorned with a stylised but splendid American eagle. 'Actually,' Moggs said, as soon as she had Kennedy sat down on the sofa, 'this might be the kind of thing where we need to fortify ourselves with some more coffee. I'll go brew a fresh pot.'

She scooted back through into the kitchen and after a minute Gayle followed her, muttering something about helping to carry the tray. Left alone, Kennedy read the walls while her heart rate slowed to normal. The walls were covered with photographs, and Eileen Moggs herself showed in none of them. There was a wall of portraits, some of which Kennedy recognised: Webster Gayle (twice), George Clooney, Jesse Jackson, Bill Clinton, Bono, Donald Rumsfeld scowling like the devil on crack. The facing wall was all places: the Grand Canyon, Route 66 complete with iconic sign and biker flotilla, Anasazi ruins, cactuses, the state legislature being mobbed by hundreds of demonstrators, and one very disturbing image of a desert setting where a group of uniformed police or state troopers (Kennedy didn't know the uniform code well enough to tell for sure) posed solemnly around the corpse of a black man.

Gayle came in carrying three mugs on a tray, backing through the beads with his head ducked down. Moggs followed with a plate of cookies and – a little incongruously – a bottle of Jim Beam. Gayle set the tray down and Moggs twisted the cap off the bourbon. 'I usually have a shot of this in my coffee,' she said to Kennedy. 'Just a small one. Symbolic, really, but it takes the edge off edgy things.'

She spiked her own drink, looked at Kennedy with the bottle raised and ready.

'Are we going to be talking about edgy things?'

Moggs grinned. 'Didn't we already?'

'Go ahead,' Kennedy said, and Moggs poured.

'I'll pass,' Gayle said. 'I gotta go back to work after this.'

'I'm still on the clock,' Moggs growled.

'Sure. But everyone expects a newshound to be drunk.'

They ribbed each other with the easy intimacy of lovers. They didn't need to laugh at each other's jokes. Moggs went across to an over-sized L-shaped desk in a corner of the room and returned with a very thick olive-green file folder, which she put down on the table between them, pushing the plate of cookies over to one side to make space: the pièce de résistance.

'Okay,' she said, with the air of someone getting down to brass tacks. 'This is our dead-men-walking file.'

Kennedy hadn't been feeling any thrill of anticipation, but experienced a sinking feeling, all the same. 'The ghosts of Flight 124?' she said.

'Absolutely,' Moggs confirmed. 'Take a look. I promise you revelations, signs and wonders.'

'I'm ... not a believer in this stuff,' Kennedy protested, queasily but without much force.

'Oh, me neither, Sergeant. Read it anyway. Then we'll talk.'

A half-hour later, Kennedy was still reading, watched by her indulgent hosts – but the signs and wonders had yet to put in an appearance. In fact, the contents of the file were exactly what she would have expected them to be: a warmed-over soup of urban legends, done-in-one-sentence spooky stories and sad self-delusions.

All the usual suspects were in there: the man who sent emails full of indecipherable gibberish from his office computer when his body was lying on a slab in an Arizona morgue; the woman who felt her dead husband's hand on her shoulder and his kiss on her cheek at the exact moment that the plane went down; the car left running on a driveway in the middle of the night ('My wife's keys were in the ignition – she had them on her when she died, I swear it!'); the mother-and-child stick figures drawn in the condensation of a nursery window, and the sweet old lady identifying them unhesitatingly, and tearfully, as the work of her granddaughter ('She always drew herself with curly hair, even though she grew the curls out a year ago'). And so on, and so forth, with minor and uninteresting variations. The tales people tell each other to convince themselves, against all the odds, that death is not the end.

Kennedy closed the file, still only half-read, to signify that she was done with it. If anything, she'd drawn it out because she felt more or less convinced now that Gayle and Moggs were evangelists for one of the more surreal American churches and she was about to have to tell them both that their sandwich quotient was deficient for picnicking purposes. 'Like I said,' she repeated, as neutrally as she could manage, 'I don't really subscribe to the whole life after death thing. This is interesting, but it's really not my kind of—'

'Interesting?' Moggs was incredulous. 'Why would you say that, Ms Kennedy? Why, most of this is the same garbage the supermarket crap-sheets try to feed us every damn day of the week. It's so far from interesting, I can't get through six pages of it without losing the will to live.'

'Well, then ...' Kennedy foundered. 'Why show it to me?'

'That's the right question,' Moggs said. 'And I'm gonna answer it with another question. What do you notice about this nonsense? What's the pattern?' There was something a little sly or smug in her voice: the tone of the teacher who already knows the right answer and is waiting for you to chip in with the wrong one.

Kennedy went back to the file, scanned the first few pages again with no more enthusiasm than she'd managed the first time. 'No actual sightings,' she said. 'Not much that's verifiable. Nothing at all that couldn't have been faked or imagined. It's perfect tabloid-fodder: facts and names kept to a minimum, so it's hard to cross-check anything and there's maximum room to manoeuvre. Stories from one agency picked up and polished by another ...'

'Absolutely,' Moggs said. 'I've seen it all before, Ms Kennedy. Listen, can I call you Heather? Thank you. I've seen it all before, Heather, and it sounds like you have, too. But like they say, you have to look to the exception to prove the rule – and this time around, the exception is a pretty big, glaring one.'

Kennedy shrugged with her hands. 'I'm not seeing it.'

She could see Gayle yearning to break in but holding himself back – presumably seeing this as Moggs's show rather than his own.

'The truth is,' Moggs said, backing off just a fraction, 'it took me a pretty fair time to see it, too. Web was driving me crazy with this stuff. Even when he wasn't talking about it, he had a look on his face that said he was thinking about it. So I picked up this here scrapbook, basically so I could beat him round the head with it – show him all the different ways it was moonshine. Then it hit me – I think because it was all in the same place, and Web had tried to sort it by date and time and everything. That was sort of the key. Go back to the start, Heather, and bear in mind that the file's in chronological order.'

The first article concerned Peter Bonville, the clerk whose work routine was so powerful that death couldn't hold him back from turning up at the office, fixing himself a cup of coffee, firing up his computer and working through his inbox. Something nagged at the edge of Kennedy's attention. She checked the dateline: the fifth of July. Three days after CA124 went down.

'This isn't the first,' she said. 'There was one datelined on the fourth.'

'Sylvia Gallos,' Moggs confirmed, approvingly. 'Right. That threw me, too, at first – but it's a parallax error. You see, Gallos called into a local radio station – late-night talk show, same night it happened. So there's no time lag. It happens on the fourth and it's filed on the fourth. The Bonville story hits a day later but it happened two days earlier. It's just that it didn't turn into news until someone thought to notice.'

Clearly, they were getting to the meat of the matter now. Moggs didn't actually lower her voice but she leaned in close as though what she was about to say deserved the theatrical attributes of conspiracy. 'There were a lot of different versions of Peter Bonville's story, with a crazy range of details about what he supposedly did when he checked into work that day. Like, Bonville swiped in with his own ID. Wrong. No one found any evidence of him coming or going. Bonville fixed himself a cup of coffee and left it half-drunk in his cubicle. Wrong. As far as I can tell, only the office area, which was open-plan, got a visitation: the kitchen space was elsewhere and it wasn't touched. Bonville talked to some of his fellow employees, who didn't know they were seeing a ghost until later. Wrong. Nobody saw him. All the evidence that he'd been there came from his computer, his work-station, which had been turned on and used.'

'Used for what?' Kennedy asked. She felt a prickle of tension on the back of her neck, on her forearms. Was there actually some pea of truth buried under the damp mattresses of all these lazy, overused fairy tales?

'Well, again, there's different versions,' Moggs said. 'Some of them have Bonville surfing porn sites. Most of them say he sent emails: either full of random gibberish or scary complaints about being lost in a desert somewhere where the sun never comes up. Again, I checked all that with Bonville's employers, the New York Department of Public Works. They didn't have to talk to me, of course – wouldn't even have had to talk to Web, if he'd called, because his jurisdiction ends at the county line. But they wanted to talk. They were kind of griped by all the crazy stories going around and they wanted to set the record straight. They said Bonville's mail program hadn't been opened and neither had his browser. All he did – all whoever it was did – was access a few files and delete them. So they assumed it had to be a routine hacker attack rather than a ghostly visitation.'

That preliminary prickle had become something a lot more urgent now, which had Kennedy sitting forward too, as though she was about to lean across the table and kiss Moggs – which might have caused Sheriff Gayle to revise his good opinion of her. 'Which files? Do we know what they were?'

'No, we don't. And they don't – because the department's

main server got a big viral infection later that day and all the back-up storage got wiped clean before they could do anything about it. All that was left was a registry table with the names of some of the files on it, but they're not informative. Data 1, data 2, data 3, stuff like that.'

Kennedy's first thought was an obvious one: *Rotgut?* But no, that was vanishingly unlikely. If anyone on Stuart Barlow's team had been talking to a minor official in a public agency in New York, she would have come across the data trail long before now. This was different: not Rotgut. But sufficiently like Rotgut for the response to have been the same. Send in Michael Brand.

Moggs was still talking. 'So there's not much to work from at that end. But here's what got me going, Sergeant. I said this was the earliest of the ghost incidents. I didn't tell you just how early. That registry table had precise date stamps for the last time each of the files was modified – which was when they were deleted. They're clustered really tight together, in a five-minute period starting at 11.13 a.m. on July the second. In other words, the files got wiped while Flight CA124 was still in the air: a good ten minutes or so before Peter Bonville became a ghost.'

Kennedy checked the times for herself and then observed a minute of silence for Moggs's detective work: or five seconds of silence, anyway. 'You're right,' she said, full of admiration. 'You're totally ... you nailed it, Miss Moggs. Eileen. This was a pre-emptive haunting.'

Moggs laughed, clearly liking both the term and the praise. 'Pre-emptive haunting, then two days of nothing, then all these other ghost stories kick in. So by the time Bonville's supervisor figures out they're missing some files and tells head office, all this other stuff is already starting to come out. And that's how it was reported – another ghost from Flight 124.'

Kennedy nodded slowly, thinking backwards and forwards

along that chain of logic. 'That's actually really clever,' she murmured. 'You cover your trail as far as you can, but when you realise it's not covered enough, you throw out a whole lot of false trails so it looks like it doesn't lead anywhere.'

'"The elaborations of a bad liar",' said Moggs. It sounded like a quote but Kennedy didn't get it and didn't feel like asking. She turned to Gayle instead. 'So you think someone took advantage of this guy's absence to get into his computer and take something out of it? And then when he died instead of coming back to his desk, they worked out a supernatural cover story?'

'That's exactly what I think,' Gayle agreed.

'I think you're wrong, Sheriff.'

Gayle blinked a few times, hit squarely in the face by the harsh words. A moment ago, they'd all been conspirators – and conspiracy-busters – together: now it seemed like Kennedy didn't want to play.

'How's that?' he asked her.

Kennedy turned to Moggs. 'Have you got the passenger list from 124?' she asked.

Moggs nodded. 'Got every piece of information I could legally hold about this whole business, and then a little bit more.'

'Can you go get it?'

Moggs went over to her desk and fired up her computer. Sheriff Gayle went with her and stood behind her as she keyed in her password. His hands dropped to her shoulders, a gesture of protection and solidarity. They'd shown their baby to Kennedy: was she about to throw it out with the bathwater?

Moggs tapped a few keys, opened a file. 'Okay,' she said. 'Got it.'

'Find Peter Bonville.'

'Got him. He's near the top, obviously.'

'Okay, I'm going to tell you his seat number.'

Moggs shot her a puzzled glance. 'What, from memory?'

'I never even heard his name until just now.'

'Then how would you know his seat number?'

'Maybe I don't. In a lot of ways, I hope I'm wrong. But is it 29E?'

Both of them, in unison, read the screen and then turned to stare at her. 'How'd you know that?' Gayle demanded.

Kennedy reached into her inside pocket and took out the folded sheet Gayle had given to her the day before: the photocopy of the marked dollar bill that Brand had carried. She held it out. Gayle took it and scanned it, but Moggs got there first.

'The three lines on the note,' she said. 'They run right across the serial number here, at the bottom.'

'Well, I'll be goddamned!' Gayle exclaimed in wonder, getting there a second later. The three red lines crossed out an E, a 2 and a 9.

'The first thing I thought when I saw this note was that it might be a coded message of some kind,' said Kennedy. 'The people I've been tracking ... they love codes and hidden messages. They think they're the smartest people in the room, I guess, and that they can operate right out in plain sight so long as they put up a smokescreen over their comms. This is right in their line, as far as that goes.'

'So how does this mean we're wrong?' Gayle asked.

'Because you were assuming the raid on Bonville's computer was opportunistic. It wasn't. Whoever gave this note to Brand was telling him who the target was. Which means that Brand got on that plane with the express intention of killing Bonville. And for reasons we're never going to know now ...'

'Oh sweet Jesus,' Moggs murmured.

' ... he killed them all. Everyone on board. He completed his mission by bringing down CA124.'

49

In some ways, after that, it got easy.

Bonville didn't board at Los Angeles. He was with 124 all the way from its point of origin: Benito Juárez International Airport, Mexico City. Kennedy asked Sheriff Gayle – despite the jurisdictional issues that Moggs had already mentioned – to place the call to Bonville's former supervisor, a woman named Lucy Miller-Molloy, at the New York Department of Public Works. What had Bonville been doing down in Mexico? And while they were on the subject, what did Bonville do, period? What was his job, in the department? What was his area of specific expertise?

Power routing, was the short answer. The slightly longer answer: Bonville was a respected thinker in the expanding field of peak usage flow-back equalisation. Miller-Molloy knew far too much about the subject herself to explain it clearly to a layman, but she told Gayle enough so that he could give a bare-bones summary to Kennedy and Moggs without contradicting himself.

'Say you run a city and you've got a generator that's providing electricity for the city,' he said. 'Sometimes you'll need a lot of power, sometimes not so much. So you use the trough times to charge up auxiliary generators – or, say, to pump water upriver a few miles, past a dam with a hydro plant. Then when you get to a peak time, you've got that extra charge saved up like money in the bank and you can pay yourself back somehow – increase your capacity at the peak times.'

It seemed there were many different ways of doing this flowback stuff, some so cheap they paid for themselves. What Bonville did was look at power systems and say, 'Well, you've got room to do this, this and this, and it will cost you this much for each erg of power.'

The New York Department of Public Works had used Bonville as an outside consultant for a while and then had put him on salary – a pleasant corollary of which was that they could generate additional revenue by sending him out on loan to other municipalities. Mexico City had been the latest of many of these gigs.

'So he was down there telling them how to economise on electricity,' Gayle summarised, when he reported back to Kennedy and Moggs. 'The idea was that he'd look at their power usage. Then he'd tell them where they had spare capacity in their system and how they could use it.'

By this time it was after midday, they were on the fourth pot of coffee, and Gayle had relaxed his strictures against the bourbon. He took a slug of it now, in a tiny shotglass labelled in red letters, 'A Present from Tijuana'. Silhouettes of a sombrero and a cactus provided additional verification.

'I'm not seeing how this picture fits into your picture,' Moggs said to Kennedy, scrolling through her Bonville notes, to which she'd been adding in the course of the morning. 'Your Judas people kill anyone who finds out about their secret bible, right? Are we assuming that Bonville came across this Rotgut Gospel somewhere down in Mexico?'

Kennedy had been pondering the exact same thing and had

come up with something like an answer. 'I think they cast their net wider than that,' she said, as Moggs resumed her rapid typing. 'The point about people not seeing the Gospel of Judas isn't just a blind article of faith. If it was, they'd have killed everyone who read the mangled version that surfaced a few years back – the Codex Tchacos. I think the point is that they don't want anyone to know that they exist or that they ever existed. The complete version of the gospel, the one Barlow got from the Rotgut, talks about their internal rules and the divisions of their society. It makes it clear that the worship of Judas was something that defined a community. A tribe. That seems to be what they want to keep secret.'

'An ancient Judean tribe? There's still no logical throughline.'

'Well,' Kennedy said, 'maybe there is. We know that Bonville travelled the world, advising people – local government people, public agencies – about power usage. So he had access to a whole lot of data about that stuff, about patterns of power flow and power consumption, at different times, in different places. Suppose he found a piece of data that didn't fit into the pattern?'

Moggs' hands, poised over the keyboard, froze. She turned to stare at Kennedy. 'Power usage where there shouldn't be any,' she said.

'Exactly. Or just heavier than it ought to be, for a particular place and a particular population density. He could have found out where the Judas people are based, purely on the basis of those statistics. He wouldn't even know, necessarily, what it was he'd found. But he started to ask the wrong questions or look in the wrong places. And they shut him down before he could put two and two together and get four.'

Gayle cast an anxious look at Moggs's computer. Kennedy

433

could read his mind. 'We've got to be really careful who we tell about this,' she agreed. 'In fact, I'm thinking we should keep it between the three of us for now. Eileen, do you have a laptop?'

Moggs nodded.

'Save those notes on to a pen-drive and move them over to the laptop – and keep the laptop off the net. If they could get to Bonville's computer, they can get to yours.'

'Maybe I should unplug my home computer, too,' Moggs muttered. 'I can use the machine down at the *Chronicler* office for internet stuff.'

Kennedy shook her head. 'No, keep your machine here plugged in. If they were to check up on you, we'd want them to find nothing at all out of the ordinary. Everything as it should be and everything smelling of roses. If they see us coming, they'll come for us first. Believe me, you do not want that to happen.'

'What's the next step?' Moggs asked.

'Santa Claus,' Gayle answered, before Kennedy could get the words out. 'We go on up to the evidence store again and we see whether anything of Bonville's is either in his box or in among the anonymous stuff. Anything that might tell us what it was he found.'

'That's my feeling, too,' said Kennedy. 'And we do that right now. If we get no joy there, we go back to the New York office and ask for a list of all the places Bonville went in the past year, say. That gives us a shortlist.'

'Might give us more than that,' said Moggs. 'If you cross-referenced that list against the files on the New York server, you might find that there was only one discrepancy – one place that doesn't have any data saved for it.'

They agreed, in the end, to work both ends at the same time. Moggs would stay at the apartment and place that call. Gayle and Kennedy would drive out to the storage sheds at Santa

Claus and search for smoking guns there. That was Gayle's expression and it made Kennedy wince.

'As a personal favour,' she asked him, 'can we just say "search for evidence"?'

50

Highway 93 was clear as far as the horizon, in both directions, again. All the same, Kennedy couldn't keep from checking the rear-view mirror every minute or so. She didn't trust the desert to remain empty.

'This is going to take some explaining,' Gayle ruminated. 'And as soon as we start into explaining, it's going to be federal. I don't know if that's a good thing or a bad thing. Those people got the resources after all. And I guess once the risk is spread that wide, it ain't a risk any more. There'll be no reason for anyone to come after us, if all this stuff gets to be out in the open. But the feds have got their own rules and they're powerful hard to negotiate with. You might find your Arizona vacation a little longer than you expected, Sergeant. If they think they're likely to need what you know, they'll want to keep you right here ready to hand. And I know you ain't got your own people to go to bat for you. But keeping you out of the picture ... well, that'd be real hard at this point.'

'You don't have to lie for me, Sheriff,' Kennedy told him. 'You play it exactly the way you think it needs to be played and if any rules have gotten broken or bent along the way, feel free to put that on to me.'

'Well, I wouldn't do that.'

'Okay. But I bulled my way in here by lying to you – and the lie's on record. Nobody but us needs to know that you saw through it. You were helping a fellow cop. It all rolled out of that.'

'Okay,' Gayle said. 'I like that version.'

The Biscayne backfired, the report sounding like an embarrassed cough.

They rolled off the highway, parked the car and went on into the storage shed. It was mid-afternoon now, even hotter than it had been on their first visit. Gayle switched on the AC and they took refuge in the Biscayne until the tiny, outmatched unit could start to make a difference.

'You and Moggs been together a long time?' Kennedy asked.

Gayle actually blushed a little. 'Oh,' he said, 'that's kind of ... you know, what you hear ain't always ...' He tailed off, hitting the limits of articulation, then rallied with a question of his own. 'What about you? There a Mr Sergeant Kennedy, Sergeant Kennedy? There a special man in your life?'

His evasiveness made her sick of her own equivocations. 'I'm gay,' she said. 'But there isn't anyone right now. Been a while since I got down to any serious misbehaviour.'

Gayle's blush deepened. 'Right,' he said. 'Well ... different strokes, for ...' That was another sentence that wasn't destined to be finished. 'I reckon we can probably make a start,' he said, and got out of the car again.

It was true that the storage shed had cooled a little now. They went straight to the right-hand aisle, picking up the red folder along the way.

Like a general, Gayle outlined their plan of campaign. He'd brought two pairs of non-reactant gloves, one of which he handed to her, and a bottle of spray disinfectant. 'It's everything from here through to here,' he said, pointing with nods of the head as he anointed both his own hands and hers. 'We made an effort to group similar types of thing together, but to be honest, it depended on who was writing it up. Anstruther had his own categories, which didn't make a whole lot of sense to me, and Scuff is just plain lazy, so I don't think there's much we can afford to leave out.' He was slipping the gloves on as he spoke. 'One thirty-eight to one ninety-seven is clothes, and we turned out all the pockets, so let's keep them as a last resort. Chances are, there'll be real slim pickings there. One ninety-eight is right here, so that gives us ... five units, or sixty boxes, give or take. I guess I'll start from one end, you can start from the other, and we'll meet in the middle.'

Kennedy nodded and went to her place, putting her hands into the gloves as she went and wriggling the fingers into place. Gayle called out after her.

'Sergeant?'

She turned. 'Yes?'

'I don't care who you share your bed with. I was just brought up not to talk about it. No offence meant.'

He looked ridiculously earnest. Kennedy smiled.

'None taken,' she said.

'Okay, then. Good hunting.'

'And to you, Sheriff.'

The contents of the boxes were a tragi-comic miscellany. She'd gotten a glimpse of them, of course, when she opened the red folder the first time around. Now she had to sort through them, and it turned out to be a task filled with horror and pathos, like trying to read the future in the entrails of dead children. But it was the past she was trying to read and she couldn't afford to be squeamish.

The objects were banal in themselves. What made them terrible was their specificity: a wallet with photos of two grinning kids, a boy and a girl, the girl slightly cross-eyed; a silver fountain pen inscribed *MG – for forty years*; a key chain whose fob was a chunk of crystal into which a 3D image, the portrait of a patrician older woman, had been laser-etched; an MP3 player in a case decorated with comic book panels, on to which the name *Stu Pearce* had been written in smudged black marker. The stumps of sheared-off lives, still raw, when the screaming had long since stopped and the bodies were underground.

She steeled herself against the emotions rising inside her: they'd only slow her down and make it harder to think. She was looking for something that might conceivably have belonged to Peter Bonville and might in some way contain a message. A CD, a USB stick, a voice recorder, a Walkman, a diary. Eventually they'd get to the phones, and Gayle would have to wrestle with the Fourth Amendment and his conscience.

But it was Gayle who struck gold, in the end, and it probably didn't even take all that long, counting by the clock. Subjectively, every minute spent poring through these cardboard burial vaults was a day.

'Sergeant.'

She turned to look at him. He was holding up a notebook: A5, or maybe a little smaller, with the words WALMART VALUE emblazoned across its red cover.

'Definite?' Kennedy asked. 'Or only maybe?'

Gayle turned the pages with gingerly care. 'Well, right at the start here we've got a list of addresses, headed up with the words "Switching stations". Then there's a second list of "Hubs". Lot of figures in columns, and then we get this. "Visit, Saturday: Siemens power generation service, Poniente 116 590, Industrial Vallejo, Metro Azcapotzalco, Mexico City, Distrito Federal: matters arising". It's looking pretty solid, I'd say.'

Kennedy thought so, too. She came and read over Gayle's

shoulder as he turned the pages. Most of it was unfathomable, but it all stank of electricity. Measurements in amps and volts, references to generating capacity, peak and off-peak averages, resistor tolerances, fluctuation by time and by district, where the districts had names like Azcapotzalco, Alvaro Obregon, Magdalena.

Three pages from the end they found another table, with the heading in block capitals, XOCHIMILCO ANOMALIES, and lists of numbers, some with multiple question marks appended as though they defied all logic and reason.

'What do you think?' Gayle asked.

'I think it's paydirt,' Kennedy said.

They had to decide whether to continue with the search or not. There could be more: digital data in some form or other that would corroborate and substantiate these handwritten notes. But what they had already was enough to bring the house down and the feds in, effectively filling all the blanks in their evidence trail. Michael Brand led back to Stuart Barlow and forward to the sabotaging of Flight 124. Flight 124 led to Bonville and Bonville led to . . . this. A place called Xochimilco. A place in Mexico, presumably. A place that was important, in some way, to the Judas tribe, and would prove their existence.

Kennedy weighed that against the numbing prospect of trawling through yet more boxes of mortal remains. The equation yielded only one answer.

Her eyes met Gayle's and he nodded, seeming to acknowledge everything she'd thought but hadn't said. 'It's enough,' he said. 'Feels like it should be anyway. Let's leave it to the big boys to figure out from here.'

Just as he had with Michael Brand's dollar bill – which he now took the opportunity to put back – Gayle insisted on following evidence protocols, signing the notebook out into his own possession. Kennedy waited by the door, feeling a weird sense of calm descend over her. Now that she had something, some weapon – however small – to aim at the bastards who had killed Chris Harper, it was as though she only had to let herself go now and gravity would reel her in. She knew that wasn't true – that in fact she had another gauntlet to run back in the UK very soon – but it was a pleasant feeling to indulge just for a moment.

'Okay,' said Gayle, closing the folder. 'I guess we're done.'

There was another wait while he locked the shed up and then they headed for the car, Gayle a few steps in front.

'Should we call Eileen?' Kennedy asked him. 'I'd like to know how she got on with the New York people.'

'I'll call her from the car, on the hands-free,' said Gayle. 'I'll feel a lot happier once we—'

Arriving simultaneously with its own sound – a sharp snap like the cracking of a whip – the bullet took him through the shoulder, close to the neck. It must have passed clean through because even as blood fountained forward from the entry wound, Kennedy could see a red ring widening at the back of Gayle's white shirt: expanding and filling out like a sun coming up, then drooping and losing its symmetry like one of the melting clocks in a Dali painting. The sheriff gave a grunt of astonishment and pain. He toppled sideways, crumpling into an ungainly shape as he hit the ground.

Kennedy was too shocked, too dumbfounded, even to dive for cover, and in any case there was no cover to be found: the Biscayne was the nearest, and that was ten yards away, in the same direction from which the shot had come. Tearing her eyes from Gayle's sprawled body, she looked past the car towards the leering Father Christmas on the porch of the nearest chalet.

Santa wasn't the shooter, though: the shooter stepped out from behind him now, the gun raised in her hand. It was the woman from the bar, at Benito Juárez airport. The woman who had left the silver coin for Kennedy to find. She wore no make-up at all now, so the red, scorched flesh that marred the beauty of her face was shockingly distinct.

'Just you and me,' the woman said, in a voice indefinably accented but still distinct. 'That was how it should have been last time, you murderous whore. But who knows what God wants of us? He made me wait. And now – finally – He'll make you bleed.'

51

This close, in full daylight, there was no mistaking what the woman was: underneath the burns, she had the same death pallor as the other assassins, both those in Luton and the ones Tillman had killed at Dovecote.

Unarmed and in the open, Kennedy knew she had no chance. She took a step back and to the side, away from the woman, hesitant, uncertain, as though she might run, in reality putting herself a little closer to the car.

The woman laughed, with real amusement. She held up her hand and silver flashed. Not a coin this time but the keys to the Biscayne, which Gayle had left in the ignition because who the hell was going to steal them way out here? She flicked them into the air, made to catch them but at the last moment let them fall at her feet, trod down on them with her boot heel. 'There isn't anywhere,' the woman said. 'I wasn't so stupid. But look. Now I will do something stupid.'

She lowered her gun, turned it over and slammed the heel of her hand down on the mag-catch. The magazine slid out partway, on to her palm. She drew it the rest of the way and threw it down in the sand. Then she tossed the gun over her shoulder with a negligent gesture. She looked at Kennedy and shrugged theatrically. *Well, now.*

Kennedy's reaction was immediate and instinctive – and wrong, she knew, even as she was doing it. She ran hard at the fish-belly-pale woman, who just stood with her arms at her side and watched her come. With a wordless yell, she swung a punch at that cold, contemptuous face that would have ended up halfway down the woman's throat if it had connected.

The woman caught her wrist, turned and threw her – a move that seemed almost improvised but was performed with snake-tongue speed. Kennedy flew through the air on a short, tight arc, smashed into Father Christmas, shattering him to matchwood, hit the wall behind and landed hard.

She started to scramble up but a dead weight slammed her down. The woman knelt astride her, right hand and left forearm combined to grip her throat in an agonising lock, lifting Kennedy's head while her knee, dead-centred in-between Kennedy's shoulder blades, kept Kennedy's torso pinned flat against the ground.

'This will hurt you much, much more than you imagine,' the woman murmured, close to her ear. 'And it will last for a very long time. Your friend will bleed out and die, as we do this. Your other friend, the journalist, is dead already. And the gun that killed them both will be found in your hand – the knife that kills you, in the sheriff's. Fight. Fight against me, you filthy, broken thing. Let me break you some more. I offer up your pain to God, who loves it.'

She slammed Kennedy's head hard against the planks of the porch. Stunned, her ears ringing, Kennedy tried a sideways roll that was unexpectedly successful because the woman was already gone, had stood up and stepped away from her.

Kennedy climbed groggily to her feet. The woman waited for her and then half-turned to kick her in the stomach with devastating force. Kennedy folded, saw the shovel-hook punch coming but couldn't dodge it, and was sent staggering backwards. This time she went clean through the door of the chalet, the desiccated wood exploding into dust and splinters.

The woman strode through the door right behind her and was on her again while she was still disentangling herself from the wreckage of the door. She was so *fast*. Kennedy put up a block: the woman's hands locked on her arm, one above and one below the elbow, and she leaned, very slightly, from the waist. Intolerable pressure was brought to bear suddenly on the bone of Kennedy's upper arm. She heard the snap as it gave. She opened her mouth to scream and the woman's forearm came up from below, hammered her jaw shut, so the sound was just a ratchet clicking of teeth and tongue and half-swallowed breath.

'Be patient,' the woman said, severely. 'Pace yourself.'

A hard rain of punches and jabs drove Kennedy backwards one lurching step at a time, until she slammed into an interior wall. No, it was a solid beam, that jarred every bone in her body. Her vision blurring, she saw the woman shift footing for another attack. She threw herself to the side: the reverse round-house kick scythed through the space where she'd been. The wooden beam, five inches square, broke like a twig.

There were two upsides to this, from Kennedy's point of view. The first was that it wasn't her neck that had snapped. The second was that the roof fell in on them both.

It was a wooden shingle roof, and it held together initially, swinging down at an angle like a giant fly swatter. It hit the woman first, just because she was standing. Not hard enough to take her out but hard enough to hurt her and distract her. Kennedy had a second or so to see it coming and rolled away – agony flared in her broken left arm as the weight of her body bore upon it – but the roof was breaking up now anyway, like a calving glacier, raining sheets of wood and tempests of dust on them both.

Kennedy elbowed and kneed her way to the left – both knees, only one elbow, her left arm trailing uselessly – as far as the side wall, then got half-upright and made a run for the open doorway, which she could just about see through the suspension of wood pulp, dust and assorted debris.

She almost made it.

The knife hit her low down in her back, on the right-hand side, and it went in deep. It felt like a punch at first, and then pure, perfect cold spread out from the impact point. It wasn't pain: it was the herald of pain, and it brought the pain in its silent, shrieking wake.

Pure momentum kept Kennedy moving. She took a step, then another, stumbled through the doorway into the clear, baking air, but crashed down on to her knees and pitched forward off the porch into the sand.

She heard the woman at her back and then the woman's shadow fell across her.

'No poison,' the woman said, her voice harsh and ragged. She coughed, once and then a second time. Good! At least the damned dust had got to her. 'No poison on the blade. Nothing to be found here that would link your death to any other death. And it will be slower this way. We'll sit together, you and I. I'll sing to you as you die.'

Kennedy tried to crawl, one-handed again, her heels scuffing sand, her feet and her right hand finding no purchase. She tried again, levered herself forward a little, slumped again on to her stomach, gulping shallow breaths. Her side wasn't cold now: it was pulsing with a sort of raggedly rhythmic fire. She didn't dare to look. She didn't want to know how much blood she was losing.

The woman began to tidy away her things, picking up the gun and the magazine, the keys. The keys were fifteen feet or so away and as she bent to retrieve them, she had her back to Kennedy for a moment.

Kennedy abandoned her pantomime of total immobility and launched herself into a much faster crawl, quickly covering the distance that separated her from Gayle's body. The woman turned, saw her, began to break into a cold smile and then realised, an instant later, what Kennedy was aiming for. As Kennedy reached the sheriff, the woman slammed the magazine home into her semi-automatic, aimed and fired in one quick, liquid movement. Too quick: the cartridge hung up as it entered the chamber and the gun clicked to no effect.

The woman dropped the gun and ran towards Kennedy.

Kennedy pulled the snap-lock strap away from the holster on Gayle's belt and drew the FN Five-Seven from its sheath. She didn't even have time to see whether he was still alive, still breathing. She thumbed the safety as she rolled on to her back. Was that the safety? It was where she would expect the safety to be, to the back of the grip and on the left, but maybe she'd just ejected the magazine.

The gun seemed too light and had a plastic feel, like a child's toy. The sun was in her eyes now, but the woman's body as she ran towards Kennedy occulted the sun. That plus the distance compensated for the clumsy, one-handed grip and the blurring of her vision. She thrust her arm out straight in front of her and fired.

People who like the Five-Seven are impressed by its capacity of twenty rounds. Those who hate it are appalled by the muzzle flash it spits out sometimes, like a searchlight beam full in your eye. Through strobe bursts that seared white on black against the inside of her eyeballs, Kennedy pulled the trigger again and again and again in a steady, mechanical rhythm, moving her wrist through small increments to right and left to give a quartering fire.

Finally, the gun was empty and the trigger wouldn't yield any more. She let it fall from her hands.

When she could move again, the first thing she did – even before ripping up her shirt with her right hand and her teeth to make tourniquets – was check on the woman's condition. As it turned out, only two of those twenty shots had hit, and one was a surface wound to the woman's calf.

The other had gone through the left side of her chest, and from the sounds she was making, it was pretty clear that it had punctured a lung.

There wasn't a whole lot that Kennedy could do for her. In any case, Gayle came first. Stanching the sheriff's shoulder wound with only her right hand in play and the bones of her left arm grating against each other whenever she moved was like juggling chainsaws with barbed wire mittens on. It took a long time and by the time she'd finished, the blood in her own wound was flowing sluggishly, starting to clot. She didn't dare pull the knife out and start it flowing again, and she couldn't dress the wound with the knife in place, so she just left it there.

Gayle's breathing was so shallow his chest didn't even seem to move. Kennedy could only detect it by putting her cheek to his mouth and feeling the slight stir of air.

She called the incident in using the radio in the Biscayne, probably not making much sense by this time because her mind was starting to float away a little. She heard Connie – the bulldog at the despatch desk – shouting, 'Is Web okay? Is Web okay?' again and again. Then, 'Anstruther. Anstruther's coming.' Then silence.

In the silence, the woman's voice: an obscene chorus of choking, bubbling sounds. Kennedy stumbled across to her, found her livid face painted red like a Hollywood Indian, with the burns and with her own blood.

Gayle had left his jacket on the Biscayne's back seat. Kennedy was able to wad it up and get it under the woman's head and shoulders, which she thought might clear her airways marginally. It didn't seem to make much difference, though.

The woman was still trying to talk: in some foreign language at first, full of liquid labials (much less pretty to hear when the liquid was blood) and occasional glottal concatenations, but then in English and finally in some sort of pre-linguistic mewling.

Before she died, her dark gaze fixed on Kennedy's face with a feral intensity, she whispered a secret.

It seemed to give her some comfort that Kennedy heard it and that Kennedy wept.

PART FOUR

GINAT'DANIA

52

The thing about despair was that it didn't move. It stayed right where it was, like a train abandoned on a siding.

Tillman had avoided despair for thirteen years, simply by virtue of having an agenda. There were things that needed to be done, and he did them, going from A to B to C with ruthless focus and inexhaustible patience. It might even look impressive from the outside – some kind of achievement, some great act of will – but in fact it was just his refuge, his salvation.

Now, suddenly, he had nothing to do. Michael Brand was dead and the trail was cold. Maybe Kennedy could keep her Rotgut investigation alive by mining something out of those discs and papers, but it seemed impossible now, that the trail would lead him anywhere close to Rebecca and his children.

They weren't even children any more. Grace, the youngest, would be in high school now, discovering make-up and rock music and boys. Actually, she would have discovered those things already: the thresholds shifted, decade by decade, so that girls and boys started becoming women and men that much earlier.

Rebecca was old. Or dead. The children were adults. Or dead. The bridge was out. The case was closed. The end of the line.

And at the end of the line, in the exact same place where it had always been, was that windowless train. It had never moved, in all those years. It had just stood on the siding, waiting for him to get on board.

In a rented room in a damp-stewed B&B in a grimy west London suburb, Tillman sat on the bed, the gun in his lap. It had six rounds in it, but only out of pure habit. He was thinking of firing just one.

It had taken him a while to get to this point. Kennedy had rung his cellphone often in the first few days; and back then, which already seemed like a long time ago, he'd picked up, spoken to her. She told him about her suspension, and then, almost immediately, about her resignation. It had been the perfect stitch-up, from the way she described it. If she stayed in the force, the investigation into Combes's death would reveal enough procedural irregularities to justify handing a dossier to the CPS and asking them to consider a prosecution against Kennedy for criminal negligence and possibly even manslaughter. If she agreed to stand down and to sign a confidentiality agreement, her DCI had told her, they wouldn't come after her. They wanted her gone more than they wanted her hurting. Far more than either, they wanted an end to media speculation and some room to breathe.

So Kennedy had said yes, and she'd signed, and then she'd worked out her few last days in what she called 'the bear pit', closing off and handing over cases, clearing out her desk, performing the ritual obsequies over the death of her own career. She'd had to fight even for this concession: the higher echelons wanted her gone immediately, and would have preferred her to serve out her notice at home, but Kennedy stubbornly insisted on walking all the stations of her personal cross.

That, at least, was how her fellow detectives viewed her

454

continuing presence in the division. And some of them gave her a grudging respect for that; but at a distance, as befits someone who's seen two partners into the grave inside of a fortnight. Nobody wanted to help Kennedy make the hat-trick.

Kennedy allowed them to think what they wanted, while she used up favours, abused reporting protocols and raided other people's files at a rate that would have been suicidal if there was any chance at all of her still being there when the chickens came back to the homestead. If anybody asked, she was just tidying up. She did exactly enough tidying up to make the cover story stick.

The most important – and the most flagrantly illegal – thing she did was to find out where Professor Emil Gassan was being kept, and to forward him the copy she'd made of the Dovecote disc. She added a brief covering letter in which she asked Gassan, if he succeeded in unravelling any meaning from the files on the disc, to request a meeting with her. The request had to come from him and it had to come while she was still nominally a cop. Also, it had to come through Specialist Ops, the department that had found the safe house for the professor and was looking after him there. Unlike Central, Specialist Ops wouldn't necessarily know about the axe impending over Kennedy and would have no particular reason to check. She could hope, at least, that they would put the request through to her directly, rather than via the DCI.

All of this, Tillman got from Kennedy in the first couple of weeks after the night of the Dovecote fire. He couldn't remember now what he himself had been doing during those two weeks: couldn't remember weather, meals, places, or any significant action that he'd performed. He was running down, using up the last of the stored energy that had got him this far.

After the second week, he stopped picking up the phone.

Kennedy kept calling, kept leaving messages. He put the phone on silent, threw it out of sight, maybe into a drawer. Somebody moved, outside the door of his room, and a little later in the room next door. He heard a scratching at the base of the wall, almost too faint to catch. It couldn't have been Kennedy, checking up on him, because he'd never given her – or anyone – an address. Then again, she was a detective, and she'd turned out to be pretty good at her job, so maybe she'd found a throughline to him. That meant he should move, at once: if Kennedy could do it, his enemies could do it, too.

He stayed put, and waited. He didn't admit to himself what he was waiting for, until it became apparent that nothing was going to happen.

He was waiting for death: for the pale killers to smash the door down and cut his throat, or shoot him, or do whatever they felt like doing to take him off the map. That would have been neat, and logical, and it would have saved him the effort of thought and action. Thought and action seemed to be all but beyond him now. Or maybe he'd struggled so hard, for so long, against the obvious, that his own stubbornness, like a canker grown up inside him, had frozen him in an attitude of denial and defiance. So now, when all he wanted to do was close his eyes for ever, he couldn't bend to take the obvious and necessary steps.

Time kept passing, brought nothing. More and more nothing, piling up around and inside him, as though the room were the interior of his mind and this a continuum that went on endlessly, within him, beyond him, level upon level. The man sitting on the bed: zoom in, find on the curved surface of his retina the man sitting on the bed.

Six bullets in the gun. The empty speed-loader in his left hand. Fastidious – it was hard to source them in a size that

456

matched the Unica's configuration – he reached out to put the loader on the bedside table. He misjudged the distance: it fell on the floor at his feet, rolled under the bed and clunked up against something there.

He raised the gun, stared into its single black eye.

But the speed-loader was out of sight now. It would be missed. Lost. Probably never matched up with the Unica again. Why should that even bother him? Was he looking for an excuse to live?

Slowly, ponderously, as though he had to remember all over again how to move, he rose from the bed and knelt to reach under it. His hand closed, not on the speed-loader, but on the phone. So that was where it had ended up. He stared at the thing, reminded of a past life in which it had had a function.

Amazingly, the phone still had some charge left in it. On the tiny screen inset into its lid, a figure danced: a cartoon unicorn, trailing a cartoon banner that read, 'YOU HAVE NEW MESSAGES'.

The figure blurred suddenly. Tillman was blinded by tears, ambushed by a sudden, peremptory grief that ransacked and dismantled him. Mr Snow was drowned. So was the little girl who had once held fiercely on to Mr Snow as she fell asleep, raising him like a grubby bulwark against the cares and fears of the world. He'd let her down in the end. Everything had let her down, in the end. He knew, then, with a terrible certainty, that she was dead: that they were all dead. Rebecca. Jud. Seth. Grace. If they were anywhere in the world, he would have found them. He had been fleeing for thirteen years from this one, simple admission. Now it swirled through him in filaments like ink through water, and as he stood, as he straightened up, that small movement stirred the blackness, spread it to every corner of his being.

He pressed the gun to his forehead.

But with dark-adjusted eyes, he saw the room differently. He saw, at that pivotal moment, the anomaly, the new thing: it was a note, slipped under his door. He crossed to it and picked it up.

It was not a note. It was a photograph. Rebecca. Rebecca in her late teens or early twenties. He knew her at once, even though he had never known her at that age. Rebecca sitting at a table on a café terrace, people walking by in the background, down a wide street. The light was strange, greyed out as though a storm was coming. Rebecca ducked her head shyly and grinned, hiding from the camera but knowing that the shot would be taken anyway.

The shot. The synchronicity dizzied him.

It was as though he heard the camera shutter, snickering suggestively as it cut a single moment of time out of the endless ebb tide; as it made the transient eternal and immutable.

He wouldn't hear the bullet, though. Not unless consciousness adhered to pulped brain tissue. Eternity was waiting, and it was almost out of patience.

He turned the photo over. On the back, in a small, neat script, five words were written.

She said you wouldn't stop.

There was an interim. What it consisted of, Tillman didn't know. He punched something: the wall, or a door, or a piece of furniture. He punched it repeatedly, until hammering and shouted protests were coming from above, below and across the corridor.

It wasn't enough. The pain in his hands was starting to cut through the fog and the ink and the dullness, but it was too far away. He had to connect himself to the world again, before the world went away.

He punched out the window and selected a piece of broken

glass of a size that he could conveniently hold. He used it to make incisions in his arms and chest, judging the depth of the cuts judiciously so that no nerves or major arteries were severed.

Some progress there.

He heard shouts in the hallway outside his room and someone banged on the door for a long time but finally gave up and went away.

Tillman lifted the glass to the level of his eye, stared at his own blood, dripping from the narrow end. He used that map to find himself: in the red and the mess and the dangerous ruck, not the clarity of the nothing ever.

The photo. And the phone. *You have new messages,* said Mr Snow. *You have new messages from your dead wife.*

He found the phone again and pressed the voicemail key.

Kennedy's voice. 'Leo, there's something I have to tell you ... '

When the messages had all played out, Tillman sat in silence on the bed, staring at the furious red gashes on his arms.

Kennedy's message and Rebecca's smile roiled behind his eyes: not ink now, but oil and water. Oil and water didn't mix.

Kennedy said that Michael Brand was the changing symbol of something that endured. Not a man but a mask that any man could wear and then throw aside.

Through the words on the photo, Michael Brand had said, *Come and find me.*

Tillman got up, on legs that trembled a little, and began, slowly, methodically, to do a number of things that needed to be done.

He found the speed-loader and put it back in the duffle bag where he carried all the weaponry and ammo that weren't on his person at a given time.

He checked that there were indeed six bullets in the Unica. He'd been so far away for so long that he couldn't be entirely sure without verifying by eye. He was thinking that he might live after all, and so it mattered again that the gun was in working order.

He showered – he stank like something dead – and shaved off what might be a month's growth of beard.

He left the rented room for the first time in however long it was, found a cheap restaurant and ate until he was no longer hungry. It didn't take long: the ravenous appetite he felt when he sat down turned out to be one easily sated by a few crumbs. His hand shook a little as he ate. He'd have to rebuild his strength, but that was a practical problem and he knew how to go about it.

Back in the room, he read the Gassan files that Kennedy had sent him, and familiarised himself with what she'd learned about the Judas tribe.

Last of all, he picked up the phone again and placed a call.

'Leo!'

'*Hoe gaat het met jou*, Benny?'

'Could be better, could be worse. It's not like you to keep the same number for so long, Leo. You're still in Britain? How did things go there? Did you manage to get some face time with Mr Brand?'

'Not yet, Benny. But maybe soon. Maybe very soon.'

'Well, that's maybe good news, then.' Vermeulens' tone was cautious.

'In the meantime, I was hoping you could do me a favour.'

'This I had guessed, Leo.'

Tillman found he was ashamed. 'On the far side of this,' he said, 'if it turns out I'm still alive, I'll make it up to you, Benny. I'm close to … something. Something big. But I've got to travel again, and Suzie – Insurance – isn't selling to me right now. I think if you offered to buy on my behalf, she might make an exception.'

'What was it you wanted?'

'Basic package. A passport, to my spec. Credit card in the same name with a couple of thousand ready to draw. Legend and supporting papers good enough to stand up to more than one glance.'

'That's not a small favour, Leo.'

'I'm good for the money. I can pay upfront by a wire transfer from the Dominican account.'

'I don't think about the money. I think about my job.'

'Nobody ever gets to know.'

'From you, perhaps, nobody ever gets to know. You can't make the same guarantees for anybody else.' A silence fell between them. Tillman didn't push: he knew there was nothing he could say that would influence Vermeulens' decision, and he didn't want to twist the man's arm any further than he already had just by asking.

'Something big,' Vermeulens said at last. 'Big enough that this might be over finally, for you? Or only big in being a station on the way to something bigger?'

Tillman thought about the gun, and the first bullet in the gun. 'It will be over,' he said. 'One way or another, this will finish it.'

'Then I'll do what I can. Stay by the phone, Leo.'

'Thanks, Benny.'

'Remember what you owe me is nothing. But this ... perhaps this is the *last* nothing.'

53

In Ginat'Dania, there were no seasons. Every day was like every other day, untouched by tempest, changeless as God's countenance: a piece of eternity, fallen into the fallen world but still perfect, still miraculous.

It had been five years since Kuutma had last been home. He stood out now, like a stranger, and as he walked up the grand alley to the Em Hadderek, all eyes flicked round to stare at him. At his aberrantly dark skin. At his gait, his movements, the expressions that crossed his face. All were wrong in gross or subtle ways, and since he was clearly not a woman, he could not be of the Kelim: the wrongness marked him out as one thing, and one thing only. Everyone he passed bowed to him, or saluted him, or murmured the '*Ha ana mashadr*' – 'We sent you out' – as he passed, touching his shoulders lightly with the fingers of their right hands. Kuutma took this as his due and kept on walking.

But just as they saw his strangeness, he saw theirs: he felt the raw tension in the air, a mood of expectation, half-fearful and half-enthralled. Kuutma didn't like it. It betokened change, here in this place that was immune to change. It troubled him and it reproached him.

From the Em Hadderek he turned left, past the farm sheds

and the animal pens, the shops of Talitha, then the place of gathering. Just beyond was the Sima, where the elders met. Kuutma walked directly to its door, where four men of huge girth and slab-solid muscle stood. He saluted them with the ritual words. '*Ashna reb nim t'khupand am at pent ahwar*': I have returned to the house from which I set forth.

They gave the proper answer, speaking all in unison, with solemn formality. '*Besiyata Dishmaya*': with the help of Heaven.

'I need to speak with them,' Kuutma said, lapsing into English, the linguistic switch a finessing move, in a sense, reminding the guardians of where he had come from and what he'd done. It made it very difficult for them to say no. Still, they couldn't have him intrude on the elders without being announced first, and so one went into the Sima while the others stood to attention before Kuutma, in a heavy silence, until their comrade returned and indicated to him that he should go inside.

None of the guards came with him, but two more were standing just inside as he entered, and they fell into step to either side of him. Kuutma went to the Kad Sima, the debating chamber. The vast space was empty apart from the three elders sitting on the dais at its centre.

Kuutma's honour guard waited at the threshold of the room: they had not been summoned. Kuutma himself genuflected, making the sign of the noose, then walked down the steps to the centre of the room.

The three stern men, two ancient and one still young, watched him come. They did not smile to see him, but they accepted his obeisance with curt answering nods. By tradition, they were known as the Ruakh, the Sheh and the Yedimah: in the language that preceded even the true tongue, these names signified the Oak, the Ash and the Seed of That Which is to Be.

Only the last role, that of the Yedimah, could be filled by a man younger than sixty years of age.

The Ruakh spoke first, as tradition required. 'Kuutma,' he said, his voice high and a little querulous with extreme age. 'You've struggled against tremendous difficulties. Truly, tremendous difficulties.' That seemed to be the limit of what he wanted to say. He glanced left and right at his two yokemates, inviting either of them to take up the reins.

'Unparalleled difficulties,' the Sheh agreed, dry and caustic. 'Never in our history have two threats of such magnitude come side by side. Perhaps, Kuutma, that is why you have failed to acquit yourself with your usual thoroughness and attention to detail. Things have been done badly. Things have been done late. Some things have not been done at all, and still need to be looked to.'

Kuutma had no alternative but to bow before the three and accept the censure. Feeling a tremor in some part of himself that could not physically shake – his soul, perhaps – Kuutma knelt.

'Revered ones,' he said, his eyes on the ground, 'I carried out my duties as well as I was able. If that was not enough, your servant humbly begs pardon.'

'The scholars in England,' the Sheh allowed, 'were dealt with expeditiously. And yet, as it transpires, you left loose ends even there. The man, Tillman, you neglected until he became a canker. The American was killed in a way that guaranteed scrutiny. An entire plane brought down, and hundreds killed! Most unforgivably, the woman – the police sergeant, from London – has now been allowed to put these things together. When she went to the United States, it should have been obvious to you at once that her death outweighed all other tasks then depending upon you. You should have killed her yourself, not trusted the task to the youngest and least experienced of your Elohim.'

Still kneeling, Kuutma allowed himself to look up into the face of his accuser.

'I recommended thirteen years ago that Tillman be killed,' he pointed out. 'I was overruled, Elders, because your predecessors did not see him as a threat. His survival is the random factor that has bedevilled so many of our recent actions. The police-woman, for example, would have died had she not had Tillman with her. And the information Tillman brought allowed her to make the link to the operation in America.

'As for the downing of Flight 124, I gave no such order. The agent I sent to deal with the American was told to kill him before he boarded the plane. He chose instead to destroy the plane and himself with it. It was madness.'

The Yedimah spoke for the first time. 'Perhaps your agent was inadequately briefed,' he said, mildly – but underneath the reasonable tone Kuutma discerned an edge.

'Nehor,' Kuutma said. 'Nehor Bar-Talmai. You will remem-ber, Elders, that I asked you to recall him to Ginat'Dania five months ago. I said then that he was coping badly with being in the world, and that I felt his suitability as a Messenger needed to be re-examined.'

'We remember,' said the Yedimah. 'We decided that with proper shepherding – proper guidance – he could grow into the role we had ordained for him. Clearly, at the end, he lacked that guidance. Had you given him more explicit and more practical instructions as to how to deal with the American clerk, he would not have improvised so desperately and made so disas-trous a misjudgement. In the end, we believe, it must all come back to Kuutma – the Brand. That, after all, is the significance of the name. Kuutma's will is a fire, and the marks he leaves on the minds of others are written there as with hot steel.'

Kuutma knew as well as did the Yedimah that this was false

etymology. He knew, too, that he could not win this argument: he could not even begin it. 'Your servant begs pardon,' he said again.

The Sheh waved his hand in a vague and unconvincing benediction. 'It is granted,' he said. 'Stand, Kuutma. We ask no penitence of you.'

The Yedimah raised an eyebrow at this, as though the Sheh had overstepped the bounds of his authority. 'We have, however,' he murmured, 'determined that this will be the last time you take the field as Kuutma. From now on, your skills will be deployed closer to home.'

Kuutma let no emotion show on his face: he did not even stiffen. But something at once hot like a coal and sharp like a drawn wire ran through his brain. He felt as if he were becoming weightless. 'Here in Ginat'Dania?' he asked, so there could be no mistake.

'In Ginat'Dania,' said the Sheh. 'But not here. We prepare for *mapkanah*.'

It was true, then. Kuutma had known it as soon as he stepped through the gate and felt that tension in the air: the people were preparing to be gone from this place that was their home, and find a new home in a far distant place. This had not been done for two centuries, and then, as now, it was because the location of Ginat'Dania had been compromised. Underneath the pain, underneath the shame that was being heaped on him, Kuutma felt the stirring of a strange joy: the joy of things coming together as they finally must.

'It is not for me to say,' he murmured, his eyes cast down again.

The Yedimah breathed through his nose, almost a sniff of indignation. 'No,' he agreed. 'It is not. Kuutma, there are those alive who may now know who we are and where we are. Their deaths will be procured, in due course, but as of now their deaths are not even a priority. We have gone beyond such concerns. First, before all else, we must protect the people.'

Kuutma bared his teeth in a snarl, but kept his head bowed so that nobody would see it. 'They have always been my care, Yedimah.'

'We know it. And we know you must feel this as a reproach. Still, it must be done, and we must see it done. We look to your support in this, as in everything.'

Kuutma stood. Strictly speaking, he ought to have waited for permission to rise, but this seemed to be a time when protocol bled away into the spaces between thoughts and words, words and deeds. He stared at the Yedimah for a long time in silence, and the Yedimah waited for him to speak. All of them, the Oak and the Ash and the Seed, waited on the words of the Brand.

'With *mapkanah* comes *maasat*, the paying of the balance,' Kuutma said, stating the obvious.

The Ruakh nodded, once.

'When?' Kuutma demanded.

'Two days from now,' the Ruakh said.

'So soon?'

'So late,' said the Yedimah, grimly.

Kuutma made the sign of the noose, yielding the point. 'I want to stay,' he said. 'To efface my failure, let me be the one to hold the scales and make sure the balance is paid. Grant me this, Elders, and I will give up my place as Kuutma with a light heart.'

He was holding the Yedimah's gaze. So many things were hiding in the thicket of that sentence, unspoken, so many shy, skittish meanings. What would it be like if I failed to surrender my place? Or if I did it resentfully, unreconciled? He spoke no word of threat, but his eyes prophesied.

467

'The systems are automatic,' the Yedimah said. 'It needs no one to be here.'

'Can a machine deal justly with a man?' Kuutma intoned, with austere savagery. 'Can a switch or a lever answer, before God, and say, "This is the balance, this thing is rightly done"? Elders, when a thing becomes possible, it does not therefore become inevitable. Grant me this thing. Let me stay.'

He waited them out.

One by one, they bowed, the Yedimah last of all.

'You will hold the scales, Kuutma. You will pay the balance.'

He thanked them gravely. They accepted graciously.

And then he went from that place, with a terrible hurt and a terrible hope warring in his breast. He was still Kuutma: until Ginat'Dania ended, and was reborn, he held his name in his hands.

His name and one thing more.

54

It took Tillman a little longer to travel to Arizona than it would have taken anyone else. There were things that needed to be done before he could embark on that journey, and none could be skimped or compressed.

First, he had to collect the documents that Benny Vermeulens had bought on his behalf. Insurance had asked for an insane fee – twenty times higher than she would normally have taken for a package like this – and she'd demanded payment up front. That wasn't an issue: Tillman had emptied his various accounts and sent the money. But the arrangements for the hand-over were more problematic.

Benny understood that Tillman wouldn't provide an address or even turn up at a post office box to take receipt of the passport, the credit card and their attendant proofs. He knew, too, that Tillman would be concerned about how far he could trust his weight to the documents, given Insurance's withdrawal of goodwill.

Benny solved these problems by travelling to London himself on the false passport. He and Tillman were very similar in build, so all that was needed to produce a reasonable resemblance was hair dye and coloured contact lenses. He arranged to meet Tillman at Heathrow, in the Café Rouge in the departure area of Terminal 5. Tillman arrived first, ordered two double espressos and sat with his hands folded in his lap and his gaze fixed on his hands, pondering imponderable things. When the chair opposite him creaked, he looked up.

Benny slid a bulky envelope across the table. He was dressed in a suit of obviously expensive cut. Somehow it made him look less respectable and more dangerous than he'd ever looked in combat fatigues. Or maybe it was his physical impersonation of Tillman that was unsettling. 'Here, Leo,' he said. 'Happy Christmas.'

Leo took the package without examining its contents. Vermeulens had earned that trust a hundred times over. 'It's July,' he pointed out.

Benny shook his head. His jowled face was solemn. 'December,' he said. 'Late December. The turning of the year, when nobody's really sure whether or not the sun will come back.'

Tillman smiled awkwardly. 'I didn't know you were a poet, Benny.'

'I'm the least poetic man alive, Leo. I'm telling you what you already know. You're going off to do battle against the forces of darkness and you don't think you'll be coming back. That's the only reason you're cutting yourself to the bone like this.'

'The money? I can always get more money.'

'I meant the tone of your voice when you called me. The look I see in your eye, now that I'm here. Leo, I was on the roster at Xe longer than you were. I've seen a lot of men kill themselves in a firefight because they thought it was their time to die. They behave in ways that are . . .' he gestured '. . . unsustainable. They forget to watch their backs or secure an exit. They lower their guard because they think their guard is irrelevant.'

'I've seen that, too,' Tillman agreed. 'But that's not me,

470

Benny. I'll get in, I'll do the job and then I'll get out. Like always.'

Benny laughed a funereal laugh. 'And what's the job?'

Tillman didn't answer.

'Not the same,' Benny said. 'Not the same as what it was. Don't bother to lie to me, Leo. This is a slash-and-burn mission, and the last thing you burn will be yourself. I hope it's worth it.'

Leo turned the envelope in his hands, feeling its weight and solidity.

'I think so,' he said at last. 'I think it will be.'

Then there was the provisioning, the sourcing of equipment – not in London but in Los Angeles. He didn't trust Insurance for this. He had his own contacts in America, and although it had been years since he spoke to them, they were still there when he called. Guns? Guns of any size and specification could be obtained. Explosives? Likewise. Electronic eavesdropping items, even of professional standard, were universally available these days, as were crowd control devices like pepper sprays and tear gas. Tillman put together a long list, to be paid for C.O.D.

After that came the journey. Normally, he avoided planes because they were – by definition – enclosed spaces with no exits. Flying put you in the hands of people who might wish you harm. This time he didn't spare a thought for those concerns. They belonged to a life in which there was a distinction to be made between 'safe' and 'perilous'.

Normally, too, Tillman bore the tedium of long journeys well: he sat still, his mind working through logistical puzzles that needed to be solved. This time his thoughts were locked on a single idea: revenge. He spent the flight in contemplation of that monolithic ambition, like a supplicant kneeling at an altar no one else could see.

He'd paid for reconnaissance, as well as guns and ammunition, so he knew by this time that Arizona state police were holding Heather Kennedy – ex-sergeant – under guard at the Kingman-Butler Hospital in Kingman, Arizona, charged with first-degree murder, impersonating a police officer, false representation and a raft of lesser offences. He'd established the conditions in which she was being held, as well as her injuries and the likelihood that she'd be conscious at any given time of the day or night.

Tillman drove from Los Angeles, in a car hired under the temporary name he'd bought from Insurance. It took the best part of a day, with stops along the way, but it had the advantage of making his precise location difficult to determine, even if Insurance had sold the name and credit card details on to third parties.

From Bullhead City, he called the hospital and demanded to speak to Heather Kennedy. It was a calculated risk. He had to wait while the nurse put him on hold – to check with the police guard, he guessed – then she came back on and asked what this was concerning.

'A death in the family,' Tillman said. 'Her mother. God forbid you keep this from her, ma'am. She needs to know, and it's her right to know.'

Another wait. Then a gruff state trooper came on the line and asked a few more questions. Mechanically, his thoughts elsewhere, Tillman invented a lingering illness for Kennedy's mother that had gone through a great many permutations but left her alive long enough to gasp out one final message for her only daughter.

'Only daughter?' the cop grunted. 'Our information is she has a sister. What's that about?'

'Half-sister,' said Tillman. 'Same father, different mothers.'

'And you are?'

'Half-brother. Same mother, different fathers. Listen, does any part of your state or federal law allow you to hold Heather incommunicado? Because if it doesn't, you should stop asking these stupid questions and just put her on the phone. I'm recording every word of this, officer ... what was your name again?'

It turned out his name was 'Wait a second.' Tillman waited, and the next voice on the line was Kennedy's. She sounded groggy and very tired but not drugged into stupor.

'Who is this?' she asked. There was a time-delayed echo on her voice: maybe just a bad line, or maybe a bad wire-tap, set up very quickly with no real quality control.

'It's Leo.'

A long silence. 'Tillman.' More silence. 'Thank God.'

'So. Murder? Conspiracy to murder? It's like I don't know you any more, girl.'

'You remember Dovecote Farm?'

'Sure.'

'You remember hearing a woman screaming?'

'Seems like I do.'

'She did the murdering, and the conspiring, too. The local sheriff will vouch for me, but he's in deep sedation right now. Bullet wound to the upper torso. He might not pull through. If he doesn't, there goes my alibi. There was a woman who could have spoken up for me, but she's dead, too.'

'Sounds like you're screwed.'

'Doesn't it.'

'We miss you, Heather. All of us.'

'All of you?' She sounded wary. He wondered if she knew that the line was bugged. He'd have to assume that she did. There was no time to finesse this.

'Me. Freddie. Jake. Little Wendy, with the squint eye. You're in our thoughts all the time.'

'I ... miss you, too.'

'You're just being kind,' Tillman said. 'It's no secret to anyone that you and I haven't been close in recent times. I want you to know that's going to change.'

'Well, you always say that.'

'I mean it, Heather. I'm going to see you again soon. I promise.'

'Okay. Whatever.'

'Are you ready, do you think? To see me again?'

'Any time, Tillman. Name the day. Name the hour. Or just surprise me.'

'I guess I'll surprise you. You, um, you get many visitors there, Heather?'

'Not that many, no. Just two big burly cops at the door to keep me company, and two more on the main corridor where it branches after the elevators.'

'They don't want you to go wandering off and get lost.'

'Evidently. But in case I do, there's always the GPS tag locked to my ankle.'

'I see. Well, at least you're among fellow cops. You guys can all sit around and talk shop.'

'My shop's a corner store in Queen's Park. Theirs is a strip mall in Monument Valley. You'd be amazed how little ...'

Her voice faded out and the cop came on again. 'I'm limiting you to five minutes,' he told Tillman. 'You can call again tomorrow, if you want.'

'I didn't even tell her about mum yet,' said Tillman. 'I was still working my way around to it. At least let me—'

'Tomorrow.' The line went dead.

Tillman put the phone away and drove on, his mind starting

to move again at last. It was a relief to have something practical to think about. And it would be, he knew, an even bigger relief to have something he could set his weight against and push.

55

The girl named Tabe lived alone, although she was too young, strictly speaking, to be allowed to do so. Before that, she had lived in orphans' house with the helpers. She had always been an obedient and courteous child, but as the helpers said, *beiena ke ha einanu*, her soul moved on silence. She seemed to live alone in a small, self-bounded world, barely aware of the people who lived and had their being around her.

This is not to say that she was selfish. Tabe was a warm-hearted girl, and kind, and even considerate, on the occasions when she surfaced from her own thoughts long enough to inter-act with others. But she was an artist: colours and tones and textures formed the dimensions of her world. Mostly she painted still lives. In the past she had painted people, too, but she had scandalised the helpers by asking if she could sketch a boy, Aram, with his robes removed. That had been the end of Tabe's career as a painter of the human figure.

Now she lived alone in a room on the fourth level of Dar Kuomet. But her paintings could be seen as far afield as Tethem towards the daybreak and Va Ineinu towards the night. She seemed happy alone. The boy, Aram, was betrothed now and Tabe had painted their married rooms with images of happy, dancing children. She seemed to bear no grudge against the lad, but then her interest in him had been primarily an aesthetic one.

In her room in Dar Kuomet, Kuutma found her. She was drawing with a stick of black oil pastel on a bedsheet nailed to the wall (on the other walls, painted directly on to the plaster, were murals of strawberries and redcurrants in earthen bowls). It took her some while to realise that she wasn't alone. When she finally registered Kuutma's presence, she bowed her head to him and whispered, '*Ha ana mashadr*', blushing a red more hectic than the fruit painted on her walls.

Kuutma signed to Tabe to sit. 'You knew me for one of the Elohim,' he said to her. 'Was that by my complexion?'

Tabe rubbed the tips of her fingers together nervously: they were black and greasy from the pastel. But she met Kuutma's gaze directly. 'Not only that,' she said. 'I remembered your face. You came to visit us once at the orphans' house and I asked one of the helpers who you were. She said you were Kuutma. The Brand.'

Kuutma nodded. 'And so I am. Until *mapkanah*, at least.' At that word, her eyes lit up, which somewhat surprised him. But to the young, anything new seems exciting just by being new. And then again, she was an artist: wherever Ginat'Dania went next, the light would be different and there would be new scenes to paint. For Tabe, *mapkanah* might seem like a rebirth.

'When I came to the orphans' house,' Kuutma said, 'it was to see you – you and your two brothers. I had an interest in verifying for myself that you were happy there. I knew your mother, you see.'

The girl's face clouded for an instant. 'My mother ...' she said, tentatively, and left the sentence unfinished. Kuutma sensed something of bitterness in her tone, and he frowned.

'You know she was sent forth, like me,' he said.

Tabe's stare was hard: it gave no ground, no quarter. 'Not like you.'

'The work of the Kelim is every bit as important as the work we Elohim do,' said Kuutma. 'More so, even. We both work for the survival of the people: but our work is glorious, theirs is bitter and degrading. We're honoured and they're reviled.'

Tabe shrugged, but made no other answer.

'I would have you think well of her,' Kuutma said, stiffly. 'Your mother. I'd have you be generous to her, in your memory. Think what her sacrifice meant for you, as well as for us.'

Tabe looked down at her blackened fingers now. He could see that she was longing for him to be gone, so that she could get back to her work.

'I know your father, too,' he said.

Her gaze snapped up again, and her eyes as she stared into his were like two dark wounds in the unblemished whiteness of her face. But to the Elohim, all things look like wounds. Kuutma had made love only a handful of times in his life, plagued each time by the terrible thought that a woman's sex is like the site of an old injury, partly healed.

He waited, allowing the girl the space in which to speak. She only watched him.

'You don't ask me what he's like – your father,' he said at last.

'No.' Tabe was categorical. 'How would it help me to know?'

'He's ... a brave man, by his own lights. A soldier, like me. But he's a soldier who fights against us. Our enemy.'

Tabe considered this. 'Then will you have to kill him?' she asked.

Kuutma smiled reluctantly. 'That's why I came to see you today,' he admitted – although he'd had no intention, when he came, of telling her all this. 'I think killing your father may be the last thing I do, as Kuutma. I have ...' He hesitated, picked

478

his words with care. 'I can see a pathway that leads us to meet. And when that happens, I'll certainly have to kill him. Would I have your blessing, if I did that?'

Tabe's dark gaze was unwavering. 'Oh yes,' she said. 'Of course. *Ha ana mashadr*, Kuutma. Everything you do, you do in our name. Of course you have my blessing. He's only the father of my flesh, not of my spirit. But if he's as brave as you say, I hope he doesn't hurt you. I hope he dies quickly, without striking a single blow against you.'

Kuutma saw the radiant innocence and earnestness in her face. He felt humbled by her simplicity – he who, out in the wider world, had become as complex and subtle as a snake. But snakes were holy, too, of course: snakes were holiest of all.

He knelt before her. '*Touveyhoun*, daughter,' he murmured, his voice thick with emotion he could not bear to examine.

'*Touveyhoun, Tannanu*,' she said, but she was unnerved by the wrongness of his kneeling to her. He realised that he had disturbed her calm and probably ruined the painting that she was making. With a muttered apology, he left her.

Tabe paced the floor a while after he left, clasping herself hard and leaving black fingerprints on the flesh of her own forearms. But she had become used to turning strong emotion into some less transient form. Soon enough, she took up the pastel and resumed her effort to capture the swollen, pregnant belly of a storm cloud.

56

Tillman took his time. He'd come up with a reasonable plan, but it involved a great many moving parts, and he had to start from the assumption that he was in enemy territory. Getting Kennedy out of the hospital wouldn't be hard in itself, but the Arizona police would mobilise quickly once she went off the grid. At that point, he had to disappear her quickly and unanswerably. Otherwise the operation would pretty much be doomed.

He parked down the block from the hospital and walked up to its grounds, where he reconnoitred thoroughly, moving at a brisk pace so that he wouldn't be challenged. He had floor plans to work from, but floor plans were useless unless he could link them to reality: he started that process by visualising the building as a three-dimensional space, with physical entrances and exits mapped on to the schematic diagrams he had in his head.

The good news was the flat roof, three storeys below the window of Kennedy's room; or at least, below the space that corresponded with Ward 20 on the plans. The bad news ... well, the bad news was manifold. He'd timed the distance from the nearest police station: at the speed of a flat-out chase it was three minutes, no more. The flat roof was on the far side of the building from the car park, and he'd found no closer approach.

Bullhead City and Seligman both had police heliports, and there were only two main roads out of town – State Highway 40 and Interstate 93. Closing both of those roads would be the work of a minute once the alarm went up.

He thought about how to adapt the plan, given the lie of the land. He couldn't come up with a single elegant or fool-proof solution. But one led the others by virtue of being intensely confusing and chaotic. If you haven't got any good cards, play a wild card.

Tillman walked back to the car and drove on up to the hospital, parking not too close to the police black-and-white he'd already located in the car park out front and not too far from the street: a fine balance, on which a lot was going to depend.

He'd already chosen and packed his kit, in a plastic bag-for-life with the name and logo of a local florist blazoned on it and the leaves of a potted plant sticking out the top. He went in through the front doors, walked right by the reception desk and kept on going like a man who already knows his destination.

In the gents' toilets on the first floor of the main building, Tillman unpacked the bag and transformed himself into a hospital orderly by means of a long white coat and an official-looking ID badge. The badge was a fake, and not even a very good one, but it would fool someone who didn't spend all day every day looking at the real thing: a cop on temporary guard duty, for example.

In a wide hallway next to the service elevator, he obtained – as he'd hoped – an empty gurney. He'd been prepared to wander the wards a little until he found one, but the less time he spent walking around in the whites, the less chance he had of being challenged.

Tillman rode the elevator to the fourth floor and stepped out, wheeling the gurney in front of him. The two cops who

Kennedy had warned him about – the first two – were waiting where the corridor forked. They looked tough and humourless and alert. Tillman walked on up to them and nodded to indicate that he intended to pass. 'Transfer from Ward 22,' he said.

The nearest of the two cops checked Tillman's badge, which Tillman helpfully held out with the thumb of his left hand. His right hand rested on a sap that he was holding below the push-bar of the gurney, but he was hoping not to have to use it: improvisation at this early stage would be a bad omen for the whole damned enterprise.

The cop waved him through. Tillman rolled the gurney on down the branch corridor that led to Kennedy's ward among several others.

At Ward 22, he abandoned the gurney and the whites. The long coat would just encumber him and from here he'd have to move fast. From the storage bin underneath the gurney, he retrieved his bag, tossing the pot plant.

Kennedy's ward, number 20, was around a right-angled bend about ten yards further on. Tillman took the corner at the briskest of brisk walks and found himself heading directly for two more cops who looked just as solid and serious as the first two.

He dropped the bag and raised his hands to shooting position. In each hand he held a bottle of OC spray, and his index fingers were already clamped down on the nozzles. This wasn't pepper spray, as such: it was a Russian-made product, a derivative of pelargonic acid, the nastiest thing of its type Tillman had ever encountered, weighing in at four and a half million Scoville units. The two men went down in agony, clawing at their faces. Tillman slipped on a surgical mask and carefully and unhurriedly knocked them out with desflurane soaked into a handkerchief. He also anointed their faces with a milk and detergent mix that would mitigate the worst of the spray's effects. He had no intention of killing law officers on this jamboree, even unintentionally.

He left the men where they lay and walked through double swing doors into the ward. It had been sub-divided into several bays, but he got lucky: Kennedy's bed was in the second of these areas. Tillman saw her just as a nurse came out from another bay further down and registered his presence. A second later she registered the Unica in his hand: not aimed at her exactly, but impossible to ignore.

'Go back inside,' Tillman told her. 'Don't say anything or do anything. Just wait.'

With a nearly voiceless squeak of panic, the nurse backed away out of sight. Tillman turned his attention back to Kennedy.

'Tillman. Good to . . . see you,' she croaked. She looked in a bad way, her left arm in a cast and taped to her side, which was also swathed in thick bandages. She was herself, though, and better, she was mobile. She levered herself up out of the bed with a grunt of pain and effort and came to meet him. Tillman was already hauling the bolt cutters out of the bag.

'GPS tag,' he said tersely. 'Which leg?'

Kennedy showed him and he knelt to cut the strap. It was tight enough that he could only get the blade of the cutters halfway under, but it snapped all the way across when he applied pressure.

'Open the window,' he told Kennedy. He threw aside the bolt cutters and reached into the bag again for the rappel rope, which he uncoiled with a flick of the wrist.

Alarm crossed Kennedy's face when she saw the rope. 'Tillman,' she said, tightly, 'there's no way I'm swinging out of the goddamned window. Look at me. I've only got one functional arm!'

'You won't have to take your own weight,' he said. 'I'll carry you.' He was unfolding the grapnel, slipping the rope through its eyelet, checking the friction hitch on his belt.

Kennedy didn't waste any more time arguing. She unlocked the window and opened it. A security lock stopped it from moving more than a few inches. Kennedy held out her hand for Tillman's gun, which he handed over with some reluctance. She smashed the lock off the frame using the butt of the Unica, three measured blows, and gave the gun back to him. By this time, Tillman had the rope doubled through the friction hitch and the grapnel firmly wedged into the steel frame of Kennedy's bed. He pushed the bed up against the window so it wouldn't slide in that direction when they put their weight on the rope.

'Ready?' he asked her.

She nodded.

Tillman helped her over the sill, then climbed out after her, his left arm around her waist, his right arm on the control lever of the friction hitch. It took a few seconds to find a grip that was firm enough, yet didn't press against her injured arm. He leaned backwards to test the weight and Kennedy swore, off balance above a gulf of air and not liking it a bit.

They heard an alarm begin to sound back inside the room: either the nurse had raised a shout or someone had found the two downed cops. From now on, it was all on the clock, and Tillman had to measure off every second against the perfect, Platonic version of the plan in his mind.

He kicked off from the window ledge and abseiled down the hospital wall in a series of clumsy, gingerly hop-and-jumps. If it had been a rock face, or the wood of a climbing tower, he'd have made the three storeys in three quick see-saw leaps, but this wall was mostly glass. If they went through, it would be a toss-up whether or not they bled out before hospital security or the troopers from the corridor found them and slammed the cuffs on them.

As it was, by the time they landed on the felt-and-gravel flat roof below, heads were already beginning to peer out of the windows above. One of the heads was accompanied by an arm, at the end of which was a gun.

'Stay where you are!' a voice yelled. 'Kneel down and place your hands on your heads!'

Tillman took careful aim with the Unica and squeezed off a shot. The cop drew his head hastily back and didn't return fire. Not yet anyway.

Tillman scooped Kennedy up in his arms and sprinted along the roof to the end, where he launched himself into space. Kennedy, who had managed not to make a sound during the hair-raising descent from the fourth floor, gave an involuntary yell now: but Tillman's feet landed with a resounding metallic clang on the lid of the dumpster he'd pushed in against the wall at that exact point, and from there they made it to the ground in three steps – from dumpster to regular rubbish bin to plastic drum full of contaminated sharps, and so to asphalt.

'Can you run?' Tillman asked Kennedy.

'I can run.'

'Then let's run.'

57

The first shots sounded as they sprinted around the side of the building, through the ambulance bay to the main parking area. Slowing a little, Tillman led the way to the third aisle, where a bright red Noble M15 awaited them. Kennedy stared at the indecently conspicuous car in horror: its gaping side-vents reminded her of a shark's gills.

'Jesus,' she said. 'Tillman, they'll pick us up before we've gone a bloody mile.'

'Get inside,' he told her, tersely.

She shot a glance towards the hospital's front doors. No pursuit visible as yet. Maybe if they got out of the car park on to the street before the cops emerged, they'd have a fighting chance.

She hauled open the passenger door, shinnied inside and then struggled to belt herself in one-handed. She looked towards the driver's side, filled with effervescent impatience.

It was fully twenty seconds before the other door opened and Tillman climbed in, moving without undue haste. 'Come *on*,' Kennedy yelled. 'Get a move on.'

Tillman turned the key and revved up the engine, but stayed where he was.

'Tillman!' Kennedy bellowed. 'For Christ's sake!'

'Wait for it,' he murmured, looking over his shoulder towards the doors of the hospital, where now two figures in dark tan uniforms came running out into the sunlight. Tillman let them get halfway to their car before he reversed out directly into their path, forcing them to leap aside to right and left. He peeled rubber as they picked themselves up, and was gone around the end of the line of cars as they drew and aimed. The shots they got off were more to make a point than anything else.

'They *saw* us,' Kennedy wailed. 'You let them see us.'

'They didn't hit us, though,' Tillman said. 'That puts us well ahead of the game. Open the glove compartment.'

Kennedy did. Inside, she saw a squat block of black plastic with green and amber LED lights on its fascia and the words UNIDEN BEARCAT BC355C in the lower right-hand corner. A tangle of wires at the back suggested that it had been hooked up to the car's battery in some ad hoc way. Kennedy knew a radio scanner when she saw one, and although this model was new to her, she had a reasonably good idea what to do with it. She looked for the tuner and found it already set to the VHF hi-band, around about 155MHz. A little tweaking on the up and down keys quickly brought in the local police wavelength – where, unsurprisingly, the gossip was all about them.

'—in pursuit, and we've got visual,' a man's voice was saying. 'They're on Oak, north of 93, and they're going east. Repeat, they're eastbound on Oak.'

'Roger that, four-seven,' a woman's voice took up. 'We've got cars incoming on Maple and Topeka, and another unit coming down Andy Devine. They've got to be heading for I-93. We'll set up a roadblock at Powderhouse Canyon, over.'

'Copy.' It was the male voice again – probably the driver of the black-and-white stuck dead centre in their rear-view mirror, a fair way back but holding on for grim life.

Tillman took a right, on two wheels, and shot down a narrower road at precarious speed. It was a steep slope and Kennedy thought for a second that the black-and-white would overshoot, or at least lose ground, but it made the turn just as adroitly as Tillman had.

'They took a right,' said the man's voice. 'We're on 4th.'

'Copy,' the woman said. 'Okay, I can see exactly where you are. They'll probably turn left on to—'

They shot across a major intersection, almost clipping the back bumper of a leaf-green soft-top that was poodling across their path. The doppler wail of a car horn followed them south.

'Okay, scratch that,' the woman muttered. 'Guess they're not headed for I-93 after all. Car five-oh, you've overshot. They just . . . they crossed Topeka and they're still going south.' How the hell did she know that? 'They're not heading out of town at all. They're gonna double back.'

Another man, his voice incongruously slow and laconic. 'Might wanna think about another roadblock down on the 40, then – and one on 66. Ain't nowhere else they can go, unless they're fixing to grab some dinner at Mr D'z before they light out of here.'

'Covered,' the woman said, and then, 'We've got a chopper in the air, coming out of Bullhead. ETA six minutes.'

Kennedy swore bitterly and obscenely. The original black-and-white was still hanging on to line of sight with them, the woman at despatch somehow keeping track of them. And now they'd have to contend with an eye-in-the-sky on top of everything else.

'We should give it up,' she muttered. 'If we hit one of these roadblocks, they'll fire on us, sure as hell. People will die, Tillman – probably starting with us.'

'Nobody's going to die,' Tillman said, with such complete assurance that Kennedy stared at him in wonder and fell silent for a moment.

The silence was broken by the chatter from the scanner. 'Car five-oh, where are you now?'

'Faked south and we're turning on to Hoover, right now, at 2nd. Where are they?'

'They're still north of you. That's great. You can get to 4th ahead of them and cut them off. Repeat, they're south on 4th, and you got the drop on them.'

Tillman slammed the accelerator to the floor: the Noble's three-litre engine made an oddly muted noise, like a giant trying to utter a roar of menace without waking up a small child. The car shot away like a speedboat, seeming to leave the road surface altogether.

They crossed the next intersection at something close to the speed of sound. A second police car had been heading towards them from the west at a fair lick, but they shot by in front of its nose, forcing the driver to brake to avoid hitting their original tailing car full-on.

'They got past us!' car five-oh's driver bellowed.

'Damn! Sorry, five-oh, I guess I misread the distance. Four-seven, you still on them?'

'Just. They're a ways ahead of me now.'

'Five-oh, you turn around and stake out on Old Trails Road. They're driving into a goddamn cul de sac and that's the only way out, far as I read it. Four-seven, keep them in sight but don't engage until you've got some back-up. The man is armed.'

'I know he's armed, Caroline. He damn well shot at me back at the hospital.'

'There's no need for language, Leroy.'

'There is if you want to say something to someone. Listen, I'm losing him. That boat has got a turn of speed on her. How long till the chopper gets here?'

'Two minutes. They're over the 68 right now.'

Tillman looked in the rear-view, where the police car was now almost too far away to see. He slowed a little, took a sharp left, then a right on to a road that ran parallel with the one they'd been on. Two blocks south Kennedy saw a bridge where this road crossed a smaller road. Another glance in the rear-view, then Tillman pulled off the road and drove straight down the bank. For a few seconds they were skidding on sandy soil and weeds and scrub. Kennedy thought they'd slew sideways and roll end over end, but Tillman somehow kept the car under control and wrestled its speed down. At the bottom of the bank, he rolled in under the bridge and stopped. Directly across from them was a parked car, halfway up on to the pavement: a dark-blue Lincoln sedan, a little rusted-up around the front wheel arches.

'That's our ride,' said Tillman. 'You didn't have any luggage with you, did you?'

He got out without waiting for an answer, covered the distance in two strides, and was behind the wheel of the other car before Kennedy had time to react. He threw the passenger door open and beckoned to her peremptorily.

When Kennedy followed, she found him fiddling with the controls of an identical radio scanner in the glove compartment of the Lincoln.

'I've lost them!' The driver of car four-seven, in a flat panic.

'Negative, four-seven. They're still ahead of you.'

'What? Where?'

'South on 5th. They are south on 5th, four-seven. You keep right on going.'

The bridge was a steel-frame construction, with concrete and asphalt overlaid: they heard the black-and-white pass over their heads like muted thunder.

Tillman gave it a decent interval, then rolled out and drove east. After a while, they heard the chopper coming in from the

490

west. They took a left, keeping a convenient line of taller buildings – three- and four-storey apartment blocks – between them and the eye-in-the-sky.

'I don't have them, Caroline, and I'm running out of road.'

'You're right on top of them, four-seven. Maybe they got out of the car already. Look for a woman moving on foot.'

Look for a woman? Why say that, instead of a woman and a man? Kennedy realised then what Tillman had done, what it was the woman at the despatch desk was tracking. 'Son of a bitch,' she said, with scandalised awe. 'They're chasing my GPS tag, aren't they? Where did you put it?'

'Taped it underneath their car,' Tillman said, 'back in the hospital parking area. That was why I wanted them to follow us – close enough so they'd misread what they were seeing on the read-out. These tagging rigs usually aren't accurate to more than twenty feet or so.'

Kennedy slumped in her seat, almost catatonic as the after-effects of the prolonged adrenalin surge hit her system. 'Son of a bitch,' she said again.

Tillman was putting on dark glasses, a so-so fake moustache, a Yankees baseball cap, all from the glove compartment where they'd been stuffed above the scanner.

'Still got to get out of this bottleneck and on to the Interstate,' he murmured. 'But it definitely helps that they're all looking in the wrong direction.'

A couple of police cars drove south down the cross streets on either side of them as they kept on heading north.

'Where are we going by the way?' Tillman asked her at last.

'Mexico City. Xochimilco.'

Tillman sighed heavily.

'What?'

'Crossing the border. Complicates things a little.'

Kennedy laughed in spite of herself. 'What, breaking me out of hospital and beating on the asses of the Arizona police department didn't count as complicated? You set the bar high, Leo. You set the bar halfway to the bloody moon!'

58

Watched with the right level of detachment, the process of *map-kanah* was not unlike the process whereby water swirls down a drain. A gathering, a patterning, the gradual replacement of random turbulence with a powerful and directional flow, which then imposes itself, inexorably, on a whole continuum.

Kuutma felt like a cork bobbing on the surface of that flow, too light to be touched by it. He watched the people packing away not their own belongings – already packed and stowed long before – but the infrastructure of their world. They lowered the vats from the hydroponics plants, drained and still dripping, from upper windows to the ground, where waiting teams rolled them on down to the cargo bays. A loom from the textile factory rolled by on a cart pulled by a single, straining ox. Kuutma heard the drover murmur reassurances into its ear: 'Only another three after this, my lad, and then we start on the carding machines, which are so much lighter.' Most surreal of all, a burly man struggled by, carrying on his shoulders the carved wooden lectern from the Kad Sima. In his sweating face shone a boundless pride: it was like hauling a piece of the Godhead.

The city was packing, folding itself flat, along one plane and then another, until finally it would disappear through an auger hole.

Kuutma, meanwhile, needed to be trained in his new responsibilities. He went to the pump station and reported to the watermaster there, a woman named Selaa who was younger than Kuutma by a full decade. She was *suoma'ka*, red-haired. It was a recessive trait among the people, and very rare, so that those who possessed it moved through life surrounded by whiplash double-takes. To Kuutma, with the mantle of the outside still upon him, it merited neither a glance nor a thought.

'I'm Kuutma,' he said, knowing she'd already been briefed.

She was a businesslike woman, and clearly very busy with the task of dismantling the parts of the water plant that would no longer be needed here: the purifiers, the meters and gauges, the two largest of the pumps. Nonetheless, she bowed respectfully to Kuutma and touched his shoulder.

'*Ha ana mashadr*,' she said. 'Do you know the equipment already, Kuutma? I know many people spend a season at the pump station, when they're young, to learn the rudiments.'

'That practice came in after my time,' Kuutma said. 'I'm good with machines generally, though, and I'm familiar in theory with what you do.'

'Of course.' She nodded. 'And I imagine that the only machines you'll need to operate tomorrow will be the sluices.'

She showed him where they were and what they did. There were four, two drawing from the Cutzamala reservoirs and two directly from the aquifer below the city which was all that remained of Lake Texcoco. Selaa was very proud of the system, and she had reason to be. 'In the last decades,' she boasted, 'the city outside has suffered continual crises of water shortage. It's sinking into the lake bed at the rate of three inches a year, Kuutma. Did you know that? That's how quickly Ciudad de Mexico is using up the resources of its own water table. But our water flow has never been interrupted. It's never even suffered a drop in pressure. The people take what they need, as God allows.'

Kuutma pulled her back to the practicalities. 'One of these sluices has been modified, I assume,' he said to her. 'Which one, and how does it work?'

'It's not a sluice,' she said. 'It's just a tank here – one of the purification tanks – which will feed into the flow through the sluice when it reaches the third station. That's this bank of controls here. The water comes in at station one, runs through the aqueduct under Em Hadderek, and out through these branch channels. But all the branch channels will be closed after we leave. The water will flow straight through and back into Cutzamala – back into the main water supply of Ciudad de Mexico. All you have to do is open the sluice gate with this lever, and then whenever you're ready, dump the concentrate from the tank into the water.'

She made the sign of the noose. Kuutma raised an eyebrow.

'I'm sorry,' Selaa said, a little sheepishly. 'I'd feel sad even for the death of so many animals.'

'But you wouldn't ask God to bless their carcasses.'

'No. I suppose not.'

'Thank you, watermaster. I think this will be easy enough. Isn't there a control, though, called the *tsa'ot khep*?'

Selaa looked puzzled. 'The "Voice of the Flood"? That's a defence mechanism, Kuutma. There won't be anything left that needs to be defended.'

'I know. But I'm curious. Please show it to me.'

'With the biggest pumps removed, it won't work in any case. Not as it's meant to work anyway. It's this control here: the sluices slaved to this lever, and the channels re-routed through the slides – ten of them in all – along here.'

'Will all these controls still be functional tomorrow?'

Selaa nodded. 'The power runs to the whole bank,' she said. 'I can't turn off parts of the station house: nobody ever saw a need to.'

'No. Of course. Again, thank you for your time. You must be very busy. I presume you have a set of keys to hand to me?'

She gave him her own, taken from a loop on her belt. 'There's a copy set in my office,' she said. 'But it should be these that lock the doors for the last time: they were given to me by Chanina, who was watermaster when I first came here. Please keep them when you're done, Kuutma. It would make me happy for you to have them. Unless you think you'd have no use for such a souvenir.'

'I'll keep them until I die,' he promised her. He bowed formally and withdrew.

I'd feel sad even for the death of so many animals. It was a sentimental thought, and sentimentality was something he'd seen little of in Ginat'Dania. It felt and looked like weakness – a weakness the people, because of their tiny numbers, could not afford to indulge. But what of his own weakness? What of the holes in his own armour, made by equally indefensible emotions?

He was going to kill twenty million. And yet he only cared about one.

Nethqadash shmakh, oh Lord. Help me to draw a breath in which there is only You.

59

Crossing the border turned out to be easier than Tillman had imagined. But thinking about it in safe hindsight as he threaded the back roads of a nameless hinterland just south of Chihuahua, he could see why it worked that way.

The resources of the state of Arizona were bent on stopping Mexicans from coming north across the border. What patrols they saw – and he knew there were a whole lot – had all been looking at the traffic in that one direction, and were not inclined to view one white man heading south in a suspicious light.

One white man, alone, because Kennedy lay slumped in the back of the Lincoln under a blanket, completely out of sight and asleep most of the time. She was still in a lot of discomfort from her injuries. Tillman didn't have much to give her by way of pain relief, but he did have some more of the desflurane. When the pain got to be too much, he gave her a little of it to sniff on a paper tissue, after which she fell into a deep, scarily motionless slumber.

For the border crossing, he shifted her, with apologies, to the wheel well in the boot. Kennedy was afraid that folding herself into the narrow space would open up the wound in her side, but Tillman insisted. They couldn't take the chance that a casual search would find her. He was proved right when the guards at the border station north of Nogales threw open the boot and rummaged through his luggage – the innocuous parts of it anyway, since the guns and explosives were inside the gutted and rebuilt rear seats – before sending him on his way.

He stopped as soon as he dared, about two miles further on, and helped Kennedy out of her confinement. The bloodied bandages at her side showed that her fears had been justified. Tillman got her to strip to the waist and changed the dressing quickly and expertly. He admired her breasts as he did so, because they were impressive and right there in front of his face, but he tried his best to edit out the memory afterwards, or at least to keep his mind on other things. Normally when he doled out medicine to fellow soldiers, they were neither man nor woman to him: you needed a level of detachment when doing running repairs on the failing body of someone you'd been swapping jokes with an hour or two earlier.

This seemed to be a good time to give Kennedy the clothes he'd brought along for her: anonymous blue jeans, a black T-shirt, a loose-fitting black jacket, serviceable trainers. Kennedy struggled into them, Tillman helping to manoeuvre her bound-up arm. Nothing fit her perfectly, but it was all more or less okay, and there was no denying she was a lot less conspicuous now. Like a tourist from north of the border, trying to look stylish but casual and failing in both aims.

'I don't think I'm going to make this,' Kennedy groaned. 'It's another seven hundred miles. A whole day's driving – a day and a night probably – and every time we go over a bump it's like someone stuck a knitting needle in my kidneys.'

'Take some more desflurane,' Tillman suggested. 'You can sleep all the way. Then we'll take a couple of hours once we get there for you to put your brains back together.'

Kennedy shook her head emphatically. 'I need to be awake for this,' she said.

'A day and a night,' he reminded her. 'You're not going to stay awake the whole time, Heather. And if the pain gets to be too much, you might go into shock. Then I'd have to take you to a hospital, where they'd most likely match us up to the descriptions in some police APB. We just need to meet one person who's more than half-awake and we're solidly screwed.'

Kennedy chewed it over. 'Yeah,' she said at last, glumly, reluctantly. 'Okay.'

She stretched out on the Lincoln's back seat and Tillman doped her again: a stronger dose this time, but still well below the red line on the dosage chart he'd gotten along with the drug. Desflurane was a general anaesthetic after all, and sending Kennedy down too deep – into the realms where she'd need mechanical assistance even to breathe – was a real danger.

Tillman looked down at her, lying insensate, and experienced an unfamiliar twinge of conscience. Had he sucked Kennedy into his own madness or had they just met each other at a moment when she was mad enough to resonate on the same frequency? He covered her with a blanket, strapped her in at shoulder and waist with the seatbelts. He felt glad anyway, that he hadn't told her her bed was mostly made of plastic explosive.

He kept to the back roads, even though the back roads were rougher and more treacherous. As night came on, he flicked the headlights to full beam and slowed down to forty, a compromise between their need to cover the distance before the search for them crossed the border and the more immediate need to drive around the crater-deep potholes instead of into them.

The desert night was as wide as a continent, and they were its sole inhabitants: a ghostly caterpillar threading the dark, with the beams of their headlights for its body and the Lincoln rocking along at its tail end. Tillman found himself drifting into reverie: Rebecca and the children spoke to him, or at least he saw their faces and heard sounds suggestive of their voices. There were no real words, though, and no need for him to reply. The burden of what they were saying was: *soon*.

Outside Zacatecas, with maybe three hundred miles still to go, he looked for a billboard next to the road. When he found one, he pulled off the asphalt and eased the car in behind it, so it would be out of sight unless someone was actually looking for it.

He didn't bother to lie down. He just slid the seat back a couple of inches, closed his eyes and slept at the wheel.

His dreams were formless and hideous things, but Rebecca's face floated above all of them, calling him onwards.

60

Kennedy woke around seven, with sun-up. She muttered and turned, but couldn't keep the light out of her eyes. Her throat was so dry she couldn't swallow, dry to the point of agony, and her head throbbed to the rhythm of her own heartbeat.

They were still moving, or maybe moving again: the car yawed on its clapped-out shocks like a rubber dinghy in a squall.

'Jesus,' Kennedy groaned, thickly. 'Where . . . where are we?'

'Lopez Mateos,' Tillman said. 'It's been all built up for the last thirty miles or so, but we're not properly in the city yet – and Xochimilco is to the south. Say another hour.'

Without taking his eyes off the road, he reached over the back of the seat to hand Kennedy a bottle of water. She sat up, groggily, to drink it. She kept the first sip in her mouth, swilling it around, and then let it trickle down her throat in tiny increments. Even so, it made her stomach heave and her head spin. She persevered, while Tillman drove on in silence. Once the swollen membranes of her throat had eased a little, she could take larger swigs. Eventually she emptied the whole bottle. It did nothing to dull the ache in her head, but she felt a little more able to think around the pain.

She watched the anonymous suburbs and barrios roll by,

while her mind came back into focus by fits and starts. When Tillman pulled in, about halfway along an interminable row of one-storey breeze-block buildings, she didn't realise at first why he was stopping. Then the smell of cooking reached her: eggs and bread and something spiced. Kennedy's stomach turned a few more aggrieved pirouettes, but underneath the nausea she found she was hungry.

In the rear corner of the bare and busy cantina, they ate huevos rancheros and tiny bread rolls still hot from the oven. Kennedy kept the jacket on, draped loosely over her shoulders to hide the cast on her arm, and ate one-handed. The food tasted unexpectedly delicious, and Tillman let her wolf the breakfast down in silence. When she finally came up for air, he got straight to business.

'I need to know where we're going,' he told her. 'Xochimilco, you said, and we're almost there now. But is there an address? Some place specific we're headed?'

'There's no address,' said Kennedy, pushing the empty plate away. She'd popped two Tylenol along with the eggs and sausage and, between the food and the lessened pain, was starting to feel more like a human being. 'But I know it's in the area served by a particular electrical generating station – and I think it's going to turn out to be something big. Something like a whole office block or a row of office blocks.'

She told Tillman about Peter Bonville and the unexplained hiccups in power usage that had first put him on the track of the Judas tribe. Tillman frowned in concentration, drinking the information in. He waited until she'd finished before he asked any questions.

'This was all recent?'

'Up to a couple of months ago. Bonville was on his way back from Mexico City when Flight 124 went down – why he was on

502

it. And the crash happened on the same day Stuart Barlow was murdered.'

'But you don't think there was a connection?'

Kennedy shrugged. 'It doesn't sound likely. As far as we know, Barlow and Bonville never met and never communicated. They didn't exactly move in the same circles. The only connection is that they both represented a threat to Michael Brand and his . . . well, his people, I suppose. The people who sent him out into the world.'

She fell silent, thinking about the words of the Judas Gospel: the Elohim and the Kelim, the two types of emissary that this group of ancient sectarian ninja maniacs sent out into the world. She made a connection suddenly – probably because her brain was cross-wired right then, and begun working in ways slightly aslant to its usual functioning.

'Your wife,' she said to Tillman. 'Rebecca. What was her maiden name?'

'Kelly. Why?'

'There was another Kelly who disappeared. Tamara? Talulah? Something like that. It was one of the cases Chris tied Brand to, before he died.'

Tillman stared at Kennedy, waiting for her to tease the thought out. 'You flew here,' she said. 'I mean, to the States. From London.'

'Yeah.'

'But not under your own name?'

Tillman put down his fork, his eggs only half-finished. 'I usually buy travel documents from a woman who specialises in fake identities. She's ex-CIA, has friends in the corporate mercenary community and mainly works for people in that line of business. Espionage, but espionage that's being done a level or so down from what the government gets up to. Heather, where are you going with this?'

503

'Brand always uses the same name,' she said. 'It makes his job harder, makes it more likely that someone like you will pick up his trail, but he never, ever switches to an alias. Why is that?'

'You tell me.'

'Maybe it's because he doesn't want to lie. And if it is that . . . then maybe . . .'

She was feeling dizzy again, and the eggs, which had tasted so good going down, threatened to rise catastrophically. Tillman saw from her face that she was going through some sort of crisis, reached out to touch her forearm.

'You want to leave?'

'I'm fine,' she lied. 'Tillman, Emil Gassan said that Elohim, in Aramaic, means something like Messengers. In the regular Bible, angels get called that. I wonder if maybe Brand's killers – his team of assassins – see themselves as guardian angels for their people, and so that's the name they use.'

'Okay. Go on.'

'Well, if I'm right, the Kelim would have to be something else.' She hoped he'd complete the chain of logic for her, but he didn't. She was really saying: what if the Kelim, like Brand, walk among normal people without scrupling to lie about what they are? What if they choose a name that advertises their origins, or their purpose, or their nature.

Rebecca Kelly.

Tamara Kelly.

Maybe a whole lot of other Kellys. Why hadn't she run a search on missing women with that surname?

What if they were the Kelim? Coming out like Brand and his team to complete some sort of mission in the world, then disappearing once that mission was done. And if they'd had a life in the meantime, raised a family, the family came back with them.

504

'Possibly just ranks or specialised roles in the one organisation,' Tillman said. 'Probably they all work for Brand. But I think you're right that he doesn't want to lie. That's why he leaves the coins, too. If there's a link to Judas – and you said this gospel mentions silver pieces in terms of some kind of bargain these people struck with God – then the coins could refer to that. They announce that one of their kind was there.' He chuckled – a sound so much at odds with her mood that it almost made her give a physical start. 'But it's some handicap, for a hit man – not being able to lie. I can't see why they'd tie their hands behind their backs like that.'

Kennedy found that she could. 'Why do Catholics give up comforts and luxuries for Lent?' she asked, rhetorically. 'Same thing maybe. They offer up their suffering to God – and the Judas people offer up, I don't know, their truthfulness.' Even as she said it, a better explanation hit her. 'Or maybe they get absolution in advance, for specific sins – the way bishops used to bless soldiers going into war. But they're only cleared for murder, not for every kind of sin they feel like committing. So they have to be moral in other ways and that includes not lying.'

'That's insane,' Tillman pointed out.

'Did you really think that we were dealing with sane people here, Leo? After everything that's happened?'

He didn't answer. Instead, he signalled to the waiter with a wave and a nod that they were ready to pay.

'They've lived like a big secret society for at least the last two millennia,' Kennedy murmured. 'But actually, that's a lousy simile for what they are. Because they're also a race. A secret race. A secret species almost. They don't see themselves as anything like the rest of us – less like us than we are like monkeys maybe. They hold themselves apart. They ought to have their own country somewhere, but what they've got is . . .'

'An office block in Mexico City.'

'Or something. So don't expect sanity, Leo. Whatever we find at the end of this road, I can pretty much guarantee that it will not be sane.'

They drove on south, through a city that seemed to come at them in waves. Endless expanses of adobe and concrete slums – the old and the new thrown together in bleak discord – gave way to business districts where steel-and-glass fortresses stabbed at the sky. But then the same thing would happen in reverse, the gleaming towers and ramparts would die away and there would be more avenues of dust and breeze blocks and despair.

Finally, Tillman's pocket map – bought from a gas station while Kennedy was still sleeping – told them that they'd arrived in Xochimilco.

It was not what Kennedy had been expecting. Knowing what she did about the sheer scale of the resources available to Michael Brand – resources sufficient to launch teams of murderers across whole continents and swat planes out of the sky – she'd thought she must be approaching some hub of power. One of the sky-threatening towers seemed appropriate, or else a complex of buildings on their own gated campus, like a modern fortress sealing itself off from the city that sprawled all around it.

Xochimilco held nothing even remotely like that. It was a factory district, mostly derelict. Weeds grew up in profusion through the asphalt of the wide streets and the only cars parked at the kerbside were burned-out wrecks. It was as though they were driving through a city that had hosted some private apocalypse. The buildings that rose on either side of them were huge, but they were only shells: every window broken, every door gaping dark and vacant like a dead man's mouth.

Something tugged at Kennedy's memory, something with overtones of death and disaster.

Tillman took turns at random. 'Going to be a long job without an address,' he muttered. 'It's not like there's even any kind of a grid or we know what we're looking for.'

'Generating Station 73 South,' said Kennedy. 'Where Bonville found the weird patterns of power usage. That's where we have to go.'

Tillman nodded, but without conviction. He pulled in at the kerb, took out his phone and started to dial. He hesitated, looked over at Kennedy. 'A friend,' he said. 'But he doesn't know you and he's strict about who gets to know his business. You mind?'

'Go ahead,' she said. 'I could do with stretching my legs anyway.' She got out of the car, surprised to find that the air was cool. A breeze had sprung up from somewhere and there was a thick overcast in the sky, changing the light to something numinous and silver-grey. Thunder rumbled in the distance. Summer thunder, and a cleansing rain. Kennedy felt grimed to the core of her being and longed to be washed in any water, hot or cold or in-between, until her body felt like her own again.

She walked slowly towards the end of the street. She could hear nothing. There was almost total silence here, in this city of over twenty million souls. None of the twenty million, it seemed, lived in Xochimilco. She crossed to a café, or at least the frontage of one, which called itself – with heroic hubris – El Paraiso. The windows had been boarded up with corrugated steel, and the good things advertised on the sign (ENCHILADAS! CHILAQUILES! BISTECK!) seemed unlikely to materialise.

The restaurant was a dwarf on a street of behemoths, but it was just as dead: the crisis of late monopoly capitalism, like the angel of death, spares no one who doesn't have the magic sign of God's favour painted on their doorposts.

Kennedy reached the corner and stopped. Facing her across the road – a dual carriageway avenue wide enough to have a row of trees planted in the middle of it, but completely empty of traffic – stood a warehouse complex. A single massive structure with uncountable outbuildings, all built from the same pre-stressed concrete and painted battleship grey. A few tiny windows high up on the walls so deep-set in the brickwork that they couldn't have let in any light at all. A still-solid fence and a set of gates bearing a massive padlock. Above them, bristling nests of CCTV cameras mounted on steel posts surveyed the street to either side.

Kennedy laughed aloud – out of sheer incredulity.

She heard Tillman's step behind her, and turned. 'All of it,' he said, indicating the area around them with a wide sweep of both hands. 'Station 73 South serves everything within about a two-mile radius of here. We'll have to try something else, Kennedy. Maybe if Bonville spoke to someone here about what he was working on, or filed a report, we could triangulate from that. Otherwise, I think we should try looking at . . . '

He broke off, at last, seeing that Kennedy was pointing: across the street, to the great grey warehouse.

'We're here, Leo,' she said. 'That's it.'

It was the building from the photo underneath Stuart Barlow's floor – the one on the back of which he'd written the list of scrolls and codices that contained John's Gospel.

The end of their journey had been written into its beginning.

61

It took Tillman ten minutes to ascertain that the cameras were dead.

He noticed first of all that they sat on mobile mounts, designed to increase the viewing arc by swivelling from side to side: but they had been locked in one position, not even the most practical or advantageous position. The one on the left was aimed more or less directly ahead, but the corresponding one on the right had pivoted inwards to point towards its partner. Effectively, both were looking at the same area of ground, leaving a dead zone to the right.

That could have been a mechanical malfunction, leaving the cameras frozen but still seeing. Tillman used the dead zone to creep across the street and edge in close to the base of the nearer support pole. With a digital multimeter from his kit, he tested the wires and found no current flowing to them.

Since there was no need for stealth now, he crossed directly back to Kennedy, making the throat-cut gesture. 'Nothing,' he said. 'Power's out. Either they've been shut down at the board or the whole area's had a power cut.'

Kennedy pointed. The first streetlamps were blinking on a few blocks further on. The lamps closest to them had all been smashed, but clearly if there was a power cut it was a very local one.

Tillman considered.

'I think this might be where we part company,' he told Kennedy.

'What?' Kennedy was shocked. 'What the hell do you mean, Tillman? We're in this together. I know I can't fight, but I didn't drive a thousand miles to send you off with a wave and a kiss on the cheek. I'm going in with you. Count on it.'

He didn't seem to have heard her. He walked away while she was still talking, heading back towards the Lincoln. Kennedy broke into a jog-trot to catch up.

'I'm serious,' she said. 'You can outrun me but you can't stop me from going in unless you tie me up and gag me or something, and if you even try that, I'll struggle hard enough and make enough noise that they see us coming a mile off. I repeat, Leo: we're in this together. All the way.'

They'd reached the car by this time. Tillman threw open the rear door, then turned to meet her gaze. 'You're a cop, Heather,' he said. 'You uphold the law.'

'I stopped being a cop when they made me resign, remember?'

'But it's still what you're here for. Because people were killed and it's your job to make sure that the killers pay.'

'You're not listening, Leo.' Kennedy struggled to keep her temper. 'It's not my job any more. Anything I do down here is illegal two or three times over. I'm out of my jurisdiction, I'm off the force, and I'm a wanted fugitive. This stopped being about the law a long time ago. It's about justice now.'

His stare was still locked on her, waiting, weighing her, looking for some sign. 'What kind of justice?'

'What?'

'What kind of justice is it about, Heather?'

She stared back, bewildered, threw up her one good arm. 'Is there more than one flavour?'

510

'Lots of flavours. And the one I'm interested in is the worst of them all. The really filthy one. An eye for an eye. They killed my wife and they killed my kids. They took everything from me – everything. But they didn't have the decency to kill me. Thirteen years. Thirteen years in this world that they left uninhabited. All that's left now for me is to give them back what's rightfully theirs.'

He reached into the car and wrenched off the seat cover, revealing two machine rifles, four handguns, clips and belts of ammunition stacked and coiled, and a number of glossy black plastic bags, about the size and shape of bricks, bearing the WORDS M112 CHARGE DEMOLITION C4.

Kennedy's mouth opened and closed. She struggled to get any words out, and when she did, she knew they weren't the sort of words that were going to be any good. 'Leo ... you're wrong. You're wrong about this.'

Tillman didn't seem to take offence. He just smiled sadly. 'What, you think there's still a chance my family are alive, Heather? After thirteen years?'

And like some holy assassin, Kennedy crashed head-first into the impossibility of the lie. It died in her throat.

'No,' she said. 'I ... I don't think they're still alive. But if we're right about anything, that building is going to be full of people who had nothing to do with killing them. Other people's families, Leo. Are you so hungry to get even with Michael Brand that you'd be ready to turn yourself into him? Because if you are, get out that fancy pistol and put it right up against my head because I swear to God, you're going to have to start with me.'

They stood facing each other in the street, for some uncountable number of seconds. Tillman winced, as though thinking about this was costing him physical pain.

'I didn't come here to kill kids,' he said.

'Good.'

'The plastique—'

'Yes, Leo? What about the plastique?'

'I had no idea what we were going to find here. Or how we were going to get in. I wanted to be ready for anything.'

Kennedy nodded. 'So that's good,' she said. 'We're ready.'

'Right.'

'But we're here for Michael Brand, right? All the Michael Brands.'

'No.'

'No?'

Tillman shook his head slowly. 'Someone sent them. Someone chose them, and trained them, and equipped them. Someone told them what to do to me, and mine. And your young lad, Harper. And Christ knows who else. We close them down, Heather. Not just Brand. The people behind Brand. We close every last one of the bastards down.'

'Pass me one of those guns.'

Tillman did. Kennedy felt a prickle of déjà vu as she took it. It was a G22, identical to the one with which she'd killed Marcus Dell. But that was in another country and that Heather Kennedy was now officially dead.

She gestured with the gun, raising it butt-first to show the mag-base. Tillman got the message, selected a clip from the rich array inside the hollow of the gutted seat and slapped it into place for her.

'Couple more,' she instructed him.

Tillman took one in each hand, slid them carefully into the pockets of her jacket.

Kennedy thanked him with a nod. 'By virtue of the authority invested in me as an ex-cop way too far from home,' she told him, 'I'm deputising you. You know what that means, Leo?'

512

He seemed afraid of how this was going, of how much of his decision-making he was entrusting to her. But the slope they were on had become so steep now neither wanted to look down. And at this point, Kennedy knew what was at the bottom better than Tillman did because she'd heard the last words of the lady assassin back at Santa Claus: words she was determined Tillman would never get to hear.

'No, Heather. What does it mean?'

She tucked the gun into the waistband of her jeans and tugged the jacket closed over it. 'It means we're an armed response unit. Let's go respond.'

The easiest way into the warehouse compound turned out to be at the side, where an adjacent building – a one-storey shed of some kind on a site that had once been a U-Store depot – ran close to the fence and allowed them to jump across.

Tillman went first, and when Kennedy jumped he caught and braced her so that she didn't fall. She hadn't realised until then how weak she still was, in spite of the long sleep and the meal. Her side felt stiff and sore, her broken arm ached worse even than her head, and the anaesthetic was still in her system – dulling her thinking without doing a damned thing for the pain.

Tillman had transferred a whole lot of light and heavy ordnance into a kit bag that he carried on his back. In his hands, in place of the Unica, he carried a FA-MAS Clairon assault rifle in the French army configuration, complete with bayonet and grenade launcher. The thing terrified Kennedy: it looked like the Swiss army knife of sudden death.

They followed the wall of the main building, looking for a way in. The only door they found turned out to be welded into its frame. All the windows were way above their heads, and since Kennedy couldn't climb, the ropes and grapnels would have to be a last resort.

They saw more camera posts at intervals along the fence: none of them moved, and all showed negative for current when Tillman tested them with the multimeter.

When they reached the front of the warehouse, they looked out cautiously on an open stretch of asphalt like a parade ground, its surface pitted and broken, with copious weeds everywhere. But there were odd anomalies, which they pointed out to each other in whispers. The fence looked in perfect repair, the chains and padlocks rust-free and solid: and the weeds inside the compound had been flattened down in straight swathes, as if by recent and heavy traffic.

Tillman was reluctant to step out into the open, even though he knew they had nothing to fear from the cameras. He counted too many vantage points from which they could be watched. They went round to the back of the building instead, where the asphalt gave way in places to dust and earth, and where narrower spaces separated the main structure from some of the many satellite buildings.

Exploring these outlying structures, they discovered that all the doors were like the first they'd seen: welded shut and clearly no longer in use. At last, though, Kennedy found tyre tracks in the dirt, fresh and clear, and followed them back to the up-and-over door of what appeared to be a garage or hangar. The place looked shabby and disused, but the tracks suggested otherwise.

The door was fixed with a padlock. Tillman took a crowbar from his kit bag and snapped the hasp with a single movement, grunting slightly from the effort. He swung the shutter up and they stared into the interior of the building.

It took a moment or two for Kennedy to process what she was

seeing. They stood at the top of a ramp that extended downwards into perfect darkness. It seemed to run the full width of the building, about forty feet, and its incline was a gentle one-in-ten. They heard no sound and saw nothing else. The building housed the ramp and nothing more: or rather, whatever else it contained was below them, at the ramp's further end.

'You got a torch in there?' Kennedy muttered, nodding at Tillman's bag. Her voice echoed in the eerie stillness and took a long time to die away.

Tillman produced two: sturdy cylindrical flashlights with rubber sheathes, each about a foot and a half long. They seemed to have been designed to serve as truncheons as well as sources of illumination.

Kennedy flicked the switch and aimed the strong, steady beam into the darkness below. Tillman followed suit. All that accomplished was to show them that the ramp extended a lot further than they'd thought. The beams still didn't reach the bottom.

Tillman glanced at Kennedy, who gave a single nod. Nowhere to go but down. Her unease deepened with every step. No scenario that she could imagine reconciled setting up this degree of security and then being so lax in its oversight. And who'd live in a wasteland like this in the first place? They'd obviously found a supply depot of some kind, rather than – as she'd thought – their enemies' heartland.

The ramp extended about three hundred feet, and took them down at least thirty below street level. At its bottom end, a corrugated steel roller-door stretched from end to end of the ramp, blocking their path. Kennedy shone her flashlight beam on the wall, looking for controls, but found none: probably they were on the other side. She was about to suggest looking elsewhere when Tillman's light, aimed at the floor, revealed that the way wasn't blocked at all: there was a foot of clearance between the bottom of the steel shutter and the floor.

Wordlessly, they got down on hands and knees – Kennedy grunting in pain as already abused muscles registered their protest – and slid-shuffled under the door.

On the other side, they stood up, still in complete darkness, but Kennedy could tell from the movement of air on her face that she was in a very large space. Her flash, flicked at random around her, picked out nothing close enough for the light to touch it.

Tillman put out a hand to touch this side of the steel shutter and followed it along. Kennedy shone her torch ahead of him and, as he reached it, put a perfectly centred spotlight on a bank of switches. A red light to the left of the array announced that here at least, there was still current.

She came to join him and they examined the switchboard together: there were three large slide controls at the left-hand side and then four banks of ten smaller switches, none labelled.

'We touch these,' Kennedy whispered, 'and we're throwing up our hands and shouting, "Look at me".'

'Listen,' Tillman whispered back.

She did. No sound at all, anywhere: not even the sounds of distant traffic that count for silence in most cities most of the time. Tillman was right. The noise they'd already made in sliding under the shutter – even their footsteps on the ramp, though they'd been as quiet as they could – would have carried a long way in this absolute hush. If there was anyone here, their arrival was surely no secret. But if there was anyone here, why hadn't they already been challenged?

Tillman didn't bother to get Kennedy's approval this time. He just pressed the sliders all the way down and flicked the top row of switches, one at a time.

The sliders didn't seem to do anything much, but when Tillman pressed the switches he was conducting a symphony of light: not bulbs or strips or spots but huge panels, inset in the walls and stretching from floor to roof, stirred into life like a chain of sunrises all around them.

Kennedy gasped.

They stood in a space as high as a cathedral but much longer: a subterranean avenue whose walls were blocks of sheer, almost painful radiance. Kennedy covered her eyes with her right forearm, dazzled, blinking away tears.

'Wait,' Tillman murmured. 'Okay. Got it.'

It was because he'd floored the slide controls first. He cut them back to about two-thirds, and the light dimmed to something more bearable.

They took stock of their surroundings, and it was slowly borne in on Kennedy that they were in the right place after all.

This was a street: an avenue, rather, thirty feet wide and seventy or eighty high, which stretched away into the distance in both directions. Small wooden booths like the stalls in a market lined the street on either side, and behind them stood more permanent structures with doors and windows of their own: an indoor thoroughfare in an indoor metropolis.

Two thoughts struck Kennedy at once. The first: that the market stalls were all empty, one or two of them clumsily ransacked. The second: that the space couldn't actually be that high, given that they weren't far enough below ground. She stared up at the ceiling, appraising it more carefully. It had been painted to resemble clouds and blue firmament, and it curved in a vast arch. It was – it must be – the inside of the warehouse roof. They stood underneath the main structure, which had been hollowed out inside to provide a vault of sky for this underground concourse.

'This is the craziest thing I've ever seen,' Kennedy said, her throat suddenly dry.

Tillman said nothing, but he moved on down the street and gestured for Kennedy to follow him. She fell in at his side. She'd swapped the now useless torch for the G22, and she gripped it tight.

The market stalls extended for the first twenty metres or so, but the structures behind them were a continuous feature. Some had wide windows, like shop windows, with shelves and platforms to display goods. All were empty, except in places for a scatter of boxes, the occasional plastic strip or bag, and in one display a single yellow scarf hanging from an otherwise empty rack of polished wood. There were signs above the doors, written in a script that looked to Kennedy like Hebrew. The enigma hit her anew: assuming the Judas people had arisen in ancient Judea, as the *sica* knives seemed to suggest, why come from the Holy Land all the way to the arse-end of Mexico City?

Probably she'd never know, but she felt certain, suddenly, that it had nothing to do with the fluctuations of temporal power. Twenty million people, and an urban sprawl that covered six hundred square miles – that made a great desert to hide a grain of sand in. Maybe they did this often. Maybe the Judas tribe were a nomadic people, going wherever the best camouflage, or some other resource that they tracked and followed, was to be found.

And riding on that thought, another, terrible possibility, which she didn't dare to voice: maybe we missed them.

They were approaching what must be the northern limit of the warehouse site. The roof high above them was sheared off clean by the plunging vertical of the front wall, and the trompe l'oeil clouds bent at sharp angles suddenly as though they'd crashed into some invisible barrier and gotten broken.

Kennedy expected the vast space to close in now, but the gulf of air that had been over their heads was replaced, unexpectedly, by a gulf that opened beneath their feet: where the warehouse ended and the ceiling closed in, the great alley opened downwards on to a vast parade of descending steps, which then broke apart into subsidiary flights heading off to right and left and straight ahead. More streets led off this one but they were stepped and went further down into the ground.

Tillman took a stairway at random and they descended into another thoroughfare, just as wide and almost as high as the first. Here there were no shops, but what looked like houses instead. Rows and rows of windows lining the walls, terraces on which chairs and tables had been set out, ornamental urns and sculptures at corners and on balustrades. But some of the urns had toppled and shattered, and some of the doors gaped open on dark interior spaces. Someone had gone to a lot of trouble to make the huge indoor complex look homely – and then had ransacked it.

Tillman's face was set in a scowl. He stopped suddenly, his gaze darting to left and right before finally settling on Kennedy. 'People can't live like this,' he muttered, his voice thick with something like anger. He must be afraid now, as she was: afraid that they'd come too late and that solving the puzzle meant nothing after all.

'Yeah,' she said, unhappily. 'I think they could. These lights in the walls probably include UV frequencies, so they wouldn't go crazy from cabin fever. Maybe they get to go upstairs every once in a while, although I'm guessing they don't do it often. They've lived underground long enough for most of the melanin to have leached out of their skin, which is why even their field agents are about as tanned as snow tigers.'

Tillman didn't appear to be listening, so she stopped talking. He'd crossed to a decoration of some kind, hung over the edge of a balcony. It was a white sheet, on which someone had painted a strikingly beautiful image. It was the moment when sunlight breaks through storm clouds, announcing either that the storm is over or that it's not going to come. The storm clouds were black, swag-bellied horrors: the sunlight that broke through them was a filigree of the most delicate gold, only there when you looked at the painting from a certain angle and the light bounced off it just so.

Tillman ripped the sheet down and tore it in two.

'To hell with this!' he bellowed. The words bounced back at him from every wall and cornice, redoubled and fractured, a chorus line of expletives that kept on tripping over its own feet.

'Leo—' Kennedy began, but he silenced her with a wild glare. He didn't want sympathy or condolence right then, and really she didn't have a whole lot to offer. She felt cored out, tired beyond words. To have come this far, only to find this mausoleum, was too cruel.

In the end, having nothing to say, she left him there and went back up to the top of the steps. The whole vast complex was like a sounding board, so Kennedy's own movements came back to her, overlaid on themselves in ever more complex discords. She thought of the Duchamp painting of the nude on the staircase, shedding angular, stroboscopic fragments of her own being as she walks. How much of herself would she leave in this place? It seemed a fair question, given how much she'd had to sacrifice to get here.

She couldn't make it all the way to the top of the stairs in one go. On a terrace just past halfway, she leaned on the balustrade and rested. Her side was aching again, and her arm, too. She should have asked Tillman to put the bottle of Tylenol in his kit bag along with the crowbar, the guns, the ammo, the kitchen sink.

She saw him moving below her. He was checking some of the houses, maybe to see if anyone had gone to ground there. One of the doors didn't give. Kennedy watched Tillman kick it open, sending a sound like chambered thunder through the vast space.

But the thunder grew, rather than fading. And now it seemed to be coming from above her, instead of below. Kennedy walked the rest of the way to the top and looked back the way they'd come.

The corridor seemed to be melting, like wax in a flame. Then she saw that the moving, rippling mass was something independent of walls and floor and sky-painted ceiling. It was a battering ram made of water, that filled the space from top to bottom.

It struck Kennedy like a kick in the teeth from God, and then it trod her under.

62

Kuutma held the sluice gates open for seven minutes. The first thirty seconds gave him the volume of water needed to mix in the concentrate. After that, the only use the water had was as a weapon.

Although he'd switched off the external cameras, he kept the security systems inside Ginat'Dania itself up and running, and so he was able to watch as first the woman and then Tillman succumbed to the flood. The woman was incapacitated, of course, with an arm broken and bound in a cast, but it would have made little difference if she'd been fully fit and mobile. The water came down the grand alley towards the Em Hadderek under enormous pressure, moving very fast. The strongest of swimmers would have been in dead trouble.

The woman went under, and as she went under she fell backwards down the steps of the Em Hadderek. The flood would fill the space below, vast as it was, inside a minute, and there'd be nowhere for the *rhaka* to surface unless she swam all the way back to the Em Hadderek itself and found the upper level again – or went forward and found the Em Sh'dur. Swimming with one arm, either would be quite a feat.

Paradoxically, although he was already on that lower level, Tillman had a much greater chance of survival. He could see the wall of water coming, then breaking and roaring down the stairways like a dozen questing, groping tentacles. He had time to brace himself, gripping to the iron lattice of an ornamental balcony. The water hit him but he held on fast and kept his grip – for the first minute.

Then, with the lower spaces filling fast and the water pressure slackening as it found its level, Tillman launched himself upwards with slow, powerful strokes. He'd lost the machine rifle, but still had the kit bag strapped to his back. He looked around, presumably for the woman, but then all the lights went out as the water flooded junctions and fuse boxes. This meant that Kuutma could no longer keep track of Tillman's movements. It also meant that Tillman's chances of finding the woman before she drowned went from slim to – effectively – zero.

Kuutma turned off the flow of the water, then proceeded to collect his own weapons and equip himself for the business to come. Six *sica* blades, three to each side of his belt. The Sig-Sauer in its shoulder holster, with a full clip and two spares in the pockets of his flak jacket. His movements were methodical and unhurried. He knew beyond and beneath logic that this was meant to be. This was why Tillman had survived for so long. Why he himself had leaned down, with dark and terrible mercy, to interrupt Tillman's suicide.

Tillman didn't have the right to end himself in that way, and furthermore there was something he needed to hear before he died: to hear, and to understand. A balance had to be restored, and Kuutma had been blessed: the balance lay in his keeping.

He locked the doors of the pump station and walked down the steps to ground level. He would have to come back one more time, of course, to release the water back into the Cutzamala reservoir. That would be the last thing he did before he left this place for good and closed the doors on the whole of his life up to this point.

He made his way to the grand alley. The great, imperious mass of the water had drained away into the lower levels, but deep puddles still remained. Kuutma knew this from the sounds his feet made as he strode through them: he couldn't see them because the alley remained in complete darkness. There was a manual system for providing light in power failures and he knew where its controls were. He went to the nearest of these stations, slid back a panel in the wall and turned a cranking wheel that he found there.

High overhead, slats in the steel roof of the warehouse – the shell that covered Ginat'Dania – slid from tightly overlapping diagonal positions to near-vertical. The day outside was overcast: only grey light filtered down, but it was enough.

At the further end of the grand alley, a splashing and thrashing announced that Tillman had breached, like a whale. Staring in that direction, Kuutma couldn't see the man at first. But then a flailing shape reared up at the top of the Em Hadderek steps, where they were widest and most beautiful: reared up and fell again, and crawled with spastic, uncoordinated movements out on to the dry land of the grand alley.

Kuutma strode towards his adversary, holding in each of his hands, the familiar, exquisitely balanced weight of a *sica* blade.

63

When the waters closed over Kennedy, she did most of the wrong things.

First of all she forgot to breathe. Stumbling backwards into the foaming chaos, she clamped her jaws tight shut, when she should have gulped in a massive lungful of air to last her until she became reacquainted with oxygen.

Next, she fought against the irresistible surge that held her and moved her, wasting her strength in a futile struggle to break the surface. Her body's natural buoyancy was going to carry her upwards in any case: she needed to use all the strength and agility she had to avoid hitting any of the buildings and structures towards which she was being carried like a toy in the hand of a running child.

She slammed hard against a wall and almost opened her mouth in a gasp of shock and pain. That would have been the end for her, she knew. Getting her instincts back under control, she twisted and wriggled until she was facing in the same direction as the rushing water, and kicked out with her feet to move herself left, then right, avoiding two further collisions by inches.

It was a little like flying, Kennedy thought dazedly. She could see the tiled floor of the lower level, the indoor streets and indoor houses, rushing past below and to both sides of her, a blue-shifted blur through which light spangled and starred in wild refraction.

Then the lights went out and she knew she was in even worse trouble.

Her lungs were already beginning to protest at the absence of air; to demand the right to inflate again. Kennedy had maybe half a minute, at best, to get herself to some place with air, and she had no idea where such a place might be.

Motes of light danced before her eyes in the rushing darkness. They expanded into underwater suns, and Kennedy was dazzled by them, even while she recognised, objectively, that they weren't there at all. She was starting to lose it. Oxygen deprivation was plucking at the loose strings of her brain.

She tried to think. Pockets of air trapped inside the houses? From what she remembered of high school physics, that seemed possible – but she had no time for a house-to-house search, and in any case she had no police ID to show.

Focus, Heather. Focus.

Fight the flow or ride it?

Go up, down or sideways?

It wasn't likely to make a whole lot of difference, but it felt important to decide. Her father had always told her to impose herself on situations. Just drifting along was almost always a mistake.

64

Tillman struggled to his feet. His own heartbeat sounded loud in his ears, but there was no other noise, and there was no light. His head was spinning: it also seemed to be expanding and contracting in time with his heartbeat, as though his heart orchestrated the pulsing heart of the universe itself.

He laughed incredulously. *It's a small world after all*, he thought. *And I'm right here at the centre of it.*

But his stomach lurched and he felt suddenly sick. The megalomanic thrill subsided and nausea dropped him to his knees. He vomited into the last of the ebb tide: a noisome flux that tasted of chilli and coriander, probably because it contained the remnants of the meal he and Kennedy had eaten on their way down from ... somewhere.

It was cold and it was dark. Cold and dark as the grave. Tillman shuddered. But light descended, abruptly, from above him, soft and feathery like a fall of grey goose-down. Tillman tried to control his racing heart, his throbbing head, his shaking hands. He shouldn't feel this bad. Something was wrong with him.

And Kennedy. He had to find Kennedy, make sure she was okay.

He gritted his teeth, closed his eyes and counted to ten. At least, he tried to. But the numbers mostly wouldn't come.

'And now,' said a gentle, cultured voice from above him, 'here we are.'

A solid impact at the side of Tillman's jaw sent him sprawling, rolled him on to his side in the fouled water. He gasped, flailed, tried to come upright again. A second kick, to the ribs, and he folded in on himself, a tight ball centred on the sudden, violent pain.

'Please,' the voice said, 'take a moment or two to orient yourself. I hope you didn't swallow too much of the water. I'd hate it if you died before we had time to talk.'

Tillman stayed down. Staying down – so long as there were no further attacks – allowed him some space to think, however skewed and dulled his thinking had become. Something in the water? That seemed only too likely. He didn't remember swallowing any, but it wasn't possible that he'd avoided getting any at all in his system. And maybe the something, whatever it was, didn't need to be swallowed. Maybe you could take it in through skin contact. Maybe it was evaporating off the water and he was breathing it in right now.

'Get up,' the voice said.

Tillman uncurled slowly, rolled over on to hands and knees, came up in a reverse kow-tow.

The man facing him looked his own age, more or less. Very tall but not too broad at the shoulders. Well muscled but lean – the physique of a dancer or a runner. He had a shaved head, his dark slender face bisected in the dim light by the vertical slash of an aquiline nose. He had about him the solemnity of a statue or a priest officiating at a ceremony.

'Michael ... Brand,' said Tillman, his rubbery mouth slurring the words.

'Yes,' the stranger said, with something like satisfaction; something like pride. 'That's who I am. Michael is a Hebrew

528

name. It means "who is like unto God?" The brand – in our own tongue, *ku'utma* – is the mark that Laldabaoth, the god of the fallen world, left upon the forehead of our father, Cain. I try to be honest, Mr Tillman. I try never to lie. A lie diminishes the man who speaks it, however noble the motive. I am Kuutma. I am the Brand.'

With a huge effort, Tillman struggled to his feet. He strode at the man before him, his fists raised.

The man's hands moved swiftly. Tillman felt a lance of cold air drive into his lower belly, but when he touched his fingers to the place, there was pulsing warmth.

He looked down at his hand. It held a cornucopia of blood, which filled it again endlessly as it poured out between his clumsily parted fingers.

'And now,' Michael Brand said, 'we must speak quickly. You don't have much time left, and there are things that must be said.'

65

Symmetry, Kennedy told herself. It wasn't much to go on, but it was something.

Everything they'd seen here, everything they'd passed, had been constructed to a simple, elegant schema. The broad main street, its placement beneath the warehouse roof, the swooping falls of stairs that led down from the plaza where the street ended. All symmetrical, presenting to the inhabitants of this screwed-up, troglodyte world a pleasing, ordered vista.

So maybe at the far end of the lower level, there would be another set of steps and another plaza.

Kennedy swam with the flow of the water, using her legs more than her one good arm because the movements of her arm swung her sideways, out of control. She had her eyes tight shut, for some reason. But there was no light to see by, so she probably wasn't missing anything.

The pressure in her lungs, the darkness in her head built and built. The ceiling of the vast corridor brushed her head. Kennedy kicked off against it and angled her body downwards, terrified of getting tangled up in a light fitting or smacking her head against a cornice. If she did that, it would all be over.

It was all over anyway. She was out of oxygen and out of time. Up or down, equally damned. She gave up and let herself float upwards, expecting the ceiling to press against her back and her struggling limbs, holding her in place. When that happened, Kennedy would open her mouth, probably on a profanity, and drown.

She broke surface with a splash that tore into the darkness on either side in endless susurrations. It was as though she'd ripped through the vault of the sky. Grey light filtered down from somewhere and showed her the indoor lake in which she floated.

Kennedy couldn't remember, for a moment, where she was. In Arizona, she knew. But no, that was before. They'd driven south, into Mexico. This was Mexico City.

Mexico City was a lake of darkness, in which nobody fished and nobody swam. Except her.

She turned a slow circle in the water, breathing in deep, ragged gulps as though she was breaking off pieces of the air and chewing them, forcing them down her heaving throat. To her back, a sheer wall rose, studded with the dark vaults of windows. She'd come up from underneath it, where the streets of the lower level ran invisible, flooded from floor to ceiling.

To either side, and in front of her, multiple stairways like the ones that opened from the other plaza. Kennedy had no idea where they led. The distances receded and then advanced upon her in a sinister lockstep. Her brain was a limp, floppy, saturated thing through which thoughts refused to move.

But from a long way away, she heard voices.

66

'She died,' Kuutma told Tillman. 'She died a long time ago.'

The waters had receded a little further and he'd taken a seat at the top of the main steps. Tillman knelt a little way away, both hands gripped tightly to his wound. Despite what Kuutma had told him, the wound had been carefully placed and would take a good while to kill him yet. The blade had not been anointed. The flow of blood would slow gradually, and perhaps even stop so long as Tillman didn't move. Right then, Tillman looked incapable of moving.

'Rebecca,' Tillman muttered. His voice was weak, ragged. The voice of something profoundly broken.

'Exactly,' Kuutma agreed. 'Your Rebecca. I killed her. With a knife just like this one.' He held up the *sica* so that Tillman could see, turned it over in his hand so it caught what light there was. No gleam, in that twilight: the blade looked like a dead thing, in his hand. The world was a dying world, almost unpeopled. 'But I didn't toy with her, or torment her, the way I'm tormenting you. I cut into her chest, between the fourth and fifth ribs, and cut her heart into two pieces. She died very quickly.'

Kuutma wasn't even looking at Tillman as he spoke, but he saw out of the corner of his eye the movement as Tillman stood and lurched towards him. He'd been expecting it, was even waiting for it.

He came to his feet as Tillman reached him, the *sica* still in his right hand, but used his left to block Tillman's clumsy punch, then hook-locked him with left arm and right foot and threw him down on to the top of the steps with a force that might easily have cracked the man's spine. Only then did he lean in and open up Tillman's cheek with the blade: a single slash running from brow to chin.

'Good,' he said, approvingly. 'Hate me as I hate you. Hate me with every breath you draw, until the hate becomes thick enough that you choke on it. This is what I wanted from you.'

Kuutma moved away to the other side of the steps and sat down again. The violence had brought a certain release, but it had set his heart running quickly in his chest. He needed to find the quiet heart of the violence, and inhabit it, as he did when killing out in the world. But this was not the world, it was Ginat'Dania. And this was not a killing like any other killing: it was the paying of the balance.

Kuutma watched the slumped body until it twitched and stirred, which indicated that Tillman was both alive and conscious. Then he resumed his narrative.

'Death was Rebecca's right,' he said. 'It's the right of all the Kelim. But I never thought she'd choose it. I told her, when she came to me, that there was no need. For others, yes, possibly, but not for her. Never, never for a moment ...' He stopped. This was not how he had meant to start: he had to keep his mind on the goal and build logically towards the revelation that would destroy Tillman.

Kill his enemy's soul and only then despatch the body.

Kuutma began again, although calm still eluded him. 'We live apart,' he said. 'That's one of the commandments laid on us. We

533

keep our bloodline pure. Not since Judas only, but since Eden that was, we hold ourselves apart.

'But purity comes with a price. The people number less than a hundred thousand and in such a small community, certain sicknesses – sicknesses that come with birth – spread quickly. We know the genetic basis for this now, as you probably do too, Mr Tillman. In a small breeding community, double recessive genes pair up with disastrous frequency, and congenital defects, weakness of heart and body and mind, become endemic. Without a periodic influx of new genetic material, the community cannot thrive.

'The Elders conferred, many centuries ago, and reached a judgement. A wise one. We could not give our precious blood to the degraded mass of half-animals you call humanity. But we could take strength and vigour from them, where we needed to. We could enrich our stock with graftings from the best of theirs.

'The women who were sent out were called Kelim – vessels. Where the Messengers carry death, outwards from Ginat'Dania to the world, the Kelim go out into the world and bring back life. That's their sacrament. Their glory.'

Tillman had got partway upright again, resting on an elbow. He stared at Kuutma with a feral intensity. Kuutma put away the *sica* and took his gun from its holster. The next time that Tillman charged him, he would shoot out one of the man's knees: the right one, probably.

'The water,' Tillman slurred.

'The water?' Kuutma frowned at the irrelevance of the comment. 'The water's poisoned. *Kelalit*. The same poison we Messengers take to give us our strength and our speed. In concentrations greater than five parts per million, it will paralyse and kill. You've had a very small dose because when the water hit you, the sluice had only just begun to empty into it. It's been emptying all the while we've been talking, the concentration building to LD 100 level: the level at which a single sip will kill within a minute or two. Ciudad de Mexico will be a vast grave-yard. When the people move, they leave nothing behind them, Tillman. We sow the earth with salt and the sky with ash.

'But we were talking about Rebecca. Rebecca Beit Evrom.'

Tillman tensed and gathered himself. He would move soon, Kuutma felt sure of it. But in this condition, befuddled by the *kelalit* diffused in the water and weakened by his injuries, he presented no threat.

'The Kelim are chosen by lottery,' said Kuutma. He felt as though he were building a scaffold on which to hang Tillman, a noose for his neck, a trapdoor for his feet to stand on. 'They go out into the world, with false identities provided by the Elohim, and they marry. We access the medical records of any potential husbands and vet them for diseases carried in their seed. If there's no risk, the union is approved – for breeding only. It's not, of course, a marriage in the religious sense.

'The Kelim bear three children, and then they return. The husband comes back to an empty house – the woman, to her real home and the bosom of the people. Her exile is finally at an end. As you'd imagine, this duty – though sacred – is hard to endure. It is a terrible ordeal, to pretend to love someone for three or four or five years, to live so long under the shadow of a lie.'

'No!' Tillman gasped. He made it to his feet and took a step towards Kuutma. Kuutma raised his gun and Tillman stopped.

'It was a horrible mischance,' Kuutma said, with more vehe-mence than he'd intended. 'The odds against it ... two or three thousand to one. I never thought she'd draw the red ball from the bag. That she'd be chosen. But because I was Kuutma, I thought, it would not be so bad for her as it was for others.

535

I would watch over her. I would still be with her, in a way, even if I couldn't speak to her.

'I sent her to England. She met you. She shared your bed and had your children. Judas, who in your presence she called Jud. Seth. Grace. I watched them grow and I waited my time. To the last day and hour, I waited my time. Until finally the day came when I was allowed to call her home.

'My God, Tillman, that was a bitter time!' Kuutma found that he was talking through clenched teeth, his voice harsh and clotted. 'She committed no sin, you understand? She was blameless. And yet she wallowed in your arms at the end of each day and surrendered herself to ... abomination. I felt for her. I felt for her so much.

'Sometimes ... ' Why was he saying this? Why had he gone so far from the words he'd prepared? 'Sometimes, people forget this. They're not mindful of the sacrifice the Kelim make for us – the sacrifice of their own flesh. Sometimes the women find, when they return, that nobody wants them. As wives, I mean. Wants to be bonded to them. *The vessel is clean*, scripture says, but how can something still be clean when it's been dipped nightly in filth and ordure for so many years? You understand? It's a mystery. A holy mystery.

'But I offered ... I offered her ... myself.' Kuutma blinked away tears. He got to his feet and took a step in Tillman's direction. There was a magnetism that drew him: it had to draw Tillman too, and reel him in to the next stage of his dismantling.

'I told her that nothing had changed between us. I said I'd take her and marry her, and raise her children. But she chose death. She felt so fouled by your touch, so deeply spoiled, she couldn't meet an honest man's eyes again or accept his love. You hear me, Tillman?'

536

'I hear you,' Tillman mumbled. 'You sad little prick. She turned you down. She turned you down because she still loved me.'

Kuutma screamed. He couldn't help himself. The sound was torn out of some part of him too deep for reason. He covered the distance between him and Tillman in three strides and smashed the butt of the pistol into the bridge of the man's nose, shattering it. Tillman staggered and started to crumple, but Kuutma turned like a dervish and planted a kick in the centre of his stomach before he could even hit the ground. As Tillman lurched back, doubled over, Kuutma smashed him again with the gun, in the side of his head, and finally he fell.

'She didn't love you!' Kuutma bellowed. 'She never loved you! You don't kill yourself because you love someone!'

Winded and helpless, Tillman knelt on all fours at his feet. Kuutma racked a bullet into the chamber of the Sig-Sauer and flicked off the safety. He put the gun against the back of Tillman's head.

But he got himself under control again before he could pull the trigger. He was almost ready: almost. But he couldn't send Tillman into the dark on that note of absurd and insulting defiance. He had to tell him the rest and watch him weep his soul into the dirt.

'Your daughter,' Kuutma said. 'Her name isn't Grace now. It's Tabe. She was raised by strangers – and taught to hate you. She's so happy here, Tillman. So happy with us. She's an artist. She paints. There's such beauty inside her that it spills from her fingers into the world. You hear me? Your daughter *loves* the life I gave her! Before I came here, I went to her. I told her that I was going to kill you and I asked for her blessing. She gave it joyfully. "Why should I care what happens to the father of my flesh?" she said. And when I'm done with you, Tillman, I'll go

537

back to her. I'll tell her how you died, and she'll kiss my hand and bless me all over again.'

Tillman was shaking. For a moment, Kuutma thought it was fear that made him tremble, but then realised that the man's once-powerful frame was wracked with wrenching tears. 'Alive!' Tillman sobbed. 'Grace is alive! My Grace is alive!'

In an excess of rage, Kuutma clubbed the huddled, helpless ruin in front of him again and again with the butt of the gun. 'She hates you!' he bellowed. 'Didn't you hear me? She hates you!'

Kuutma's own hands were shaking now and there was little force to his blows. Crouched like a rat in a rainstorm, Tillman weathered them.

Kuutma touched the Sig once again to the back of the man's skull. He still had the final, the unanswerable argument. It was a sublime instinct after all, that had made him start with Rebecca and save the worst for last.

'Your sons—' he began.

Movement from above caught his eye. Something falling. Kuutma jumped aside and the ornamental urn, pushed from a balustrade on a terrace way up over his head, smashed to the ground exactly where he'd just stood. Jagged shards of stone hit his face and body.

'How much does God love you, Kuutma?' a voice said, speaking from the air all around him.

It was Rebecca's voice.

67

Six months in narcotics: the shortest posting you could take and still claim it on your CV as valid experience. What Kennedy didn't know about drugs would fill whole libraries.

Ironically, what she knew about methamphetamine came from a homicide bust. A woman who'd killed her two flatmates and fellow addicts in their sleep with the spiked end of a mallet intended for tenderising steak. She'd tenderised them very thoroughly indeed. She'd also been happy to explain why: they'd been trying to kill her with microwaves and with poison soaked into the fabric of her pillow.

One in five long-term meth users will eventually succumb to an intractable mental illness known to clinicians as amphetamine psychosis. And Brand had been using regularly for at least thirteen years. He had to be at least a little crazy, even by the exacting standards of religious maniacs.

Kennedy walked slowly down the stairs towards Brand – or Kuutma, as he seemed to call himself – and Tillman. She'd lost the gun Tillman had given her, but she had a chair leg that she'd picked up along the way. She held it close to her side, where she hoped it would be hard to spot.

She was improvising desperately. All she'd really wanted to do was to stop the bastard from finishing that sentence. But she seemed to have got his attention anyway: all she had to do now was keep it.

'How much does God love you?' she repeated, in the same cold, stern tone.

Kuutma didn't answer. He seemed unable to speak. He stared at her as she came towards him, and took an involuntary step back.

'Seems to me,' Kennedy said, 'that those he loves, he protects. He gives the faithful their reward on earth and he smites the heathen. That's how it goes, isn't it? And you're the arm that does the smiting, so I reckon you should know if anybody does.'

Kuutma laughed suddenly, which wasn't at all the reaction Kennedy was expecting – or hoping for. 'Just you!' he said. 'I thought for a moment ...' He seemed to pull himself away from an interior precipice, a shudder running through his body. 'God loves the people, *rhaka*. His covenant is with us. Only the fallen one cares about you.'

Kennedy had reached the bottom of the steps now, only ten feet from Kuutma. She looked at her watch, then met his stare and shrugged. 'Getting a little late, isn't he?' she asked, mildly.

Kuutma's eyes narrowed. 'You're going to die with a blasphemy on your lips,' he told her.

Kennedy went on as though she hadn't heard him. 'More than twenty years late. You were supposed to wait for thirty centuries and then you'd get your turn in the big chair. But thirty centuries came and went, and you're still living here in the dark like roaches. Hiding from the rest of the world. Sticking more and more fingers into more and more holes in the dike because the world is getting smaller all the time. Satellite surveillance, data monitoring, biometric passports and genetic fingerprinting. Even your electricity bills betray you, Kuutma. And you wait, and you wait, and still God doesn't turn up, until you must feel

540

like the shy girl in the corner who never gets asked up for a dance.

'And what are all your murders worth, in the end, if you're not holy? If God didn't bless you and tell you to fight, then what about all that blood on your soul?'

'There is no blood on my soul,' Kuutma said. She'd slowed to a halt and now he took a step towards her. The gun still in his hand, and aimed at her heart, he unhooked one of the nasty, angled knives from his waist. 'I am forgiven.'

'But only for killing,' Kennedy reminded him. 'Not for lies. So tell me the truth about one thing, Kuutma, before you kill me.'

Holding the knife at chest height, between index finger and forefinger, he tilted the blade to a sixty-degree angle and crooked his hand back to throw.

'Ask me,' he invited her.

'Was the whole of this sorry spectacle because you couldn't do the nasty with Rebecca Beit Whatever-her-name-was? Because I've heard of lovers' balls, man, but this is really, really sad.'

Kuutma threw the knife.

Kennedy made a judgement call and threw herself to the right. It was the wrong direction, but the movement saved her anyway: her plaster cast had been built around a steel frame and the knife hit one of the struts, exposed by its recent baptism. The blade creased Kennedy's cheek as it bounced up and away into the dark.

Kuutma drew a second blade. Kennedy threw herself forward, and with a wild swipe of the chair leg knocked the knife out of his hand. That just left the Sig-Sauer. It came up while she was still off-balance, and Kuutma had begun to pull back on the trigger, when the deafening peal of an explosion made him look

541

down, in shock, at his own chest. A supernova of blood expanded there, covering the whole of his torso in two vertiginous seconds.

Tillman hadn't trusted his aim: he was too sick, too dizzy, his hands too unsteady. Even getting the Unica from his belt and thumbing the safety had taken every ounce of concentration that he could bring to bear.

He'd dragged himself laboriously to his feet, while Kuutma debated theology with Kennedy, and moved towards them one baby-step at a time. Kuutma hadn't seemed to notice him, but Kennedy had. She held her ground and kept on talking, presenting the world's easiest target.

And Tillman had brought the gun up at last, a scant inch from the back of Kuutma's hand-woven linen jacket.

Had held it on the right line.

Had pressed the trigger.

Had pressed harder because the trigger didn't want to give way under his sapless grip.

Had fired and lost the gun at once to the unexpected kick of a recoil he normally took in his stride.

But one shot was all it took. Kuutma sank to his knees, still staring at Kennedy in blank-eyed astonishment.

'God . . .' he choked. 'God is my . . .'

'God thinks,' Kennedy told him, her cold voice grinding like a stone dragged across the mouth of a cave, 'that you're a lying, murdering bastard.'

Kuutma opened his mouth to answer but death got there first.

68

SUMMARY INTERVIEW WITH OFFICER FELIPE JUAREZ, CIUDAD DE MEXICO
PTD, CONDUCTED BY LT JESUS-ERNESTO PENA, POLICIA FEDERAL.
START TIME: 3.30 P.M.

LT PENA: Did the call for assistance come from the site?

OFFICER JUAREZ: I thought so at the time, Lieutenant. But the call wasn't properly logged, as you know, and in such a densely populated area, interrogating the cellphone companies' logs has turned out to be ... well, not very practical.

PENA: It was a man? A man's voice you heard?

JUAREZ: Yes.

PENA: And he specified a location in Xochimilco?

JUAREZ: Exactly. A warehouse, on a site formerly owned by the United Fruit Company. Its current owners are hard to determine. There is a maze of companies apparently, most of them based in Africa or the Middle East. A great deal of confusion.

PENA: Tell me what you found when you arrived at the site.

JUAREZ: Lieutenant, it's almost impossible for me to describe. It was an underground complex, almost

	like a small city. It had been flooded, but still it was largely intact. An incredible thing. If someone had told me that such a place existed, I would have laughed at him.
PENA:	I've seen the pictures, Officer Juarez. And I agree, it's impressive. I believe you found two people there when you arrived?
JUAREZ:	A man and a woman. Both of them injured – the man seriously. He had a wound to his abdomen and another to his face. The woman had been beaten and it's possible that she had an injury to the left side of her body. She had a jacket draped over her left arm, so that I couldn't see.
PENA:	Also there was a dead body.
JUAREZ:	Yes, that's true. A second man was present and he was dead. A gunshot wound clear through the upper torso at very close range. My immediate assumption was that either one or both of these people must have killed him, and so I attempted to perform an arrest. I was unable to do so, however. The man outdrew me and forced me to surrender my side-arm.
PENA:	He outdrew you. Despite his wounds?
JUAREZ:	Lieutenant, he moved as quickly as a snake. This man had been a soldier. I don't have any doubt of that. You saw the guns and ammunition he left behind – a whole arsenal. Also, he seemed a little insane. Unbalanced. If I had brought back-up, I might have had a chance against him: against the two of them, I should say. Alone, I had none.
PENA:	So. There you were with your gun in your holster and your dick in your hands.

544

JUAREZ:	Masturbation I leave to you federales. I try never to compete with an expert.
PENA:	I want that to remain in the transcript.
TAQUIGRAFO:	It's your choice, lieutenant.
PENA:	Tell me what happened next.
JUAREZ:	They took me to a staircase and showed me that the lower levels of the complex had been flooded. They explained that the water was poisoned – a neurotoxin of some kind – and that it must not, under any circumstances, get back into the water table. It had to stay where it was, under guard, until it could be pumped away and disposed of. Was that the truth?
PENA:	That's need-to-know, Officer Juarez. You're not on the list.
JUAREZ:	No. Of course not. But I know that the site was closed for nineteen days. An area three blocks wide was sealed off, with haz-mat signs at every corner.
PENA:	Need-to-know.
JUAREZ:	And the satellite feeds? I heard a rumour that for two days before this, hundreds of trucks arrived at this warehouse and then drove away again. But nobody knows what they were carrying.
PENA:	Need-to-know.
JUAREZ:	And that there were tunnels, leading to other sites, also in Xochimilco. That there were houses and granaries and storerooms and swimming pools and gymnasia and—
PENA:	Tell me what happened next.
JUAREZ:	What happened next? The man and the woman told me an incredible story. Incredible anywhere

else, I mean. In the place where we were at that time, it didn't seem quite so hard to believe. The man had lost his wife and his children. The woman her partner. The man they killed had murdered a great many people and had tried to kill my city. My family. My friends. Everyone I knew. Can you imagine!

PENA: Yes. I can imagine. What then?

JUAREZ: They tied my hands, but not tightly, and the man told me it would not be good for me if I followed them.

PENA: Did you try to follow them?

JUAREZ: Eventually, yes. But by then they'd gone. There was no sign of them.

PENA: How much time had passed at that stage?

JUAREZ: Perhaps fifteen or twenty minutes.

PENA: It took you fifteen or twenty minutes to free your hands, when there was a knife – logged as item 21 – lying directly at your feet?

JUAREZ: It was dark. I didn't see the knife.

PENA: Until it was safe to do so.

JUAREZ: It was dark. I didn't see the knife.

PENA: Or any of several other knives, in the belt of the dead man, in the kit bag logged as item 16?

JUAREZ: It was dark. I didn't see—

PENA: Yes, thank you, Officer Juarez. I believe I understand. Let's turn to AMC inter-force bulletin 1217. This concerns a woman who escaped from a hospital in Kingman, Arizona, where she was under police guard, with the help of a man who lowered her down the wall of the building on a rappelling rope.

JUAREZ:	Yes. I read it.
PENA:	Look at the photographs. Is this the man and woman you saw?
JUAREZ:	My understanding is that the charges against the woman were dropped on the evidence of the county sheriff, who said the woman had actually saved him from an attacker.
PENA:	The man is still wanted. Look at the photographs.
JUAREZ:	It seems to me, if the water was really poisoned, that the man who died at the warehouse might have been a poisoning son of a bitch who deserved to be shot clear through the upper torso at very close range.
PENA:	It seems to me that if I wanted your opinion on that, I'd ask for it. Look at the photos.
JUAREZ:	That was not the woman and that was not the man. I wish I could help, Lieutenant.
PENA:	I wish I could put your balls in a vice.
JUAREZ:	So few people are ever truly happy in this world.

69

She went home.

She had a home to go back to.

It was a room, in which her father waited. She told him the story of where she'd been and what she'd done, although she knew he didn't understand. She didn't understand his story, either, come to that. The best you could do was bear witness and to listen whenever the chance came up.

Someone else waited, too, in another room, not too far away. There was dirty talk, and afterwards, some other things for which talk wasn't necessary.

'I always, always, always thought you were straight,' Kennedy murmured, into Izzy's ear.

'Hell, no,' Izzy giggled. 'Not since I was fifteen.'

'But you talk the talk so well ...'

Izzy straddled her and smiled – for Kennedy alone – a smile that would melt platinum and open the legs of an angel. 'Oh, the talk's universal, hon. It's the walk that counts.'

70

He went home. It was still empty.

But the emptiness felt different now. He knew that his wife had died loving him, thinking of him. That she hadn't wanted to leave him, and couldn't imagine a life without him, any more than he'd been able to build one without her.

He knew that his children were alive, somewhere in the world, and that they were happy.

He felt that his solitude was a shrine, in which he kept the holiest of things: his memories of their brief time together as a family, which nobody else alive now remembered.

Because he lived, it was all true. Because he remembered, they were with him.

Next to that, what else mattered?

71

'Letter for you, Web. Got the Queen's head on it, so I reckon it's from England. Who'd you know in England?'

Connie handed the letter across the desk to Sheriff Gayle, and then hovered around with the air of someone who still has something else to do and is about to do it real soon.

'Thanks, Connie,' Gayle said.

'Oh, you're welcome,' she told him. But he didn't make any move to open the letter, and in fact put it aside with a negligent air, so eventually Connie had to retire defeated.

When she was gone, Gayle took the envelope up again, shivved it open with his little finger and took out the letter. It was from Heather Kennedy. He'd guessed that already because she was the only Brit he'd ever met.

Dear Web,

I'm so sorry I wasn't able to make Eileen's funeral. The truth is, I got out of Mexico by the skin of my teeth, and I had this worry that if I came back to Arizona, they might not let me go again. I know the original charges were dropped, but then there was all that damage Tillman did when he busted me loose, and some more stuff in Mexico that was even crazier.

That's why I'm writing, really. I feel like you've got a right to know how it all turned out. You lost more than I did in this thing, and it's not a loss that can ever be made good, so this – the story – is all I can give you. That and my thanks, truly heartfelt, for everything you did for me.

Gayle read on, for the best part of an hour. He only stopped when Connie brought him coffee and did some more hovering. Once he'd waited her out again, he took up where he'd left off.

It was crazy, just as Kennedy said it was. It was an easy secret to keep because nobody would ever believe it. Maybe that was the best thing they had going for them, these Judas guys: they were so damned preposterous, folks could stumble right across them and then talk themselves out of it again. Couldn't have happened: too stupid, too wild, too ridiculous to have happened.

But what a story it would have made, for Moggs! How she would have given it gold paint, and shiny chrome, and wings and fins and flourishes.

It was only when he got to the end, to the last page, that he saw how it really was. He changed his mind about a lot of things then. It wasn't an easy secret to keep at all: not for Kennedy anyway, who knew this Tillman guy and owed him her life and all. And Moggs wouldn't ever have got to tell the story like it was because she just wasn't anywhere near cruel enough.

I went back to Gassan's translation, *Kennedy wrote*, and got caught up on some of the fine detail. It made a lot more sense once I'd seen that place for myself. The children of the Kelim keep the names they were given at birth, so long as those names were chosen by the mother. If the father chose, the kids are christened again by the people.

I think with Rebecca's children, Brand just wanted to wash away as much of their past as possible. There was nothing wrong with the names they already had, but he gave them new ones anyway. And I knew what the names were. The woman who almost killed us both, up in Santa Claus, told me as she was dying.

Grace, the girl, became Tabe.

The boys – Ezei and Cephas – died at Dovecote.

Gayle folded up the letter and put it in his desk drawer. Then he thought better of it and put it through the office shredder. Then he had an even better idea and used Anstruther's lighter to burn the confetti-like strands of it until there was nothing left.

Watching through the glass from the outer office, Connie contemplated with longing a good piece of gossip that she'd never get her hands on.